Sharon Marie Provost
Stephen H. Provost

EVERMORE

Sharon Marie and Stephen H. Provost

Acknowledgments

The basic storyline for *Evermore* was an idea I had been playing with for some time. Then, one day, I asked my Facebook followers to tell me their biggest fears and gross-outs, giving them a chance to win one of my books if I used their idea. Sandie La Nae described her biggest fear, which inspired some of the intriguing details in my story.

And thank you to my biggest fan, my supportive husband, Stephen, for being so fascinated by my story that he wanted to participate in its creation.

Sharon Marie Provost,
May 18, 2025

Thank you to Sharon for agreeing to share this work, which she conceived, with me. Her incredible talent, work ethic, and cooperative spirit are an inspiration to me.

Stephen H. Provost,
May 18, 2025

*"Eventually soul mates meet,
for they have the same hiding place."*
— Robert Brault

*"I will not have you without the darkness that hides
within you. I will not let you have me without the
madness that makes me. If our demons cannot dance,
neither can we."*
— Nikita Gill

Contents

Roman Britain, c. 410

The Maiden and the Knight

Sharon Marie and Stephen H. Provost

The Maiden

Edge of the World

It's lonely here on the edge of the world. Once upon a time, this place was the symbol of the empire's grandeur, its seat of power in these hinterlands that became civilized... if only for a brief glimmer of time in the full course of things. But it seems timeless when you're living it, when it's all you've ever known.

Until suddenly it's not.

The sun never set on the empire, until it set on us, here on its western rim a few years ago, never to rise again.

It wasn't always this way.

I played in its streets when I was a girl, secure behind the walls that protected Colonia from the outside world. That's what we citizens called it: Colonia. Those born of this land knew it by a different name. I was born here, but I called it Colonia, too, since my parents called it that. My father was a high official, assigned here from Gaul to serve as governor of the province. That meant he was responsible to oversee the tax collection and the city treasury.

My father said he wanted to oversee the provincial finances directly, but it was only later that I learned the truth: The empire was finding it more and more difficult to fund Colonia's government, and had therefore heaped more duties on poor Father's shoulders. Not only did that mean more work, but serving as tax collector also made him the most hated man in Colonia. He was considered a pariah by those who lived outside the walls, many of whom still clung to their pagan roots and followed a druid who called himself "The Falcon."

The Falcon styled himself after their legendary witch warrior, Boudicca, who'd led a great rebellion against the empire here centuries ago—a rebellion that was crushed when the witch was slain. But the Falcon was proving to be more irksome. Rather than mounting a full-scale revolt, he had undertaken a campaign of strategic resistance. I'd overheard Father say the Falcon had obtained the tax schedules and therefore knew when his collectors, the *publicani*, were due to arrive at each farm. He then stationed men there and ambushed them, wiping out many of Father's best men.

By the time Father knew what was happening, word had spread among the *publicani* that collecting taxes had become dangerous.

Too dangerous.

So they simply refused.

In the not-so-distant past, when the empire was strong, such defiance carried severe consequences. In cases of mass desertion, one man in every ten would be flogged and decapitated as an example to the rest. Losing more men was not an option in a frontier city that found itself increasingly isolated—and vulnerable to hostile forces beyond the walls that were growing bolder by the day. There was even talk that The Falcon had anointed a ruler to take Father's place as governor of Colonia.

When these rumors reached my ears, I was scared. Who wouldn't be? But that fear was nothing compared to the dread I felt when the legion was dissolved, leaving no one to protect us against the barbarians. It wasn't as though the legion was recalled to Rome; things had gotten so bad by this time that the soldiers—unpaid and outnumbered by the Falcon, simply laid down their swords and faded into the trees or hid in the marshes. What became of them was largely a mystery. Some may have found their way across the channel, but most of them likely made common cause with the barbarians and simply blended into their tribes, abandoning their former identities.

"Traitors!" Father shouted, slamming his hand down on the wooden table. "How long can we hold out and wait for reinforcements from Honorius?"

"I would not speak so of the emperor, if I were you," Felix Anguselaus warned. Angus, as he was known to most, was the head of my father's personal guard. His reputation for loyalty—both to my father and to Caesar—was well earned. His name meant "one choice," which spoke to the strength of his devotion. As to "Felix," it was a nickname that reflected his optimism and good fortune.

That seemed less fitting in light of our current dire circumstances. Still, Father needed someone to give him hope, and Angus gave him that. The fact that the fiercest fighter in the west had stuck by him in such dire circumstances was a sign that he might still prevail.

Or so he believed.

It was testament to Angus' fidelity that he had remained by Father's side when the entire legion had deserted him, and that he still spoke with respect toward the western emperor, even though it was clear to nearly everyone that Honorius had abandoned us.

Tacitus Atticus, my father's chief counselor, fixed Angus with the kind of stare that would have made most men hunker down in their seats.

Angus just met his gaze and held it there.

"Enough of this pretense, Felix," Atticus scoffed. "The emperor will *not* be sending reinforcements. He has enough to deal with on his own doorstep, where the Goths and Huns and Vandals are camping out, just waiting for the chance to sack Rome herself."

"We do not know that," Angus said sternly.

"Perhaps *you* do not, but it is abundantly clear to the rest of us, and it has been for years now."

Angus pursed his lips and shook his head, his eyes still locked on Tacitus. The two men were testing each other, seeing which of them would avert his eyes first.

Tacitus finally gave way and spun to face me.

"What is *she* doing here?"

That was possibly the worst thing he could have said. Father was extremely protective of me, and since we had become vulnerable to invasion, he had insisted on keeping me in his own presence or under Angus' watchful eye. Angus was as loyal to me as he was to Father. And since he and Father were both here in the council chamber, I was here too.

I assumed that Father would react first to Tacitus' audacity, but it was Angus who flew out of his seat, pulled a dagger in the space of a heartbeat, and stuck the point of it at Tacitus' throat, drawing one thin trickle of blood. "*She* is here because she is the governor's daughter," he hissed. "And she is here because she is in *my* charge. If you did not honor her position in Colonia, that would be offense enough. But what is worse beyond measure is that you see before you only 'a woman' and therefore do not grant her the deference her character demands. She is of age, well educated, astute, and observant. In fact, I'd wager she has more insight into matters you *pretend* to understand than you or almost anyone else. What say you, princess?"

I flushed redder than the breast on a bullfinch and looked away from him. "I am not a princess, Angus."

He bowed stiffly. "Of course, of course. Please forgive my gaucherie."

Father laughed, and Tacitus—the blade now withdrawn from his neck—harrumphed. "Tell me, Alba," my father said, addressing me by my given name. "Since Angus has broached the subject, what *is* your opinion of these matters?"

Tacitus' eyes widened, but he held his tongue.

"Father, I..."

"Do not be shy, child. We are soliciting your opinion, and you've never been timid about sharing it before."

I blushed again. I *did* like to express my opinion, but on my own terms. I hated being put on the spot. Especially when my answer was unlikely to find favor. I looked up at Angus, who was staring down at me expectantly. My father's eyebrows were raised in a look that said, "Well?"

I cleared my throat and avoided looking at Angus. "Father," I said, "I believe Tacitus is right. We've sent word to Rome and haven't had a response. Six calends have passed, and still there is no word."

"If I may," Angus interjected. "Bandits or rebels might have waylaid our messengers on the road."

"Does that matter?" I ventured. "Whether they were rebuffed after arriving in Rome or prevented from completing their journey, the result is the same."

"Precisely!" Tacitus nearly shouted. "Either way, no help will be forthcoming."

I looked at Angus out of the corner of one eye and could see he was fuming. For one whose loyalty was beyond reproach, betrayal was the ultimate sin. He saw my opinion as a betrayal, even though I was only being honest.

Angus turned away from me. "Then I shall go myself!" he declared. "I will deliver our call for reinforcements to Rome. I stake my honor on it. My very life. Let there be no more excuses, in this council chamber or in the emperor's halls, for failing to save our province in this time of need. I shall do so myself if I must, and it looks increasingly as though I must!" He shot me a reproving glance, but this time, I met his gaze and saw something else behind it. Was it disappointment? Sorrow? If it was either, I did not want the knowledge of it, because I already suspected my own glance reflected those feelings... and something else I did not wish him to see.

But I knew he had.

Angus whirled around and rushed toward the door, calling back over his shoulder, "I ride forthwith!"

"Angus!" my father called after him. "I have issued no such command. If you do this, it is treason! You have been charged with keeping watch over my daughter, that nothing befall her in this dark age."

Angus stopped in his tracks, turned around, and stared directly at my father. "I *am* keeping watch over her! When the Roman legions return at my back, they will deliver not only her but all of Colonia from the pagan scourge."

"Then what?" Tacitus scoffed. "You will install yourself as governor and cast Alba here into a cell for opposing you?"

"I have no interest in governing, only in serving. But if you are so worried about such an outcome, could it be you think I might succeed? Perhaps my cause is not so hopeless as you wish the governor to believe. Perhaps it is you who wishes me to fail so that *you* might be the one to seize power—without opposition from Rome. But watch and you will see, ye that accuses me of treachery. I shall stand in the gap between heaven and hell, and the gates of hell will not prevail against me, for I am pure of heart. My conscience is clear. The God of miracles will acquit me."

Sharon Marie and Stephen H. Provost

The Maiden

The Falcon and the Bear

Angus had deserted me—had deserted us. And with him had gone the last of our good fortune.

A few weeks later, a traveler arrived at the gates of Colonia Victricensis with a message for my father. Tacitus bore it to the house of government, and it was one of ill omen for us all.

"It's from the Falcon," he said stoically.

"Well, what does he want?"

"He demands your immediate surrender of this city, its public works, and all the weapons in its armory. Without condition." He paused.

"And?" My father could tell there was something more.

Tacitus cleared his throat. "And you are to turn yourself over to face their judgment. Your children are to be surrendered as well, and will be reduced to servitude as a sign to all that we are their inferiors."

Father looked at me. I was his only child.

I did my best to put on a brave face.

"And if we refuse?"

"He says the Ursidae will take Colonia by force, slaughter its citizens, and give their property over to those he calls the 'true Britons.'"

I looked at my father and saw the apprehension on his face. It was clear from that expression that he had no plan to counter this threat to the city.

"Ursidae?" he said. He was asking the question to give himself time to think.

"It says here that they are followers of the Bear, whom the Falcon has anointed as high dragon of all Britain."

My father scoffed. "Under what authority?"

"His own, I suspect," said Tacitus. "This Falcon styles himself as a kingmaker. This 'Bear' is no doubt some crude and unkempt brute he has installed as a figurehead to galvanize his forces. The Falcon wields the true power behind this rebellion. He no doubt wrote this demand himself, being the only literate soul among these heathen wretches."

"Have you heard a report from the battlements?" Father's tone was laced with barely a whisper of hope.

Tacitus nodded. "There is a force assembled not a quarter-mile from here," he said. "They are formidable in number. Our watchmen think there might be 3,000 of them."

"That's nearly a full legion!" I burst out. "Even if Angus returns with Roman support..."

Evermore

"He's not coming back," Father said wearily. He slumped in his chair. "It is over."

"Father, no! You can't..." My head was swirling. Nothing in my life had prepared me for anything like this. I'd been insulated from the intrigues of Colonia's politics, which Father had always seemed so good at navigating. He'd been in a position of authority for as long as I could remember, trusted to carry out his duties to Rome for one simple reason: He always succeeded. I wasn't used to seeing him like this. When I saw him helpless, it made me *feel* helpless. Everything was collapsing around us, and if he couldn't hold himself together, how could I?

"Tell me what else I am to do, Alba?" he said. "Our defenses are not just depleted, they're nonexistent. We could seal the city, but who's to say they couldn't force their way in? And even if they lacked the means to do so, they would lay siege to the city and carry out their threats once our food was gone. If we surrender, perhaps they will be merciful. We can at least pray that our Lord may stay their hand."

He was asking *me* what to do? I was barely fifteen years old—old enough to marry... but I still felt so young. It looked like I would have to do the rest of my growing up in a hurry.

"These are ruthless men," Tacitus said, speaking softly. "They demand that our surrender be unconditional. This can only mean they intend on carrying out their intentions whether we submit willingly or not."

"We could make them some kind of offer," I suggested. "To appease them."

Tacitus glared at me. "Pay attention, child. They're going to take whatever they want anyway."

"Well they won't take me," I said defiantly. "Their message said they intend to make slaves of your children. As your only child, that means me. But if they want me to be their slave, they will have to guarantee your safety, Father. Otherwise, I will take my own life. I refuse to give them the satisfaction of enslaving me without at least getting something in return."

Father's eyes widened, then narrowed. "I will not permit it."

I stood and put my hands on my hips. "And I will not permit you to merely surrender without condition. I won't let you suffer that kind of humiliation. I won't let Colonia be disgraced so, and I won't allow myself to stand by and do nothing if I have it in my power to retain my dignity. I *do* have that power. And I *will* exercise it."

I turned and stomped out of the chamber before either my father or Tacitus could do anything to stop me.

This is madness, a voice inside my head was screaming, but I refused to listen.

I marched down the main road, Decumanus Maximus, toward the western Balkerne Gate. I could hear the whispers all around me.

"Is that Alba?"

"The governor's daughter?"

"What is she doing?"

I quickened my pace and tried to block them out, staying focused on my purpose as I maintained my course. All the while, I was trying to convince myself that this was a good idea—that the Falcon's army wouldn't simply ignore my teenage bravado. That they wouldn't storm the gates with a battering ram, force their way into the city, and kill everyone inside. Myself included. How could I really think that these barbarians cared at all for keeping me alive, simply to parade me around as a slave? It made no sense. But what was the alternative? I couldn't see one.

So, when I arrived at the gate, I planted my feet and looked up at the watchtower. Then I cupped my hands to my mouth and called up to the guard stationed there.

"Tell the Falcon's messenger this: My father, the legally appointed governor of Colonia Claudia Victricensis, will yield to you the city, its water works, its weapons, and all its properties. In exchange, you must promise to spare the people of this great city and guarantee my father safe passage from this realm. These are his only terms, and he will accept no less. Should you fail to meet them, I, his only daughter, will slay myself here where I stand, and you shall not have the satisfaction of possessing me as your servant and 'trophy.' I await your answer."

I could hear the people on the streets gasping, followed by the sound of feet scurrying away as they disappeared inside the buildings that lined the street and bolted the doors behind them. It occurred to me that they hadn't been told of the danger.

Of course they haven't. Father would not have risked causing a panic... the way I just did.

I sighed and awaited the inevitable.

It seemed like hours, but it was just a few minutes later when I heard a voice call through the gates.

"After some consideration, we have agreed to accept your terms," the voice said. "The governor will not be harmed, nor will the residents of this city. We ask that the governor's daughter accept our hospitality to come and live among us freely as our guest. She will not be harmed, nor will she be made our servant. You have our word in this. Far better that she submit to us freely than we be forced to subjugate the town by force of arms."

I didn't believe the man's assurances for a second—and I was annoyed that the speaker was referring to me in the third person, as though I hadn't been the one addressing them in the first place.

"My thanks," I said. "You have my word that I will accept

your speaker's word on this"—two could play at this third-person game—"and that we will surrender to you in due course, if you will only allow us some time to prepare..."

"No, we will not." The speaker's tone shifted, shedding any semblance of courtesy. "We will give you no time to 'prepare' for us by placing archers on your rooftops, burying your weapons in some bunker, or otherwise seeking to deceive us. You will open these gates now, or we will open them for you!"

I looked anxiously over my shoulder. I'd expected my father and Tacitus to come running after me and try to stop me, or at least speak on the city's behalf rather than leaving that to me. But there was no sign of them, and even as I tried to figure out where they might be, I heard a massive thud against the wooden gate that shook it on its hinges. They were wasting no time.

"Hold!" I shouted.

There was a second thud, reverberating through the wood like a thunderclap.

"Hold, I say!"

But they weren't listening. The sound of wood splintering accompanied the next impact, and it was clear the gates would not hold for long. I was standing there alone now; I couldn't move my feet. The streets were deserted, with still no sign of Father or Tacitus. I backed up in case a horde of cavalry came galloping through when the gates failed, convinced that my gambit had failed.

I was definitely *not* going to open them now. If they broke them down, these heathen invaders would have to deal with the damage once they secured the city. More work for them. The thudding against the gate sounded all the more ominous against the backdrop of utter silence that had taken Colonia.

Then, abruptly, it stopped.

Evermore

I waited for a moment, trying to make out any sound from beyond the gate, but the first noise I heard came, instead, from behind me. Horses' hoofbeats were approaching, not at a gallop, but at a leisurely trot.

I let out a sigh of relief. "Father!" I gasped as I turned. "I thought you would never..."

My words trailed off into a terrible silence. There, in front of me, rode two horsemen, with an army of others coming up now behind them. They bore the banner of a golden dragon on a white field, poised as if to attack. The man at the left wore a gray hooded cloak that obscured his face; to his right was a large man dressed in a conical helm and a bearskin draped over chainmail, which covered his barrel chest. His thighs and upper arms were thick with muscle, and he wore an arrogant smile on his thin lips. He looked to be in his mid-thirties, but his bearing made clear that he believed he already knew everything worth knowing.

I barely noticed any of it.

My attention was drawn to two men directly behind the pair in front. They weren't dressed in any formal uniform, yet they were undoubtedly soldiers by their demeanor. Each of them was holding the prone, lifeless figure of a man drenched in blood. They came forward, passing on either side of the two riders, and dropped the bodies unceremoniously in front of them. A cloud of dirt rose from where they had been dumped, but it was their faces that held my gaze.

I fell to my knees, sobbing, as I buried my face in my hands.

"Father! Oh, Father!" I moaned. Waves of grief flowed up from inside of me, making me shudder and convulse.

My father wasn't breathing.

The lifeless body of Tacitus lay next to him.

"How could you!" I shouted, looking up at the two men and

19

shaking my fist in a useless display of defiance. "You promised!" I wailed. "You promised!"

"Oh, but we have kept our promise," the bear-skinned man taunted. "We pledged to give your father safe passage from this realm, and that is exactly what we have done. We have granted him safe passage across the River Styx and into Pluto's Underworld." He reached beneath the bearskin and pulled out a pair of drachmae, flipping them onto my father's body. "Here," he said. "We will even pay the ferryman for passage."

The hooded man must not have approved of his humor, because he stayed silent, his eyes fixed on me. I looked up at him through hollow eyes, and he gestured for me to stand.

I did so, like a ghost rising up from the grave. I felt numb. Something deep within told me that to disobey might cost me my life, but the rest of me cared not. My father was dead. Colonia had fallen. Gone was my resolve to end my own life rather than being delivered into their servitude. In the wake of what had just happened, I no longer cared what they might do to me. They could defile me, whip me, or even crucify me for all I cared. None of it mattered anymore.

The man tilted his head as he stared at me, like he was scrutinizing some new piece of cargo that had just been delivered by a trading ship from some exotic land.

"I suppose you will make me your slave now," I said, spitting at his feet.

He just laughed, and I fell to my knees again from the burden of sorrow, exhaustion, and my own terrible failure.

"Get up!" the bear-skinned man shouted. "You demean yourself, and by extension, you insult your king."

The hooded man nodded once. "What he means to say is that your current posture, on your knees in the dirt, is not fitting for a lady who will be a queen. You will not embarrass your master by acting in any way other than proud and dignified."

The hooded man dismounted and extended his hand to me. "Rise, most fortunate one. I am the Falcon, who will remain perched upon your shoulder henceforth. Do not trifle with me, or you will find yourself a field mouse in my clutches. It is my pleasure to inform you that you have been chosen as consort to the high dragon, heir to the throne of the Britons and new emperor in the West. Do obeisance to him, and to me for his sake, and you will prosper. Defy us and..." He left the rest unsaid.

That brutish companion of his, the man he had referred to as "high dragon," seemed to have very little interest in me, his would-be consort. He wasn't even listening to the Falcon's words as he demanded that his bannerman hand over his standard, bearing his personal crest. This he took hold of and slammed it into the soft earth, so it stood there, a golden dragon rampant against a snow-white background.

This done, he cast me a sidelong glance, and announced. "I am the dragon. This wench is my pure white field... which I intend to plow until she gives me an heir!" He laughed, and the other men laughed with him.

I felt sick to my stomach.

"I claim this capital of all Britons in my own name, for the Ursidae," he shouted up to the sky. "I will make it the heart of my glory, the center of my kingdom."

"Thenceforth, this place shall no longer be Colonia," the cloaked man added. "But it shall be known by its ancient and rightful name, Camulodunum, the mighty fortress on the hill. All hail the age of Camulod!"

"All hail the age of Camulod!" the soldiers echoed.

"All hail the Bear King, the high dragon of Britain!"

Sharon Marie and Stephen H. Provost

The Knight
Fool's Errand

For the first time in my life, I felt lost.

I'd always been supremely confident in my judgment and abilities. I'd never been bested in single combat or wounded on the battlefield. That was how I'd earned the nickname Felix: "the fortunate one." But though no blade had ever cut me, no man had ever bested me, I suddenly felt anything but fortunate. Had I made the right decision in leaving Colonia... more specifically, in leaving Alba? I'd sworn to the governor that I would watch over her and defend her with my life—that, indeed, was my very purpose in making this journey.

But what if I had chosen wrongly? What if I were unable to secure assistance from the empire, and in my absence, Colonia was overrun by the pagan horde? Tales of the Falcon's cunning had reached Colonia, and tales of the Bear's brutality had followed. If Alba should fall into their hands...

It had stung when her father had accused me of treason for not staying to watch over her, but that had not been the worst burden laid upon me. That burden had been conveyed to my shoulders by the look in Alba's own eyes when I announced I would be leaving. I could sense she was disappointed in me and scared to see me leaving. Not because she couldn't handle herself. She could.

But because...

I shook my head. There was no question we had built a bond between us, she and I, from the simple fact that she had been put in my charge. That was all it was, surely... that and the crisis that had come upon us. That desperate passion that arises at the moment you think you might never see someone again—someone who has become integral to your life and purpose. I tried to block from my mind the purity of her pale skin, the subtle curve of her lips, the way her chest rose and fell with each glorious breath.

God forgive me!

She is but a child still, one voice within me said.

But of marriageable age, said another. *And if you do not cast your lot with her, another will. Or perhaps steal her away by force.*

My mind immediately fixed itself on the Bear, though I knew not why. I had never seen the man, but already I hated him. His whispered reputation was one of callous cruelty. I knew not if that were true, but the possibility could scarcely be ignored, aligned as he was with the Falcon, that so-called druid whose subtlety and artifice were widely known. That wizard practiced the arts of Satan himself, and only the Lord's champion could resist him.

Christ himself had so ordained me, and I had proved myself

his champion. Yet here I was, heading *away* from the threat posed by the Falcon and the Bear. Away from my true love... What was I saying? This was madness. And the madness was spreading, making me question everything. My only recourse was to put my faith in the one true God and trust him to restore me to myself.

It had been a fortnight since my departure from Colonia, and I'd found the state of the western empire even worse than I'd imagined. The empire's swift decline wasn't limited to Britannia, either. Eluding the barbarian marauders there had been simple enough. I knew how to keep to the shadows in the forest and stay hidden in the tall reeds of the marshlands near the coast.

I had more trouble than I expected, though, in procuring a boat for passage across the channel. I arrived to find the docks empty and abandoned, waves lapping softly against the shore beneath a layer of fog that hung over everything like two leaden wings on the angel of death. After two precious days lost waiting, a boat finally put in just up the coast, but it wasn't a trading vessel or fishing boat. It was just a relatively small, narrow ship with a bow rising up like a dragon's head to pierce the waves.

At first, I thought it might belong to the Bear's men, who had supposedly begun calling him "high dragon." I'd seen a group of soldiers camped under his banner. A disorderly lot, they were nonetheless greater in number than I could have imagined. They didn't appear to be going anywhere in particular, but so many of them wouldn't have been gathered in one place if they didn't have a clear objective. If that objective was to take Colonia, I would have to move quickly. A disciplined Roman legion would likely get the better of them, but not without enduring heavy losses... and I feared that nothing less than a legion would be a match for them.

I had kept out of their sight as I skirted their camp and made for the shore, but now I faced a new obstacle: The ship I'd spied was manned by a dozen men wearing furs, which made them look like animals, and conical helms. Armed with swords and battleaxes, they looked like they were getting ready to come ashore—probably to get the lay of the land. But I already *knew* the lay of the land, which gave me an advantage in confronting them. I couldn't take them all at once, I knew, but I could pick them off one at a time.

Hidden behind the trees, I drew a bead with my longbow and let my arrow fly toward the one I surmised to be their captain. It hit him square in the shoulder and knocked him down, producing a cry from his crew, who began running around like they'd gone mad. They didn't waste time seeing to the injured man, but instead began charging toward the arrow's point of origin like so many mad bulls in a stampede.

I had already moved several yards away and was preparing to fire again from my new position. Without delay, I loosed two more arrows, both of which found their marks. And by the time they realized what had happened, I'd scurried to yet another new location and launched three more darts. The first whizzed by the ear of one man, but the second caught a companion square in the chest, and the final one buried itself in another man's stomach. They weren't wearing mail, which made my task that much easier.

I thought seeing six of their number so quickly felled might dissuade them from any further charge. But, to the contrary, it only seemed to anger them further. Like wounded animals, they became more enraged and shouted battle cries to unknown gods in a strange language I had never heard. Then forward they came again.

Evermore

But I was no longer in front of them.

I'd taken the opportunity to circle around to the edge of the forest and dart behind them, putting myself between my enemy and the shoreline. I was now fully exposed, pitting myself alone against the half-dozen of their contingent who remained. Even though no more arrows were coming at them from the woodland, they plunged like madmen into the forest, running around blindly in pursuit of their quarry... and leaving their ship unmanned. I lost no time in making full use of my advantage, rushing into the water and toward the ship, splashing through the shallows and reaching it in short order.

Perhaps my biggest challenge would be to get the vessel under way before the heathens discovered my deception and returned. The sail was still raised, and a dozen pairs of oars flanked a row of seats down the center. I took my position at one of them and started rowing furiously. I strained and pulled, but the ship barely moved.

"You might need some help with that."

I shot to my feet and drew my sword in the same instant. It seemed I wasn't the only one adept at hiding.

Before me sat two men, peering out at me from behind a pair of planks. Each was bound at their ankles and wrists by thick rope.

In an instant, I had the tip of my sword poised to strike at the nearest man's neck.

"You speak the Roman tongue," I said, surprised after hearing the barbarous war cries and cursing from the others.

"We were taken captive by those foreigners along the north coast," one of them spat—the one who didn't have the point of my blade at his throat. "Said they'd been there before. They even said they'd named our village after themselves. Imagine that! The town and the river that flows into the sea there are called Wyke, which they said means 'creek' in their tongue. Of course, the same word means 'encampment' to us." He laughed bitterly. "We'd never seen anyone like them. But they insisted they'd come to reclaim it, calling themselves the 'people of the creek,' which is *vikingr* in their tongue. The townsfolk managed to drive them off, but not before they took the two of us as slaves."

"Enough of this talk," his companion added, speaking hurriedly before turning to me. "You might as well lower that thing," he said, referring to my sword. "You're going to need all the help you can get."

He pointed to the beach, where the *vikingr* were bursting out of the trees and starting to run across the sand toward the boat, axes raised and looks of fury on their faces.

I cut the two men's ropes with my sword, sat down and took hold of two oars.

"Row!"

When I informed the two men we would be crossing the channel, they objected loudly. They'd been of a mind to hug the coast and head to Londinium, but there was no way I was going to waste time on such a detour. I reiterated that we were bound for Gaul and threatened to throw them into the sea if they protested.

They didn't.

Our destination would be Lutetia. Despite its name, which meant something like "the swamp," Lutetia was a thriving city and had even housed the provincial capital for a brief time some years ago. The emperor's kinsman Marcellus had been installed as legate there, and as he was a man of my acquaintance, I was hopeful that he might be persuaded to dispatch a force of men to

Colonia.

I soon realized that this would not be the case.

From the moment I arrived, it was clear that Marcellus faced some of the same travails in Lutetia that beset Colonia. Barbarians had been raiding the surrounding area with increasing frequency, sparking rumors that they had set their sights on sacking the city itself. They proclaimed themselves heirs to the Parisii, who had burned the old city rather than letting Rome collect its spoils. Though these Parisii been defeated, they were still regarded as heroes among the native-born peasants, who referred to it as "Paris" in their honor.

When I asked Marcellus for help, he laughed out loud. "Have you seen what is transpiring in the country around about here?" he said. "I cannot spare a cohort of men, or even a century—certainly not my entire legion. They are, as you yourself have seen... preoccupied, Lakeman."

"Lakeman" was a play on my nickname, Felix, which sounded like "Fe-lacs" to uneducated ears... "lacus" being the Latin word for "lake." Ironically, I had been raised beside a lake, by a woman who I called my mother, though in truth she had taken me in after finding me abandoned to die of exposure. I didn't like being called "Lakeman," but was far less concerned with how Marcellus had addressed me than *what* he was saying—and the sick feeling that it had produced in the pit of my stomach.

I *had* been wrong to leave Colonia. To leave Alba. Had I been there, I could have spirited her away from danger. But in my absence, there was no telling what terrible fate might befall her.

I tried one more time. "Marcellus, I came here on a crusade ordained by Christ himself. I must not fail. The fate of Colonia, of all Brittania hangs in the balance."

Those words were barely out of my mouth when a courier

came rushing in.

"What news?" Marcellus asked. He was badly winded, having obviously come a long way.

The courier bent over, putting his hands on his knees for a moment to catch his breath, then straightened again and bowed before Marcellus.

"Dire news from the west, commander," he said. "Colonia has fallen."

The Maiden

Bird's-Eye View

"What have you done?" I demanded.

"What must be done." There was not even a shred of regret in the man's voice.

"That is not what I asked."

The hooded figure in front of me didn't answer. He *knew* what he had done—and, I was sure, had already planned out what he was going to do next. He thought he could toy with people like they were pieces on a latrones board. He tried to intimidate everyone with that long white beard, those piercing eyes, and the low measured delivery, full of gravity and dramatic pauses.

It was all for show. I'd seen the same thing from emissaries seeking an audience—and usually some favor or privilege—from my father. They all tried to sound more important than they really were. But Father saw right through them, and I had learned, by observing him, to do the same.

This Falcon was a little different. He wasn't trying to act impressive as much as he *considered himself* impressive.

I wasn't falling for it.

The man in front of me was a sparrow in falcon feathers. And he needed me, or I'd already have been shackled in the city dungeons. Or dead. The way my father was. I could not think about that anymore, though; I couldn't afford to show weakness. I remembered the way Angus had always stood firm in what he believed... even if it meant challenging my father.

Angus wasn't here, but I felt like he was standing right behind me. It wasn't so much his strength that I felt, but his heartfelt belief in *my* strength.

It was strange sitting at my father's council table, across from this stranger who now occupied his chair.

I had to restrain myself from retching.

"Why am I here?" I asked in an even tone.

The Falcon spread his arms across the table. "Because this is your home, Alba."

I scowled at him. I had no patience for condescension from a pagan. "You have not earned the right to address me with familiarity."

He nodded his head, never deviating from his stoic expression. "Which is, to answer your question, precisely why you are here before me. You have been judged to be the ideal consort for the rightfully anointed king of Camulodunum."

"Colonia Victricensis."

"With respect, milady, this city is no longer a colony of Rome."

I was growing increasingly impatient with his tone,

courteous on the surface but laced with unspoken threats. "Let us speak plainly, Sir Falcon, if that is what you call yourself. You have no respect for me. Why do you name yourself for a bird of prey? You and that child you call a king appear more like fowl to me, strutting and preening like roosters who've had their heads cut off."

He raised his eyebrows.

"Because he has no mind of his own, and neither one of you has any humility."

He just kept staring at me. I couldn't remember him shifting his gaze or even blinking during the entirety of our conversation. "The name by which you know me was bestowed upon me," he said, ignoring my insults. "It's suits me because I can see things to which others are blind. The past, the present, and the future, as if I am looking down on the doings of men from on high. Like a falcon. I see the ways of men, yet I manage to remain above them."

"You speak as though you were God himself. Yet you are a godless pagan."

For the first time, his expression changed, a thin smile spreading across his lips. "Pagan. Christian. I see little value in such labels. I myself have been on this Earth for thousands of years. People knew me as the prophets Samuel and Elijah, and the storyteller Aesop, and a hundred other men whose names you would not know. Yet I have lived all these lives and have vivid memories from each of them."

"You are mad. I don't believe you."

The Falcon shrugged slightly. "As is your prerogative."

"I also don't believe you have any plausible reason for holding me here against my will."

"In point of fact, I do. Whatever you believe about my

personal motives, I have no wish to see you harmed. Without my protection, those men out there would have passed you around among themselves, defiled you and likely left you dead.

"The alternative I offer is far preferable, I am sure you'll agree. You will be wed to the Bear King, my protégé, and rule at his side as queen of all Albion."

"Albion?" I had never heard that name.

"The name of this island, which the Romans call Britannia. Surely you recognize it. Albion means 'white,' as does your given name... Alba. It is a sign that this is your true destiny. I have seen the future. You cannot change it."

He didn't have me in bonds, but his words were crafted carefully to make me feel as though I was. "I am a baptized Christian," I said. "I will not be unequally yoked to your pagan brute."

I am already betrothed to Angus...

Where had that come from? Angus had never proposed marriage, either to me or to my father. But I couldn't deny the appeal of the idea. I had fantasized...

Stop it! I told myself

That thin-lipped smile had returned to the Falcon's face. He didn't say anything, but there was a twinkle in his eye that seemed to indicate he knew what I was thinking... even though he couldn't have.

"I can put your mind at ease concerning your impending nuptials." He spoke as if the wedding he'd arranged had been written on stone tablets. "The Bear has been baptized into your faith, as was *his* destiny. The old ways are passing away, and the ways of your Christ are ascendant. To unite this kingdom, it was necessary that the Bear embrace your faith. Just as it is necessary for him to take a bride who can help his people make the transition from Roman Brittania to the new age that lies ahead. You can be that bride. But the choice is yours, and it must be made freely."

Then why did it feel like he was giving me no choice at all?

The days passed, and I waited, hoping against hope that Angus would return with a cohort of Roman soldiers to deliver Colonia from its occupiers.

But the days turned into weeks and the weeks into months, yet still he tarried. I fought a growing bitterness that rose within me. How could my Felix have abandoned me? He hadn't. I still felt his spirit deep inside, reassuring me. And the more I thought of him, the more I yearned for him. With my father gone, he was the only source of hope that remained to me. The longer he was away, the more discouraged I should have become. But I didn't. Instead, I clung to that hope even more fiercely.

In the meantime, the day of my wedding to the Bear was fast approaching, and the Bear had done nothing to improve my opinion of him. Why the Falcon stood steadfast in support of him, I knew not, but the Falcon saw only what he wished to see. I saw him for what he was: a filthy barbarian unfit to rule the smallest village. The first question he asked me wasn't about my father's approach to governing or how to win over the masses. It was whether I had ever lain with a man before.

When I told him it was not his place to know, he only laughed and said he would find out in our marriage bed.

"If you have been despoiled by another before I seed you, I will have you cast off the chalk cliffs and into the sea. Or perhaps burned at the stake. You must understand that, from this moment forward, you are mine. Mine to bed. Mine to summon. Mine to command. Mine to do with as I please."

I straightened my back. "I am to be a queen."

"You are to be the oven for my seed. That is all. A pale reflection of my glory. And if you are barren, I will send you to a nunnery, where you shall live out your life in shame, forgotten and unwanted."

I told myself then that I would never allow myself to be anything to him but the "oven" he demanded. That was all. I would not seek his approval, but his humiliation. By refusing to please this awful man, I would disgrace him in his own eyes. I would not move a muscle, but lie prone beneath his rancid body, refusing to look at him or even acknowledge his existence.

I would play my part in public for the sake of my country and my people. I would smile and wave; I would curtsy and speak with flattery when it was called for. Then, when the king had retired and the people had all gone home, I would lie alone in my bedchamber, dreaming of the day when my Angus would return to me.

The Bear didn't beat me when I "failed" to give him an heir.

It was *I* who failed: That's the way he put it, never considering the possibility that his own virility might be in question. He didn't beat me, because he had to keep up appearances. It wouldn't do to have a bruised and battered queen holding court beside him. But he stayed his hand, more importantly, because the Falcon forbade it. The hooded figure was not a constant presence at court, as I would have expected a senior advisor to be. He came and went, seemingly whenever he chose. The Bear never protested, perhaps because he feared the Falcon might replace him—the way Samuel had withdrawn his blessing from Saul and placed it on David.

Evermore

The Falcon claimed he had *been* Samuel in a past life, but this was impossible: The Lord of Hosts gave us each a single lifetime to prove our faith, after which we would rise to heaven and become like angels or descend into the depths of fiery hell. When I told him this, he merely shrugged and reminded me that he did not share my faith. His purpose was merely to serve as a bridge from an age of darkness into a new golden age: one that would forge the best of old and new into a common crucible.

Just as Samuel had been a bridge from Saul to David.

I didn't want to take that parallel any further, for it would cast my father as some new version of Saul, who needed to meet his death for the "rightful" king to claim the throne. The Bear seemed nothing like King David.

Although he did have his best friend murdered so he could sleep with the man's wife.

He was like David in that way.

After a short time, he began to tire of me simply lying under him, motionless, to serve as a receptacle for his seed. He visited my bed less often, instead satisfying his immense ego with women who pretended he pleased them: Either they feared his wrath if they disappointed him or they were conniving to replace me at his side. I was only too happy to let them have him; by the time we had been three months together, his visits to my chamber were perfunctory and few. He returned to my bed only at the moon's proper phase, so he might try again to conceive a child.

I had no fear that the Bear would replace me. His own fear—of the Falcon—kept any impulse to do so in check.

The Falcon seemed to be protecting me. At first, I thought it was because I fit in so well to whatever purpose he believed was destined to be fulfilled. That was true, to be sure. But as time passed, I realized there was something more as well. He felt some personal connection to me. Perhaps he felt a responsibility to look out for the girl he and the Bear's men had orphaned (and I *was* still a girl to him, though he seemed to realize I was something more.)

The Falcon and I sat and talked for hours sometimes. Partly because I was lonely, and partly because he sensed he could speak with me honestly, at least when it came to matters of the heart. He told me of a woman named Vivian, with whom he'd fallen in love. In wooing her, he'd taught her the ways of a seer, and she shared her bed with him. But she'd told him, to his disappointment, that she could not conceive.

As time passed, she began to distrust him over his refusal to confide in her regarding what the future might hold for her. That distrust grew to fear, and that fear to resentment, until one day she told him she had seen *his* future: that this life would be his last.

The Falcon had not expected this: that she would use the skills he had taught her against him.

He'd flown into a rage and, in an unguarded moment, had told her what he had foreseen about *her* destiny: She had lied to him, he told her, for she would in fact conceive a child—their child—and that the son she would bear would share the fate of the Falcon himself: He would live and die and live again, a near immortal on this Earth. And not only that, but he would remember every detail of all the lives he lived, being unable to forget a single thing he ever experienced over a thousand lifetimes.

Evermore.

"This is a blessing and a curse," he told me. "It has allowed me to avoid making the same mistakes I have made in lifetimes past... most of the time. Yet it has also shown me *what* my destiny will be in each new life to come—in everything but love."

I tilted my head and fixed him with a questioning gaze.

"I knew that Vivian was the only woman I could ever love. We were bonded in a way that surpassed anything either of us could conjure. For this reason, I had resisted looking into her future until then, not wishing to know what it might hold for us. But in that moment of fury, my passion betrayed me. I looked... and saw that she and I were not fated to be together, in this life or any other. It broke me, and I resolved then and there that this life would be my last, for I could not endure going forward with this knowledge throughout eternity. And I realized then that I was setting the course for the very thing Vivian had foretold of me. My fate was aligned with my wishes, as so rarely happens. Yet in this case, it was true, and sadly so."

I felt terrible for him. I could not imagine what such a cruel sentence must feel like, even if it were merely the dreadful realization of an aged man coming to terms with the fact that life had passed him by.

My father had spoken of this once, at the death of my mother: "Once we accept that death will claim us, we begin to reflect on all the things we have done—and failed to do—in our time upon this Earth. This is to prepare us for the judgement God will render at our passing, and bring us to that peace that passes understanding: The assurance that He is with us, even as we pass through the valley of the shadow of death."

Now, I believed, I was seeing the same in the Falcon, though he professed no faith in the risen Christ.

One need not believe in something for it to be true.

I did not believe what the Falcon was telling me. I still believed him to be deluded, perhaps by the torment of love denied him. Yet like Eve, I could not resist the temptation to ask for divine knowledge of one who claimed to possess it.

"What, then, is my fate to be?"

The Falcon, though, was no serpent. He had not tricked me into asking for this, and he even seemed troubled that I should have broached it. "I would spare you this, child," he said softly. "For if it were good, you would lose your taste for it, having already experienced it in your mind's eye. And what we see with our minds is always more perfect than what we see when we are living it..."

Almost always. Angus...

"...and if it were for ill, you would torture yourself in attempting to escape that which must happen. And you would go mad when you finally realized that you were powerless to do so. However, I will grant you the answer to one question about all these things that I have told you, with only this condition: You must choose something you are sure will have no impact on your own destiny."

That hadn't been what I wanted to hear, but I could tell the Falcon believed he was protecting me.

"You have appointed yourself the guardian of my interests," I said.

But he shook his head: "That task has been given to another."

I raised my eyebrows. He could only have meant Angus. But how could he have known?

"Your question, fair Alba. What is it?"

I thought for a moment, then chose a question about the story he had told me that I was certain had no impact on me: "Whatever became of the son that Vivian bore you?"

The Falcon's face turned a ghostly shade of pale, and his eyes widened... "I told you my condition..."

40

"That I could only ask you a question I was sure would not affect me. And so I have done."

For the first time since I'd known him, the Falcon appeared beside himself, uncertain, and... regretful.

"So I did," he said finally, resignation in his voice. "I spoke in haste and carelessly, as you could not possibly have been sure what might affect you in the future. Yet now I am bound to answer your question, for I have given my word."

Be careful what you wish for, a voice inside my head was saying. *You shouldn't ask questions if you are wary of the answers.*

But how could the fate of Vivian's son possibly matter to me? I had never met her or her son, and I had only known the Falcon since the fall of Colonia. And how could this man's destiny have any impact on my future?

I would soon find out.

"Vivian's son is a man you know," the Falcon said slowly. "That man's name is Angus."

Sharon Marie and Stephen H. Provost

The Knight
Uneasy Alliance

Asking Marcellus for help had been an even bigger mistake than I'd first realized. Not only had he laughed at my request, but then he'd turned it on its head. He'd asked... no, *demanded* that I help him defend Lutetia from a barbarian tribe called the Franks that was advancing from the north.

As a loyal Roman citizen, I could not refuse, but when I saw the numbers of the Frankish horde, I realized no single legion could stand against them. I pleaded with Marcellus to call in provisions from the surrounding tributaries and prepare a strong defense. These Franks, I knew, were marauders who lacked the patience or discipline for a protracted siege.

But he wouldn't listen. He insisted on sending the legion forth and taking the fight to the enemy.

It was a terrible mistake.

The imperial force endured tremendous losses before finally withdrawing again behind the walls... but without the provisions

I had begged them to store up. Now, it was too late. The marauders had already burned the fields of grain and set fire to the peasant dwellings outside the city. Now throngs of homeless people were clamoring at the gates to get in, with neither food nor water to sustain them.

Marcellus refused them, and the barbarians cut them down with their backs literally to the city walls, slaying the men and brutally defiling their women before finally ending their lives at the point of a sword.

I had seen enough. I had no taste for being slain or starved out with the rest of them. This was a sign that I was needed, not in Gaul, but where my first duty lay.

To Colonia.

To Alba.

It had always been thus, and now I knew it evermore would be.

By the time I finally returned to Britannia, it was too late.

Everything had changed.

Colonia had fallen.

I found my lands occupied by pagans who had plundered my cellar and slaughtered my livestock. These were not the legions that had besieged Lutetia, but a handful of opportunists who had set themselves up as mock lords of an abandoned hall. This was my punishment for thinking I could garner help from the emperor. I flew into a rage and massacred the lot of the usurpers, cleaving heads from shoulders and arms from torsos. I thrust the point of my sword into each of their bellies and pulled their entrails out with my bare hands, venting my wrath at my own failure on them.

Evermore

When I was done, I set their heads on posts along the boundary to my land, around the lake that had been my mother's home before me. It had been she who had bequeathed me my blade, which she said had been forged with Vulcan's hammer and quenched to harden in this very lake. I did not believe in Vulcan—or any of the pagan gods—though I could never dissuade her from doing so. What I did believe in was the power of an iron blade, the point of an arrow, and the tip of my lance. Such things, wielded by the proper hand, would do what no false god could accomplish.

When I was done reclaiming my lands, I stood there, chest heaving and drenched in blood like a man possessed.

And I *was* possessed: by the righteous spirit of God.

"Are you satisfied?"

The voice took me by surprise, and I turned to see a figure emerging from the forest. He wore a cloak and carried an oaken staff, which he used to steady himself as he walked toward me, his back slightly bent from age.

"I am not," I said.

"Good."

"Who are you, old man? Speak plainly, or I swear to the heavens I will cut you down where you stand."

He put his arms out to either side, so that his cloak appeared like wings spread out.

"The Falcon," I hissed. "You are the one behind all this madness."

"Madness?" he said. "You are the one here who appears taken by mania."

"By God, old man, I am..."

"Angry? Embittered? Lusting for vengeance? I know. You can direct your lust toward me, but it will not be quenched. Neither

45

will it accomplish anything. Your god has set before you a purpose, and I am here to help you fulfill it."

"By destroying Colonia? By setting your men to defile my household?"

He shook his head. "Your estate's condition is not my doing. The men you killed acted on their own. And as to Colonia, it has not been destroyed but is being transformed even now into the greatest capital this land has ever known, Camulodunum. Throne to the high dragon, on whose behalf I have come to you this day with an offer."

"*You* claim to speak for *him*?" I laughed. "I judge it to be the reverse: He is a puppet on the devil's strings, guided by your hand."

"I *am* a guide, but merely to keep his feet pointed straight on the path to his destiny. I am the same for you."

I spat at his feet. "I don't *need* your guidance!" I shouted.

"Is that truly so? Or do you not wish to be restored to your position as Alba's protector?"

"Alba lives?"

"Not only does she live, she reigns as queen in Camulodunum."

My eyes widened in shock.

"And the Bear? I thought *he* was to be king. I thought…"

"He does reign, indeed, with Alba as his consort, as has always been fated."

I stared at him, my heart filled with fury. Alba was *mine* to protect! And this charlatan had allowed—even arranged for— that beast to claim her? I moved my hand slowly toward the hilt of my sword.

The Falcon must have seen I was preparing to end his life,

because he raised one hand and said, "I can help." He tried not to make his pronouncement seem hurried. He was practiced at keeping his cool. But even so, I could sense just the slightest hint of concern in his voice. Of fear.

"How?" I snarled, keeping my hand a hair's breadth from my blade.

"As I insinuated, *if* you'd been paying attention..." The haughty impatience in his tone did nothing to alleviate my rage. "...it is within my power—and it is also my sincere intention—to restore you to your rightful position as Alba's protector."

"And why would you do that?"

"Oh, I have reasons, and good ones. I don't normally share my motivations, but since you insist on keeping that blade of yours at the ready..."

"It is said you can see the future, wizard. If this be true, you should know if I'm going to use it," I scoffed.

He smiled. "I see the future as the falcon sees the forest below, on a grand scale. The details are less clear to my eye. But I have been fated to live one life after another, each in a different mortal skin, and I remember everything I've learned in each previous incarnation. Thus am I able to predict with a fair degree of accuracy what will come next. I am nearing the end of my journey through these many lives, but yours is just beginning. Have a care, for few possess the gift we share—the ability to remember lives past—and fewer still master it before it drives them mad."

The gift we *shared*? What was he talking about? None of it made any sense. He was an old man given to wandering off on tangents that had nothing to do with the matter at hand. It was my task to refocus his attention on what we were *supposed* to be discussing. "Why would you want to reinstate me as Alba's protector?"

"If you would allow me to finish," he harrumphed, "I was getting to that. As I was *about* to say, my reasons are these. For one thing, I fully recognize that the high dragon is a volatile and capricious man. I need you there to protect Alba from him. But more than that, I have foreseen that he will not succeed in fulfilling his destiny without your help. Even now he is assembling a group of knights to fully secure his place as their ruler and build what I have foreseen for Albion. You are the most renowned warrior in these lands, and I would have you at his side—not at his throat."

He wanted *me* to *help* this uncouth pretender strengthen his hold on a city he had stolen from its rightful rulers? *My* city? My fingers moved back to my blade and curled themselves around its hilt.

"I would be careful about trying to use that."

Was he *warning* me?

I smiled ruefully. "You yourself called me the most renowned warrior in this land," I reminded him. "Do you think you can stand against me?"

"Whether I can or not is immaterial..."

Not exactly the best way to back up a threat.

"...but if you do not accept this invitation, I will be unable to restore you as Alba's protector, which would, I fear, leave her vulnerable to the Bear King's moods and whims. Do you really want that? This course of action is in *all* our interests. Indeed, it is the only possible course that lies before us."

He was asking me to make a deal with the devil, and leaving me no choice in the matter. I gritted my teeth and narrowed my eyes. I could, of course, try to breach the city walls myself and take on however many knights he'd already assembled to fight for his cause. I was confident in my abilities, but not *that* confident. My best course of action would be to take the Falcon up on his "offer" and infiltrate the Bear's inner circle, then look for an opportunity to spirit Alba away from that place. Once I'd accomplished this, I could work on consolidating my own forces to retake Colonia.

I knew the Falcon would be expecting such a move, but he'd just admitted that he only saw the forest, not the trees. He might know my intentions, but he would be blind to when or how I might decide to carry them out.

"If it must be so," I said coldly, "then I accept your offer. But if anything goes wrong... if Alba is harmed in any way... blood will spill. Yours. The Bear's. And anyone who dares to stand against me."

He smiled coldly back. "As her protector," he said, "it will be your task to ensure that does not happen." Then his face softened, and in a whisper he added, "I owe this to your mother."

The Bear had gone mad—if he'd ever been sane to begin with.

Upon arriving at court, I found he was engaged in some ridiculous scheme to find and procure the chalice of Christ's communion. The idea that this object should be in Britannia seemed absurd enough, but his "plan"—such as it was—involved simply dispatching his warriors to run about blindly through the hinterlands, looking for it without having any clue where it might be.

What he hoped to gain by this was even more fanciful. He seemed to believe that this chalice held the power to yield up unlimited sustenance, thereby enabling him and his men to withstand any siege. Beyond this, he had gotten it into his head that the cup could heal his wounds and grant him eternal life. He seemed to have missed the entire point of what Christ had said at the Last Supper: that his *blood*, not the chalice that held it, was the key to eternal life... and then in the kingdom of heaven, not here on this mortal plain.

What the Falcon thought of this, and whether or not he had endorsed it, I did not know. His knack for remaining inscrutable, even to the keenest eye, was uncanny. But the preparations for this foolhardy quest kept him preoccupied—so much so that he barely noticed my comings and goings in the new palace he was building inside the city walls: a hollow and gaudy monument to his own misguided ambition.

But I had little concern for such things, apart from the fact that sending his warriors out on a futile "quest" left the city largely undefended. He'd sought to dispatch me, as well, but the Falcon had convinced him not to pursue this: "Angus is your best fighter. Keep him here, close at hand, that your queen and your capital might be well defended in the absence of your warriors."

This turn of events could not have been more auspicious. The king's absence would make executing my plan much easier, with no one but the Falcon to oppose me.

I wouldn't have much time until they returned, which meant I would need to win Alba over quickly.

That, however, proved to be more difficult than I'd hoped.

She'd aged less than a year since last I saw her, but she seemed to have transformed herself from a girl into a... queen. I knew I couldn't seek a private audience with her. As her protector, I was charged with guarding the door to her chamber and accompanying her in public, nothing more. And even in this capacity, she refused to speak to me beyond perfunctory commands that she delivered in a haughty tone.

She scrupulously avoided looking my way, and if she happened to do so accidentally, turned her head quickly so our eyes would not meet.

It was apparent that she held my long absence against me, which wounded me to the soul. I already felt I had failed her, and would never forgive myself; I did not need her coldness toward me to remind me of this, and I longed to remind her of our Lord's injunction: "Be kind to one another, tenderhearted, forgiving one another, even as God for Christ's sake hath forgiven you."

Yet I dared not... at least not within the city walls.

So I waited until she went riding in the countryside—an outing on which I was, as her protector, charged to accompany her.

"Must you always be my shadow?" she demanded as we came near the edge of the forest. "Following me like the shadow of the lapdog you are. The Falcon's lapdog." Her words were cutting, but also encouraging: It was the first time she'd spoken to me other than to order me about.

"I am charged with being your protector, Lady."

"And a fine job you did of that the first time," she scoffed. "How could my husband countenance such a breach?"

"I took counsel with the Falcon, and he himself arranged it."

"The Falcon!" She spun around on her horse and gave me a withering look. Then she jumped to the ground and marched toward me, her hands balled up in fists and shaking as she approached. She looked like she was heading off to war. "So you *are* in league with him? The man who arranged my father's death? The man whose forces laid waste to Colonia while you were off God knows where? The Falcon does not arrange things for me. I follow my own dictates, not his."

"From what I understand, he arranged for you to be married to that idiot of a husband who shares your bed," I shot back. "But I will grant you this: The Bear does nothing without the Falcon's assent, so perhaps you should at least thank that crooked old man for making our fair city habitable again. You yourself reside in a palace, do you not?"

"ARGHHHHH!" she screamed at me.

"I know the Falcon spared your life during the invasion," I hissed.

"An invasion that would not have happened in the first place if not for the Falcon. And during which I would not have been taken captive if not for... You. Not. Being. There."

"So what is the Falcon to you, then? Your enslaver or your benefactor?" She could not very well defend and condemn him at the same time... although I myself had done the same. This fact, it turned out, was not lost on her.

"And what is he to *you*?" she shot back. "Your enemy or ally? Do speak plainly, sir, for I tire quickly of this banter."

"He is my means to see you again!" I shouted, putting my hands on the sides of both her shoulders.

She struggled for a moment, but I held her fast, then pulled her to me. I could feel her heart beating faster in her breast... or was it my own? Perhaps they were beating in time.

"Unhand me..." The phrase burst forth from her lips determined, then sank meekly in upon itself amid growing regret.

She was shaking now.

"Please...," she said, her voice quavering. "You cannot still care for me... Not now... that it is... too late."

"But it is *never* too late," I whispered in her ear.

"I am wed to another. I am a queen..." Her protests sounded hollow, as though she were arguing with her conscience.

And losing.

She was sobbing uncontrollably, her body collapsing into mine and roiling it with waves from a tortured breast. "I held out hope for so long, dear Angus... What was I to do? Why did you not come sooner?"

I knew no answer I could give would satisfy her, for none existed that could satisfy me. The truth, perhaps, least of all.

"I must tell you something," she whispered back through tears.

"I love thee," I said softly.

She nodded into my shoulder, as though she had taken my pronouncement as a question. "Yes, I love thee, Angus," she said. "I always have."

The Maiden
Undone

My husband the king was away upon his quest, so it was barely noticed when I invited his bravest knight to my bedchamber when all was dark and quiet.

And the following evening.

And the evening after that.

Night was the only time Angus himself was not charged with guarding my door. Another guard was posted there, which allowed Angus a few hours of rest in his own quarters. Yet he was not resting. He was with me.

He came in through the hidden entrance from the backstairs that my husband had installed, ironically enough, to come and go as he pleased without being noticed.

Our love, though kept in the shadows, blossomed as the lilacs and bluebells do in the fullness of springtime sun. Being parted from him during his long absence had been painful enough, but now that he had returned, each brief moment apart seemed like that very same eternity—torture now compounded by knowledge of his love.

The daylight hours were filled with longing. As my protector, he stood beside me, but neither of us dared betray the passion that burned within us. As the queen, it might have been assumed that I would take my husband's place on the throne in his absence, seeing to affairs of state. But that was not the way of this world, in which women were mere appendages of men, their authority extending no further than their own attendants and serving girls. It was the Falcon, not I, who spoke in the king's name, and though part of me took offense at this, another part of me was grateful that I could remain out of the public eye, that no one might guess the constant yearning of my heart.

The Falcon, of course, knew without guessing. He'd made it known with a single glance that he was well aware of my trysts with Angus. It was a glance that said, "Be careful" and "Enjoy yourself" at the same time. But when I asked him discreetly of news on when the king might return, he told me merely that the Bear's party had traveled to a place that was past the extent of even his keen eyesight.

I did not for one moment believe him.

"If this does not convince you that we are fated to be together, what then will?" Angus asked me, kissing me lightly on my wrist as we lay together.

"It is not the fates I mistrust, but the Bear," I said. "And my own desires. How will we escape the Lord's wrath for flouting his commandments: For coveting each other so and brazenly defiling the marriage bed?"

"If we are guilty of sin, let it be the sin of love," he said, nibbling at my neck. I wrapped my arms around him and drew him closer, gasping slightly.

"But..."

"The king himself is guilty of fornication. His whole company knows it. The king beds whomever he pleases, and he may have a dozen bastard sons in the city and outside it." His lips worked their way down to my shoulder, kneading my flesh and biting gently as he flicked his tongue against it. "Those poor wretches, spurned by their father, were not the product of love, but of a dark spirit bent on feeding the man's insatiable carnal lusts."

He ran his hand down my outer thigh, then back up the inside slowly, like a serpent slithering up me.

I could barely think. "What we do. That... does not... make it... right."

I gasped as he cupped his hand over my mound and slid a single finger slowly inside. "How... are his... lusts... any less... carnal... than yours...?"

A second finger followed, pressing up deeper, as he lowered his head to kiss my breast. He raised it just long enough to say, "Your husband lay as a very young man with his own lawful sister, with whom he conceived a bastard child."

I had not heard this.

He slid on top of me and pulled me to him, looking me in the eyes as he began to move on me. "He brought the child here out of guilt and even knighted him."

"What?" I gasped, but didn't focus on his answer.

He was moving faster now, and I with him. "His name is... Medraut," he grunted. "The king has knighted him, and he... sits at... his table... But the Bear did not trust him... enough... to have him... accompany him... on his quest... He..."

My lover's thrusting had grown more insistent.

I squeezed my eyes shut, lost in a swirl of imagined sound

and color.

Whatever more he had planned to say was stolen away from him by the urgency of his own passion.

"Alba!" he cried, arching his back. "My Alba!"

"I am yours... forever!"

"Yes, forever!"

"We are fated. We are one!"

"We are..."

"Discovered!"

Angus tumbled off me, falling naked to the floor on all fours, then springing to his feet. The backstairs door was open. Had we, in our haste to find each other's arms, neglected to bolt it? There stood, as though in answer to our summons, young Medraut himself, backed by two members of the king's guard.

"Yes, discovered," he said in a self-satisfied tone. "By the very one of whom you spoke!"

He turned to the guards, and cried, "Seize them!"

There was nowhere for either of us to run.

We were separated after that, and I was thrown into a dungeon underneath the palace to await my husband's return.

I prayed that he might have been killed on his quest.

Such prayers, I knew, would never be answered by a righteous God, and I remonstrated myself for saying them... then said them again and again and again.

In due course, the Bear did, in fact, return. He did not come to me in person, but sent guards who paraded me barefoot and in rags before the people of the city, from the dungeon to the common square. All along this "journey of penitence," as he called it, I was tugged by a chain fastened to a collar around my neck. I slipped and fell time and again in the mud and manure that littered the streets, only to be hauled roughly to my feet again and dragged forward.

My eyes searched the crowds for Angus, but they found only eyes filled with loathing and hate. Many of those eyes belonged to people I knew. Friends. Acquaintances. People to whom I had shown kindness and who had shown the same to me... but no more. In this moment, transformed from queen to whore on the word of a bastard, none of them hesitated for even a moment to buffet me with tomatoes and cabbages and heads of lettuce until my skin was a blotched canvas of red and purple.

The king was waiting for me in the square, seated on a palanquin borne aloft by members of his court.

Jeers and curses rose from the crowd, continuing unabated until the king raised his hand for silence.

"What do you have to say for yourself, whore?" he demanded.

I looked up at him, steeling myself, but saying nothing.

A lash came down upon my back.

"Will you not answer your king? Your *husband*?"

I shook my head slightly, and the lash came down again.

"Then I will answer for you," he shouted. "Alba the Fair, I judge thee guilty of fornication, adultery, and treason to your king. And I further find that thou hast bewitched my faithful knight Felix Angus, luring him with your wiles to thy bed, that ye might corrupt him and turn him from the way of the Lord."

"Angus! Where is he?" I shouted.

The Bear just laughed. "The crime of adultery a gentle husband might forgive," he said, then turned his head and spoke to one side, as though confiding something to his friends. "Though no one has ever accused me of gentility!"

The crowd erupted in laughter.

"The crime of treason is another matter, yet even this pales in comparison with the crime of witchcraft that you have committed. For this crime, the punishment is that you must be burned at the stake until dead, *dead*, DEAD!" He laughed again, and motioned with his hands for the crowd to join him.

He turned to the throng. "As for Angus, he has left us. Where he has gone, I know not. But he is welcome to rejoin my knights, should he wish to, with the only conditions being that he swear fealty to me and renounce the witch who stands before you now... by spitting on her grave once she is dead. Until then, the valiant Medraut shall sit by my right hand, at the head of my table." He turned and looked to his side, and Medraut stepped out of the crowd to take a bow.

I spat at him.

"Die, witch, die!" the crowd responded, and it became a chant, repeated again and again.

"Die, witch, die!"

"Die, witch, die!"

"DIE, WITCH, DIE!"

More tomatoes and cabbages were thrown at me, and I ducked but failed to avoid all of them. I sank to my knees in the mud and covered my head with my arms. Then, all of a sudden, it stopped.

"Hold!" a voice at the back of the crowd demanded.

I looked up, and every head turned.

It was Angus. "I invoke the right of challenge!"

Everyone turned to look at him, riding in on his horse, his eyes fixed on the king.

The Bear opened his mouth to speak, but the next words came from close beside him. "The right of challenge has been invoked," the Falcon said, stepping forward to stand before the king, raising his cloak with his arms. "By law, once invoked, no king may refuse the right of challenge. But he may, by right, choose whomever he wishes to act as his champion."

All heads turned to Medraut, but he shrank back.

The coward.

"And," the Falcon continued, "also by law, the person who would be the king's champion must come forward *willingly*."

No one moved. The knights all feared the king, but they sensed that the Falcon stood ready to shield them from his wrath... and they also sensed that neither the Falcon nor anyone else would protect them from Angus in a joust or swordfight. The outcome of such an encounter, for *any* knight, was not in doubt.

"And if," the Falcon said further, raising his voice, "no one will come forth to act as the king's champion, the king must accept it as defeat and spare the life of Queen Alba."

"Nooooooo!" the king bellowed. "I do not accept this!"

The Falcon fixed him with a steely glare. "It is the *law*, your majesty."

The Bear stood up in his seat so suddenly that the men holding it were unable to steady it. He tumbled off the palanquin and onto the ground.

"I know the law, old fool!" he screamed, getting to his feet and trying in vain to brush the mud from his vestments... instead smearing it into the fabric. "And I also know this: that it is my right to select a lesser punishment should no champion come forward." His eyes moved in a slow circle, encompassing all the warriors who had refused to answer his call. "I therefore decree that the queen shall be stripped of all title and possessions, and shall retire to the abbey at Almesbury, where she shall dedicate the rest of her days to the Lord in chastity, penance, and solitude."

I looked to the Falcon, my eyes pleading, but he shook his

head.

"I invoke the right of challenge!" Angus shouted again, desperation in his voice this time.

"Your challenge has been issued and met," the Falcon said, raising his staff. "You have no more standing here, unless you wish to accept the king's gracious offer to swear fealty and return to him."

"Never!" Angus shouted. "I shall not rest until you pay for this, King Nothing! I shall hound you to the ends of the earth, and I shall win my love back, if not in this life, then the next one!" Then he lowered his voice. "I vow it on my life, and I curse you in my mother's name, whose sword I wield: You shall *never* find the chalice of the Supper which you seek, for the Lord will withhold it from now until eternity. Your bones will rot in your grave, King Bear, but the queen and I will attain life everlasting. Together."

With that, he spun on his horse and departed.

And from that moment, I was lost.

The Maiden

Nevermore

The Falcon did not escort me to the abbey. He did not visit me there—nor did anyone else.

I never heard from the king, though rumors reached my ears that he had descended into madness, had waged war against Angus, and had ultimately died in battle, slain by the same bastard son who discovered our betrayal.

I did not hear from Angus, either. Once again, he had abandoned me.

After a time, I resigned myself to my fate, and I resolved in my heart that I would never break the vow of celibacy I'd taken. My passions had betrayed me once, but never again. I had been sentenced to this place by my own doing, and only the Lord's clemency had spared my life.

But what life? What *kind* of life was this?

Had the Lord been merciful or vengeful in consigning me to live without the one person who understood me? The one person who had ever loved me? I knew not whether he even lived. Had he been slain seeking vengeance against the king? Had he died of some plague or off on some quest to redeem himself? There was no word; no way of knowing. I knew one thing: I could not wait for him to return any longer. I had put myself through that sorrow—sustaining myself on prayers and wishful thinking—once before, when he had left me at Colonia, and my heart could not endure it a second time.

So I sat down and wrote him a letter. Into it I poured the last of my failed wishes, so I might be free at last the burden of them once and for all:

> *My dearest love,*
>
> *These will be my last words to you, and in truth, I hope you never read them. For I would far prefer that you live out your days in ignorance of my fate, and in forgetfulness of what we might have had together.*
>
> *I was sent to this place that I might renounce the world and all things in it, yet my heart would not allow me to renounce the one thing that mattered: you, my darling. The only thing I can do to be free of this curse is to renounce the world in truth by ending this tragic journey at last and for all time. Know that I would have lived forever with you had it been destined, but since the fates have conspired against us, I take my own fate now and rail against them one last time.*
>
> *I know that by this deed I will seal the door that leads to heaven, but what is heaven without my true love? Our lives have been lived in hell on earth, so perhaps it is in hell below that we shall meet. I bid you now farewell. For now and for always, you are my knight in shining armor.*

Evermore

I took the rope that bound the plain white garment at my waist, removed it and flung it over one of the low rafters in my quarters. I secured it there, then looped it around itself and tied it in a knot.

I stepped up on the only piece of furniture in the room, a small wooden stool, and slipped the rope around my head.

Then I closed my eyes and kicked the stool away, feeling the rope jerk tight and dig into my skin.

I gasped, flailing for a moment, and opened my eyes one last time.

My gaze fell upon the small window across from me, and there I beheld, in my final moment, the sight of Angus running toward me, calling desperately. As I drifted away into that final sleep, I thought I heard him crying out, as if in a faint echo: "Alba! Alba! Oh, my God, NO...!"

Sharon Marie and Stephen H. Provost

New England,
Late 18th Century

Eat Your Heart Out

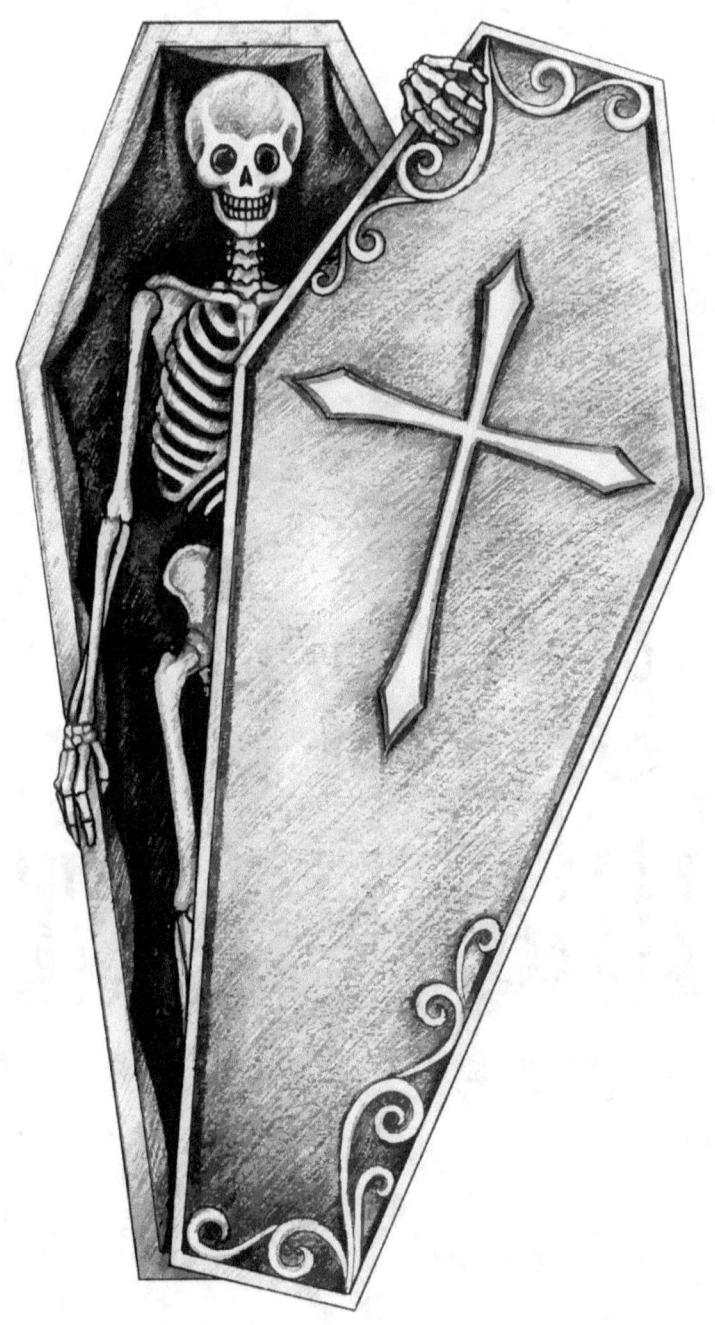

The Miller's Son

PALE

"Wake up!"

I shook Teagan softly, but she didn't stir. She'd been in the midst of a nightmare a moment earlier, but now she had gone completely stiff, as though dead.

I shook her more frantically.

"Teagan, it was only a dream. Wake up!"

Her eyes popped open and she sat straight up, a look of terror on her face, and she began coughing and sputtering violently.

"Oh," she sighed, easing herself back onto the pillow. "It's you, Lawrence." She smiled faintly. At least I still had a soothing effect on her. Would that I might have been able to enter that fever dream of hers and slay whatever demon had been assailing her.

"Your dream... do you remember it?"

She nodded slightly. "Some of it, brother. There was a dark creature hovering over me, held aloft by... I know not what. I saw no wings, and the face was obscured in shadow. But those eyes... they were brighter than fire, and it shed crimson tears, oozing rather than running from its eyes. I felt them... run off of him and onto me. When they hit my skin, they both burned and chilled me. There was blood coming out of its mouth, too, and spurting out onto me as it laughed or choked... I could not tell which."

I nodded and brushed her cheek with the back of my hand. Oh, how I loved my dear Teagan! We'd shared our mother's womb, and so much else I dared not tell her. These dreams of hers—they had vexed me as well, but not with the same consequence that my precious sister endured.

Teagan had been frail since birth, though no one could explain why. Our mother had perished giving birth to her; she had remained stalwart all during her first delivery, but no one knew a second twin remained within her, struggling to emerge. When she did, the cord was wrapped around her neck, depriving her of the air she needed to live. The wetnurse, in her haste to save the child, had cut the cord too close to our mother's body, unleashing a torrent of blood that she could not stem.

Father blamed Teagan for our mother's death, and swore that she must be a demon child. Even now, he spoke of how he should have left her out in the forest to be consumed by wild animals or taken by the early winter chill. "If she'd been lucky, one of the savages would have found her," he said. "This demon is no child of mine."

In the Old Country, he said, the devious fae would steal human babies from their cribs and replace them with lookalike demons. "Who's to say they didn't steal my *true* daughter from

70

her mother's womb as well?" he shouted, flailing his arms about like a windmill.

It was merely a folktale, based on nothing more than fearful imaginings. I might have been just sixteen years old, but I *knew* this. My father either did not know, despite being more than twice my age, or was using it as an excuse to blame poor Teagan for his own failings. He was always complaining that she had been born a girl, and a frail one at that, who could not pull her weight in running the mill. She wasn't strong enough to hoist the grain to the top floor of the mill, move sacks of flour, or adjust the gap between the millstones. Even simple chores such as sifting the flour were often too much for her.

To our father, this meant she was useless.

For me, it meant more work. But I never minded. I thought of it as helping Teagan, not helping Father—and anything I could do to help her, I would. But it was never enough. When a beaver dammed up the waterway that turned our millwheel, he blamed it on Teagan. "There be witches in this new country," he told me. "I've heard tell of it. They call simple animals to them, which they enslave to their will and passions. Most use cats. But this demon child has bound a beaver to work her will for her."

I shook my head. "Even if it were possible, why would she do such a thing? The mill is her livelihood as much as ours."

My question earned me a hard slap across my cheek. "How can one who does no work speak of livelihood? She does this solely to vex me. To *vex* me, I tell you!" He struck me again, this time backhanded. He was convinced that Teagan was somehow his enemy, and that she would take any opportunity to thwart his designs.

But Teagan had neither the time nor energy for such things. I could stand by and take it when my father hit me, but if he ever did the same to Teagan, I didn't know what I might do. Though I doubted the church's teachings, I somehow knew that some power far greater than myself had ordained me as her protector, and I loved her fiercely, with the kind of love that burns in the heart of a man for a woman. When I looked at her, I saw not my sister but my mate: the one person on this Earth who understood me, and the one person I could confide in. I dared not breathe a word of these feelings, to her or to anyone else, because they were forbidden. But no prohibition could banish them from my heart, which was one with hers even if our bodies could never be one.

I both blessed and cursed the day that we were born: the former because I was spared the arduous task of seeking her out and the heartbreak of one second lived without her; the latter because we could never consummate our love. Yes, I knew she loved me in the very same way, though she too could never give voice to it. I could see it in her eyes and in the way her chest rose and fell when we spoke; I could feel it in the way she clutched my hand tightly when she held it, and in how she held me close when we embraced—an embrace that defied her weakness.

Today, though, she was even weaker than normal. Fair of complexion from birth, she had grown even paler these past few days. She woke but seemed as though she might slip back into slumber at any time, despite the risk of being confronted once more by the nightmare of which she had spoken.

"Rest, darling," I said, scooping her up into my arms. This time, though, she did not match my warm embrace with her own; she simply lay there in my arms, unable or unwilling to exert herself. I laid her back down as gently as I could, but even this slight change in position triggered another coughing fit. This time, though, she was coughing up blood.

"Father!" I shouted.

Evermore

"What do you *want?*" he shouted, as though I had interrupted some vital activity, without which the world would come crashing to an end. He always sounded like that, though, even when he was napping or simply watching the wheels for some sign that they might be too far apart.

"Teagan is ill," I said.

"What of it?"

I swore inwardly that I would go downstairs and throttle him then and there if he didn't respond with at least some small measure of decency and compassion.

"The post is due for delivery on the morrow. I shall send for the doctor then."

"She will worsen by then. I shall go to town myself and fetch the doctor."

"I need you here to work the mill," he said. "We cannot simply shut it because that witch child is sick."

"You can see to the mill," I shouted back. "Or go into town yourself if you prefer, and I will man the wheels."

There was a moment of silence, but I had no doubt how he would answer.

"Very well," he scoffed. "I will go and fetch Doctor Peterman. You stay here. But *you* will pay the doctor for coming to call on us and for any tincture or therapy he might prescribe. And if anything goes wrong here in my absence, you will pay for that as well."

"Doctor Peterman?" my voice caught in my throat. "But Doctor MacGregor is..."

"A *Methodist* who charges twice the fee," my father shot back. "We are *Presbyterians.* Or have you forgotten?"

I had not forgotten that *he* was a Presbyterian; I attended Sunday services because he insisted, not because I believed anything of the preaching that came out of the Reverend Archibald's pulpit. I had been born, in my father's words, with a doubting nature and a haughty spirit. In that much, he was correct. I could not deny it. But I had reasons for my lack of faith that a hard-hearted man like himself would never understand.

What I did understand is that Doctor MacGregor practiced modern medicine. He inoculated his patients for smallpox and performed highly effective surgeries to set bones and remove rotted teeth. More importantly, he eschewed the barbarous "cures" administered by Doctor Peterman, who prescribed mercury for everything from skin rashes to obstructed bowels, and used leeches to bleed his patients of their "ill humors."

Sure enough, when Peterman returned with Father, he brought with him leeches that he was certain would restore Teagan to health in no time. "She has been bleeding from her nose, correct?" he asked me, his mouth apparently moving somewhere behind the prodigious mustache and mutton chops that obscured it.

"Hrrumph," Father said. A single nod of his head was the only thing to indicate that he meant "yes."

"It is clear, then, that she is too sanguine, which is to say, she has too much blood in her system. The same must be drained to restore the proper balance of the four humors: blood, black bile, yellow bile, and phlegm. Once we have corrected this imbalance, she will gain strength and be up and about again within the week!"

"How do you know?" I asked, and saw Father shoot me a warning glance that I was at risk of being struck for my insolence. I didn't care.

"It is simply a matter of common sense, boy," Peterman said. "And it is standard practice dating back centuries to the time of

Galen. Because blood is the dominant humor, it must be drained to correct most imbalances, except of course in the case of a cold, where phlegm must be addressed, or cholera, which is caused by an overabundance of yellow bile."

I shook my head and whispered "balderdash" under my breath.

Unfortunately, my father heard it.

"Now see here," he said. "You were the one who insisted that I fetch the good doctor. If you wish to dismiss him before he has got the chance to administer his treatment, I care not. But have no doubt that the next time a physician is required, I will not be so willing to engage his services."

Peterman nodded approvingly. "Just so," he said. "Now, may I commence?"

"By all means," my father said, before I could get a word out.

"Very good." Peterman reached into a fabric bag he had brought along and withdrew a jar full of the parasites. He then pulled them out, one by one, between his thumb and forefingers, applying four to each of her arms. He opened her mouth to place one inside her lower lip, and put one of the things in each of her nostrils.

Teagan gagged and tried not to swallow, but this caused another coughing fit, which produced more blood and sent the leech inside her lip flying across the room.

My father went to retrieve it, but apparently it had fallen through a space between the floor boards.

Peterman patiently removed another leech from his jar and put it in place of the first one before declaring, "The blood is inside her lungs, I am afraid. We must therefore apply our little friends to her chest, that they may withdraw the blood from that place as well."

75

He reached down to untie her top and removed her shirt, leaving her naked with her breasts exposed. "I will place two on her chest, just below her neck, to clear her breathing tube, two more on her abdomen, and one on each nipple... just so."

I was shaking with rage as I watched him, yet I dared not intervene—if only because Teagan herself was shaking her head slowly as she watched me and was enduring the torture being inflicted on her so well.

I went to fetch a blanket to cover her, but the doctor grabbed it out of my hand. "We must leave her uncovered for the next hour or so while the leeches do their work. We do not want to risk jarring them loose."

At this, I could no longer stay silent. "It is freezing out!" I protested. "Even if, as you say, the leeches heal her, what good will it be if she catches a chill and contracts winter fever?"

The doctor did not answer; from the expression on his face, it appeared he had failed to consider this.

"You only did this to cast your eyes upon my sister's naked body, did you not?!" I shouted.

The doctor gasped, and my father's hand leapt forward and caught me by the ear. "I am done with this insolence of yours, boy," he said. "Perhaps it is you who should be exposed to chill air. Then you will either be proven right, and winter fever will rid me of your irksome presence once and for all, or else you will be proven wrong and disgraced for having spoken so rashly."

He smiled, satisfied, as though he had backed me into a corner. That, however, was the least of my worries. All I could think about was the prospect of losing Teagan because of this doctor's malpractice, and thinking of that drove me near to madness.

The Miller's Son

EXSANGUINATED

Teagan fell unconscious almost immediately after the leeches were applied, which the doctor declared to be an auspicious sign. "Fainting is a sign that our friends are doing their work."

Or was it?

Peterman had said the leeches would continue to feed on my sister for up to an hour, but after no more than a few minutes, they started to fall away, leaving red spots where more blood was oozing out of Teagan's body.

"This is... irregular," the doctor said. "There must be so much blood in her system that the leeches are becoming engorged almost at once. Her condition is worse than I feared."

"So what do we do now?" my father asked, feigning concern.

"We must apply more leeches, of course, and to other parts of the body where buildup may have occurred." He reopened the jar and plucked out more of the squirming creatures, setting them on her stomach, hips, and thighs. "Women bleed each month from their nether regions," he commented. "Perhaps placing our friends in this vicinity will ease the congestion within her."

That is not menstrual blood, I wanted to cry out, but I held my tongue.

The leeches dropped off my sister even more quickly this time, and the doctor shook his head in bafflement. "It is as though she has been consuming blood herself; in fact, I can think of no other reason there should be so much of it in her system."

"Consuming blood?" I said.

"I always knew she was a demon!" my father exclaimed.

Just then, Teagan sat up in bed, opened her mouth, and released a fountain of vomit full of bile... and blood.

"She is accursed!" my father shouted. "As the Good Book proclaimeth: 'Ye shall eat the blood of no manner of flesh, for the life of all flesh is the blood thereof. Whosoever eateth it shall be cut off.'"

"Amen," the doctor agreed.

They were insane. Teagan had not ingested anyone's blood. She was merely coughing so hard that she'd started bleeding inside. I was sure of it. Leeches would be of no help in such a situation—if they were, indeed, helpful in any situation.

I picked up the jar of leeches and hurled it across the room, where it shattered against the wall, freeing both the parasites and the pond water that preserved them. "Get out! Both of you! You'll kill her before you heal her. And I swear by Almighty God, I'll kill you if that happens!"

"Blasphemy!" my father exclaimed, balling both fists up as he took a step toward me.

Evermore

The doctor, however, seemed too unnerved to be angry. He bent down to pick up his medicine bag, bowed hastily to my father, and darted out the door.

"Her death be on your head!" my father shouted.

"She will not die!" I vowed.

But Teagan was shaking her head.

Sharon Marie and Stephen H. Provost

The Miller's Son

THE ACCURSED

In the days that followed, Teagan's condition only grew worse. She could not keep any food or fluid down; trying to do so would only trigger another coughing fit, after which she would vomit up whatever she'd ingested.

"Have you had any more nightmares?" I asked her.

She shook her head and responded in a raspy voice that was barely a whisper. "I only dream of waking up in a different body which has not been so ravaged by this affliction."

I put my head in my hands as I sat beside her.

"Do you think it is true what the Bible says? That when we grow weary of these present bodies, the Lord will give us heavenly bodies as new garments that will withstand all manner of affliction?"

I did not want to answer her. I had no faith that this was the case, but I had no wish to bring her spirits lower.

"I think," she finally continued, "that if this is so, death will be welcome as a tailor to fit me with these new garments."

I took her hand in mine and squeezed it. "You cannot submit to death so readily, dear Teagan. What would I do without you?"

"Come after me," she said. "Come away from all this and find peace with me."

I shook my head. "What if I come after you but fail to discover where you have gone? What if I am accursed, fated to spend all eternity pursuing you and never coming near to you again? I cannot risk it. I cannot."

"The Lord would not let that happen to us."

I gritted my teeth. "And why not? If the Lord were merciful and benevolent, how then could he condemn us to suffer so? To have taken our mother away and left us subject to a father who cares nothing for either one of us? To be constrained by birth from sharing our bodies as well as our souls? And now, to inflict such suffering on you that we are left with the choice of continued anguish or parting anew?"

"There is no choice, my love," she said softly. "The longer I tarry here with you, the more I suffer, and the less conscious I am of your presence. I am being torn from you piece by piece, day by day, our bond rent slowly but inexorably asunder by the horrors of this disease."

"No!" I shouted. "You cannot leave me!"

"Come after me then. I will wait for you."

"You cannot promise that. You have no knowledge of what lies beyond the veil."

"If our love is here, it will be there, as well. If you have no faith in the Lord, have faith in me. I will await you. This I promise. You have shown me so much kindness in our life together. Show me therefore one last kindness now." She reached beside her bed and laid her hands on the leather cord that had bound her skirt tight around her waist. She'd never tied it around herself again after the doctor's visit. Then, I had thought, it was because she was too weak or forgetful, but now I saw the truth of it.

She handed me the cord, placing one end in my right hand and the other in my left before closing both my palms around it.

"If you love me..." she said, her voice trailing off as she closed her eyes.

If I loved her? How often had I shown her the truth of this. Was she testing me or taunting me? Was she telling me I could only prove my love by taking her life? By removing her from my presence?

Her eyes fluttered open again briefly, and she nodded. "I know you love me," she said. "And I know you will do this for me."

She closed her eyes again, and I pulled the cord taut between my two hands, clutching its two ends so tightly my fists began to turn red. I would not give her the satisfaction of killing her on her terms, based on the lie of a promise that we would unite again in heaven. She should have known better than that. The God she worshiped was a phantom, and the act I would now perform would serve as a requiem to this phantom god.

Even as I looked down on her, the love drained out of my eyes and gave way to dawning fury. This was not an act of love, and she would not *make* me perform it in service of love. If I were to grant her request, as I knew I must, it would be on my own terms. In service not of love but of bitterness. Of fury. Of defiance.

I pulled the cord as tight as I could, leaned forward and pressed down hard on her throat.

She gasped once, and her eyes opened.

A look of shock fell across her face, and I knew it was not from the surprise that I had dared to carry out her request. It was from the look in my own eyes that must have seemed so foreign to her. In that moment, for the first time, I hated her. I hated her for denying me the only thing that meant anything in life.

Her presence.

She gagged and seized, more blood spurting out of her mouth as I pushed the cord down so hard it cut into her skin. I began yanking it back and forth, sawing through her flesh and deep into her throat. I was not killing my sister now. I was killing my darkest enemy.

And when it was all over and she had breathed her last, I was alone.

Just as I had always been.

The Minister

A Plan is Hatched

The graveyard behind our church had been growing quickly of late. Too quickly. A plague of unknown origin had come upon us, sent by Lucifer to test our faith or by God Himself to punish us for some transgression, though I knew not what.

As pastor and leader of our session at Covenant Presbyterian, it was my duty to discover the source of it. I could not simply entrust this duty to another, but had to see to it myself. Therefore, I set up a chair beside the headstone of our most prominent deceased member, deeming it most likely to draw out whatever evil had beset us.

I felt almost as though the spirit of Samuel Smith was looking down at me from heaven's gates, reproving me for disturbing his slumber. I took small comfort in the knowledge that my own slumber was fitful at best, wrapped in a woolen blanket that barely shielded me from the chill. Sleep was not my objective, in any case. I had charged myself to stay alert for any noise or movement that might signal something was amiss. Every time I fell asleep, my eyes would open with a start at the tiniest hint of some activity in the graveyard.

An owl taking to the wing.

A light breeze brushing my forehead.

A frog croaking out by the pond.

Something unknown skittering through the underbrush.

It was long past midnight when I was awakened by something else: A gaunt, pale man—not more than a boy, really—wearing an old knee-length gown. The moon was in its first quarter, providing enough light to see, but not clearly. The candle I had brought with me had gone out, so I struck flint against silver in my tinderbox, which made a noise that I feared would alert the intruder to my presence.

But he ignored it, and me, as though he were in a trance, walking slowly but deliberately toward one of the smaller gravesites, unmarked except for a small stone carved with the name Teagan. It was, I knew, the resting place of a girl who had been taken less than a fortnight ago by the plague that still beset us.

Fully awake, I watched with keen interest as the stranger walked over to the grave and first sat down, then lay himself prostrate upon it with his arms spread wide to both sides.

I heard his voice, low and still but carried to my ears upon the breeze.

Evermore

"Teagan, my love. Forgive me. I love thee still. Forgive me."

He repeated these last two words perhaps a dozen times between sobs before at last falling silent, his body growing still as he fell into either slumber or paralysis or the death-sleep. I knew not which.

I dared not disturb him, fearing that he was possessed by an evil spirit that might spring forth from him and attach itself to me.

The Lord is my shepherd. I shall not want. He maketh me to lie down in green pastures: he leadeth me beside the still waters. He restoreth my soul: he leadeth me in the paths of righteousness for his name's sake. Yea, though I walk through the valley of the shadow of death, I will fear no evil: for thou art with me...

The twenty-third Psalm had always brought me comfort in the past, but not this time. The words rang hollow inside my head as I stared at the almost ghostly form of the man, lying still as he was atop the grave. It was almost as though he wished to lie with the girl within, in some unholy coupling of the living and the dead.

I could not watch, but neither could I turn away. I sat transfixed, staring at him as he lay there. I thought I could make out his body rising and falling slightly, impelled by the intake and exhalation of air... or perhaps I only imagined it.

The next thing I knew, the rays of the sun were washing warm over my face.

I sat up straight with a start.

The candle had expired, and the young man who had been lying on the grave was gone. I wondered now whether he had ever really been there, or if he might have been a phantom from some fever-dream induced by Satan. I was perspiring heavily, and I felt not the usual hunger to break my fast. I coughed once, then a second time as I rose.

Then a thought occurred to me, of a sudden: Had the young man spread the plague to me?

My hands were shaking as I penned the note alerting the ministers of our sister congregations to what had befallen us. I had met with the elders of the session, and we had determined together that we faced some form of demonic infestation. The situation had grown dire, with more congregants falling ill, both in our own church and nearby. The entire presbytery would be required to deal with the situation.

At our meeting, it was determined that the only course of action must be to exhume the body of the first person to fall ill when the plague was discovered. Doctor Peterman had informed me of Teagan's illness and its peculiar nature: that the girl had spit up blood, which trickled from her lips, and that her body had repelled the leeches he had brought to give her succor.

"The nature of her illness is clear to me now," he said as he stood before the assembly. "This is, I fear, a case of vampirism. The blood on the girl's lips was not her own, but belonged to others on whom she was feeding."

"Did anyone who fell ill visit her in her failed convalescence?" The voice was that of Cyrus Hoagland, one of the senior deacons in our own congregation.

"I was only there for an hour or so," the doctor demurred. "But they must have. There is no other explanation."

Harlan Blackmore, one of the elders, spoke up: "Remember, her father was found dead only one day after she was lain in the ground, gutted by a pitchfork in his own home. She must have risen from the grave in the dead of night, returned to the home, and killed him to partake of his blood."

Evermore

"This is absurd," Michael Alden said. He was one of the youngest members of the council and one of the least apt to follow the others' opinions. Those others, it was not surprising, did not welcome his presence among them. "A dead woman rising from the grave? Have you taken leave of your senses?"

"Hardly," Elder Blackmore sniffed, looking down his long patrician nose at the young deacon. "Or have you forgotten the scripture? It states plainly that, when our Lord breathed his last, the graves were opened, and many bodies of the saints which slept arose."

"Saints and vampires are quite different things," Deacon Alden retorted.

"Nevertheless, the dead may be truly animated by the will of God, or may be brought back in a facsimile of their former selves by the prince of darkness, who will send many in the Lord's name declaring 'I am Christ.' Perhaps this is owing to the fact that they, like Christ, have been raised from the dead—yet unnaturally, by the devil."

"What does it profit us to bicker so?" Deacon Hoagland said. "If she is not a vampire, no harm will have been done. Minister Fillmore can consecrate the ground anew, and she can be left in peace.

"But if she *is* a vampire, we can put an end to the scourge she spread by exhuming her remains. This practice, gentlemen, is well-established. If the corpse is in a lifelike state and blood is found within her, we will know she has been turned. Then we can move forward with the procedure of beheading her, pulling the heart from her chest, and burning her body. The heart we can reduce to a tonic that all the townsfolk may receive to inoculate them against this evil."

A murmur of approval arose around the table.

"And what of the young man Minister Fillmore saw visiting her in the graveyard?"

"We can only hope that destroying her corpse will release him from her thrall, and that the tonic will cure him if he is infected," Deacon Hoagland said.

"And if it does not?"

"Then," Elder Blackmore announced, "we will have to kill him."

The Miller's Son

CONSUMED

I had visited the graveyard every night since they buried my Teagan. How could I have given into my rage so and strangled her as she lay beneath me? I had to let her know of my remorse, of my sorrow. I had to go to her and beg her forgiveness.

Yet this earthen layer upon her grave separated us. I lay there, every night, so near to her yet so far away. My ears longed to hear her soft, whispered voice. My fingers needed to caress her skin. My loins ached for her.

In my rage, I had killed my father as well, run his bloated belly through with a pitchfork. But I felt no remorse for this. None at all. It was just recompense for his ill treatment of my Teagan. Still, when I heard the rumors in town that Teagan herself had risen from the dead and slain him, I did nothing to quell them. I had no wish to be imprisoned or hanged for the crime of patricide, and it seemed only right that Teagan should receive blame—no, credit!—for dispatching that vile creature.

But just as Teagan had taken ill, so too I was feeling the effects of the disease she had contracted. Had she spread it to me? It mattered not. If so, she had done me a kindness by allowing me the prospect of a swift death, that I might be without her for only a while.

As I approached the graveyard behind the church, I was surprised to see the light from flames dancing on torches, held aloft by men I recognized. Minister Fillmore and others from the church, including, of course, that mountebank "Doctor" Peterman. As I edged closer to them, peering out from the shadows cast by moonlight through the trees, I could see they were gathered around Teagan's grave. Her stone marker had been knocked over, and I could see shovels lying on the ground beside it, and a mound of dirt.

What were they doing?

I could hear voices, and soon I knew.

"The body is pristine," Peterman was saying. "It is as I feared."

"She is a vampire?" someone else said.

"Yes. And she has been rising from the dead each night to assail us in our slumber, draining the lifeblood from us as we sleep until we are left as the monster's ghostly spawn, with ashen skin and hollow eyes."

I thought of the nightmare Teagan had shared with me—of the red-eyed monster that had appeared so vividly before her. But that had been only a dream, and Teagan herself could not have risen from her grave in the dead of night, or I would have seen it. What they were saying was a product of their own paranoia; of something that defied explanation in their limited minds, so they felt it necessary to concoct some fantastical interpretation of the facts before them.

I drew closer and saw they had raised Teagan's body from the earth and lain it beside her open grave. Then I watched in horror as one man raised a sharp axe meant for woodcutting and brought it down upon her. I saw the body shudder as the blow connected... only to lodge itself in her neck, which was left hanging there, partly severed.

A second blow completed the task, and her head rolled off beside her, coming to rest at the axe-wielder's feet.

I was frozen where I stood, unable to move a muscle. What I was witnessing was too bizarre to comprehend. As I stood there, my breath caught in my chest, I saw Peterman step forward and plunge a knife into her torso. Cutting into her flesh to expose her ribcage, he pulled the ribs apart to reveal her heart, which, with some difficulty, he finally succeeded in removing. This done, he held it triumphantly aloft. "This, gentlemen, is our instrument to defeat the plague that has ravaged us," he declared. "This consumption of human flesh and soul will be ended, Lord willing, once and for all."

An *instrument*? He had called my beloved sister's heart an *instrument*?

It was her *heart*. It was *my* heart. It belonged to us both, we who had shared our mother's womb; who were bonded eternally by a love that only we could understand. They meant to steal it like common thieves and do... Who knew what they might be contemplating?

Rage and indignation surged through me, overcoming the weakness visited on me by the plague and propelling me forward into the midst of their wicked assembly.

"No!" I cried. "You shall not have her!"

The men turned toward me, but I had taken them by surprise and was past them before they could react. I slammed my body into Peterman's chest and grabbed at his hand, wresting Teagan's heart from his grip as he writhed on the ground, gasping for air. But before I could regain my feet, the others had encircled me, torches in hand.

"He has gone mad from the consumption!" Peterman shouted. "Lay hold of him, but be careful that the heart is not damaged. The entire organ must be burned, unsullied, that the ashes may be used in the tonic I shall prepare to end this vampiric nightmare!"

I watched as they closed in on me, arms outstretched, reaching for me like tendrils belonging to some unearthly demon. I could not let them have Teagan's heart. I could not. But what could I do to stop them? There was no avenue of escape, and I lacked the power to stand against them. There was only one solution:

I shoved the heart in my mouth, biting off a piece of it and swallowing it whole.

The men gasped and took a step backward.

"It is too late!" one of them cried. "He is one of them!"

Before they could recover their senses, if they had any to begin with, I swallowed the piece of heart in my mouth, feeling it slide down my throat. It was almost as if it gave me new strength, new purpose. Teagan and I were one now, finally. She was part of me, as she was always destined to be.

I bit down hard, ripping another piece of heart from the organ, and gnawed at it furiously, savoring the taste of it this time as my eyes flashed from one face to the next in triumph and defiance.

The horror in their expressions only fueled my lust.

Evermore

I shoveled the rest of the heart into my mouth, like a wild beast tearing into the flesh of its prey. I was meant for this, I knew. The fates had proclaimed it.

The last thing I felt was the thud of a wooden board against the side of my head.

When I awoke, it was daytime, but I could barely see the sun through the haze that was rising up around me. My hands and feet were bound, and I was tied to a stake. Flames rose upward from a pile of branches and kindling beneath me, but I could tell by the voices that the entire town had come out to witness my destruction, here at the center of the public square.

I was a spectacle. I was the damned.

The fire lapped at my heels like a rabid dog, slithering up both legs toward my torso. I was strangely calm amid it all. The pain was there, but something had numbed it: the knowledge that Teagan was mine for all time now. With that knowledge, pain was of no consequence. Neither was the smoke that invaded my nose and mouth, choking and gagging me, mixed with hot cinders that seared my throat.

"Burn the vampire!" a voice in the crowd shouted.

"Burn him!"

"Destroy the demon!"

"Purge us! Purge us!"

But I was the one being purged and refined by their hatred into a pure vessel for the love I shared with Teagan. These fools could no longer touch me now. I was beyond their reach. I felt my consciousness fading slowly, but I was unconcerned. I had defeated them.

And these... these vulgar simpletons, they were too ignorant even to realize it.

Sharon Marie and Stephen H. Provost

England,
Early 19th Century

An Accomplished

Young Lady

Emma

And Then I Grew Up

I'd spent most of my life at our country estate, Mattley Manor, in Derbyshire. I'd always felt the most alive in the hilly landscape around our home, although I did enjoy the hustle and bustle of London when Mother and I occasionally accompanied Father there for business. Our dear friends, Baronet and Lady Beaumont, lived a few miles away in Chatterley Hall, and our two families were very close. Mother had tea daily with Lady Beaumont, and I had been best friends with the Beaumonts' son, Ennis, since the two of us were born, only hours apart.

Mother wanted to raise a proper daughter capable of attracting the best match when it was my turn to enter society.

However, she did not think that meant I shouldn't enjoy the joys of childhood or only be restricted to friends of the female persuasion. Mother always said, "The key to taming a spirited daughter is to let her run the wildness out." In that regard, she was right because I couldn't imagine the life without exertion that women were expected to live: nothing more lively than going for a walk, dancing, or riding on horseback.

To that end, Mother let Ennis and me spend our afternoons exploring the countryside and walking through the heather on the moor. When I returned home in the evening, my hands were filthy from catching frogs and lizards all day, and the bottoms of my skirts were damp and muddy.

I spent my mornings with my governess, Miss Elkington, studying reading, writing, mathematics, and French. After my studies, Sir Wallace arrived for my pianoforte lesson. Mother insisted my afternoons be left free for me to play. Then in the evenings, I learned to sew and embroider at Mother's side by the fire while Father read to us. My life was perfect, and I never wanted to grow up.

I dearly enjoyed the evenings that my family or the Beaumonts held house parties at our estates. Mother and some of the other women would take turns playing the pianoforte, harps, lutes, or guitars while the guests danced. The other children and I spent time in another room, away from the adults, but where we could still hear the music. Ennis and I would spin in circles until we collapsed to the ground, exhausted and dizzy. As the hour grew late and guests began to leave, I loved to join Father in the ballroom and whirl around the floor in a waltz or learn to dance a reel or quadrille.

Lady Beaumont and Mother always watched us play with knowing smiles on their faces. As they saw us mature and grow closer, their conversations drifted more and more to plans for our future... together. One day, shortly after I turned fourteen, I walked inside to ask the maid to bring us out something to drink. As I turned to head back outside, I overheard the two of them talking quietly in the sitting room. It was common knowledge that our mothers wanted us to be a match, but this day, I heard something new and concerning. I stood quietly at the edge of the door frame, unnoticed, listening in.

"Emma is such a beautiful, dear girl. She will make a wonderful addition to our family. I could not have asked for a better daughter. She's already so attentive to his needs," Lady Beaumont whispered to Mother.

Mother smiled and nodded.

"And Ennis, it's clear he worships her. The glimmer in his eyes as they follow her every movement. I swear he never lets her out of his sight."

Lady Beaumont laughed and leaned over conspiratorially. "I'll tell you a secret. At home, he calls her 'My Emma' as if she's his, alone, already."

"I don't think we need to worry about anyone coming between them. He's the first person on her mind each morning. I'm glad the governess is the one who has to draw her attention to her lessons. They are 'meant to be' it seems. It is a great comfort to me that someone will be looking out for her with as much devotion as I have."

Lady Beaumont's eyes glistened with unreleased tears. She placed her hand reassuringly on Mother's arm and leaned forward. "I'm sure everything will be fine, Lady Blackwell. Dr. Thomas is the best in the county. He will have you better in no time. Or you could always travel to London with Sir Blackwell to see specialists there, and I would be happy to look in on Emma in your absence."

"Thank you, Lady Beaumont. I'm sure you're right. I just feel so weak as of late, as if I'm fading away. I'm probably just worrying too much. You are such a caring friend."

Just then, the maid returned down the hall, calling out my name, so I darted out of sight and slipped back out the front door. Ennis came running up to the porch when he saw me.

"What's wrong, Emma? You look upset."

"I'll tell you later."

I grabbed his hand and pulled him down the porch stairs and over to the bench in the garden. I peeked through the rose bushes and saw Mother and Lady Beaumont come out of the manor, with the maid following behind to look for us.

"Children, where are you?" Mother called out.

"Be right there, Mother."

We emerged from the garden and found them waiting on the veranda. "Come inside, children, and get some lunch." Lady Beaumont motioned for us to follow the maid inside. I looked at Mother's face straining to detect any cause for concern, but other than looking a little tired, she appeared normal to me. As I passed, she gave me a quick kiss on the top of my head.

The maid served us lunch in the dining room. As we sat there eating, Ennis kept staring at me, hoping I would open up. But I could never discuss what I'd overheard in the presence of the staff. I ate a few small bites as Ennis quickly devoured the cold meat and bread with jam. As he stuffed the last bite in his mouth, he grabbed my hand and led me out to the stone bench by the fish pond in the side garden.

"Tell me, Emma."

"I think Mother is sick. I heard her talking to your mother about not feeling well. She's been seeing a doctor."

"I'm sure you have nothing to fear. The doctor will cure her."

"But she said she felt like she was fading away. And she said..."

"Said what, Emma?"

"She's glad that I have you and that you'll watch over me like she does. It's as if she's going to leave me. I love Father. Truly I do, but he doesn't understand me like Mother... or you. He leaves me to Mother's care, but I know he doesn't agree with her when it comes to all matters."

"Like what?"

"You. Our friendship. He thinks it's improper for me to be friends with a boy and to be in your company alone, even though we grew up together. He wants me to pursue my studies all day and learn all the 'needed' skills sought after in a wife. I don't think he even realizes that my lessons have progressed much further than is considered appropriate for a young girl. Mother thinks my inquisitive mind should be encouraged, and Father thinks women are only fit for running a household."

"I agree with your mother, Emma. I would never treat you like an object. You are my equal." He looked away from me, blushing. "My other half."

"I don't know what will happen to me if I lose Mother. Father is much too busy to raise a young lady preparing to enter society in the next few years. And what if he separates us?"

"We cannot be torn asunder, Emma. I simply won't allow it. It's just not possible. No matter what, we will find each other. Besides, you must remember, we're the same age. I will come to London when it's time and court you officially. Our own families have always seen us together."

"Our mothers have. I don't know about Father."

"How could he not? We are of the same station in life. I'm an appropriate suitor."

"Promise you won't forget about me, Ennis. No matter what happens. I simply couldn't be matched with anyone else. No one else would understand me or accept me. I would simply go mad if I could only go for a walk. I want to run with the wind in my hair. Ride like the wind on Jasper, not relegated to a sedate walk sitting sidesaddle in a long gown."

"And you will do just that. I would never change you, Emma. We..."

Lost in his eyes, I finished his sentence for him. "Were made for each other."

My mind and body were swirling with emotions, thoughts, and feelings I had never experienced before. We had both just expressed sentiments that, while they seemed obvious given our bond and destined future together, neither one of us had ever given voice to. My whole body felt flushed with fear and excitement. My heart raced. My mouth watered. I could smell the heady scent of his perspiration after our lively games of croquet and bowls. My eyes wouldn't stray from his full lips that I wanted to do nothing more than kiss.

He raised his hand and placed it on my shoulder, tentatively at first as he began to lean towards me. We both jumped when we heard Father's voice just as he rounded the corner of the hedge at the edge of the garden.

"Where has Emma gotten to?"

"Oh my! You had a bee on your shoulder. There... I think it's gone now," Ennis said as he nervously brushed his hand across my shoulder.

Father narrowed his eyes as he looked over at us. "You need to come inside now, Emma. This instant! Your mother needs you. Goodbye, Ennis."

"Farewell, Ennis. I'll see you tomorrow." It was difficult to tear my eyes away from his face. I scampered out of the garden and headed towards the house.

"Emma, need I remind you that young ladies do not run?"

"No, Father." I slowed my pace to a brisk walk, risking one last glance back at Ennis before entering the manor. He was smiling at me.

The next few weeks passed in a blur of activity. I'd blossomed from a girl into a young woman in the blink of an eye. And that young woman soon became lost in a society of rules and expectations that she didn't fit into—with no one to guide her.

I spent every free moment possible with Ennis, but that was getting more and more difficult. Father had called me in that day because Mother had collapsed. She blamed her swooning on unseasonably warm weather, but I could tell it was more. As the days went by, she became weaker and wanner. I'd noticed that her appetite had decreased as of late, which wasn't uncommon for her in the warmer months. But soon, she couldn't pass more than a few small bites past her lips.

She soon took to her bed for frequent small naps that, before long, turned into her being bedridden. Lady Beaumont spent all her free moments at Mother's side, comforting me each day before she left that all would be well. But I could tell she didn't believe that any more than I did. I knew that Mother's life was slipping away when she had me spend the evenings snuggled in bed with her, going over all the duties and expectations of a lady running a household. She was preparing me for what I would soon need to do here and for a future for which she would not be present.

Father would often peer in the door and stop to listen to

what she told me. More often than not, he would continue on down the hall, shaking his head. I knew that he didn't agree with her reassurances to me that I wouldn't have to change to suit my husband. All my fears about Father separating me from Ennis began to overwhelm me. He could only disagree with what Mother said if he had no intention of agreeing to our union.

But why? I couldn't understand what disagreement he could possibly have with Ennis. Baronet and Lady Beaumont had been close friends with my parents since before I was born. We visited each other's homes daily. The Baronet and Father engaged in long, serious discussions about business, politics, and the Napoleonic wars. Father was also a baronet, so Ennis was a suitable match for me.

I knew Father loved me, but I began to believe he had lost faith in me. Maybe he thought I would bring embarrassment to the family name. Maybe I was the one who wasn't a suitable match for Ennis. But then what would become of me? Without Mother to fight for me, I feared to imagine what my future held in store for me.

I'd always been afraid to grow up. Childhood was such an agreeable time in life. Who would ever want to mature and give up all the joy and fun to be had with friends? Mother and Lady Beaumont had planned for Ennis and me to marry, but that had always seemed like such a foreign, distant concept to me... until recently. Ennis and I had always lived in the moment. To our minds, separation was impossible. Life was already perfect, so why change anything?

Then everything *did* change in the span of a few short weeks. I'd reached my womanhood recently and thought I was dying of blood loss. Too afraid to tell Mother and worry her when she was already ill herself, my governess had found me crying at the side of my bed. She explained it all to me, and then she'd taken me to Mother against my protestations. Mother was so proud of me, as if I'd accomplished some great feat, rather than nature taking its course.

Ever since that day in the garden, I found my urge for Ennis to be by my side had been growing. I saw how the curves of my body changed and how Ennis' gaze lingered on my burgeoning bosom. I began to feel awkward in the loose gowns of a young girl and found myself desirous of the shape-hugging, supportive gowns of a young woman—an idea that I had abhorred not long ago. And all of this came as I watched Mother, my confidante, fade from my life.

Despite all her assurances to the contrary, Mother only lasted for another two months. One morning, I woke to the sounds of a flurry of activity. I rushed down the stairs to find that Mother's body had been moved to the drawing room, and the room had been draped in black cloth and lit with candles. No one had woken me to let me know of her passing. She had been placed on ice, and her body was awaiting preparation for viewing.

My governess heard my wail and came to comfort me. Father strode down the hall angrily behind her.

"Emma, this is simply not behavior befitting a young woman. It is time that you prepare your mother before visitors come to pay their respects. I told Isabelle that she had not raised you properly to prepare you for the duties of a grown woman of your station."

I sniffled and fought to hold back my tears. "Yes, Father. I apologize."

"Don't apologize. Just do your duty."

Miss Elkington led me to Mother's room to find an outfit for her. We returned to the mourning room to bathe her body and dress her. Then we wrapped her in a black woolen shroud. Father returned a short time later to let us know that mourners would be arriving soon and, given the warm weather, her funeral would be held two days hence. I retreated to the garden to gather Mother's favorite flowers to place around the room. I don't remember much about the next two days, other than Ennis being by my side every chance he got.

Miss Elkington, mother's chambermaid, and other servants took turns sitting with her body until her funeral. Then, that morning, I donned the dress Mother had favored most on me. It was not considered an appropriate dress for mourning, but I'd had it dyed black and removed some of the frills. Father met me at the bottom of the stairs.

"Turn around and go back up the stairs, Emma. You will not be attending. It's not appropriate for ladies to go to funerals. Your sensibilities are much too delicate for such an occasion."

"That's not true, Father. You know me. I must pay my respects to Mother. I'm a strong girl, even if you don't want me to be."

"It's high time that you act appropriately. I will not tolerate any daughter of mine flouting society's rules and expectations. You will do as I say. Your mother is no longer here to defy me, and I won't let you take up in her stead."

I turned and fled up the stairs, sobbing uncontrollably. I felt like I had returned to being a little girl.

I heard Father's mocking voice as I reached the top of the stairs. "Just as I said... you're much too delicate."

A short time later, I saw the Beaumonts arrive. Lady Beaumont came upstairs to invite me over to Chatterley Hall during the funeral. I politely declined her invitation, and she went back downstairs to return home in her coach. I snuck down the back stairs in hopes of finding Ennis. As had been the case many times in the past, we were of one mind... he was waiting for me. He rushed to my side and embraced me, looking around to make sure we hadn't been seen.

"Dear Emma, how are you holding up?"

"Not well... not well at all. Father won't let me attend the funeral. But I simply must."

"Are you sure you're up for it? You were so close to your mother."

I looked at him, steely-eyed. He raised his hands in surrender. "What was I thinking? Of course, you are. It won't be easy, but I'll get you there... somehow. You know I'd do anything for you."

"Thank you, Ennis. I don't know how I'd get through this without you."

Ennis returned to the other men and made his excuses for not attending. Surprisingly, Father agreed to let him visit with me, as long as my governess chaperoned. Miss Elkington always had a soft spot for me, as well as Mother. I knew I could convince her to cover for us.

I rang the bell for the maid and sent her to find Miss Elkington.

"What can I do for you, Miss Blackwell?"

"Father has forbidden me to attend Mother's funeral."

"And let me guess, you intend to be present?"

"Yes. He has agreed to let Ennis sit with me during the funeral as long as you watch over us. But Ennis has agreed to help me sneak over to the family plot and hide amongst the surrounding hedges."

"I love you, dearie. You know I can't deny you, just like your mother never could. Don't get caught. Otherwise, it might very well be my last day here, and then who will you conspire with?"

I wrapped my arms around her, before darting out of the room to collect more flowers from the garden to place at Mother's grave after the others left. I knew I would have time to return unnoticed by Father because he would be busy with the guests at the funeral dinner. Ennis and I ran across the fields and approached the family cemetery from opposite the direction from which Father would be coming, so we could watch for him. We had safely ensconced ourselves in the hedgerow by the time the mourners arrived.

I watched as the clergyman gave his brief speech and passed around sprigs of rosemary. "We have entrusted this, our sister, Lady Isabelle Blackwell, to God's mercy, and we now commit her body to the ground: earth to earth, ashes to ashes, dust to dust: in sure and certain hope of the resurrection to eternal life through our Lord Jesus Christ, who will transform our frail bodies that they may be conformed to his glorious body, who died, was buried, and rose again for us. To him be glory for ever."

I burst into tears when her coffin was lowered into the ground, and one of the groundskeepers began to replace the dirt as the mourners slowly filed off. I buried my face into Ennis' chest to stifle my sobs. He wrapped his arms around me and held me tight. When I had cried myself out, I raised my head. The groundskeeper had completed his task and departed. Ennis gave me one soft kiss on my lips before helping me to my feet. We walked over to the grave, and I placed the bouquet.

Life as I knew it—my childhood and my freedom—had died along with Mother. I didn't know it then, but nothing would ever be the same again.

Emma

Sent Away

Father had all of my dresses dyed black, befitting the mourning period I would be in for the next six months. I wasn't prepared for the response I got when I protested.

"You loved your mother, did you not? Are you a cold, unfeeling snipe, too selfish to mourn your mother as you should?"

"No. Of course not, Father. I only meant, what will I wear when the mourning period ends? I just did not think that *all* of them needed to be black."

"You need not concern yourself with that. You won't be needing those simple girlish frocks anymore. You're a young woman now. It's time you dressed as one, and *acted* as one as well. The current state of affairs will no longer be tolerated."

I wasn't sure what he meant at the time, and he didn't bother to explain himself. I was far too lost in my grief at the moment to care. All that mattered to me was that nothing had changed. I wasn't supposed to have visitors over—other than family or close friends—which was fine with me. Lady Beaumont and Ennis continued to visit as usual. Father had decreased my free time greatly, insisting I spend more time on my studies, music, and dancing lessons.

Father was too busy, at least at first, to notice that Ennis and I still had the run of the estate, unaccompanied, for hours each day. We spent that time reading to each other, discussing our future, telling stories about Mother, and wondering what it would be like when we were formally introduced to society. We were destined for each other but, for the sake of appearances, I would be forced to entertain other suitors. Propriety dictated that my dance card not be filled with only Ennis' name.

I knew Father loved me, but in his grief, he'd become so distant and harsh with me. I understood that he felt pressure to provide me with all the skills and etiquette needed before I entered society. He just didn't seem to realize that, while Mother had been lenient with me, she'd been doing just that. I'd far surpassed the level of education expected of a young lady. I was above average in my proficiency playing the pianoforte, even if I chose not to boast of my skill. I might have acted silly when Father danced with me at those house parties, but I had learned how to dance a reel, a quadrille, a waltz, and any other dance I'd encountered.

The only piece I lacked was practice in formal social encounters with people I didn't know. I'd known all the people of society in Derbyshire since I was a young girl, and our trips to London over the years hadn't usually involved me meeting new people.

That was soon about to change.

Three months after Mother's passing, Father returned home from a trip to London and found me sitting out in the garden with

Ennis.

"Ennis, it's time for you to go home. The two of you know better than to be socializing alone without a chaperone. You know how that could affect Emma's reputation."

"Sir Blackwell, I would never do something untoward. You know Emma's virtue is safe with me. Besides, Emma is my intended... and always has been."

I blushed and turned a chaste smile towards Ennis.

"Check that arrogant attitude of yours. That is yet to be determined. She hasn't even officially entered society yet. I will not pursue this conversation any further with you at this time."

I briefly placed my hand on Ennis' arm and bade him farewell.

"Emma, go inside now. We have much to prepare before her arrival."

"Who, Father? What's going on?"

"I need not explain myself to you. But your Aunt Elizabeth, Marchioness of Arundel, shall be here tomorrow. I'm not sure what your mother taught you, but go plan a menu and have the servants make all the appropriate preparations for her arrival. I'll check on you in a bit to make sure you've done it correctly."

"Yes, Father."

I'd never formally met my aunt. She spent nearly all her time in London with the Marquess. When I was five years old, I'd seen her in passing once when we were in London, but Father had deemed me too ill-mannered to meet her at the time. Why was she coming here now? Mother had taught me what to do if a high-ranking guest should come, but I still feared Father would find fault no matter how well I did.

I couldn't understand why Father seemed to hold such resentment towards Mother now that she'd passed. And it seemed like that was being passed down to me now as well. My only guess centered on the fact that he didn't have an heir. Mother and Father had tried for years to have another child, a son, but to no avail. I know Mother blamed herself and felt terrible disappointment in herself, as if that were a matter under her control.

Father might not have agreed with all the choices Mother made in my rearing, but he never complained to her or demanded that she change certain practices. He'd been a stoic man by nature, but he'd always seemed proud of me. While he was never a part of discussions, formal or otherwise, about a future for me with Ennis, he certainly knew and never expressed disapproval at the idea. Now I'd begun to fear that he intended to raise the family's stature by arranging a marriage with someone bearing a title... someone in the nobility. If I wasn't good enough, why didn't he just remarry and have the precious son he wanted so much?

I called all the staff to meet me in the sitting room. I gave them the directions for preparing the guest room and the menu for dinner when the Marchioness arrived. Mother was very close to Miss Elkington because she had been my mother's governess when she was young. Mother couldn't bear the thought of anyone else educating her own child other than Miss Elkington, so she'd brought her along when my parents were married. She had worked as Mother's chambermaid until I was born.

Miss Elkington was the only servant still on staff that had been employed the other time the Marchioness had visited, shortly after my birth. She remembered that the Marchioness was very particular about how the servants were to treat her, what food she wished to be served, and the special accommodations she required. Miss Elkington informed me and then made sure to pass that information along to the other servants. When Father arrived to check on the preparations, he was quite pleased.

"You did much better than I expected, Emma. Maybe you won't be as difficult for Elizabeth to handle as I'd thought you might be."

"Handle, Father? Whatever do you mean?"

"We'll discuss all that tomorrow when she arrives. It's of no concern to you now."

"But, Father..."

"That will be all, Emma. Go practice on the pianoforte. I'd hate for you to embarrass me tomorrow night when she asks you to play." He threw me a hard glance that left no room for me to protest further.

"Yes, Father."

I spent the next hour playing a variety of musical compositions until I heard him leave. As I passed through the entryway to go upstairs, I heard a soft knock at the door. I opened it to find Ennis standing there.

"What are you doing back here?"

"I hid in the garden and waited for him to leave. What was all that about your aunt coming?"

"I don't know yet, but I fear he is going to send me away to stay with her. He mentioned her 'handling me' as if I were some object."

"You can't leave, Emma. I would miss you so."

"I would miss you too, Ennis, but I can't disobey Father. That's not how Mother raised me to act. He's been through so much since Mother's passing. Hopefully, it will just be for a short while. I can't imagine it being any more than that."

"But your mother is gone now, Emma. Your father acts as if

you are just a bother and worthless. You're everything to me."

"I must respect Mother, in death as I did in life. I think he is just grief-stricken and lost right now. He is still my father, and I must obey him. It will all work out. I just know it. You'd better go before Father returns."

Ennis placed his hand on my cheek, then turned and disappeared through the garden. I went up to my room to read. I'd lost my appetite. Miss Elkington said she would bring me up some tea and toast later. I needed to get some rest early in preparation for my aunt's arrival.

The next morning dawned bright and early. I could hear the servants scuttling through the house, making last-minute preparations. They sounded as nervous as I felt. I put on my best dress, even if it was black, and took extra time to make sure my hair was perfect. I pulled it up into a loose bun with masses of tight ringlet curls on my forehead and around my ears. I even wore Mother's strand of pearls. As I was just finishing up, I heard a knock at the door. Miss Elkington entered to check on me.

"Emma dear, you look stunning. Now don't you worry one bit. The Marchioness is sure to be pleased. How could she not?"

"Thank you, Miss Elkington. I'm terrified just the same. Do you know why she's coming?"

"Umm... no, dear. Your father hasn't told me."

"Miss Elkington, I can tell you're hiding something from me. What do you know?"

"Well... umm... you see."

"Just tell me, please."

"I overheard your father talking to Sir Weatherington. They were up till late in the sitting room last night. It seems that you will be going to live with your aunt in London to make sure you are ready to enter society."

"What? Why? I have been trained by you... and Mother."

"I know, dear. But it seems your father doesn't think you have received the proper guidance, or enough. He wants you to make a suitable match."

I felt a stab of pain through my heart. My ears must have deceived me. I fought to hold back the tears that welled up in my eyes.

"What did you say?"

"He... uh... wants..."

"Suitable match? What does he mean?"

"Dear..."

"He doesn't think Ennis is the proper match for me? He's going to stop me from marrying him? That can't be! I won't accept it! We've been fated to be together our whole lives. Mother and Lady Beaumont have been planning since we were toddlers."

"I know, dear."

"I love him, and Ennis loves me more than anyone else ever has... besides Mother or you. He accepts and loves me just the way I am, even if I don't follow all of society's precious little rules. No one else will do that. I'll be forced to change and be the same boring, simpleton that all the other women are in society. I'll simply die if I have to do that."

"Dear, I'm sure it will all work out. Look at your mother. She wasn't a boring simpleton. She was very happy with your father and, most of all, you."

"I know. I didn't mean to imply that *she* was a simpleton. But Mother was so much more agreeable than I. She always called me headstrong in the most flattering way, even though that's unacceptable for a woman in society. I just can't live without Ennis."

"You never heard this from me." She raised her eyebrows and gave me a look of innocence, turning her back as she began to speak again. "You must have parental consent to marry younger than the age of twenty-one. If you could say wait until that time, or if you should say... visit Scotland, on the sly, the two of you could marry, and no one could stop you. Your father cannot force you to marry someone."

"Really?"

"Yes. But you must think long and hard before you make such a decision. You would be disinherited and forfeit your station. You would lose the life you have always known. Your father would never speak to you again."

"I could never do that. Mother would be mortified. Father is all alone."

"Your mother would want you happy, first and foremost. You meant the world to her. And she always intended for you to marry Ennis. No one could have foreseen what happened."

"But what will happen to you if I leave?"

Miss Elkington's eyes filled with tears. She turned away quickly, trying to hide them from me. I heard the tiniest little sniffle before she turned back. "Don't worry about me. One way or the other, no matter which you decide, it's the same. It's time this old spinster retired. I'll go live in the country."

I ran and wrapped my arms around her. She was the closest thing I still had to a mother. I couldn't lose her too. "You can go with me. I'll talk to the Marchioness about it. I simply cannot be separated from you as well."

"It doesn't work that way, dear. You'll be fine. I want you to go to London and show them all up. Let them see what a wonderful young lady your mother and I raised. You'll be the toast of the town. The belle of the ball. Remember, you are only fourteen, my dear. Go and see what you think of the life. Give yourself time to finish grieving and mature a little more. There's still plenty of time to make up your mind."

I could no longer hold back the tears. "I'll make you proud of me, I promise."

"I have no doubt, dear. Now I really must go help the others before she arrives."

The Marchioness arrived a short time later, with even more pomp and circumstance than I had imagined. Father nearly tripped over himself rushing out the door and down the stairs to meet her. The butler helped her out of the carriage. Father grabbed her fingers and leaned down to kiss her hand.

"Dear Elizabeth, it's so good to see you. It's been much too long."

She cleared her throat and looked down her nose at him.

Father made a quick bow before her. "I apologize, Your Ladyship, that is."

The Marchioness' hard stare met my eyes as I stood at the top of the veranda. She waved her hand dismissively up at me. "And this is?"

"Emma, come down here this instant and greet the Marchioness properly."

I descended the stairs, curtsied before her, and then kissed her hand as I had seen Father do. "Pleasure to meet you, My Lady."

The Marchioness didn't respond, brushing past me and heading up the stairs. "Edmund, please have someone show me to my room. I trust you've made the necessary preparations."

"Emma saw to all of it, My Lady. I'm sure you'll find it to your satisfaction."

"That remains to be seen. I have my doubts, but those issues shall be rectified soon enough."

"What does that mean?" I knew I'd made a mistake as soon as the words left my lips, but I couldn't stop myself. Everyone in my life thought they could make decisions for me without even talking to me about them.

"This *girl* really must learn some manners, and fast, or even I won't be able to help her. I truly hope the situation is not as dire as I fear, for one can't make a silk purse out of a sow's ear." With that, she turned and continued up the stairs, as if I hadn't said a word.

I opened my mouth to say more, but then stopped. There was no winning. I'd show her she was wrong about me. I'd show both of them that Mother had been a proper woman of society and had raised her daughter in her own image. I waited for the Marchioness to get to her room and then went up to my own. It was clear the situation was just as Miss Elkington had said, so I might as well start packing.

I was left out of the dinner that I had so painstakingly planned. Instead, Miss Elkington brought my meal up to me. She told me Father had important business he needed to discuss with the Marchioness. Me—I was that "business"—not even his daughter anymore. Later that evening, I was called down to play the pianoforte for them.

I could see that the Marchioness, in spite of herself, and even Father was impressed by my skills. He hadn't listened to me play in over a year, so he didn't realize how far I had progressed. I'd hoped for a compliment, but instead I received a blow.

"Does she play the harp, Edmund?"

"No, she does not."

"And why ever has she not been trained? Seriously,

Edmund!"

"I play the lute passably well. Mother was teaching me herself."

"The lute? That's so passé. You will begin lessons immediately when we go to London. And in the future, you will speak when spoken to, young lady. Can you sing?"

"She's had lessons, but..."

I was tired of being talked about as if I weren't right there in the room. I opened my mouth, but this time I let the beautiful singing voice Mother had encouraged spring forth with a hymn. When I finished, the room was silent for a moment.

"Her voice is like a songbird..." My heart soared. Then came crashing down when she finished her statement. "But we'll have to continue her lessons." She couldn't give me one compliment without hedging. I couldn't take anymore.

"Am I excused, Father?"

"What an impertinent young lady! Go! Be ready to leave in the morning. We'll be departing for London shortly after the dawn. You need not pack many clothes. You shan't be wearing them for long. A seamstress will be meeting us at my estate to fit you for proper dresses."

"But I'm still in mourning."

"You *were*. Now you're going home with me to learn how to be a proper young lady befitting your station, and we've no time to waste. Good night!"

I looked at Father, but it was clear he wouldn't be entertaining any arguments from me. I turned and ran out of the room and up to bed. I was about to lose everything and everyone I'd ever known. And how could I possibly let Ennis know before I left? Or say goodbye at all?

Sharon Marie and Stephen H. Provost

Emma

A Lady is Born

Miss Elkington woke me nearly an hour before the dawn. She'd found me crying my heart out on the bed last night because I feared I wouldn't see Ennis ever again. Little did I know she'd sent one of the servants over to the Beaumonts to let Ennis know I'd be leaving in the morning. They'd arranged a brief meeting for the two of us to say our goodbyes—chaperoned, of course, in case we should be found.

She helped me dress and led me down to the kitchen, where she took me outside. I couldn't believe my eyes when I saw him standing there. He appeared as if he'd been crying as well, but I'd never point it out and embarrass him. I ran into his embrace in the shadows of the house.

"You must hurry, you two. We won't have long," Miss Elkington whispered before turning her back to afford us a little privacy.

"Ennis, I'm so sorry. I don't have any choice. They didn't even

123

ask me what I wanted to do."

"We could run away together. Let's go now. I have access to enough money for us to live."

"But you'd lose everything, just as I would. I can't estrange you from your parents. How would we live? We're so young."

"I can't lose you. I won't lose you! Do you hear me? You're mine!"

"Shhh, Ennis. We'll get caught."

"I don't care. This is not right. I'll fight for you."

"We'll figure it out. I promise! My heart is yours. I'm sure I can convince them with time. If I do everything they want in the meantime and follow their rules of courtship once I'm introduced to society, I'll refuse to marry anyone but you. You just have to promise to come court me properly."

"Of course, I will. But how do we live without each other until then?"

"I'm sure we'll both be so busy that it'll pass in a blink." I just wished that I could believe my own words. I fought to keep a happy, hopeful expression on my face. I needed to support him, as he had supported me my whole life, especially in the three months since Mother's passing.

"This is impossible."

"Anything is possible for the two of us. Remember, we're meant to be. Our mothers always said that. Now I really must go. We can't take the chance of ruining our plans before they've even begun. I love you. Ennis."

"And I love you. You are mine, Emma, always have been and always shall be... evermore. I will find you and take you as my bride."

I turned and ran into the house, Miss Elkington right behind me, before I could break down into tears. I returned to my room to pull myself together before Father or the Marchioness saw me. A few moments later, there was a single knock at the door, followed by Father's booming voice. "It's time to go, Emma."

When I emerged, the butler was waiting outside the door to grab my bags. I descended the stairs to find Miss Elkington waiting for me at the parlor door. She tried to hide her sadness, but I could see it in her eyes. "You'll do wonderful, sweetheart. I'll miss you. Make your mother and me proud."

The Marchioness came sweeping down the stairs, followed by several maids carrying all her bags. I couldn't believe how much she'd brought with her for a one-week excursion. The bags were all loaded onto the carriage quickly. Before stepping inside, I turned to Father.

"Must I go, Father?"

"Yes, Emma. It's for your own good. You'll have a grand time, I'm sure. Eliza... I mean, the Marchioness has much to teach you. And the wonders you'll see. I love you, dear." He gave me a quick kiss on the forehead and turned to leave.

"Let's go, Emma. We have a long ride ahead of us... nearly three days." I looked at the Marchioness' pinched face, determined not to respond, but entered the carriage feeling defeated.

I slept through much of the ride over the next three days, depression rather than excitement having settled in. In the afternoon of the third day, when we arrived in London, I couldn't help but feel some delight. It had been quite some time since Mother and I had last been there. The city was bustling with activity. When we finally arrived at the estate, my eyes could hardly take in the sight before me. I couldn't imagine the luxury that must be inside given the size and beauty of Rosewood

House.

It was easy to see why it had received its name. An enormous rose garden flourished next to a hedge maze along the eastern side of the property. I could also see a variety of other gardens in the distance. The house, if you could call it that, looked like a castle. It was a sweeping Gothic structure complete with turrets and battlements, but its arched windows were reminiscent of the cathedrals in London. There were several elegant wrought iron balconies along the second story.

In the front of the house, a large stained-glass window rose above the grand entrance. That entrance consisted of three large arched entryways that led up the steps to the portico and then on to the black double-doors. There was even a tall clock tower atop the west wing. The carriage pulled to a stop in front of the doors, and the staff came streaming out to meet us.

As the Marchioness was helped out of the carriage, she spoke to a young maid standing off to the side. "Please see Miss Blackwell up to her room. Then get her some tea and toast." She disappeared up the stairs without a word to me, and then into the grand estate. I had no idea what was expected of me, so I followed the maid inside.

I was led up the stairs and into the west wing to a beautiful room. It had a fireplace and a four-poster bed with cloth bed hangings tied back at each corner. There was a small bedside table, an armoire and a dressing table. There was even a chaise longue near the window with a small table beside it. I couldn't wait to spend the afternoons reading with such a magnificent view before me. I saw long curtains hanging down to the left of the window and realized they covered a door that led out to my very own balcony. I opened the door, giggling with delight as I stepped outside. I'd been determined to hate this whole experience, but instead I found myself exhilarated.

"I'll be right back with your tea and toast, Miss. Then you can lie down for a nap, if you like, before dinner at 8."

"Thank you..."

"Hillary, Miss. My name is Hillary."

I wasn't tired, so when Hillary returned, I asked if there was a library I could visit. She smiled and nodded enthusiastically. She sat off to the side while I drank my tea and nibbled at a piece of toast. Then she took me downstairs and into the large library. I'd never seen so many books in one location. I'd been looking around for an hour when I heard the door open.

A very dour-looking man entered, followed closely behind by one of the servants. Hillary, who'd been waiting patiently beside me, curtsied and spoke quickly. "Excuse us, My Lord. Miss Blackwell wanted to find a book to read. I'll bring her back later." She turned to lead me out of the room.

"No need to leave, Miss Blackwell. Please proceed. Delighted to make your acquaintance. So, what do you think of Rosewood House?"

"Thank you, My Lord. It's quite overwhelming. I appreciate your hospitality. I just found a book to read. I'll leave you be now."

"What, may I ask, did you choose?"

"*The Romance of the Pyrenees.*"

"My dear, that is the French translation."

"Yes, My Lord."

"I was led to believe that your education was sorely lacking."

"I am well-versed in French, My Lord. May I borrow this volume?"

The Marquess waved his hand, a bewildered look upon his face. "Yes, of course."

I returned to my bedchamber, and Hillary left me to read in the last of the afternoon light. After a time, she returned and lit an oil lamp for me and placed it on the table. At 7, she returned again to help me dress for dinner. I put on my best black dress and fixed my hair before proceeding downstairs to the dining room, with Hillary leading the way.

The Marquess and Marchioness were already seated at the table. I received a disapproving look from her, even though I had arrived five minutes earlier than I'd been told. Dinner was a quiet affair. I'd expected to be peppered with questions or condemnations, but I guessed they were being put off until the following day after a good night's rest. When I was excused from the table, I rose to return to my bedchamber.

"Are you enjoying the book, Miss Blackwell?" the Marquess asked, a gleam in his eye.

"What book is that?" the Marchioness asked, her tone suspicious.

"She's reading *The Romance of the Pyrenees*... in French."

"I'm enjoying it very much, My Lord. Thank you."

"Imagine my surprise when she picked up that volume this afternoon. My impression was that such a work far surpassed her capabilities. It shall be quite interesting to see what other marvels lie in store for us."

The Marchioness glared at me. "You may go."

As I left the room, I heard her say, "We'll see tomorrow if she has actually read that book. I'll not tolerate a fraud."

I sprinted up the stairs and returned to the chaise. About an hour later, Hillary arrived again to close the drapes and help me get ready for bed. I told her I would be up late finishing my book. She turned away to hide a small smile that crept onto her lips.

"I understand, Miss. Let me bring you a blanket from the

armoire so you don't catch a cold. I'll bring you up some warm milk later if you'd like."

"Yes. That'd be wonderful, Hillary."

I stayed up long into the night finishing the book. I was determined that I'd be ready for any questions the Marchioness would ask the following morning. I'd be tired the next day, but I'd push through no matter what. I might be stuck here, but I didn't have to let her tear me down. Confidence, not ego, was a virtue Mother had encouraged. Of course, she'd raised and educated me to be worthy of that confidence. My time here might not be so bad if she saw I was more accomplished than she imagined. Maybe that would even earn me the right to choose my suitor.

The next morning, Hillary woke me and helped me prepare for the day. She told me that a seamstress would be arriving after breakfast to see about measuring me and designing my new wardrobe. I missed Mother beyond description, but I had to admit I also missed wearing clothes in other colors besides drab black. Hillary told me that I would be on my own for the morning. I entered the dining room and found toast, marmalade and tea sitting on the sideboard. I helped myself to a small meal and then followed her to meet the seamstress in the parlor. The Marchioness was already speaking to her about the appropriate fabrics, colors and dress designs.

The seamstress accompanied me to my bedchamber and set about determining my measurements. She let me choose the colors I liked from a predetermined palette that had been approved for me. I chose white, pink, periwinkle blue, Pomona green, citron, and lilac. They'd be trimmed with lace and ribbon, ruffles, and ruching. I found out that I'd also be getting bonnets, turbans, long white satin gloves, fans, small drawstring purses, handkerchiefs, parasols, shawls, velvet cloaks, and leather slippers that matched the gowns that would be made.

The seamstress would also be making chemises to be worn under my gowns for modesty, given the thin, almost see-through sheer muslin materials. I would have to wear light-boned corsets or short stays to shape and support my torso, along with petticoats that would fill out the skirt of my gowns. I'd never worn so many layers before. I'd never shown so much skin, though, either. All these gowns would have short or no sleeves and be cut quite low on my chest. I'd still been wearing the simple gowns of young girls until this point.

I found myself titillated by the thought of wearing such form-fitting attire that would show off the figure I'd recently started developing. It was hard to believe that, only a short time ago, I hadn't wanted to grow up, but now I couldn't wait to be a beautiful young woman, admired and courted by a variety of suitors.

When the seamstress left just before lunch, I was called down to the parlor to meet with the Marchioness. She put me through rigorous questioning about the book I'd been reading, as I had expected. The more I answered her correctly, the harder she tried to stump me or catch me in a lie.

"Your father told me that your education had left much to be desired. Why did he tell me such an untruth?"

I couldn't understand why Father had said such a thing. I didn't want to voice any words that could be misconstrued as criticism of him. In the end, I did not answer. This served only to anger her further.

"Now I can see what he was talking about."

"Yes, My Lady?"

"You have no manners or social skills. You've spent too much free time running around with a young boy. You clearly haven't focused enough time on preparing to enter society. Your new tutors will arrive tomorrow. You've proven yourself adept at learning languages, so you'll be learning Italian now. Your music teacher will refine your singing skills and start teaching you the harp: the premiere instrument for a modern young lady to play. We will be assessing your reading, writing, and mathematics skills in the coming days to see what, if anything, we need to focus on. A young lady should not be seen as more accomplished than her husband. Your evenings will be spent with me refining your manners and social skills. Is that clear?"

"Yes, My Lady."

"Enjoy your last day of freedom. It will be a long time to come before you will have the right to decide how to spend your hours. You may go."

I fled up the stairs to my room and flopped onto my bed in tears. No matter what I did, I wasn't good enough. I'd proved my intelligence, but I was *too* smart, as if that were somehow a negative quality. I was very talented at playing the pianoforte and the lute, but that wasn't enough. I would need to learn the harp as well. I was fluent in French, but now I must learn another language.

I wasn't a member of the noble class the Marchioness had married into. I was from the gentry, yet my education already far exceeded most people of that station. And no matter what she thought, I was not ill-mannered. I had a suitor back home, just waiting for us to be of age. Why did I have to go through all this? What plans were being made for *my* future?

I spent the next year and a half in intense training just as the Marchioness had told me I would. I began to speak fluent Italian and played the harp like an angel on high. Each day beat me down a little more, crippling my fiery spirit until I was the quiet, reserved young lady she desired. When I looked in the mirror, I scarcely recognized myself.

I no longer laughed with the carefree abandon that spilled from my lips unbidden—now I emitted only chaste titters, my hand gracefully covering my mouth. I could barely remember what it felt like to run with the sun on my skin and the wind flowing through my long, flaxen locks. I now had my hair pinned up in a loose bun with golden ringlets that framed my face and walked at a leisurely pace through the gardens at the estate or in the park—parasol in hand with a silk fan at the ready—greeting others politely as they passed.

As spring approached after my sixteenth birthday, the Marchioness began to take me around with her on social calls—an unofficial announcement that I would be entering society with the coming season. In preparation for the imminent approach of Queen Charlotte's Ball in May—my formal introduction as a debutante—we had gone to the dressmaker's shop to have me fitted for my ball gown. It would be made of white silk with short sleeves and a more modest bodice. The bodice was covered in fine embroidery with lace trim. I would also be wearing long white satin gloves and a single ostrich plume headdress.

One evening in the middle of April, as I went down to the library, I overheard the Marquess talking to my aunt.

"I've heard good things about Emma. She's being received very well amongst those to whom you've made introductions. There's talk of suitors already fancying her."

"I'm happy to hear that. That girl was a diamond in the

rough. It's taken much work on my part to bring out that dazzling sparkle."

"I'm not sure she was really all that bad. I found her quite charming, myself."

"Easy for you to say. You weren't the one doing all the work."

"I seem to remember us bringing in a lot of tutors."

I couldn't help but smile. The Marquess was quite stiff most of the time, but he had always been very kind and supportive of me. I peeked around the door to see the Marchioness let out a sigh of resignation. Despite her stubborn resolve, even she knew when she had been bested.

"Anyhow, now I must chaperone her carefully at all times—make sure that wild, carefree spirit of hers doesn't slip back out. I can't have her reputation called into question because of a moment spent alone in the company of some roguish young man. I certainly can't let her get caught up with that Beaumont boy again."

"Is he so awful as all that?"

"Well, no."

"And he is of a suitable station... matching hers quite exactly, as I recall."

"Yes. But I didn't go to all this work just to settle. I'm quite proud of my accomplishment, and I intend to see how far I... I mean she... can go."

"Much like you yourself did, my dear?"

"Mmm... yes... no. You know what I mean. I wish Sir Beaumont the best, but he is not right for Emma." Her face was flushed with frustration, and I nearly giggled at the sight.

"Quite right, my dear. You were the belle of the ball, as no doubt she will be. I know we both just want the best for her."

"Yes, of course. I must retire for the night. There is much to do over the next couple of weeks before Queen Charlotte's Ball."

I sprinted across the foyer and up the stairs, my steps silent in the soft leather slippers. I entered my room and closed the door without a click. I dropped onto the chaise longue, despondent. I longed to experience the thrill of being courted, but I'd always thought that Ennis and I would be together. Now it seemed as if nothing had changed, regardless of all my hard work. Once more the course of my life would be decided by someone other than myself.

How could I ever say goodbye? How could I make him understand? How would *I* live without him? Would he even be here in London to court this season? Or worse yet, had he already forgotten me and moved on?

Ennis

The Time Had Come

I'd been waiting lifetimes for this moment to come. This time, nothing would get in our way. Our destiny had come full circle, and it was finally unbreakable.

It had been two years since Emma left, and I hadn't seen her the entire time. I could only imagine she had blossomed into a beautiful woman. I'd written letters to her, but had never received a response. The Marchioness must have withheld them from her. She never would have ignored me like that.

During our time apart, I had worked closely with Father to learn how to run the estate and his business holdings. That was fortuitous, since Father had passed away unexpectedly at the start of the year. Over the next four months, I'd scrambled to get everything settled in preparation for my trip to London with Mother for the season. On a visit to Mattley Manor late last year, Sir Blackwell had told Father and Mother that Emma would be debuting in the coming season.

We had arrived in London and settled into our townhome in early April. I needed to obtain all the necessary clothing for attending balls. I'd never had the occasion to wear full dress until this point. The ensuing weeks were full of social calls to establish myself as the new baronet of Chatterley Hall.

In the afternoons, I'd take Mother for walks in the park. She'd been pale and weak in the months since Father's passing, but the sunshine and social engagement of late had done much to improve her spirits. One day, not long before Queen Charlotte's Ball, I'd seen Emma taking a stroll with the Marchioness. It had taken all of my control and Mother's insistence to keep me from running up and throwing my arms around her.

"Ennis, hold back."

"But Mother, I should at least greet her."

"You're a young man now. Sir Beaumont, to be exact. You know that is not the way of the world. You must wait to be formally introduced."

"But we grew up together. We spent nearly every waking moment together."

"Yes, but she is entering society now. You haven't seen each in other years. That's the way it works."

I'd looped my arm through Mother's and begun to lead her in Emma's direction.

"So, introduce me to her then."

Mother had pulled back gently and stopped moving

forward.

"Son, just wait for the proper time at the ball. Don't you think she's as excited as you to be reunited? Let the anticipation build. It'll be worth it. It will make the moment of your reunion and formal introduction all the more special."

"I suppose you are correct."

"Mother knows best."

"Yes, you do. You and Lady Blackwell have always known that Emma and I should be together."

"*Would* be together. There was never a doubt in our minds. Before the two of you were born, we dreamed of such an outcome. But then once we saw you together... your closeness... we were sure that it would come to pass. You need not fear, dear son. Only one week until the ball, then court her over the next six months, and you will be married soon after. The worst has passed. Joy is in your future."

"And you still believe that? You don't think she will be stolen away by some *better* man? Someone with a title and money?"

"Never. There's no one better than you for Emma, Sir Beaumont. Emma loves you, and she was never one to be drawn to money or power."

The next week seemed interminable, but I had some business meetings to attend to that helped pass the time. Most importantly, I'd gone to see a jeweler to have a special piece made for Emma as a symbol of our love and commitment. I would give it to her the day I proposed. Finally, the day of the ball arrived, and I could barely contain my nerves and excitement. When I came down the stairs, Mother was waiting for me with a gift in hand. She held out Father's pocket watch.

"Every man must have a pocket watch to keep the time.

Today seemed the perfect day to pass this on to you."

"Thank you, Mother. That means a great deal to me."

I walked Mother out and helped her into the carriage.

I'm coming for you, Emma. *You are mine. Soon we will begin our lives together.*

Emma

Belle of the Ball

The morning of the ball dawned early and bright. It appeared to be the perfect spring day to hold the most important and first ball of the season. All the debutantes seeking a suitor would be in attendance, with the keenest focus on those entering society for the first time. I woke to the sounds of everyone in the household bustling about, just as Hillary entered my room, with the Marchioness not far behind.

"Why aren't you up? Do you not take this event seriously? With all I've done for you, and you can't even show me a little respect."

"I apologize..."

"It's my fault, My Lady. I just came to wake Miss Blackwell when you showed up."

"Hurry up, girl. Don't stand there sniveling. Draw her a bath... NOW!"

Hillary rushed from the room, tears in her eyes. Rather than meet my aunt's angry glare, I turned to admire my ball dress hanging from the armoire. I could hardly believe that I'd be wearing it tonight. I retrieved the chemise, petticoat, and short stay I'd have to put on first and laid them on the bed. Then I set aside the gloves, headdress, silk sash, my silk and ivory fan, and small drawstring purse. I walked over to the dressing table to make sure the pins for my hair were set out.

"You don't have time to be dawdling, Emma."

"Yes, My Lady. I was just making sure everything was ready."

"You should have done that last night."

"I did."

"Then go see about your bath. We've no time to waste. We shan't be leaving the house today with you looking like an utter disgrace to our name."

I hustled out of the room to find Hillary and nearly ran into her as I rounded the corner. She helped me bathe and wash my hair. As my hair dried, I put on my chemise, petticoat, and short stay. Then I applied face powder, a touch of rouge, and lip gloss with just a hint of pink and dabbed some lavender water on my neck and wrists. Hillary combed out my long, golden hair before twisting a white satin ribbon into the locks and arranging my hair into a loose psyche knot, leaving ringlets of curls on my forehead and framing the sides of my face.

I had just stepped into my dress and Hillary was cinching up and tying the drawstrings when the Marchioness entered. I saw a small smile creep onto her lips before she approached me with the satin sash to tie just under my bosom.

"One last step, Emma."

I turned and saw her pick up the large ostrich-plumed headdress as I was pulling on the satin gloves. She carefully placed it on my head without disturbing the curls. I turned back to the mirror and couldn't believe the image I saw before me. That couldn't be me!

"You look satisfactory for this evening. I think we're ready. Let's head downstairs and find the Marquess," the Marchioness said as she turned away.

Just satisfactory? What more could I do to please her?

Hillary gave me a broad smile and winked as she handed me the fan and my small drawstring purse.

As I descended the stairs, the Marquess came out of the drawing room.

"And who might this young lady be?"

I looked around and realized he was talking to me. The Marchioness was nowhere in sight.

I smiled and said, "It's Miss Blackwell, My Lord."

"I think you are missing one important accessory for the evening, Miss Blackwell."

The Marquess held out a delicate seed pearl necklace with a cameo depicting the nine classical muses.

"Shall I?"

The Marquess held open the necklace to help me put it on. I turned and let him drape the necklace around my neck and fasten it.

"Thank you, My Lord."

"As the Marchioness would say, we must have you live up to the family name."

"What was that about me?" the Marchioness asked as she descended the stairs.

I turned and showed her the necklace that I had just been given.

"Very nice, dear. We did have to provide her with something since her own father didn't bother to show up for her debut or provide her with any of the family jewelry."

"Have you heard from Father? He's definitely not coming?"

"Isn't that what I just said? What did you expect? He has not visited you but once since you arrived. He never was one for high society functions though. No matter. Tonight shall proceed as planned as long as you remember how to comport yourself."

"Yes, My Lady."

"We must be on our way. It wouldn't do for us to be late to court."

I barely remembered the carriage ride over to St. James Palace. One moment the coachman had assisted me into the carriage, and the next I was being whisked into the palace along with a sea of other debutantes and their sponsors. We were presented to and then curtsied to Queen Charlotte, who stood next to her birthday cake, in the drawing room. Then we were led into the ballroom.

I spent the first part of the evening beside the Marchioness and the Marquess as I was introduced to all the young men of society. Before long, my dance card began to fill up as young men scrawled their names on the card tied to my wrist, securing themselves a dance with me that night.

I saw the envious looks from the other girls and heard their mothers whispering as I drew the attention of all the young men in attendance—from baronets to barons, viscounts, earls, and a marquess. In turn, I also saw my aunt's delighted smile as I lived up to her dream for me. I was her greatest victory... other than her own, when she had captured the heart of a marquess as the mere daughter of a baronet herself. In that single moment, I had become the belle of the ball and the most sought-after bride-to-be.

I felt lightheaded and giddy as I whirled around the floor in waltzes, quadrilles, and cotillions. After finishing a lively English country dance, my face was flushed with heat. I delicately waved my silk fan as I stood off to the side, catching my breath. My eyes surveyed the room, taking in the panorama of other couples dancing, until I caught sight of a tall, handsome young man.

His dark eyes drew me in. I felt as if he were looking into my very soul. I knew I should look down. It wasn't proper for me to meet his gaze in such a way, but I felt a connection to him like I'd never felt before except with... Ennis. It was Ennis! I couldn't believe how much he'd changed in the two years since we'd last seen each other. He was taller and more muscled, and his face had changed from the roundness of a boy to the sharper features of a handsome man. He took my breath away. My heart called out to him. My whole body flushed, and I felt electrified as I looked at him.

Ennis had found me, just as he had promised. I knew I'd never be allowed to dance, or even speak to him, unless proper introductions were made. I only had one spot left on my dance card, so I couldn't take a chance of missing our opportunity. I gave a small smile and nodded at Lady Beaumont, who had just noticed me, as I made my way back over to the Marchioness. Thankfully, Lady Beaumont headed over, with Ennis following, to make just the introduction I sought.

"My Ladyship, it is so good to see you again. It's been ages since you came to Mattley Manor and picked up Miss Blackwell." Lady Beaumont turned to me and smiled. "And let me introduce my son, Sir Ennis Beaumont."

"It is wonderful to see you again, Miss Blackwell," Ennis said with a twinkle in his eye. "May I have the pleasure of a dance with you?"

I held out my wrist so he could write his name in the last

space on my dance card. Out of the corner of my eye, I could see the look of consternation on the Marchioness' face, but I acted as if I hadn't. Propriety dictated that she couldn't voice her disapproval aloud in public—after all, Ennis was a member of the gentry in good standing and of a station matching my own.

I was saved from her by the arrival of the next gentleman, Lord Fortescue, ready to collect on his dance. After our waltz, Lord Fortescue escorted me to the meal. After hours of dancing and amusement, I was famished and feeling a little faint. In all the excitement of getting ready, I'd neglected to eat anything all day. Part of me longed for the old days when I could eat what I wanted, as much as I wanted, and as fast as I liked. But manners dictated I only nibble on small amounts of white soup and some cold meats, neither too fast nor too slow.

I found my eyes roaming across the table to find Ennis, the one person I could be my true self around. His eyes were fastened on me and nowhere else. It was both exhilarating and a little disconcerting... the intensity... the single-mindedness. I tore my eyes away and replied to a comment about the meal from Lord Fortescue. As I rose from my seat after dinner was completed, Marquess Cheverell offered his hand to lead me back to the dance floor.

I only had one more dance to complete before I'd finally be reunited with Ennis... Sir Beaumont. I had to remember we couldn't act overly familiar. I fought hard to maintain my concentration on the conversation with the Marquess. It was all the usual inane chatter about what languages I spoke and what instruments I played.

It was infuriating to me that women only mattered for these ridiculous skills that they'd rarely if ever use after courting had been completed. How often would I be called upon in an emergency to sing a song or embroider a wall hanging? What about intelligence and wit? I could never enter a marriage for the sake of social standing, rather than love. But could I, would I, be allowed to refuse?

I tried to push that out of my mind as a matter to be pondered for another day. My official introduction to society at the palace was meant to be a merry, memorable occasion, not a source of stress. I had the next six months of the season to figure out how to make my dreams come true. Maybe it wouldn't be as difficult as I feared. There were no promises that I'd have any other suitors, let alone multiple ones or any more suitable than Ennis.

Before I knew it, the long evening was nearly at an end, and it was time for my dance with Ennis. I had just finished a cup of punch when I heard his husky voice behind me.

"May I have this waltz, Miss Blackwell?"

I turned and fell into the dark pool of his eyes. He held out his hand, and I slipped my gloved fingers into his grasp. He escorted me to the dance floor, and my head spun as he led me around the floor, rising and falling, in great sweeping twirls. Everything in the world felt right when I was in his arms.

"How have you been, Emma? I've missed you so much."

"I've been well. It's all been a bit overwhelming. I missed you too... not that the Marchioness left me much time to dwell. You really did come for me."

"I told you I would. You are mine. We've been fated to be together since we were born. I'd never let you go."

"But..."

"Shhh, Emma. Do not fret. Nothing is impossible for us. It will all work out in time. Let's just enjoy this moment together."

We were so lost in each other that we nearly missed the end

of the song. With only one awkward misstep, he let go of my hand, and I swung out and gave a small curtsy to him as we stepped away. I saw the hard stare the Marchioness was giving me, accompanied by the bystanders' puzzled looks. I hurried back to her side, and we left soon after.

The carriage door had just closed and the horses started with a jolt when the questioning began.

"Just what do you think you were doing tonight? Did I not warn you about the risks of making people talk? How fine a line a lady must walk to ensure proper etiquette and not start the gossip that could permanently tarnish your reputation? You *were* the most sought-after young lady of the evening. I fear to ponder what irreparable damage you may have caused with your little display out there."

"I am very sorry, My Lady. But you must have known that Ennis..." The look on her face hardened to stone. "...That Sir Beaumont and I have been expected to marry nearly our entire lives. That's what our mothers wanted. It's what I..."

"Don't you dare finish that sentence. You ungrateful, willful child. You're no more ready to enter society than the day I took you in after your father begged me. Should I just send you back home now? Your father expected more of you, but he should've known better with that wife he chose. She was no better suited to motherhood than you are to be the wife of an earl or a marquess. You had that at your fingertips tonight and threw it all away. We're probably the laughing stock of the Ton."

"No, My Lady. I am ready. I swear. I will make you and Father proud. Maybe it's not as hopeless as you think. We'll know tomorrow if I receive any calling cards. That's proper etiquette, right, Marquess? For any interested suitors to leave their card tomorrow to announce an impending visit?"

"Don't think too highly of yourself, Miss Blackwell. Time will tell." The Marchioness cut off her husband before he could answer.

The rest of the carriage ride was spent in silence. When we arrived at Rosewood House, I returned to my bedchamber and settled in for the night. It was expected that I would rise late the next day, given the hour the ball ended. I could only hope that there would be calling cards waiting on the salver by the front door in the morning. My family's respect and my future rested on it. What that future would be and with whom remained to be seen.

Emma

The Conundrum

The time was nearly here for me to make the most important, yet difficult, decision of my life. Should I follow my heart to where love lies? Or should I make the wise—the responsible—decision and choose the best suitor for my future and that of my family?

The morning after Queen Charlotte's Ball, I had been relieved to find the salver covered in a layer of calling cards... all left for me. Apparently, my misstep had not been as poorly received as the Marchioness had feared. I recognized some of the names on sight—Sir Beaumont, Sir Edwards, Viscount Stewart, Marquess Cheverell, and Lord Fortescue—but others had gotten lost in the menagerie of people I had encountered the night before. All that mattered was that the Marchioness and Marquess were pleased... very pleased. I'd lived up to their "investment."

The ensuing days were spent receiving callers. The Marchioness was determined to impress them to make up for my indiscretion. They were led into the parlor to meet with me while the Marchioness sat in the back of the room, embroidering, while she chaperoned us. I was surprised to see she even still knew how to do it. When callers arrived, they would find me playing the harp or singing a tune like the larks out in the garden. On the side table, small sandwiches, cold meats, fruit, and tea had been set out for entertaining my gentleman callers.

As time went by, my callers dwindled down to the most serious prospective matches: Marquess Cheverell, Lord Fortescue and, to the Marchioness' dismay, Sir Beaumont. My afternoons were spent walking in the park, riding horseback, having tea, and attending horse races. My evenings were taken up attending balls at Almack's or at the homes of members of the Ton. I knew that Ennis still intended to marry me. The Marquess had hinted at his intentions as well. Lord Fortescue, on the other hand, seemed to be having trouble letting go of his rakish ways. I believed he held on to our courtship more for appearances than any actual intention to marry this season.

My heart and mind were more torn than ever. On the one hand, my heart had always belonged to Ennis. My mind told me I would be happy, loved, and supported. I'd be able to return to the person I had always been. I knew I would be honoring Mother's wishes, but at the expense of Father's respect, maybe even his love. As much as the Marchioness frustrated me, I did appreciate all she had done.

Marquess Cheverell offered me a life of adventure, travel and opulence. While I loved and missed the countryside of Derbyshire, I had come to treasure my experiences in London.

He'd even promised that we could return to my home to visit for a few weeks each summer after the legislative sessions closed in July.

The Marquess was fond of me and proud of my accomplishments. He even accepted the moments when I drifted to topics not normally deemed appropriate for women to speak about. I couldn't deny my attraction to him, and I felt confident that we'd learn to love each other in time. For my family name and my future, he was the most obvious and best match... on paper. But was that the most important factor?

I knew I was running out of time. The end of the season was approaching. One or both of them would be proposing to me at any moment, and I had to decide what I was going to do. If I chose Ennis, would Father even give us his permission? If not, we would have to run away to Scotland or wait until we turned twenty-one and no longer needed legal permission to marry. Either way, our reputation and social status would be in ruins.

If I chose Marquess Cheverell, would I be happy in the long run or would I come to regret my decision? Would his attitude towards and tolerance of my behavior change once we were married? My biggest concern—what would happen to Ennis?

I couldn't make up my mind, no matter how hard or often I thought about it. Mother had always been so proud of my intelligence and wisdom when it came to decision-making. I decided to trust that when the moment came—when the first proposal of marriage was extended—I would know the answer. I didn't know that question would come the following day.

Marquess Cheverell had invited me to go on a horseback ride in the country before the ball that evening hosted by my aunt and the Marquess. With the household in full swing, busy preparing for the evening's festivities, the groom was sent along to chaperone our ride. This left us with a little more privacy than we'd normally experienced.

We stopped under a tall, old oak tree in the meadow, and the Marquess spread out a blanket for us to have a small picnic of some finger sandwiches he had the groom pack in his saddle bag. It was a perfect summer day, and I closed my eyes as I lifted my face to enjoy the warmth of the sun on my skin. The Marquess gently cleared his throat and when I looked over, he held a small gold bracelet in his hand.

"Miss Blackwell, I've become quite fond of you. I hope you will accept this gift as a token of my affection. Will you marry me?"

I was stunned. I'd known it was bound to happen soon, but I hadn't expected it to be today. I'd been holding out hope that Ennis would ask me first—a possible way to bolster our chances of getting Father's permission. Now I understood why Father was finally attending his first and only ball of the season. The Marquess and Marchioness must have known or expected this was coming and invited him so that he could give his consent.

I began to question why Ennis hadn't asked me yet. Maybe he'd lost hope. Or maybe he'd found someone else that he had come to love more. Either way, I couldn't wait any longer to make a decision. It was time that I make the only choice I felt was right and open to me. I couldn't wait any longer for Ennis to profess his love publicly and ask for my hand in marriage. If I didn't marry this season, my options would only decrease with each successive one. The Marquess was a good, honorable man, and he would make an excellent husband.

I turned to him with a few tears welling up. "Yes, I will."

"Excellent. I shall ask your father formally for your hand this afternoon, and we will make it official tonight. Your dance card is full, my love. We should return to Rosewood House so you can get ready, and I can arrange to meet with your father."

When we returned to the house, I made my way quickly up to my room and fell onto my bed in a heap, sobbing for what might have been. When my turmoil had eased, I sat up and found Hillary waiting quietly by the door.

"Miss Blackwell, I have your bath drawn. It's time we get you ready. You have a big night ahead."

I nodded and started towards her. As I walked past, she put a reassuring hand on my back for a second and said, "I'm sure you will be quite happy, Miss."

"Thank you, Hillary."

The next few hours were spent pinning my hair into the Greek-fillet style with a cascade of curls on each side of my face. I topped it off with a silver tiara with blue glass beads. Then, I put on my favorite periwinkle blue dress and felt much better when I saw myself in the mirror. I looked the proper young lady ready to announce her engagement.

"You look beautiful. Err... excuse my manners, Miss Blackwell."

"Thank you, Hillary. That means a lot."

When I descended the stairs, I met Father at the bottom, beaming with pride.

"My beautiful daughter, the future Marchioness."

"Thank you, Father. He spoke to you then, and you gave your consent?"

"Of course. I'm so happy you made such a wise decision."

"Would Sir Beaumont have been such a bad decision though, Father?"

"I would've never agreed. This subject is closed. It's improper to even be talking about this as an engaged woman. I suggest you go find the Marchioness and see if she needs anything before the guests start arriving. Including your betrothed!"

Father turned and stalked away. It was just as I had feared. I'd never had a choice when it came to Ennis. The moment Mother had died, my life had been decided for me. My only possible choice had been among the men of noble lineage, never someone from the gentry... never Ennis.

I didn't know how I would get a chance to tell Ennis properly. I would never be able to talk to him privately. It had all happened so quickly that I hadn't had a chance to send a note to him before the ball. He was going to be so hurt no matter how he found out. But it didn't feel proper for him to realize along with everyone else tonight through idle gossip and the subtle nuance of me no longer having a dance card. I just hoped I would see him early in the evening and be able to speak to him quickly off to the side.

By the time the ball started, I had forced any dark thoughts from my mind. I tried to convince myself that there was no sense focusing on a matter that could not be changed. Besides, tonight we would informally announce our engagement. I still couldn't believe I would soon be marrying Ambrose Cheverell, Marquess of Northampton. This was a night meant for celebration, for I was going to marry a good man.

As soon as the guests had all arrived and been properly greeted, the Marquess was at my side with a broad smile. It was clear from the many knowing looks and nods that he had spread the good news. He took my hand and held it out to admire the bracelet he had given me. I had put it on over my satin gloves.

Then, he whisked me out onto the dance floor.

Before I knew it, over an hour had passed as we danced the night away. As we turned about the dance floor during a waltz, I saw Ennis glare at me before turning to walk away. I was flushed with exertion and thirsty. The Marquess went to talk with some friends while I got some punch and caught a bit of the evening air out on the side patio next to the hedge maze.

Several guests were conversing off to the side when I went out. Just as I turned to follow them in, Ennis appeared, grabbing my elbow and dragging me off the porch and into the maze.

"Ennis... I mean, Sir Beaumont, stop. Let me go! You're hurting me."

"I must speak to you first."

I pulled my arm away and turned to leave.

"It's not proper for us to speak alone, away from everyone else. I must go."

He clamped his hand on my elbow once more and refused to let go.

"No! You owe me the courtesy of a conversation."

"I know. I'm sorry. It just happened this afternoon. I didn't have a chance to send you a note before the party."

"A note?! Are you serious? You owe me a lot more than that." His tone changed to more of a growl as he leaned into my face, "You're mine!"

"Excuse me? I am no one's property. You know that better than anyone. And if you don't, then clearly we were never meant to be together. Now leave me alone!"

He grabbed my shoulders, his fingers digging into the skin painfully, shaking me as he uttered, "You said you loved me."

"I was a child."

"Don't you dare say it was just childish infatuation! That's a lie, and you know it."

"Yes! I did love you! But it would never have worked. Father would never have given us permission. You know how it is with society. You must choose the best match. We don't have the freedom to marry for love in this world."

"We could have run away."

"And given up everything? How would we have lived?"

"Happy! And in love!"

My heart broke with those words because I knew they were true. True but naïve.

"Sir... Ennis, I am sorry, truly. We were children, and it was all so simple then. But now we're adults in the real world, and we are forced to make difficult—no, impossible—decisions that are painful. You will find someone, someone that deserves you and will love you the way she should."

He let go with one hand and reached into his pocket, pulling out an object that glinted in the pale moonlight. He reached out, taking my hand, just as I heard a loud voice call out. Marquess Cheverell was rounding the corner in anger.

"Unhand her now! What are you doing out here alone? How dare you sully her reputation?"

Ennis shoved the object into my hand and whispered, "Take it!" as he turned to meet the Marquess.

"I love her. I had to tell her. You stole her from me!"

"I did no such thing. And don't tell me you didn't know we were engaged. We have been together all evening. We've been the talk of the ball." The Marquess came to my side and took my hand. "Are you well, dear Emma? Has he hurt you?"

I was in shock and terrified. I didn't know how to answer. I couldn't fathom what was going to happen next. All I could do was give a weak nod. The Marquess began pulling me along beside him, leading me out of the garden and up the porch steps. A crowd had gathered and was watching the drama unfold. As we walked, I slipped the object Ennis had given me into the small drawstring purse hanging from my wrist. I would have to find out what it was later for fear of causing further harm. Once he had released me into the care of Father, the Marquess turned back to Ennis.

"Sir, I demand satisfaction! We shall meet at dawn."

The assembled crowd gasped. The Marchioness and Marquess ushered them inside away from the display. Father tried to pull me away as well, but I fought him. As I finally relented, I heard the Marquess say one last thing before coming inside behind me.

"Send your second to meet with mine to decide on the ground rules."

The ball resumed, but it didn't have the same gaiety as it had before that point. We soon went to eat, and it ended early not long after. Marquess Cheverell took me aside before leaving with Hillary standing nearby.

"I shall defend your honor, Emma. I'm sorry this has happened. I will not rescind my proposal. I could see you were just as offended as I. I will see you tomorrow afternoon."

I pressed my hand onto his and held it there a few seconds, tears welling in my eyes. "Take care, My Lord."

I turned and fled up the stairs. My tears and angst were as much for me as they were for the two men I had come to love. I knew neither one would back down. It would be a duel to the death. My life would never be the same, no matter the outcome. One of those men would die. I'd either marry the man who killed the other man I love, or I'd be a disgraced old maid—one love dead, and the other executed for murder.

I threw myself onto the bed and cried like I never had before.

When I finally sat up, weak and bleary-eyed, I pulled my purse off my wrist and remembered Ennis had given me something. I opened the bag and found a beautiful gold bracelet inside with a row of different colored gemstones, eight of them to be exact. It was such a strange assortment of gems that it puzzled me at first.

Then I remembered! I had heard about acrostic jewelry... jewelry that spelled out a secret message with different gemstones standing for different letters. I found a sheet of parchment and worked it out. In order, there was an emerald, vermeille garnet, emerald, ruby, malachite, opal, ruby, and an emerald. Evermore! He had gifted me a bracelet with the word "evermore"—one of the last words he'd said to me the day I'd been sent away, and he'd professed his undying love. He must have been planning to propose tonight, but it was a few hours too late. I'd already accepted a gift and the proposal of another.

I fell onto my bed in tears again. What was going to happen? And what would I do with this gift?

I put it on for the night... one bracelet on each arm. In the morning, I'd rise and find out which man was still alive and had my heart, once and for all.

Ennis

Dead Reckoning

How could she do this to me? After all we've been through—all the years loving each other and being fated to marry—then all the years apart, missing each other. It had finally been our time. We might have needed to wait a little longer, until we were twenty-one, to marry without her father's permission, but she couldn't have been forced to marry someone she didn't love. This time, nothing could've stopped us from being together. No heartless bastard to keep us apart. No disease to tear us asunder. But she had proved herself a harlot, literally selling herself to the highest bidder, just for the money and the power.

That strumpet! She will not get away it. We are tied together as one: Our love is like a knot that has become wet, impossible to untie, so our union cannot unravel. We are more than just soulmates... we share one soul. Twin flames melded into an inferno that burns brighter than the sun. I will not let her go. She is mine evermore. Each time she lost sight of her rightful place, she ceased to be until we met once again. I will not stop until she is mine. We will follow each other through all time, until one day we cease to be forever.

Stop it! I must calm myself. *I do love her, after all. Women can be so fickle, and there is a reason men make all the decisions. Women don't always have the sense to decide what is right. She must have seen the error of her ways by now. Without that pompous dandy by her side, I am sure she'll run away with me. Then we can be married, and I can avoid this duel nonsense. She's worth fighting for, but if I were to die, we'd have to start all over again.*

And death was very possible—I'd sent my second to deliver news of my choice of swords as the weapon since I was the challenged party. However, the Marquess' second claimed the right for the Marquess to choose given his title and that he was the aggrieved party defending his betrothed's honor and reputation. *Him* aggrieved? It was preposterous! The nobility thought they had the privilege to decide all matters because of their titles. Now I was bound to pistols at dawn in the woods outside of London. Swords had always been my strength, and now I would have to hope that my aim was true and my reflexes quick. Unless I could make her come with me and avoid all of this unpleasantness.

I arrived at Rosewood House and snuck in the back servant entrance. With the late hour, all was quiet and dark inside. Fortunately, Emma had told me where her room was, so it was a simple matter to find her. I opened the door quietly and slipped into the room.

The moonlight streaming through the window let me see her angelic form asleep on the bed. As I approached, the light revealed the bracelet I had given her earlier glittering on her wrist. She'd put it on.

She must have changed her mind. She is mine!

I climbed onto the bed and knelt beside her. I bent down and placed one soft kiss on her neck. She awoke with a start, a scream about to erupt from her mouth. In one swift move, I swung my leg over her waist, straddling her, as I placed my hand over her mouth. Her wide, scared eyes stared into my soul. Why was she scared of *me*?

"Emma, it's me, Ennis, your one true love!"

I removed my hand from her mouth. I didn't expect what she said next.

"What are you doing here? Get out of my room! I'll call for the Marquess."

"Emma, calm down. It's me. You are safe."

"Safe? Are you serious? You accosted me last night when we were alone, calling my honor into question. Fortunately, My Lord has not rescinded his proposal."

"You *want* to marry that pompous fool? And what do you mean I accosted you?"

"You pulled me into the hedge maze against my will. You held my arms tight and left bruises. You shook me like a ragdoll. And yes. Yes, I do want to marry the Marquess!"

Before I realized what I was doing, I had slapped her face hard. I could see the handprint on her cheek.

"I'm sorry."

She opened her mouth to scream, but I clamped my hand over it, with only a squeak escaping. She began to batter my face and arms with her hands. I grabbed one hand and locked it under my knee and then proceeded to do the same with the other. She strained to pull herself free, but I was stronger.

"Why are you doing this? We are soulmates. You were

supposed to choose me."

She was pleading with me with her eyes. "Not a sound, or I will make you sorry."

She nodded, and I slowly released my hand once more. I was not prepared for what she said next.

"You are a vulgar, disgusting man! I will not marry you. Now or ever! I hate you!"

Rage flooded through my body. My skin felt like it was on fire. I felt the veins in my forehead throbbing. I wrapped both of my hands around her throat and began to squeeze, so tight that they began to cramp, but yet I squeezed harder still. Her eyes bulged wide, and the color of her face darkened. Tears slid out of the corners of her eyes as she made small gurgling noises. After a time, I felt a small pop as a bone in her throat snapped from the pressure of my thumbs.

Her eyelids began to flutter—she was slipping into unconsciousness. I laughed ruefully. "I'll be seeing you." A few seconds later, her body went limp, and her eyes became vacant. I strangled her until I no longer had feeling in my hands and finally my rage had receded. But I wasn't done yet. There was one more step I had to complete. One more person that I needed to hurt.

The next morning, I arrived for the duel at the appointed time and place. The Marquess was already there, storming around like he owned the place. He was in no mood to talk, and neither was I. His second gave me choice of which pistol I wanted to use from the box, and then went over the rules for both of us. We were to put ten yards' distance between us and, when prompted, we would turn and fire once. Our seconds loaded and prepared our pistols for us.

I debated about when I should deliver the news. Part of me

was hoping to throw off his aim by delivering the news first, but then I decided it would hurt more if he heard it as he lay dying on the field. We walked out on the field and took the ten paces. I heard his second yell, "Fire!" I turned, aimed and pulled the trigger. I heard two almost simultaneous cracks as the pistols fired.

I felt like I had been kicked in the chest by a horse... and then the pain started. I fell backwards onto the grass—the pistol flying out of my hand and landing a few feet away—and saw crimson blood blooming on my shirt. *Please tell me I felled him as well.* As I lifted my head to look for him, I saw him approaching, unharmed. Damn him! I still had a feather in my cap though. I might not have killed him, but I had killed his love. I coughed as I struggled to breathe, spraying blood into the air. I wiggled my finger for him to come down to my level, so I could give him my message.

"You may have won this battle, but I won the girl. Your precious Emma lies strangled in her bed."

As my eyes closed for the last time, at least for now, I saw him fall to his knees, crushed.

Sharon Marie and Stephen H. Provost

Virginia City, Nevada, late 1860s

THE

STALKER

The Harlot
Soiled Dove

My life had not been an easy one. I was born in London, but was brought quite young across the Atlantic Ocean, then southward to New Orleans. I remained there briefly—long enough to learn the French language from a man who took the opportunity to force himself upon me and pass me around among his friends.

The man made them pay to bed me, and of course, he kept all the money, forcing me to marry him so he could control both my secret garden and my purse. But it taught me something: I could make a living selling my downstairs to men who wanted a good time, and if I could strike out on my own, I would be able to keep the proceeds for myself.

The man, who was called Smith—the commonest of names—had more love for the bottle than he did for me. Fortunately, I was able to escape his clutches, traveling as far as I could from that cursed place until I found myself at the edge of the continent, in California. I was barely 20 years of age when I arrived in San Francisco with my cousin Paul, but with so many bordellos already established there, the pickings were slim. I therefore sought refuge in the mining camps, offering up my affections there in exchange for a few silver coins.

It was in one of these places, Chinese Camp south of Sonora, that I first came across a man who called himself Jean-Marie Villain. I had taken up residence in the town's Fandango House, which rented cribs to "fancy women" who entertained the miners with dancing and that which followed.

Jean was one of those miners, but he was different from the others. A native of St. Malo in France, he clearly fancied me for more than a simple dalliance; I could tell that from the moment I encountered him. His touch was tender, not coarse, and only imparted with permission. His eyes were kind, though they masked some great burden, the nature of which I could not ascertain. It scarcely seemed to matter. His admiration for me I returned in kind, and when he came calling at the Fandango House several times, he proved to be the most tender, thoughtful lover I'd ever had. I told him he didn't need to pay, but he insisted. "At least until we can be wed."

I should have told him then and there that I was not interested in becoming a miner's wife, but I could not bring myself to do it—whether to spare his feelings or to prolong our trysts, I am not sure. Most likely, it was both of these things.

I never knew exactly why he was so drawn to me, and I to him. He spoke very little English, and then with a thick accent, so he had been delighted to learn I had some familiarity with his tongue. But there was something more to it than that, and I sensed he knew the nature of it, although he refused to share that knowledge with me.

"I never expected that I might find you here," he said as I lay in his arms, my head resting on his chest.

I smiled shyly and looked up at him. "You speak as though you were looking for me."

"*Oui.*"

"So you were?"

"*Oui.*"

"I do not understand you, Jean. We have never met before, so this is impossible. No one goes searching for a person they do not know exists."

"*Excusez-moi, mademoiselle,* but I not only knew of your existence, but that I must find you. And now, here you are! It is destiny, is it not? A *fait accompli.*"

His words, spoken so casually, made me uneasy. He acted as though he had arranged for us to meet somehow, yet he himself had said he hadn't expected to find me here. But his easy manner and confidence allayed my fears almost as soon as it had provoked them. He took my hand in his and kissed it softly, his breath warm on my skin.

"I know, *ma chérie,*" he said, whispering in my ear, "*ton coeur m'appartient.* And you know it as well, somewhere deep within you."

Ton coeur m'appartient. Your heart belongs to me. He was scaring me, yet at the same time, I sensed there was some truth behind his words.

I pulled my hand away and got out of bed, looking down on him as I stood there naked. I knew the time had come to be fully honest with him. "You presume too much, Jean," I said, my tone serious and mildly reproachful. "I belong to no man, except only for one night. It is the nature of things with me. I will not have you believe otherwise, for to allow such a thing would be to

169

wound you. I enjoy your company, Jean, but I cannot be what I sense you would have me become for you."

He grabbed my hand and held it tight this time, so I could not pull away. "You're hurting me," I said, but he did not loosen his grip.

"*You* are hurting *me, mon amour*." His voice was harder now, determined. "Do not stand in the way of our fate," he said. "You cannot, and even if you could, I would not allow it. If it is money you desire, I will match whatever amount these scoundrels pay you for your company, and I will treat you far better than they."

I scowled at him and succeeded in wresting my arm from his grasp with a hard tug. "It is not money I desire from you. It is affection and understanding. You are right to say that these low men cannot provide me that, but your promise to treat me well rings hollow." I put on my corset and hastily donned my pink ruffled skirt. "You seek to coerce me to spend time with you, rather than wooing me like a lady. Perhaps I judged you wrongly, and you are just as uncouth as they are."

His eyes widened. "Forgive me, Jule. I let my passions get the best of me. It is difficult to constrain them where you are concerned."

"But we met barely a month ago."

"That is where you are wrong, *chérie*. I have known you, and intimately, for a very long time. That is why you found it so easy to speak with me."

"When you say things such as these," I retorted, "it is not easy at all."

Half the men in the camp spent most of their time with their heads in a bottle. But Jean-Marie was not drunk. If anything, he seemed earnest and sober. Yet he spoke as a drunken man might speak, and without the excuse of whiskey coursing through his veins. It was unsettling. I was beginning to wonder if he might be mad.

I took a step back from him, and he looked wounded, almost mournful. I felt sorry for him, but I dared not close the space between us again, though part of me longed to do so. I could not trust this Frenchman. He knew too much about me, as though he had been following me stealthily, just out of view. That would explain why he claimed to know so much about me. It was the *only* explanation.

"I think we should say our goodbyes now," I said, on my guard in case he should attempt to lay hands on me. I was practiced in warding off unwanted advances from men I knew didn't have the money to pay—or, in some cases, any intention of doing so. I had suffered a few bruises resisting those men, but my regulars all liked me and treated me well. I'd never had any doubt that Jean would respect my wishes... until now, that is. It would be a shame to leave this camp behind, but with Jean acting so strangely, I felt it was best.

He didn't try to stop me, though. He just shuffled his feet and stared down at the ground in front of him, unable to meet my eyes.

"Don't do this, *chérie*. Not again."

I gave him a puzzled look. *Not again?* I had never rebuffed him before. "I must return to the dance hall. Others will be waiting for my company."

His face turned red. "I *told* you I would pay whatever they offered and more."

I turned to him, hands on my hips. "And I told *you* I have no interest in being tied to you—beholden to you, or any man."

"Your heart is mine," he growled.

"It might have been, but you have surrendered it by your

jealousy and presumption. Even so, my *body* is my own, and I will do with it as I see fit."

He laughed, almost maniacally, but I just glowered at him. "Do you not see the irony in this, *ma petite*? Your body is not yours but belongs to any man who pays the price for it. Yet, it would seem, my money is not good enough for you. You would rather be bought by some *imbecile* than loved by the one you were made for."

I whirled away so he wouldn't see the tears forming in my eyes. How could he be so cruel? How could I have been so wrong about him?

I opened the door and called back over my shoulder. "Get dressed, you oaf. This is my crib, and I expect you to be gone when I return."

He was. But on my bed he left ten dollars, twice my normal fee, and a note in French that read: "You do not know what you have done, *chérie*. Your obstinance is no match for destiny. Though you spurn me now, you *will* welcome me into your arms. I take leave of you now, but know this, *amour*: If I must hound you to the ends of the earth, I will have you. I and no other man. If you will not accept a vow of marriage from me, I present you with *this* vow instead. If I cannot have you, no one else will."

I did not see Jean in Chinese Camp after that, but it soon became clear that I could not remain there either. Fewer men came calling, perhaps because Jean-Marie had told them some filthy lie about me, or perhaps because they saw the apprehension on my face. Whatever the reason, I knew it was time to move on.

I heard talk that Jean had returned to France, which had

conscripted him to fight in the Crimean War. One part of me feared for his safety, but the other prayed he might become a casualty: Either death or severe injury would prevent him from returning to carry out his threat to me.

I had to wait for the answers to all these questions. I moved on from Chinese Camp to Nevada City, and after that to Downieville, which was in the midst of a big mining boom. Paul came with me and worked in the mines, and his presence gave me some comfort: He would defend me if Jean-Marie were to return.

For a time, everything proceeded as it had in Chinese Camp. Most of my callers treated me kindly, and one even left a small nugget of gold behind as a token of his affection. I never saw him after that. But it was the man I feared seeing, Jean-Marie Villain, who consumed my thoughts.

Word arrived from Crimea in the summer of 1855 that a group of French soldiers had stormed the Russian fort at Malakoff and had eventually taken it. It was a turning point in the war, enabling the French to capture the Black Sea port of Sebastopol two months later.

Had Jean-Marie been slain?

Had he survived?

Would he be returning to America?

For the next two years, there was no word on whether Jean had left Europe again or whether he was even alive after. I wanted to stop thinking about him, but no matter how hard I tried, I could never get him out of my mind.

Then on New Year's Day, as I stood at the window of my room on the third floor of the St. Charles Hotel, I caught sight of a familiar figure driving his wagon across the Jersey Bridge. He looked slightly heavier than when I'd seen him last, and he'd grown a full beard, but there was no mistaking him, even from that distance. Jean-Marie Villain had returned.

I wondered to myself whether it was sheer coincidence that he'd reached Downieville at the same time I happened to be there. But I knew this was doubtful, even impossible. I was sure he had tracked me down, and surer still when he parked his wagon in front of the hotel and came inside.

Paul was away in the mines, so I was alone... and in a panic. I couldn't let *him* find me here, but I knew no way of avoiding him. I slipped out of my room and hurried down the corridor until I reached the dumbwaiter, which, to my frustration, was not nearly large enough to accommodate me—not that I'd really expected it to be. I was tall and leggy (and buxom, too), which was part of my... appeal. Certainly not fitting cargo for a dumbwaiter that might have fit a child at best.

I heard footsteps coming up the stairs. Was it him?

I turned away from them in desperation, meaning to run down the hallway in the opposite direction, although I knew there was no escape that way. But as I turned, my bustle caught on a small circular table where someone had set a candle. The candle wobbled, and I reached out my hand to steady it...

Too late.

The candle toppled onto its side, hot wax dripping onto the doily underneath the candlestand. And the flame was still burning. In lunging for the candle, I'd lost my balance, and—as I realized the peril I was in—I tried hastily to right myself but instead fell forward, knocking the entire table over and sending the candle toppling to the floor.

There, it ignited the carpeting and began racing along the floor, catching on the red velvet drapes that framed a window at the end of the corridor. Smoke started rising as I struggled to hoist myself up again, thwarted for too long by that same cursed bustle that had set this chain of events in motion. Smoke was rising, forcing its way into my nostrils and down into my lungs.

The sound of footfalls on the stairs was suddenly louder, now made by more than one set of feet, and seconds later, several men rounded the corner, led by none other than Jean-Marie Villain. I saw him just as I regained my feet.

"Fire!" one man yelled down the stairs.

"Call out the brigade!"

Jean-Marie rushed toward me, having recognized me even through the smoke. "*Mon amour!*" He called out. "*Je suis ici!*"

He sounded as panicked as I felt, and his tone held genuine concern. Even *fear* for my sake. For a split second, he seemed the man I had first encountered at Chinese Camp, the sweet and caring lover who had melted my heart... only to harden it again with his jealousy and rage. At first, I felt the overwhelming urge to rush into his arms. But only for a second. Then the memory of how he had treated me when I had spurned him returned to me. *How dare he presume to "rescue" me?*

"Let me help you!" he said, reaching out to me.

But I avoided his outstretched arms and forced my way past him. "I do not need *your* help!" I spat. Had I not been fleeing from him, none of this would have happened. He'd spoken to me of fate, yet *he* was the source of this ill fortune. "Save yourself and *forget about me!*"

"But I... cannot...!" he called after me as I reached the stairs and hurried down them. "Don't you see?" His voice drifted down behind me, as if pursuing me. "I cannot forget you. I cannot forget anything. I am cursed to..."

Then I was out the front door and standing with a crowd of people who had gathered to see what was happening. The flames had already spread across the upper floor and were lunging out the windows, gasping for the air that would fuel them and spitting out embers that flew away on the wind. One of them floated down and ignited the dress of an unsuspecting woman, whose companion threw her to the ground and rolled her around in the dirt to extinguish it.

She rose to her feet defiantly, glaring at him as she brushed the dust off her half-burned dress.

"Where is the fire company?" someone called out.

But it scarcely mattered, for as I looked around, I saw other embers flying from the windows and taken by the wind. Moments later, other buildings on Main Street were aglow.

"The Fraternity Hall!" someone yelled.

"The church!" another cried.

But by that time, the gathering had begun to disperse in a panic, running hither and thither as though unsure which direction offered the clearest path to escape. I stood there for a moment longer, wondering what had become of Jean-Marie. I hadn't seen him emerge from the hotel, and his wagon was still there in the street. When it, too, caught fire, I knew I could linger no longer. I fled with the rest of them, unsure of what fate had in store for me.

Fate. There was that word again.

My past had gone up in flames, and God only knew what he had waiting for me in the future.

The Harlot

Silver Mountain

Downieville lay in ruins. One-hundred and fifty buildings had been destroyed, and they were saying that half a million dollars had been lost. Gone with those buildings was the promise of more wealth to be gained from the mines there. Five years earlier, a man by the name of Old Virginny Finney had unearthed the largest gold nugget anyone had ever seen: 313 pounds! But even its value was less than one-fifth of the damage caused by the fire.

Boomtowns always went bust. This one had just received an untimely nudge in that direction.

I only had to discover where the next boom would occur.

It didn't take me long to find out.

Some stout-hearted men, like my cousin Paul, tried to stick it out in Downieville, while others headed back to the Southern

Mines, hoping for a new strike down by Sonora.

More promising, though, was the rumor of a new discovery to the east, just across the mountains in the Utah Territory. Six months after the fire, a few Downieville residents had decided those rumors were solid enough to pull up stakes and head west to the old Mormon Fort of Genoa. A group of four men started loading up their wagons to head in that direction, and they invited me to join them—in exchange, of course, for bestowing my "favors" upon them whenever they desired. They agreed that Paul could come along, too, as long as he carried his weight.

We arrived in Genoa, but there was no silver to be had there, and the leader of our party, a man named Abraham, was rebuffed when he sought to purchase a parcel of land there. After a brief stay, he told me that he and his companions planned to establish a new town a few miles to the north, which they planned to name after the explorer, Kit Carson.

But Abraham confided something else in me, as well: The nascent silver boom wasn't in that vicinity, but farther still to the north and east, where he hoped to invest in some holdings and make a fortune. As fate would have it, the same man who had discovered that huge nugget in Downieville—"Old Virginny" Finney—had staked a claim there, as well, and they were starting to call the boomtown that was emerging there Virginia City in his honor.

I also met a man there named Tom Peasley, who said Paul and I should follow Abraham's lead. Tom was a kind soul who seemed oddly familiar to me, and I was drawn to him immediately as one I knew would protect me. For some reason, I instinctively called him "Marcus" at our first meeting, and though he hastily corrected me, I could see he felt the same familiarity—both with me and the name, even if it did seem slightly off.

He was a little rougher around the edges than I had expected, but the air of courtesy beneath that rough exterior, at least toward me, seemed familiar as well. I had an inkling, at that first encounter, that he was a person of some importance—as though he were of noble birth, bound by an old-fashioned code of honor. Without a second thought, I immediately took his word and headed for Virginia City, where, I would soon discover, he was, as I had intuitively known, a person of note.

With miners beginning to flock to the new camp, I decided it would be the perfect place to ply my trade. The town was barely more than a tent camp when I arrived, but there were more than enough miners to keep me working steadily, and more were arriving every day—men from California and farther afield: places like Ireland and Cornwall. The dirt roads were thick with dust from the wheels of wagons that barreled into town, only to come rattling to a halt because there were so many of them.

The tents soon gave way to more permanent structures, including hotels like the impressive International at C Street and Union. But this time, I didn't rent a crib there or at some bordello; I had put enough money away to afford my own place, a small wooden house just a block down the road from the International. Business got even better after that.

Living on my own, I knew, was a risk. While it set me apart from the other fancy ladies in town, of whom there were many, it also left me vulnerable. With so many foul-smelling and ill-tempered fortune-hunters jockeying for claims, I needed to be careful. The risk was high that I might be assaulted by some brutish man who didn't wish to pay for the privilege of sharing my bed.

My thriving business was the first indication that perhaps

my luck was finally taking a turn for the good. I didn't know how much I believed Jean-Marie's talk about fate and destiny, but if it *was* true, it could work both ways.

The second indication came in the person of the man I'd met in Carson, Tom Peasley. He made it obvious he fancied me, and unlike Jean, he didn't flinch at the idea of me continuing to offer up my wares to the local men... as long as they didn't abuse the privilege. It was the perfect arrangement: Tom was both feared and respected, a saloon owner who also happened to be captain of the volunteer fire company. When some of the women in town objected that I was "distracting" their husbands too much, he put them in their place by making me an honorary member of Engine Company No. 1. By courting me publicly, he said, he could ensure that I didn't receive the wrong kind of attention, and could announce that anyone who tried to cross me would have to deal with *him*.

It wasn't just for show, either. He trained me to work on the engine and told anyone who asked that I could "man a brake as easy as break a man." It was his rough-talking way of standing up for me, and I was glad for it.

The women in town still grumbled, but mostly among themselves, and the men found themselves at liberty to admire me all the more.

Tom's fiery temper and reputation as a fighter—with fists and pistols—kept anyone who wanted to start trouble at arm's length. He didn't seem to be afraid of anyone or anything.

Once, a band of masked highwaymen armed with shotguns stopped the wagon in which he was riding, alongside the mayor and the local marshal.

"We ain't got no money for ya," Tom told them, "but if you're lookin' for a fight, we'll give you better'n you got."

The men believed him and let the wagon pass.

When a drunken Irishman started spouting off about the Rebel cause in front of his saloon, Tom came up to him, gave him a swift kick in the shin, and sent him on his way. When a miner's house caught fire, he and nine other men ran inside in a vain attempt to save its occupant. Tom was the last one out.

I worried for him because nothing seemed to scare him... and because death had begun haunting my dreams. I would sometimes awake gasping for breath in the middle of the night, feeling as though someone's hands were tightening around my throat. The less heed I paid to mortality while waking, the better. Yet even when I pushed such thoughts aside, they always returned to me at night, like some ghost taunting me. It felt like something that had already happened, but also something that was destined to be.

Maybe Tom had the same kind of dreams. Maybe that was why he didn't wish to speak of things like destiny and luck. He'd sworn off pistols after shooting a man dead. I wasn't sure whether it was because I urged him not to tempt fate, or because he'd had some nightmare of his own. Either way, he seemed to think that refusing a gunfight might spare him from meeting an untimely end at the wrong end of a gun barrel.

"I care not for my own life," he told me, "but leaving you would be too painful."

No matter what I did, my nightmares would not relent. They began bleeding over into my waking life, not fading quickly with the morning light as they always had, but replaying themselves over and over in my waking state.

When I told Paul about them, he had a suggestion.

"Go see Eilley," he told me. "She'll be able to tell you the meaning of all this."

I hadn't considered that, but it seemed a fine idea. I knew Mrs. Bowers, having met her when I first arrived on the Comstock. She'd operated a boarding house south of town, and I'd taken a room there on a temporary basis before I settled down in Virginia City.

She was an extravagant lady who had a way about her. She'd throw parties at her place and do the miners' laundry for them, but she offered another service that was even more popular: She told fortunes. When she met a man named Lemuel, known to most as Sandy, and they struck it rich in Gold Hill, rumor had it that she'd foretold the success of this endeavor before the two had even met.

Did I want to know the future? I wasn't certain. I wasn't even sure I believed it *could* be known, and that was a possibility that scared me even more. But my curiosity was stronger than my trepidation, so when Eilley announced that she and her husband would be hosting a gala at the International Hotel as a bon voyage party for their trip to Europe, I asked Tom to secure us invitations.

"How lovely to see you, Jule," she said as she greeted me in the banquet room, but the smile fled from her face the moment her eyes met mine. "You are troubled," she said. "After dinner, you must retire with me to my room. I still have my peep stone with me—I trust you remember it from your time at my boarding house. I believe it may have much to say by way of illumination."

The banquet passed at a snail's pace, and I barely touched my filet, though it was perfectly cooked, or the after-dinner pastry that followed. It didn't matter that I seldom partook of such rich food and, on any other occasion, would have been grateful for the opportunity. The only thing that mattered was what Eilley might say to me after dinner. It was a question that so heightened my level of anxiety that my stomach would not permit me more than a bite or two.

My curiosity dissolved, consumed by my fear. As the end of the banquet approached, I found myself hoping she might forget about her invitation and leave me in blissful ignorance. But Eilley was not the kind of person to forget. No sooner had the plates been cleared than she rose and walked directly over to me. "Come with me," she said. "My husband can see the others out."

The urgency in her voice only heightened my unease, and when she closed the door of her room behind me, a shroud of silence enveloped us as she walked over to the bureau and retrieved her peep stone. "This," she said, "shows me all that portends for your future, good and ill. Do you trust me?"

I nodded.

"Then sit here opposite me and clear your mind while I search the depths of the stone for your answers. I could sense from the moment you arrived tonight that the fates held something in store for you. Now it is time for us to see what that might be."

She smiled and took my hand as she gazed intently into the glass stone.

"I see... a man. He stands beside you... I recognize his face... It is Tom, the fire captain, with whom you arrived this evening. I see him lying on the floor somewhere... It looks familiar, but I can't quite place it." She gasped.

I swallowed hard. "Is he...?" I couldn't bring myself to utter the next word.

"I cannot say for sure. The picture has faded, and is giving way to..."

I held my breath and searched her face for the words she

might say next, but her expression was one of puzzlement. "These images are not familiar to me," she said at last. "I see a carriage made of metal, moving down a strange road without a team of horses. I see the carriage stop abruptly when the driver catches sight of a woman walking down the road on one side. I see the driver exit the carriage quickly and run toward the woman, but she is frightened and attempts to flee from him... Tell me, do you know of anyone who might be following you?"

I knew at once she meant Jean-Marie.

I nodded.

"Are you telling me he is still alive?"

She tore her eyes from the peep stone and looked directly at me. "He must be," she said, "though in some other time and place. What the stone has shared with me looks like nothing I've ever seen—either in my mundane life or in a vision. The woman he was chasing... did not *look* like you, so perhaps you can take some comfort in that."

"What does it mean?" I asked. "This is all very confusing. Perhaps the man you are seeing is someone else... that is, not the man who has been following me."

Eilley looked perplexed. "I asked about you specifically, and the stone is bound to tell the truth, yet nothing in this vision seems related to you at all. Perhaps both these figures are related to you in some other way that has yet to be revealed. I wish I could tell you more, but that is all I can say."

"Would it help you if I gave you the name of the man who is following me?" I asked.

"By all means. Any information is helpful."

I squeezed her hand. "The man's name is Jean-Marie Villain. He is a Frenchman who was once a suitor of mine. We had a falling out, but he tried to find me. I thought he had perished in the fire, in Downieville, but... Can you tell me? Is he still alive?"

She pursed her lips and let out a slow breath.

"Yes," she said finally. "He lives. And I see something more: The two of you will both perish in the same manner. You will both die of strangulation."

It was her turn to squeeze my hand. I was shaking now, and I let out the question I was burning to ask, whose answer I did not wish to know: "When will this happen?"

But Eilley shook her head. "I see only visions, not calendars marking when they might occur."

"Are your visions always accurate? Is my future written in stone?"

She did not answer.

Instead, she rose from the table quickly, picking up the stone and returning it to her bureau. "You must excuse me, dear Jule, but the hour is late, and I fear my head is pounding. This happens sometimes after a particularly... intense... session. It is a signal that the stone will grant me nothing more to know. I am depleted and must rest. Forgive me, darling."

"Of... course," I stammered. "Yes, of course... Thank you for what you have revealed to me."

I didn't know what to make of it, which left me even more frightened than I'd been before our session. But my fear that night was a trifle compared to how I felt a few days later.

Tom was punctual to a fault. He might drink too much and get caught up in business at Carson City, where he frequently did business and had served as sergeant-at-arms for the state Senate, but he always made sure to keep his dates with me.

Seeing him was important to me, too. I needed to keep plenty of time reserved for my other callers, but he came first. Always. I loved him in a way I'd never loved any other man, though Jean-Marie had cast some kind of spell over me that I'd never experienced since. I had concluded it was a dark spell, which is why it troubled me so, and that Tom's love was its antidote.

I was immediately concerned when he did not arrive as he had promised at 7 in the evening, and that concern only mounted when he had still not come calling an hour later, or even by nine. I had no choice, then, but to welcome another gentleman into my abode, having arranged to meet him at that time. I doted on him with smiles and kisses, and glimpses at my flesh that invited him to remove my dress and corset, at no point was I thinking about him. Tom was the only person who mattered.

I dismissed that caller and welcomed another before extinguishing my candles and permitting myself the luxury of a fitful slumber. I told myself Tom would arrive in the morning with flowers and an apology, but my dreams did not reassure me. They were more of those choking nightmares, only this time accompanied by the sight and metallic smell of blood. What Eilley had told me invaded my dreams as well, and I saw a man in a horseless carriage leap out at a woman and grab her from behind. He held her fast and dug his fingers into her throat as she gasped for air.

I gasped for air along with her.

I awoke in a cold sweat. The sun, which had just broken the horizon, sent orange-golden rays through my window, but the house was still, and there was no sign of Tom.

I got up and threw on a loose wrap and prepared a pot of tea. Only a moment after I sat down to drink it, a knock came at the door, followed by the sound of someone letting himself in.

It was the Chinese man I had hired to check on the fireplace and make sure I had the wood I needed. His arms cradled a small stack of logs, which he meant to deliver. There was nothing out of the ordinary about this. But his hands were shaking and the look on his face made clear he came bearing news he was loath to tell me.

"Mr. Peasley," he began haltingly, "is... dead."

My head started spinning.

"What?" I nearly shouted.

"Yes, miss. The news is being carried all over town."

I ran out the door and up the steep slope of Union street to C Street, where I ran inside the offices of the local newspaper, the *Enterprise*. I was panting by the time I got there, but the looks on the faces of the staff as I walked into the office told me everything I needed to know. Whatever had happened, it wasn't good. Dan, one of the reporters raised his head from his desk to look at me.

"What happened?" I asked.

Dan stood up and moved around the desk to meet me.

"Remember that Carson fireman who challenged Tom with pistols last year, name of Marvin Barnhart?"

I swallowed hard. I certainly did remember it. Tom's bad temper had started the whole thing; he'd been drinking at a bar up near Tahoe when he heard someone fire off an insult. Thinking it had been meant for him, he wheeled around and knocked the man nearest to him flat.

That man had been Barnhart, who swore he hadn't said anything to insult Tom and had demanded that he submit to a duel.

"Tom wanted to fight him," I said, "but I'd told him not to do it. He grumbled about it, and in the end, swore to me he wouldn't, but..."

"Don't go thinkin' ill of poor Tom," Dan said. "It wasn't his doing. Barnhart wouldn't take no for an answer this time. According to Ed Ingham, he and Tom were mindin' their own business, playin' billiards at the Sazerac Saloon down in Carson, before heading over to the Ormsby for a smoke and then retiring for the evening."

Retiring for the evening? Apparently Tom *had* forgotten about our date. It wasn't like him. I started to scowl, but then my lower lip began trembling and I put up a hand to cover my mouth.

"Well," Dan went on, "Barnhart saunters up to him like a cock patrolling the henhouse and asks him point blank, 'Why didn't you fight me last year?' Then he draws his revolver and puts the barrel right up to Tommy's head—but Tommy ducks away, asking if Barnhart was planning to murder him."

He paused there, as if reluctant to continue the account. "What happened then?" I pressed.

"Barnhart pulled back the pistol, as though chagrined, but then thought twice about it and fired at Tom. He missed, and Tom lunged at him, but Barnhart fired a second time and hit Tom in the chest, then struck him in the head with the butt of his gun and commenced to strangling him as the two of them stumbled into the room next door."

"My God!"

"Another fellow intervened, and Tom staggered back into the barroom, but instead of falling down dead, as Barnhart must've expected, he set his back straight, drew his pistol, and fired at the door to the other room. Then he walked toward the place where Barnhart had secluded himself, put his pistol through the doorway and fired a second time... and then a third as he stepped into the other room.

"Ed ran over to the Sazerac, shouting that Tom had been shot, then hurried back to find Tom lying on the floor and

Barnhart stretched out likewise, gasping for breath. Ed managed to revive Tom..."

"Then he's still alive?" I was still clinging to irrational hope, even though he'd already told me Tom was gone.

Dan shook his head slowly. "He told Ed to go and fetch his brother Andy from here in Virginia, but by the time they got back to the Ormsby, Tom was dead. He gave as good as he got, though. His aim was true, and Barnhart expired as well."

I put my head in my hands, not believing it possible, but at the same time knowing it had been bound to happen. What I didn't understand was why Barnhart would've renewed his challenge a whole year after he'd first made it. *Some men hold grudges*, I told myself, and I didn't know Barnhart personally, but a voice inside was telling me there was something more to it than that.

I stood stiffly, facing Dan, containing my emotions as I'd learned to do when entertaining less-than-honorable clients. "Was there anything else? Anything at all?"

Dan frowned. "Well...," he began.

"Yes?"

"Jule, I wouldn't put much stock in this, but Barnhart went over the to the Sazerac while Tom and Ed was still there, and Ed remembered seeing him there only after the fact, accompanied by a foreigner and one other man. The foreigner said something in French to Barnhart, who looked like he understood it. Ed didn't know what it meant at the time but for some reason, it stuck with him. He told me the man said, '*Si tu le tues, tu me rendras un grand service.*'"

"If you kill him, you will be doing me a big favor," I said, translating as I stared blankly ahead, feeling my heart pound faster against my breastbone.

A Frenchman. I told myself it was just a coincidence. There were a few Frenchmen working the mines on the Comstock, but I hadn't run into any of them myself, and Tom had never told me about having a run-in with any of them. Yet apparently he had run afoul of one particular Frenchman, wronging him so greatly that the man wished to see him dead.

What possible motive could he have?

I already knew the answer. Eilley had seen Tom lying on the floor, and it had come to pass, just as she had said. She'd also told me she thought that Jean-Marie was still alive—a man who would have been jealous, to put it mildly, if he learned I had taken up with someone else.

My destiny appeared to have found me, and the good fortune I had believed had finally come my way was vanishing like so much smoke in the wind.

I missed Tom. But in practical terms, things didn't change much now that he was gone. The whole fire company rallied around me and swore to keep me safe in his absence. They watched out for me as I went about my business in town and saw me to my door when I returned home—some even stayed for a little fun.

I felt secure—even when Jean-Marie opened up a laundry down the street from me (and I knew the location was no accident). To my surprise, he did not come calling or molest me when I was out and about. I saw him steal a glance at me whenever we passed on the street, but he never made any move to confront me.

My business prospered, and although I was hardly rich, I was able to treat myself now and again to some of the city's amenities. Virginia had, by this time, become a city in more than name. In fact, it was the only one of any note in the state of Nevada and one that had grown to rival California's principal city of San Francisco. It had its own lavish opera house, owned by a local saloonkeeper, and one evening in January, I decided to pop in and enjoy a popular melodeon that was playing. It wasn't the first time I'd attended a performance there, and I'd always been escorted to a seat in the main section of the theater. This time, however, I was told I must sit in a special box reserved for women "of dubious morals." When I tried to protest, I was told an ordinance had been passed to segregate the audience thus, and I would have to sit there regardless of my previous practice.

The doorman told me the men of the city had no quarrel with me. The women, however, didn't want to be reminded of their husbands' dalliances by being forced to gaze upon the ladies who had "entertained them." The curtains of the box would be drawn tightly, I was told, to obscure us from view of the "proper ladies."

I had no interest in playing hide-and-seek with women whose husbands had no interest in them, so I told the doorman "Thank you" and turned to head back home. When I got there, I stepped inside and thought about starting a fire, but decided against it. It would be just as well to retire early. I'd cleared my calendar to attend the melodeon at Piper's, but with that by the wayside, I had the evening free. No one had made arrangements to see me tonight, which meant I had a chance to get a restful night's sleep for a change.

I changed into my nightclothes and lit a candle by my bedside.

Just as I was climbing into bed, though, the wind began to kick up, whistling up from the south as it did in wintertime, buffeting loose boards at the backs of saloons and cribs in the "sporting district." I heard a thunk-THUNK, thunk-THUNK at the back of my bedroom, and the wind curled its fingers underneath those shutters and tossed them about, then invaded my room, extinguishing the candle.

I crept out of bed to secure those shutters, then had to feel my way around in the darkness to find my bed again. I was glad I hadn't gone to the theater, after all. It might have been just a few yards from my front door, but that was too far to venture if a storm was coming in. Driving rain could turn the dirt streets into muddy bogs in a matter of minutes, and heavy snows weren't uncommon in January at this elevation.

The chill of the wind that had burst in through my window lingered, and I grabbed my quilt, wrapping it around myself as I climbed back into bed...

Only to hear something slam against the door in the front room.

In truth, it sounded like the door itself had been flung open, announcing some intruder's arrival by slamming against the interior wall.

Had I neglected to bolt the door?

If so, most of my callers were regulars who knocked before they entered, and even those who didn't were on good terms with me: They'd come in unannounced, playing a little game of cat-and-mouse with me that always ended with them "catching" me as a prelude to the requisite roll in the hay.

Maybe it was one of them, and the wind had ripped the door from their hands unexpectedly.

That must be it.

I felt around for the candle, but apparently the wind hadn't just extinguished the flame, it had knocked the wax and holder down onto the floor.

"Who's there?" I called. "Abner Russo, don't play coy with

me. We can dispense with our little chase. Come back to my room and let Jule warm y'up."

There was no answer, though.

The door, I concluded, must have blown open on its own, although I had no memory of that happening before. The winds were still wailing and whining as they cascaded through the streets, growing stronger, if anything, as the moments passed.

There was no avoiding it: I would have to grope my way through the darkness and into the front room to see what had happened. I struck my toe on the foot of the bedframe as I tried to navigate around it, and bit my lip to avoid crying out. If someone *was* inside, I didn't want him to know where I was.

As I rounded the corner into the sitting room, I could see the dim moonlight illuminating a pale rectangle where the door stood open.

The rectangle grew dimmer, then brighter again, then dimmer still. It wasn't raining, at least not yet, and I imagined the clouds were flying across the sky in broken formation like so many riders in a cavalry charge before the storm's foot soldiers marched in close formation behind them, raining fire down on the enemy.

I took a step forward, then two, nearing the door and reaching out my hand to shut it... when something stopped me. A hand grabbed me from behind, covering my mouth as the other hand wrapped itself around my waist. Heavy breathing in my ear joined the sounds of the wind howling and the boards of my crib groaning, creating a sickening chorus.

The man thrust me forward, grinding his hardness against my thigh and my rear as he guided me into the bedroom. I managed to squirm enough that he had to release the hand held over my mouth and use it to keep me from escaping.

"Help!" I cried, but the sound of my voice was swallowed up by the wind, and in this weather, there was likely no one out in the street to hear me.

The man pushed me down onto the bed, and I expected him to rip off my nightclothes and have his way with me. It wouldn't have been the first time. But instead of undressing me, he held me beneath him, fully clothed, his hands around my wrists as he pinned them to the bed on either side of me. The weight of his body kept me motionless, and his breath, more ragged from exertion, was hot on my face.

Then I recognized it: the scent of him. Each man has his own distinctive odor, and this was one I had smelled before. More than once. It was familiar to me, and the sense of safety and rapture it had conjured up in me before battled against the loathing and terror I now felt.

"Jean-Marie," I breathed.

"Ah, *chérie. Tu n'as pas oublié.* I might be flattered if you were anyone else. But I knew you could never forget me. Not you, my dove. You must have known I could not permit you to spurn our love... to flee our passion."

I squirmed, trying to twist my wrists free, but he only gripped them harder.

"Did you truly think you could escape?"

"I... I..."

"Did you not see what happened at your last attempt? By resisting fate, you left an entire town in ashes, laid waste by the passion of our love denied. How could you not have recognized it, my flower? Yet still you reject me, as you always have before. Even though you *know* I love you. And you love me. You cannot deny it."

"Love you?" I cried. "You never gave me the chance to love

you. Had you offered your love for me to accept, it would have been yours. But in seeking to force it upon me—as you are doing now—you have sullied it beyond all recognition."

His heavy breathing became a deep laugh.

"Sullied it? *Sullied* it? You who whore your body out to men you have never even met... *you* speak to *me* of sullying things?"

I tried to push him off of me. "Please, Jean-Marie! If you love me as you say, how can you do this?"

"How can I do what?" he shouted, rearing back and staring down at me like... like... He looked for all the world like a hunter about to deliver the kill strike on his prey. But no... he wouldn't do that. He was kind and gentle. I knew he was. He was just upset. He couldn't possibly *mean* to harm me. He was just overwrought at my refusal of his advances. If I could just calm him down... If I could just get him to remember the person he had been before...

"*Putain!*" he roared, spitting down on my face but still holding my hands down so I couldn't wipe it off. I felt his saliva trickle down my cheek and onto the pillow beside me.

Then, suddenly, he released my wrists and put his hand around my throat.

I slapped at his sides, then balled up my fists to beat against his ribcage, but he only pressed down harder.

"If you want me... take me...," I gasped with the last of my breath.

"Take you? You are already mine! You always have been, *Putain!* Don't you realize that? Can't you see?"

I shook my head, trying to free up the narrowest passageway through my windpipe. I felt his fingers digging into my throat. I had to do something; I was on the verge of passing out. Something inside resisted hurting him, even now in self-defense, but I had no choice. I brought my knee up hard into his groin, and he tumbled backward off me.

I coughed and wheezed as I sprang up from the bed, but I was too winded. Too slow. Even hurt as he was, he was quicker and stronger. I saw the shock in his eyes at what I had done, even though it was far less than what he had inflicted upon me. He didn't see what he was doing. He'd gone mad with an insatiable rage that lit up the pupils in his eyes like some demon. Perhaps it was just their reflection from the hearthfire off to one side, but I wasn't convinced of that. I wasn't convinced of anything anymore. Had he ever loved me, or had he only sought to possess me like all the other men in Virginia City and the California mining camps, and New Orleans before that?

I was still dizzy from lack of oxygen as I stumbled away from him toward the door, but he grabbed me and threw me back onto the bed. Almost in slow motion, he reached beside him for a heavy log leaning there by the fire. Then time sped up, and before I could move, he was bringing it down.

I closed my eyes tight and tried to scream, but that scream only came after I felt a searing pain rip into my skull. I tried to open my eyes, but I still couldn't see. In some far recess of the world I was leaving, I heard the log hit the ground with a thud and felt those fingers clench in around my neck once more. Harder this time... More insistent... Inexorable.

The Writer

Gallows Pole

S erendipity is a curious phenomenon. It sneaks up on men such as myself in places and at times when we are least attuned to it.

When it comes calling, it does so discretely, in the guise of an acquaintance or a stranger. It coaxes a man out for a fine evening on the town, but wears a mask throughout the evening to conceal its true identity. Then, when midnight strikes, it throws this mask down at its suitor's feet like a gauntlet, saying, "Surprise! Here I am," revealing itself as either benefactor or a scoundrel.

I was not immune to its trickery, though perhaps, had I been more observant, I might have guessed its intent. I was, after all, returning to the city where I had spent the better part of three tumultuous years. My fortunes on the Comstock had always been changeable, to put it euphemistically, and my time there had ended when I departed in haste after being challenged to a duel.

Two of them, if the truth be known.

I had returned here once before as part of a speaking tour, thinking to redeem myself in the eyes of my former neighbors with some witticisms and evidence of my growing fame. My own ego was not immune to the effects of the latter, and I suspected it might have a remedial effect on those who still held me in low esteem. The tour had been a success, but I had caught a bad chill one night when I was confronted by a group of hooligans who deprived me of my prized pocket watch and other effects. It so happened that the hooligans in question were, in truth, my friends, having fun at my expense by playing the sort of prank I had often enough played on them.

Despite this cautionary occurrence, I, being as mule-headed as any man—and, perhaps, more so than most—had accepted an invitation for a return engagement two years after my first series of lectures.

In addition to writing down my own stories for publication, I had arranged to file reports on happenings of note for various esteemed newspapers. Among these was the *Chicago Republican*, which contacted me about providing an account of a hanging in my former town of residence, which, as fortune would have it, was occurring around the time I was to appear for lectures at Piper's Opera House and in the nearby state capital.

The hanging of a certain Frenchman was to take place a few days prior to my lecture at Piper's, which allowed me some time to settle in. The man had been convicted of killing a well-known member of the fair but frail set, which is to say, a lady of the evening, whose reputation for good works far outshone her notoriety.

So popular was she in the city that a throng of men had been clamoring for the Frenchman's execution since the day of his capture.

The facts of the case, as established in court, were thus: The victim had been found on a Sunday morning in January of the previous year. A neighbor called upon her in her home, a modest house at the corner of Union and D streets, only to find her a lifeless corpse lying on the bed, her head obscured beneath a pillow but her nightclothes covered with blood. She had been, it was discovered, beaten about the head and strangled, with the killer's fingernails having punctured the skin of her neck. From her home were missing some articles of clothing, including a set of furs, two gold watches, and other adornments. The murderer's motive, it seemed clear to the casual observer, had been thievery.

But I had trained myself to be, not a casual observer, but an astute one. And if theft had indeed been the motive, then why should he have done poor Julia such violence? The soiled dove of Virginia City had endeared herself to many but, any lady in her line of employment would certainly have made enemies as well. The other women of the city had no love for her, since she no doubt entertained some of their husbands with more than a cup of tea and a glimpse at her pretty face. As popular as she was, some clients might not have received what they considered, in their minds, their money's worth, while others might have been prone to fits of jealousy when she showed excessive favor to one or another of them.

She had done this very thing to the fire captain, Tom Peasley, who had been of my acquaintance. My proclivity for drinking had conveyed me to his fine establishment more than a few times during my previous sojourn here. He was the jealous type, as well, and fiercely protective, as any fire engineer should be. That Julia had benefited from this protection, I had no doubt. I also, however, did not question that his demise would have increased the danger to her.

Was the man accused of doing away with her the agent of some enemy within the city? Or was he carrying out some personal vendetta against her? The extent of the injuries inflicted upon her suggested the latter, but I could not be sure.

The more these questions rattled around inside my head, the more determined I became to seek out the answers, and who better to provide them than the man himself, who had been identified in my hearing as one John Melanie or Millian, or some such foreign cognomen? I therefore went in person to inquire about the possibility of interviewing the man in question, confident that my reputation would grant me access to the craven murderer.

The *Republican* had asked for a story, and if I were to produce one, it would have to be worthy of my time.

To my surprise, the jailer initially refused my request.

"No one is to see the prisoner," he stated, putting a hand up to block my ingress.

I cocked an eyebrow at him and invited him to survey my person more closely.

"Oh, I know who you are, Mr. Twain, but I've been told there are to be no exceptions. That man in there is dangerous."

I responded with a short, hard laugh, directly in his face, so hard that his hair almost blew back. "Every aspect of this town is dangerous," I stated. "If you are suggesting that I'm unaware of this, having lived here myself for nearly three years, you are more unenlightened than a man of your station ought to be."

That much was obvious, but I didn't see the harm in making it plain.

"I'm sorry, Mr. Twain, but I've my orders..."

I frowned my disapproval, then shrugged. "Very well, then," I told him. "It's a pity your name won't appear in the article I'm preparing as a dispatch to Chicago."

That did the trick.

"You were going to mention me?"

"Well, of course. One must be thorough in preparing the facts for public consumption. I *was* planning to include you, but since you are no longer of any import to my story, I see no point in doing so. Wasting words is almost as grave a sin as failing to tell the complete story, don't you agree?"

He stammered something incomprehensible.

"Now, sir, if you will tell me your name, I will be sure to include it... once you grant me access to the prisoner."

"Sizemore. Joey Sizemore. But don't go tellin' on me, now. Say you came by before and that Billy O'Herlihy was the one who let you pass."

"O'Herlihy, you said? How do you spell that name, with a second 'e' or without one?"

"You mean to mention him too?"

"Or instead. If you want me to conceal your identity, I can't very well go putting it into print, can I?"

"But..." the man stammered. I had him thoroughly flummoxed now, which had been my intent all along.

"Never you mind," I said, clapping him on the back. "We'll sort this all out later. Now, if you will just escort me to the cell where Mr. Melanie is being kept, I'd be much obliged." I slipped him two bits and whispered, "Hand that to old Piper up at the corner. He'll give you some of the best whiskey in these parts." I winked, and he nodded, quickening his step back toward where Melanie was being kept.

"Who are you?" the man demanded in a manner that seemed haughtier than his appearance would have suggested. He looked about the way I had expected, with a head of dark hair, thick eyebrows. I could tell that he normally wore a mustache and Van Dyke, but that several days away from a razor had filled in the stubble on his cheeks.

"My name's Clemens," I said. "But most people these days know me more quickly by my *nom de plume*, Twain." I used the borrowed French intentionally, to ingratiate myself to him.

He smiled, whether for that reason or because he recognized me, I was unsure, but my introduction had had the desired effect either way. "And you are, I presume, John Melanie."

This brought a scowl. "The name's Jean-Marie Villain. With a V." Was he trying to spar with me using irony, or was that his true name? I could not read the answer in his expression, so I decided to assume the former. The man was sharper than I expected, having been described to me as an unschooled drifter now working as a launderer in the rough lower district. "I'm not what you expected, am I?"

He was sharp indeed. I would have to practice being more inscrutable, as, for the moment, he was besting me in that regard.

I shrugged slightly. "I've only been on this earth thirty-ought years, but I've already seen more than most men twice my age."

It was his turn to laugh this time, which perturbed me, as I had not intended to tickle his funny bone, and I only felt satisfied when my humor was purposeful. What galled me even more was that I expected him to reveal what he found so funny, but rather than doing so, he asked me a question.

"Tell me, Mr. Twain, just what have you seen?"

I was unaccustomed to being put on the defensive, but there I was.

"I've served on a Mississippi riverboat, mined for gold in Aurora, and most recently returned from a lecture tour of the Sandwich Islands. I did not, however, come here with the intention of being interviewed by a *villain* such as yourself, but of interviewing *you*."

"Then the next few questions I ask will reveal something of myself to you... and, in the process, that which is lacking in yourself."

This man was practiced in the art of verbal give-and-take, though I could not imagine how he had developed this talent. Certainly not in the California mines, whence he had come, or on the battlefield in Crimea. Furthermore, his thick French accent should have tripped up his tongue, yet somehow, it did not.

"You seem eager to cross swords with me, sir," I said.

He laughed again. "If we were to cross swords," he said, "I assure you that you would not survive the encounter... although, from what I have heard of you, you are no more competent with pistols."

I tried to disguise the surprise in my expression, though I must have failed to do so, because he smiled a satisfied smile.

"Yes," he said, a gleam in his eye. "I have read of your cowardly conduct in failing to answer a challenge issued—not even just once, but twice."

"Dueling is illegal," I stated flatly. It was true, but I knew as soon as the words left my lips that it was not an excuse that would resonate with John Melanie. Or Millian. Or Villain. Or whatever his true name was. He just smiled, however, and said nothing, confident that my own words would suffice to shame me.

"You might have visited the Sandwich Isles," he said, "which I confess I have not. But have you danced at Queen Charlotte's debutante ball? Have you stood accused of vampirism? Have you returned home to expel invaders occupying your castle, and have you put their heads on pikes as a warning against others?"

He had crossed over from irony into madness. "The next thing you will be telling me is that you sat at King Arthur's Round Table and bedded the lady Guinevere!"

His smile fell from his face, and his eyes were roiled by anger. "Her name," he said through clenched teeth, "was Alba. And that cursed Bear who set himself up as false king had no right to her. She was *mine* to protect."

Bear? It was known to me that the word "bear" was a rough translation of the name "Arthur," but how could an uncouth maniac have known such a thing? It was another question to rattle around inside my noggin, but I had a suspicion I would never know the answer.

Just as vexatious was his reference to Queen Charlotte, who had died a half-century ago. This was a gaping hole in an already fantastical story, considering the man standing before me was no more than forty years of age. The only way he could possibly have managed to be present during the age of Camelot or Queen Charlotte's reign would have been through time travel. This was the stuff of novels, not real life. I didn't know what to make of the reference to vampires. Perhaps this crackpot murderer was a clandestine storyteller trying to impress me, though I had to admit he didn't strike me that way.

Anticipating my next question, which I was, even then, still pondering, he asked another of his own: "How old do you think I am?"

Evermore

"You do not, to this observer, seem more than forty years of age at the outside."

"And you are...?"

"Thirty-three."

"*Comme je le pensais.* But as the saying goes, appearances are often deceiving. I have been on this earth, on and off, so to speak, for nearly two millennia. I have lived many lives to your one—that you know of, anyway. And I have loved Alba every single time. She was mine in the beginning. She is mine now. And she will evermore be mine!"

The madness had returned to his eyes. Had it truly ever left? I decided that now, that he was agitated and off his guard, would be the best time to pose the question I had come to ask.

"Why on earth did you see fit to kill Julia, an innocent woman, when your heart is sworn to this Alba?"

He put his hands on the bars that separated us and squeezed so tightly his knuckles lost all color. "Because, you facile *idiot*," he whispered, "Julia *is* Alba."

I passed this off as the raving of a lunatic, and instead answered him with a single word. "Was."

At that, John Melanie did something I had not at all expected: He released the bars from his grip, fell backward onto the floor, and began sobbing, his body heaving in convulsions as he tucked his knees up against his chin.

I left him there to his demented anguish.

My account of the hanging of John Melanie appeared in the Chicago Republican on May 31, 1868. It contained nothing I had gleaned from my interview with him. I'd penned my share of frontier tall tales for the newspaper, but this was even beyond anything I had ever dreamed up.

Sharon Marie and Stephen H. Provost

My official published account of the events surrounding Julia Bulette's murder focused exclusively on the Frenchman's execution, which I witnessed with interest—and disgust.

It read as follows:

> *I saw a man hanged the other day. John Melanie, of France. He was the first man ever hanged in this city (or country either), where the first twenty six graves in the cemetery were those of men who died by shots and stabs.*
>
> *I never had witnessed an execution before, and did not believe I could be present at this one without turning away my head at the last moment. But I did not know what fascination there was about the thing, then. I only went because I thought I ought to have a lesson, and because I believed that if ever it would be possible to see a man hanged, and derive satisfaction from the spectacle, this was the time. For John Melanie was no common murderer—else he would have gone free. He was a heartless assassin. A year ago, he secreted himself under the house of a woman of the town who lived alone, and in the dead watches of the night, he entered her room, knocked her senseless with a billet of wood as she slept, and then strangled her with his fingers. He carried off all her money, her watches, and every article of her wearing apparel, and the next day, with quiet effrontery, put some crepe on his arm and walked in her funeral procession.*
>
> *Afterward he secreted himself under the bed of another woman of the town, and in the middle of the night was*

*crawling out with a slung-shot in one hand and a butcher
knife in the other, when the woman discovered him, alarmed
the neighborhood with her screams, and he retreated from
the house. Melanie sold dresses and jewelry here and there
until some of the articles were identified as belonging to the
murdered courtezan. He was arrested and then his later
intended victim recognized him.*

*After he was tried and condemned to death, he used to
curse and swear at all who approached him; and he once
grossly insulted some young Sisters of Charity who came to
minister kindly to his wants. The morning of the execution,
he joked with the barber, and told him not to cut his throat—
he wanted the distinction of being hanged.*

*This is the man I wanted to see hung. I joined the
appointed physicians, so that I might be admitted within the
charmed circle and be close to Melanie. Now I never more
shall be surprised at anything. That assassin got out of the
closed carriage, and the first thing his eye fell upon was that
awful gallows towering above a great sea of human heads,
out yonder on the hill side and his cheek never blanched, and
never a muscle quivered! He strode firmly away, and skipped
gaily up the steps of the gallows like a happy girl. He looked
around upon the people, calmly; he examined the gallows
with a critical eye, and with the pleased curiosity of a man
who sees for the first time a wonder he has often heard of. He
swallowed frequently, but there was no evidence of
trepidation about him—and not the slightest air of
braggadocio whatever. He prayed with the priest, and then*

drew out an abusive manuscript and read from it in a clear, strong voice, without a quaver in it. It was a broad, thin sheet of paper, and he held it apart in front of him as he stood. If ever his hand trembled in even the slightest degree, it never quivered that paper. I watched him at that sickening moment when the sheriff was fitting the noose about his neck, and pushing the knot this way and that to get it nicely adjusted to the hollow under his ear—and if they had been measuring Melanie for a shirt, he could not have been more perfectly serene. I never saw anything like that before. My own suspense was almost unbearable—my blood was leaping through my veins, and my thoughts were crowding and trampling upon each other. Twenty moments to live—fifteen to live—ten to live—five— three—heaven and earth, how the time galloped! and yet that man stood there unmoved though he knew that the sheriff was reaching deliberately for the drop while the black cap descended over his quiet face!—then down through the hole in the scaffold the strap-bound figure shot like a dart!—a dreadful shiver started at the shoulders, violently convulsed the whole body all the way down, and died away with a tense drawing of the toes downward, like a doubled fist—and all was over!

I saw it all. I took exact note of every detail, even to Melanie's considerately helping to fix the leather strap that bound his legs together and his quiet removal of his slippers—and I never wish to see it again. I can see that stiff, straight corpse hanging there yet, with its black pillow-cased head turned rigidly to one side, and the purple streaks creeping through the hands and driving the fleshy hue of life before them. Ugh!

But even though I shared nothing of my own interactions with Melanie in this published account, something struck a chord with me as I made my way out of the jail after meeting with him that day.

As I started to walk away from the French madman, I stopped for a moment and reopened my notebook to scribble down a sudden epiphany. Maybe this hadn't been a waste of time, after all. One never knew when an idea for a novel might rear its head, and the concept of time travel seemed promising. I thought briefly, then put pen to paper and scribbled down a title: "A Frenchman in King Arthur's Court."

No, that wouldn't sell. I scribbled out "Frenchman" and wrote the word "Yankee" above it. It still wasn't quite right, but I was confident it would work itself out.

I had nothing but time.

Sharon Marie and Stephen H. Provost

Manhattan, 1923

THE BROADWAY BUTTERFLY

Dot

HITTING MY STRIDE

I'd been a wild girl from the start. There was no taming me. It seemed like I'd been born in the wrong time and place. I was never meant to be the daughter of poor Irish immigrants. They'd named me Anna Marie Keenan, but I'd changed it to Dorothy King when I grew up. Now everybody called me Dashing Dot.

Aching to get out and experience life, I'd jumped into a marriage at 18. It didn't take me long to realize my mistake. He worked as a chauffeur, that is, when he did work. The problem wasn't his bum leg, but that he was a big bum. I left him, not even bothering with a divorce. I'd finally had the marriage annulled late last year, using my own indiscretions as the reason.

Freedom, acceptance, and happiness finally came to me in

213

my roaring twenties as the tensions of war gave way to an economic boom. I wasn't the only rebellious spirit: Many people in the country were fighting for the right to consume *their* "spirits" with the advent of Prohibition.

My buxom body, blond hair, dazzling blue eyes, and freckles garnered every man's attention. Once I donned my gold silk bandeau, luxurious furs, expensive jewels, and fancy gowns, I had to beat them off with a stick.

Life as a flapper, one of the "Broadway Butterflies," was the life I'd always been destined for: money, booze, and men. I spent my nights dancing up and down the "Great White Way" going from one late-night cabaret or speakeasy to the next. And when I wasn't out on the town, I hosted wild, drunken parties up at my apartment. I had a beautiful two-room flat in a brownstone on West 57th, just a few doors down from Carnegie Hall, thanks to one of my rich admirers.

My life was full of men who wanted my attention, and I made sure to spread the love around because I certainly didn't want to end up tied down to one man again. I wasn't sure why I even got married way back when, given how much I liked my freedom. I must have thought it was a way to escape a life of hard work and poverty. Men had always seemed too possessive to me, though. Even as a child, I had this strong aversion to being seen as someone's property. Now that I'd found my own way, I'd never make that mistake again.

"Mr. Marshall," as he liked me to call him to conceal his true identity, was a wealthy married man, so I had no worries that he'd try to make our arrangement into something more than it was. He showered me with gifts of savings bonds, jewels, and furs. He'd arrive, champagne bottle in hand—wrapped in a string of pearls—accompanied by his secretary, "Mr. Wilson," another alias. Mr. Wilson would scope out the place (for what I'm not sure), and then either wait in the car or go home depending on the length of Marsh's visit. It was eccentric, sure. But how could a girl say no? Marsh was the one who'd set me up in this posh apartment for the past year and a half.

My special friend and I enjoyed each other's company, but there were never any strings attached for either of us. I didn't understand the need for all the secrecy: The three of us went out to dinner on occasion at places like the fashionable Hotel Brevoort, hardly a place one would choose to maintain discretion. But who was I to question? A quick peck on the cheek and a "Thank you, Marsh baby" was the answer for me.

Mr. Marshall was certainly a welcome distraction from that louse I called a boyfriend, Albert, a swindler with ties to the mob. I didn't involve myself in any of that, although he'd once talked me into helping him with his Ponzi scheme selling fake stocks to would-be investors. His so-called "suckers' list" of people that we had scammed was still sitting up in my apartment. It brought in more money for me, but the bruises from Albert's beatings weren't worth it. I was just waiting for the chance to finally kick him to the curb.

I walked into Vinny's new speakeasy, The Back Door Club, expecting a large raucous crowd, but I found the place surprisingly quiet for a Friday night. A few rustics, obvious walk-ins, were sitting in the back, hoping one of the flaps would look their way. I was surprised Vinny had allowed them to stay. I'd heard he was catering to a more select, upscale crowd—the kind with underworld connections. A few men I didn't recognize were dancing the Lindy with some of the girls, but other than that, the place was dead. I was about to leave and head down to The Blue Angel when Clara waved me over.

I walked to the bar, where she was sitting, and bent down to kiss her on each expertly rouged cheek. "Hi, darling. What's with the crickets?"

"A bull came in sniffing around earlier. Guess the word got around to the flatfoots that there was a new juice joint in town."

"Bet Vinny was pissed that his first Friday night was a washout! Guess that explains the apple-knockers and rubes in front and Father Time over there." I waved my hand around the room.

Clara snickered. "So, there's no giggle juice here tonight. But it's not all bad. That darb in the back corner has been quite generous."

"Guess it's a good thing I came here half-cut already." I giggled and hiccupped loudly. "That Joe over there looking for anything in particular to make him let loose of his bankroll?"

"Just some attention of the female persuasion."

As I looked around the room, my eyes were inexorably drawn to the nearly vacant right side of the room, where one strikingly handsome man sat alone. He was hitting on all sixes. The minute I looked over, he was staring right back at me. How long had he been eyeballing me with that dark, penetrating gaze? I looked away quickly—too quickly—but it was past time to do anything about that now. He sent a thrill of excitement through my body, followed by a shiver of fear. Maybe I'd had more to drink than I realized.

My hand went to my neck, and I began to massage the base of my throat—almost unconsciously. Bizarre!

I turned my attention back to Clara, who was looking at me oddly.

"That I can do. And what about that looker off to the side?"

"The one whose eyes haven't left you since you walked in the door? I thought maybe you knew him, and he was carrying a torch. But from how you're looking at him, maybe *you're* the one with the hots for *him*. The next Mr. King perhaps?"

"Never! Nobody is putting a handcuff on this finger again. I haven't seen him before, but I can sure feel his eyes. Gives me the heebie-jeebies, but if he makes it worth my time, I'm just the gal for him... for the night at least."

Clara fell forward, laughing uproariously on my shoulder. "Go get him, toots!"

"Think I'll start with the easy mark you mentioned. Let the other one build a little more steam."

I sauntered over to Mr. Fancy Pants and asked if I could have a seat. The peeper off to the side nearly blew a gasket when I delicately perched on my mark's lap. I giggled and flirted the evening away with him, pretending I didn't feel the eyes of the torchbearer boring into my back... although it was hard to ignore the deep sighs of frustration as he harrumphed at every opportunity. I nearly lost it when I found out my table mate's name really *was* Joe. He was a bit milquetoast for my taste, but when Bebe and Doris came over to join the party the hours flew by, even without the benefit of more hooch.

The girls and I danced the night away with the latecomers who came straggling in. I'd made the peeper wait long enough. It was time to go see what he had to say. With the early morning hours approaching, I headed to the loo and glanced over to where the torchbearer had been sitting. But he was gone.. Part of me felt bad that I hadn't acknowledged his attention, but I also felt like I'd dodged a bullet. Time would tell. If he really wanted to get to know me, he'd find me out on the town again one night soon.

As I was walking back to my table, Clara called me over, patting the vacant barstool next to her.

"What do you need, darling?"

"Your admirer gave me a note for you as he walked out."

"Oh yeah?"

I opened the note. It was short and sweet, if not a little creepy:

Till we meet again, ma chéri.

Again? We never met before, tonight or any other night—not one word, no dance, no drink bought for me. What the hell was he talking about? Now I wasn't so sure that I wanted to run into him again, not that I'd been eager to meet him in the first place.

Dante

PLAYING HARD TO GET

She thought she was so cute. Taunting and flirting with me the whole time while she threw herself at all those men. As if I didn't know.

She doesn't give a damn about me, but yet she wants me to want her.

She didn't need to put on such a show. She always was and always shall be mine, just as I have been hers. And if I couldn't have her, then no one would.

I'd gone out for a drink to relax and think. A fellow broker had recommended I try the new speakeasy that his client, Vinny Gamboni, had just opened. What better way to clean some cash than by making some legitimate investments?

Everything was transactional. The mob knew it, and so did I: a hard lesson learned over many lifetimes, but I'd finally caught on. Now Wall Street was humming, and I was playing along to its tune, getting richer by the moment off suckers who thought this boom could last forever. "Get it while it's hot," I'd tell 'em, neglecting to mention that every red hot cooled down once you put it in the bun. They weren't buying stock so much as they were buying a feeling: that giddy high you feel when you're *sure* something's gonna last forever—even though nothing ever does.

Except my love for her.

I was the most successful broker in Manhattan. They called me The Bull Rider because I had a knack for picking winners on the market. But none of that mattered if I couldn't have her.

Thirty years had passed in this incarnation, and there'd been no sign of her—till now. But I'd been patient. There was no hiding from me. We were fated to follow each other through life until our time on Earth was done. It had only been a matter of time before I found her.

I'd just been finishing my second dirty martini when I looked up, and there she was dazzling in the light. She was wearing a stunning, sleeveless black chiffon shift dress, bedecked in glass beads and sequins, that fell just above her rouged knees. Atop her golden bobbed locks, she wore a sequined headband with a white feather plume. My love... my dear Alba... was breathtaking. I had to have her, if only for a moment. My eyes never left her.

I knew immediately when she noticed me. I caught her look of longing and connection, but she was acting coquettish, as if she hadn't seen me or had no interest.

I knew better.

It was strange behavior for a flapper; their kind was known to flagrantly disregard societal views of decent behavior. But it was oh, so typical of her. She always knew how to make me want her more before spurning my advances. She would not ignore me this time.

She deliberately went to sit down by a man of means—whom I recognized as one of my clients—expertly working him to get him to spend his hard-earned cash on her, and before long, her friends as well. It wouldn't be long before she would be talking him out of expensive gifts. She was already wearing diamond earrings and several exquisite long strands of pearls that hung nearly to her waist.

I waited patiently for her to come to my table. It was clear she had talked about me with her friend sitting over there at the bar, but she obviously intended to make me wait. Hours passed, and still she didn't come to visit me, even dancing with some other men who came into the club later.

Two could play this game. I jotted down a quick note and left it with her friend as I paid my tab. She would not forget me. I made sure of that.

I left the speakeasy and crossed the street to wait in the shadows of a dark alley. She finally left about an hour later, looking nervous as she peered around the darkened street. Searching for something... or should I say someone?

For *me*.

One of the other flappers came out at that moment and bid her goodbye. She took a deep breath and then began her walk home.

I followed her, careful to stay hidden in the darkness. She stopped periodically to look around, but she couldn't see me. She could *feel* me, though, just as I felt her. Our bond was unbreakable, and it strengthened the moment we came together again. The streets were quiet, given the early hour, and I left plenty of distance between us so she couldn't catch sight of me. I wanted her to know she wasn't alone, even if she couldn't prove it. I wanted her afraid. She should be. Our time together wasn't over... not by a long shot.

If she thought she was scared now, she didn't know what scared was, but she soon would.

Dot

GENTLEMAN STALKER

It had been two weeks since that night at The Back Door Club.

Since then, I'd never felt like I was alone when I left my apartment. As I walked down the street, I felt like eyes were following me...

His eyes.

It didn't make sense, but that's how I felt just the same.

I tried to talk to dear Bebe—she was so sweet: She never laughed at me—but even I could hear in my head how insane it sounded. She asked me who was following me, and what could I say? Umm... him... that guy... the one that she apparently had never even noticed? It was Clara who had seen him that night, but even she'd mostly forgotten about him. When I told Bebe that I'd been having strange nightmares ever since all of this started, she asked what I meant. But what could I say? It didn't make any sense to me, so I didn't know how to explain it to her.

Finally, she convinced me to open up. I'd always been sensitive about anything around my neck. My mother had always scolded me for pulling at my dress collars, a habit that had persisted into adulthood. That's why I usually wore long strings of pearls, even though my suitors had bought me beautiful diamond necklaces. Most of them fit tighter than I preferred, so I only wore them when I was out with the particular benefactor who'd given them to me. I couldn't even bring myself to drape fashionable feather boas around my neck.

But recently, I'd been having horrific dreams, and I'd wake up every time up feeling like I couldn't breathe. I'd open my eyes in the darkness to the sensation of someone holding me down and cutting off my air. Every night, I awoke feeling dizzy and panicked. That had never happened until the night I saw him. Now I felt like I was being stalked. Like an antelope—prey to some great cheetah on the grasslands. Bebe listened to me and reassured me that I had nothing to worry about. We laughed off my fears, but they weren't funny. I was scared.

I still had his note in my clutch, but I'd begun to question if I'd imagined our encounter at The Back Door Club, because I hadn't seen him again.

Until that night.

I walked into The Blue Angel, and the joint was hopping. The dance floor was full of girls doing the Charleston with their partners of the moment—a string of young men hoping to be next in line. Bobby tapped me on the shoulder the instant he saw me.

"Hey cutie, you up for a dance?"

"Sure, Bobby. Let me get a drink first."

"I'll grab it for you, Dot."

"You're a peach."

Bobby ran off to the bar as I turned right into Albert's angry face. He grabbed my elbow, fingers digging into my skin, wrenching my arm as he pulled me toward the exit.

"You stepping out on me again, Dorothy?"

"Ouch! Let me go *now*, Albert!"

"Keep your voice down, or you'll be sorry later." He yanked at my arm again, pulling me off balance.

"You're drunk. The way you always are. How do you think I pay for the food we eat when you come over? You're just an unemployed, shiftless grifter. It's not as though you bring in a steady income."

"Why, you smartass little bitch, I oughta teach you a lesson right here."

"Do it. Albert! I dare you. You'll be..."

He pulled his fist back to punch me when another man's arm shot forward, catching his hand and twisting it behind his back.

I looked over Albert's now-hunched back to see *him*. His dark eyes glittered menacingly, at me or Albert... or *both*. I didn't know.

"Shall I see him out, Dot?"

He *knew* my name. But how? I stuttered an answer, unsure what to say or do, "Umm... yes, please."

Tony, the bouncer, appeared at that moment. "I'll take care of that, Dot. No worries." Tony escorted Albert to the door, clutching the back of his jacket at his shoulder and his belt. He gave him a great shove and let go at the last second, sending Albert reeling to the curb in a drunken heap. "Don't come back here again, or I'll break something next time." Tony winked at me and shut the door.

I could feel *his* eyes on my back. It was time to deal with this situation one way or the other. I certainly owed him a thank you for his timely intervention. I turned around and gave him an uneven smile.

"Thank you very much for your help... I'm afraid we haven't been properly introduced yet, although you did know my name. What is your name, kind sir?"

I couldn't take my eyes off of his as he stood there looking at me for what felt like an eternity. It felt like he was waiting, but for what? There was this uncomfortable sense of expectation. I shifted my weight to the other foot. My nerves felt jangly. The longer he looked at me, the more I felt like he *did* know me or I knew him... that we knew each other on some deep level. The realization both excited and terrified me.

I looked down, and my hands shook as I opened my clutch to remove a cigarette. Raising it to my lips, I looked back up to find his hand outstretched with a striker lighter. He struck the flint and held it out for me.

"Well, thank you again..."

"Dante Ambrose Martin"

"Pleased to make your acquaintance, Mr. Martin."

"Dante, please, Dot."

"And how did you know my name, may I ask?"

He nodded over to Clara. I hadn't noticed that she was sitting over at a corner table with a young man. She smiled and waved.

"I recognized her from a few weeks ago when I saw the two of you at The Back Door Club. Your eyes and mine met that night, and we had this instant connection..."

"We did? I'm sorry. I don't seem to remember that. I don't

226

mean to be rude." I couldn't let on to him that I had felt the same longing. Certainly not since, I felt an equal... umm... repulsion.

His face grew somber for a moment. "Well... I thought. Anyhow. I just had to meet you. I regretted not coming over to talk to you that night. When I saw her tonight, I asked her about you, and she said she thought you might be coming around. And here you are!"

"Yes, here I am!" My tone was far more chipper than I felt. "Well, it was just swell meeting you. I appreciate your help tonight."

I looked around to see if I could find Bobby anywhere nearby, but I couldn't see him in the large crowd around the bar. I shifted awkwardly from one foot to the other.

"May I have this dance? You seem to be free at the moment."

"I guess that's the least I can do."

Luckily, the house band struck up a fast-paced tune, and the crowd broke out into the Charleston. Contrary to my initial reluctance, I found myself having fun. But as the dance concluded and a slower song started, Dante pulled me close and tried to kiss me.

I pulled away abruptly. "Bank's closed, darling. I decide who I'm kissing and when. I should go catch up with my date. In fact, here he comes now."

Thankfully, at that moment, Bobby was approaching with two martinis in hand.

Dante's face hardened once more. "Yes. You do that then." As he turned to stalk off, I heard him mumble, "I wouldn't want to interfere with your treating."

I whirled around, infuriated. "Excuse me?"

"You heard me."

I stepped forward and slapped him across the face hard. His

eyes flashed angrily, but he held his stance. "How dare you! I'm not sure what you are trying to suggest, but I don't give away any favors in exchange for gifts of any kind."

"You never change. I don't know why I even bothered. You'll be sorry."

I tried to ignore him as I turned back around and grabbed Bobby's hand, heading toward the opposite end of the club. But I couldn't help myself: I turned back and yelled out, "Only sorry I met you, creep!"

We sat down at a table where I couldn't see him. What could he have meant about me never changing? We'd never met before, and I certainly wouldn't be interacting with him again. And was that last bit a threat? My concern about him had been warranted.

I strove to push him out of my mind and have fun for the rest of the evening. To my relief, I never saw him again in the club. I partied into the wee hours of the morning and left when there were only a few stragglers left. I walked out with Clara, and we parted ways at the intersection.

It was about a mile's walk to my apartment, but the area was still pretty quiet. As I crossed the street, I heard an engine start up behind me. I hadn't seen anyone out on the street when Clara and I left, but I tried to reassure myself that it was just another night owl heading home.

I heard the car approach slowly and looked back to see if I could make out the driver, but the headlights blinded me. I felt paranoid, the car seemed to be pacing me... staying just far enough back that I couldn't identify the driver but close enough to let me know I was being followed.

I quickened my pace, and the car sped up to match it. When I reached the next intersection, I waited at the corner for it to pass so I could cross. He—I *knew* it was him—stayed just far enough back that I still couldn't see him. I waved for him to continue, but he just idled there. Finally, in desperation, I ran across the road and continued down the street. The driver made a slow turn around the corner. I thought maybe I'd be able to see him from the opposite side of the street, but it was too dark.

I began running the 200 feet down Madison Avenue to the intersection as I saw a few cars coming down West 57th. They would, at least briefly, impede him from turning left to follow me when I made the last desperate sprint toward my apartment. Just when I thought I was going to make it, he sped up and stopped in the middle of the road to the right of me. I heard him jump out of his car and run up behind me, then felt him grabbing my arm to drag me toward it.

In my desperate fight to get free, I never managed to look back and see who had grabbed me, but I *knew* it was Dante. It had to be. Who else would it be?

I had never been so scared in my life. I threw my elbow back, connecting just under his ribs and knocking the wind out of him. I heard him grunt... which was my cue to kick back hard, connecting the chunky heel of my shoe into his shin before sliding down and grinding it into the top of his foot. It was enough of a distraction that he let me go... for a second.

And that was all I needed.

I began my panicked flight down the street toward the approaching cars, waving my arms to flag them down. At the last second, I ran out into the street, forcing one of them to stop. When I looked back, my attacker was turning away from me and heading down 57th Street in the opposite direction.

The driver offered to accompany me to a police station, but I couldn't definitively identify who had grabbed me, so I knew it would be pointless. I returned home, shaking like a leaf. I could see that John Thomas, who manned the elevator in my brownstone, noticed my disheveled appearance but didn't question me. He probably chalked it up to another night of wild partying—just like everyone else would if I told them what had happened. Flappers like me were always blamed for whatever happened to us because of our carefree, "loose" ways.

I didn't know why Dante was out to hurt me, but I knew my life was in danger. I had to prepare. I had to let others know of the danger I faced. Maybe someone would listen. In the meantime, I refused to let him or anyone else control me or dictate my lifestyle. I would simply have to be more careful.

Dot

DANGER AT EVERY TURN

I tried to convince myself everything would be okay. I changed my routine and began to frequent different cabarets and speakeasies. I avoided The Blue Angel and The Back Door Club. I told Doris, Bebe, and Clara not to give out any information to Dante or anyone else they didn't recognize. I knew I sounded a bit paranoid to them, but I couldn't take any chances.

For a few months, everything seemed to be fine. No one had seen Dante anywhere. Maybe he'd gotten spooked that the cops were out looking for him, but whatever the reason, he'd made himself scarce. I didn't have that feeling like I was being watched when I went out at night. The nightmares became less frequent and even stopped after a month. It was almost like he had never existed. I began to feel normal.

And then, there he was... again.

I had just finished dancing The Black Bottom with Francis when I excused myself and went to the loo. When I returned to the table, there he was sitting with Francis and Doris. She tried to give me an apologetic look for not warning me. He acted like nothing untoward had ever happened. He greeted me as if we were long lost friends—or more. It made me sick to my stomach.

"Hey there, Dorothy! How are you doing?"

"It's Dot. I'm... uh... fine. I should be..." My hands were trembling. The sense of impending doom was overwhelming.

"Are you okay? You look like you've seen a spook. You're certainly as pale as a ghost yourself. I could accompany you outside to get some air if you'd like."

Everything he said felt like a threat. I wasn't going anywhere with him. "Stay away from me! If you come near me again, I'll call the police." I backed away rapidly, knocking into the table behind me. Glasses fell and shattered on the floor. Everyone in the club turned to look at me like I'd lost my mind. Francis jumped up and wrapped his arm around me.

"Dot, what's wrong? Has this man done something to you?"

"A couple of months ago, he followed me home and tried to drag me into his car!"

"You did what?" Francis came toward Dante, glowering.

Dante held up his hands in protest. He shook his head, a look of innocence on his face. "I don't know what she's talking about. I did meet her a couple of months ago. We had a lovely dance and conversation. That was it. I left the club hours before she did and took a taxi home."

"Hours before me? How would you know how long I stayed after you left? See! See what I mean! He's watching me. Stalking me!"

"I just assumed. I just meant you girls..."

Francis walked forward and grabbed Dante by his elbow, pulling him to his feet. "I don't know what's going on here, but I don't like it one bit. I think it's time for you to leave, and I don't want to see you around here again. I know the owner. I'm going to have a talk with him right now." Francis dragged him to the door and pushed him out, slamming it shut behind him.

Doris wrapped her arm around me and escorted me to the bar to get a drink. "Don't worry, darling. Everything will be fine. Francis and I will take you home tonight. Isn't that right?" she asked him as he came to our side.

"I don't think he'll be bugging you again. Not if I have anything to say about it."

A couple of glasses of hooch and three hours later, I had danced away all thoughts of Dante... for that night at least.

I had hoped that Francis was right, but Dante kept showing up. At first, it was a seemingly innocent run-in at the market or out on the street. But then he appeared in the shops on the ground floor of my brownstone. Living in Manhattan, it was just too much of a coincidence for us to be frequenting the same locations at the same time over and over.

He found me no matter where I went. I couldn't understand how he always knew every place I would be. Even more disturbing, I couldn't figure out how he had access to all of them. I had started going to some of the more exclusive speakeasies whose locations were kept tightly under wraps. I was well-liked among the flapper set, so I was free to come and go as I pleased. But he was there every time, watching me every night. His hungry, haunting eyes focused only on me.

Even when I couldn't see him, I always knew when he was

nearby. That feeling of being stalked returned. My throat constricted, and it was difficult to breathe. Oppressing dread overtook me. Anxiety became my constant companion—I was just waiting for him to show up again. Waiting for him to hurt me.

I had been abused for so long by Albert, and I didn't want someone else to start. Nobody wanted to deal with the flatfoots, especially if you were a flapper who frequented speakeasies, but I would call them if Dante didn't stop. It all had to end—I cut off my relationship with Albert after he beat me again for refusing to give him money for booze.

I decided to get out of town for a week and lay low. I was exhausted and needed to rest my frayed nerves. Being early March, it was still cold outside, but a week along the shore in Atlantic City was just what I needed.

I left Atlantic City feeling rejuvenated and ready to take control of my life.

But the moment I returned to Manhattan, a sense of foreboding washed over me. When I got to my apartment, I made out a will leaving all my worldly possessions to my mother. I called her to let her know I was home, and I told her I was in fear for my life. She hated Albert as much as I did, so she of course assumed he was to blame. I reassured her that I had cut him out of my life once for and all. I didn't want to scare her, so I couldn't explain about my stalker. She tried to soothe me as only a mother can, but I couldn't put aside my fears.

Over the next couple of days, I was careful to leave for the clubs before darkness fell and find someone to accompany me home. Then, one afternoon, when I was out in the city, a woman grabbed me by the hair from behind. She threw me to the ground and began pelting me with her fists. She was screaming at me so wildly, it was incoherent. All I could do was hold up my arms to block the blows. I had no idea why she attacked me so viciously, but I was beginning to feel cursed.

That feeling was amplified two days later, when there was a knock at my apartment door. I was expecting a friend, so I opened it without looking first. Instead, it was Albert. He was drunk as usual, and angry that I had broken up with him and then left town. He accused me of cheating on him. He brutally beat me again, only stopping when I pulled a knife on him and threatened to call the police. I told him I still had the list of his victims from the stock scam and said I would go to the cops as a witness. He didn't want to go back to jail, so he finally left.

The only bright spot for me was a planned night out with Mr. Marshall the following day. Mr. Wilson accompanied us as usual, and we had a lovely dinner at the posh Hotel Brevoort. Even in their pleasant company, my nerves affected my appetite. I did enjoy a delicious bowl of celery soup. though. We returned to my apartment at about 11 p.m. Mr. Wilson came upstairs and stayed for a short while before leaving.

Mr. Marshall lingered for a few hours to have a nightcap. He told me he'd had some more good luck with his investments and wanted to celebrate, grabbing the bottle of champagne out of the icebox that I had put away when he brought it earlier. He popped the cork as he turned to ask, "Dot dear, would you like a glass?" Marsh never wanted to talk about the details of his business, but he couldn't resist bragging a little, in his own well-mannered way, in my presence. It was a little insulting but kind of cute, so I forced a smile and pretended to be excited for him. Still, I wasn't up for any champagne. My stomach was too unsettled.

"Thanks, Marsh baby, but not tonight. I think I'll just make myself some tea."

"You're not your usual bright, joyful self. You mentioned something about not having an appetite at dinner. Talk to me. Is something wrong?"

"It's nothing for you to worry yourself about."

"We're friends, dear. You know you're the bee's knees to me… the proverbial cat's meow. If you're upset, I want to help."

"There's just this man that has been following me around everywhere I go. He's stalking me. For all I know, he's waiting outside right now. He followed me home one night in his car, and he tried to kidnap me. I'm scared, Marsh."

"Is he the one who hurt you? I didn't bring it up before, but I can see a trace of some bruising under your makeup."

"No, that was Albert, but I cut ties with him. And then this crazy woman attacked me for no reason the other day too. It's all been so stressful." I broke down in tears, even though I'd told myself I would hold it together.

"Don't cry, sweetheart. I will have Mr. Wilson look into this man, and we'll have someone *talk* to him. What's his name?"

"Really? That's so kind of you. It's Dante Ambrose Martin."

"Of course, dear. Please put your mind at ease."

"This means so much to me, Marsh."

"I should be leaving. The hour has grown late—or rather early—it is nearly 2. You relax tonight and lay your weary head down to get some sleep. Everything will be better tomorrow."

I accompanied him to the door and gave him a kiss. "Goodnight, Mr. Marshall."

I locked the door and then went to bed for my first peaceful night's sleep in weeks.

Dante

TILL YOUR LAST BREATH

So many names over the years. Dot... Emma... Julia... whatever she called herself didn't change the fact that she was mine and always had been. We were destined to be together. We *would have been* by now if she hadn't given up each time.

Life is filled with struggles. No one ever said it would be easy—things worth having don't just fall into your lap. But if they *are* worth it, you fight with all you've got to get them. I'd never given up on her. I was always there by her side, willing to endure any pain, give up my very life if necessary, do absolutely anything to spend my eternity with her.

Why couldn't she do the same?

Those who follow each other from one lifetime to the next are meant to live those lives together. They're soulmates... kindred spirits. Why did she make me hurt her every time? Why did I always have to start over, trying to make her see the truth? I was tired of playing this game. If that was the way she wanted it, then I was ready. Her last breath would end this lifetime and birth our new start.

I'd been watching her apartment building all afternoon. I saw her come out with those two men. I couldn't see them clearly, but I thought they looked vaguely familiar. I shook it off. *Who* they were didn't matter. *What* they were doing did. It disgusted me to contemplate what she might be doing up there alone with them. They didn't return until after 11 p.m., and then they had gone upstairs with her. A short while later, one of them came down and left.

I waited for hours before the other man finally exited. He still looked perfectly coiffed, but what else could they have been doing at this late hour? Her behavior appalled me, but I still loved her beyond measure. I had to bide my time, though. That nosy night elevator man would still be at his post, so I couldn't take the lift and risk that he would remember me going up to her apartment.

I'd snuck into her apartment several times in the past, but always when Juanita, the young day elevator operator, was on duty. She was less than ideally attentive when it came to her job. Plus it was easy to distract her with a few well-timed compliments. I'd have to wait until the shift change to head upstairs.

I entered the lobby about 5:30 a.m., after John Thomas finally left. The building was still quiet, although some residents would be rising before long to head in to work. Juanita was lost in her own thoughts and didn't even acknowledge me. I had to tell her the floor twice before it finally sunk in.

When I arrived at the fifth floor, I stepped off into the corner. I pulled a small bottle of chloroform out of my pocket and soaked a wad of cotton in it. Just as I was about to step out, I heard someone undoing the locks of the other apartment. I quickly stashed the cotton and bottle in the dumbwaiter and dipped into the shadows in the corner of the hallway. The tenant exited quickly and never even noticed me.

I retrieved the items, stashing the bottle back in my pocket, and knocked on Dot's door. It took a few minutes before I heard her soft voice call out, "I'm coming. Did you forget your key, Billy?" Perfect—she thought I was her maid coming to straighten the room! She opened the door, dressed in a loose, yellow silk chemise, with bleary eyes and never even saw me before I swept through the door, slamming it behind me.

"You...!" she started to scream as she turned to run before I caught her, shoving the cotton over her mouth. Within seconds, she fell unconscious in my arms. I laid her body down on the bed.

I decided to leave some contradictory clues behind that would flummox the police as to her manner of death. All I wanted to do was wrap my fingers around her neck and squeeze until every last drop of life left her body. Watch her eyes bug out of her head until the light faded. Feel her fear oozing from every pore and swirl around the room in a dark turbulent cloud of pain and confusion. But there was no way I was going to draw my last breath strapped into "Old Sparky" because of her.

I overturned some furniture and threw some of her fur coats, jewelry, and other belongings around the room. I even found a pair of men's yellow silk pajamas and a black comb, probably belonging to the Casanova who'd left a little bit ago. I left those out in plain sight. Let the police go after that lech. He probably had so much money that he could buy his way out of jail. Just in case, I pocketed some of her jewelry and ransacked the place to make it look like a robbery gone wrong... the same way I'd done when she was Julia and I was Jean-Marie.

I was so lost in my thoughts I didn't hear her wake up. It was only as I heard her unsteady footfalls as she tried to run toward the door that I realized she was awake. I dove across the room and grabbed her elbow. I wrenched her arm behind her back and pushed her face-down onto the bed. Her head was buried halfway under the pillow as I wrapped my left hand with the chloroformed-cotton tightly over her mouth. She whimpered in pain and fear. Her eyes were wide and streaming tears.

It didn't take long before she slumped unconscious, but I didn't let up. I smothered her with the drugged cotton until long after she ceased to breathe. I pulled the chloroform bottle out of my pocket and left it on the bed between her legs. With any luck, if they didn't buy my robbery decoy, authorities would attribute her death to suicide or accidental overdose: Flappers were notorious for using chloroform as a party drug.

I realized that it was now well after 6, so people would be rising, especially with all the ruckus that had just occurred.

I ran to the window and pulled it open. To my dismay when I looked out, I saw that the fire escape didn't rise to her level of the building. How had I failed to notice this before? I couldn't risk the elevator, which most of the tenants would be using, and if I hadn't made an impression before, Juanita was sure to remember me if I returned.

When I left Dot's apartment, I used her key to lock the apartment door behind me. I decided to take the stairs because they had a private one-way exit to the outside. That way, I wouldn't risk being seen by anybody in the lobby. As I reached the last flight, I heard someone enter the stairwell one flight above me and begin trotting down quickly.

I didn't want to be seen anywhere near the building, so I ran down the last flight and burst out the door, crossing the street immediately.

I didn't realize I had run in front of a car until I heard the *ah-ooga* of the horn just before it hit me.

I awoke lying on the pavement with my head thundering. I felt completely disoriented. I couldn't remember where I was or had just been. I didn't even know where I was going. I couldn't even recall my own name. I just had this feeling of panic... a need to hide. I needed to get away from this place. A man was kneeling beside me, asking if I was okay and reassuring me that he would get help. But all I wanted to do was go *now*!

I rose unsteadily to my feet and waved him off.

"I'm... uh... okay... really."

"Sir, please sit down. You hit your head very hard. It's bleeding. Let me get a doctor for you."

"No, really. Gotta... go."

I turned and limped down the road quickly and made a right at the next intersection. My right knee was hurt, but I had to ignore the pain. I didn't even know where to go. After a short distance, I saw an extremely large park ahead of me. This street was busy even at this early hour, so I felt comfortable that the man in the street had probably lost sight of me.

I made my way into the park, which had a large marker designating it as Central Park. I went deep into the park and found a bench in a quiet area. I was exhausted, and my head was throbbing. I lay down on the bench to take a short nap, hoping that, when I awoke, I would remember what had happened.

Manhattan, 1929

MEMORIES ARE MADE OF THIS

Dante

SHOULD AULD ACQUAINTANCE BE...

"Five! Four! Three! Two! One!"
I might have forgotten a lot of things, but I knew what was going to come next.

"Happy New Year!"

A woman standing next to me, wearing a sequined flapper cap and holding a cigarette at the end of a long smoking stick, dropped it to her side and leaned in for a kiss. I didn't know this woman. I didn't *want* to know this woman. She smelled of smoke, and before I could stop her, she was *exhaling* that smoke from her open maw into my mouth. This was supposed to be enticing. I found it quite the opposite.

I pushed her roughly away. "Whore!"

It had the desired effect. Her face blanched, and she moved away from me as quickly as she could, tripping over her high heels and falling headlong into the arms of another reveler who, being quite drunk, stumbled into a woman standing next to him, creating the kind of domino effect you'd see on a Keystone Cops short.

"Hey!"

"Watch it!"

I laughed as the man she had fallen into helped the smoking flapper to her feet—minus her cigarette or its holder, which had both been crushed under the gallivanting feet of the mob. He took the opportunity to plant the same kind of open-mouthed kiss she had tried to bestow on me. Good. She was his problem now. Maybe he'd knock her up and ruin both their lives. It would serve them both right. They didn't deserve to be happy. No one did.

The drunken throng swayed and gyrated as they sang the same song they sang every year.

Should auld acquaintance be forgot, and never brought to mind?

The answer to that was a hearty and definitive yes. It had been six years since I'd lost my memory, and in some ways, I was glad of it. I somehow knew that my past was darker than the shadowy void of my amnesia, and I didn't want to go back there. The only thing I knew about myself was my name: Dante Martin. And I only knew that because it had been on the ID in my wallet when I woke up in Central Park.

But I remembered other things. I knew which stocks were gonna break big and which were about to go bust. It was like it came natural; probably some talent I'd had before that was still there under the surface of my forgetfulness. I might not have known why, but other people did. They started asking me for tips and said they recognized me. They asked me why I'd left Goldman Sachs and who I was working for now.

"Did that new house, Bear Stearns, snatch you up?" one guy asked when he recognized me on the street. "If they haven't, they should. It'd be a coup for them to get The Bull Rider over at Bear." He laughed. I didn't. It was a bad joke.

It took a lot for me to laugh these days. Almost every time I did, it was at the misfortune of others.

For the hell of it, I looked up Bear Stearns and knocked on their door. I sat in the office there for twenty minutes before some guy in a Herringbone and a fedora came waltzing through the door like he owned the place. Turns out he did. I didn't recognize him, but he sure knew me.

"Well, how do you do!" he said, more as an exclamation than a greeting. He leaned back and inserted his thumbs under the sides of his vest. "If it isn't Dante Martin himself! Half the world's wondering what happened to you, and you show up on our doorstep? Must be my lucky day."

I stayed seated and just stared at him, at which his gleeful smile shifted toward a guarded frown. "I see the recognition isn't mutual, and you seem to have forgotten your manners."

I stood grudgingly and took his outstretched hand, squeezing it hard. He squeezed it back just as tightly. "Joseph Ainslie Bear at your service," he said. "Or maybe you'll be at mine. We pay pretty damn well here, and we'd love to have The Bull Rider take a seat in our corral, if you catch my drift."

I'd taken a job there, and they paid me well—well enough for me to clue them in on what I saw coming: Everyone was in hock on spec stocks up to their eyeballs, and the day of reckoning was coming. All these people in Times Square were singing "We're so happy in my blue heaven," like they didn't have a care in the world. But I knew different: The Roaring Twenties were about to come to a screeching halt.

I didn't know if it was this way for everyone who lost their memory, but this is how it was for me: I remembered how to do things, just not why I was doing them or how I'd learned them in the first place. Certain things triggered a feeling that I *ought* to know about some event or person in my past, but I never knew why.

In '27, I stopped at my regular newsstand to pitch in my literal 2 cents for a copy of the *Daily News*. The front page headline referred to a story on Page 2 about a beauty queen-turned-aviator named Ruth Elder who was about to embark on a flight from New York to Paris. I was mildly interested, so I turned the page, but it wasn't her story that caught my attention. A different headline grabbed me by the throat the minute I saw it: "Scarf Kills Isadora Duncan."

I was captivated as I read the story. Duncan, the famous dancer with a penchant for wearing long scarves, had decided to buy a racing car and had a demonstrator take her out in an Amilcar CGSS. The open-air car had a seat for the driver in the front and another directly behind, where Duncan sat. Leaning back to enjoy the ride, she was suddenly yanked violently backward by her 6-foot-long scarf—which had become caught in the right rear wheel. As the scarf wound tighter and tighter around the wheel, it snapped her neck. According to the article, "she hardly had time to scream. The demonstrator stopped the car and found her dead."

The story should have sickened me, but instead, I lay down the paper in a burst of excitement. I wanted to do that. I needed to do that.

Not buy a racecar.

Break a woman's neck.

But it couldn't be just any woman. It had to be one particular woman. The problem was, I had no idea who. I stopped myself: Was this morbid excitement incentive for some future act, or was it an echo of something that had already happened? Try as I might, I couldn't determine the answer. All I knew was that the idea held more appeal to me than cornering the stock market or making a million dollars.

There was simply no comparison.

Bear Stearns survived the crash of '29—mainly because I'd told them it was coming—but instead of thanking me, they decided to blame me for not preventing it. I was The Bull Rider. I should have been able to stop it, they said. They didn't realize I'd been feeding the market all the speculation that had been making them money hand over fist in the twenties, which meant the bubble had to burst. Was it my fault they didn't understand simple economics?

To them, it was. So they kicked me to the curb along with a bunch of other brokers, and I couldn't find another job. By 1932, I was flat broke and forced to stay wherever I could find a place to lay my head for the night. I'd sleep on boxcars or sneak into a movie theater and stay hidden until after closing. After a while, I wandered down to Paterson and stayed at the Hooverville on Molly Ann Brook, a ramshackle collection of thrown-together siding, wood panels, screen doors, and stovepipes.

The people who ended up there didn't look much better, and they didn't get along. Hard times bred ill will as readily as mosquitoes and fleas spread diseases. There were plenty of those in the Hoovervilles that were spread all across the country, havens for the homeless and the down-on-their-luckers.

They weren't just hobos and ex-cons, either. A lot of them wore suits they'd bought during the flush economy a few years earlier, now threadbare and soiled. There were no dry cleaners in a Hooverville. I tried to keep a low profile. Out-of-work stockbrokers weren't exactly popular after the crash, and I didn't want to get my head caved in by some former client taking out his frustrations on me.

I kept to myself and grew a long beard—which was easy, since I couldn't afford a razor—and took to wearing an old green-and-yellow plaid shirt that I'd found washed up near the place where the Molly Ann emptied into the Passaic. It wasn't flattering, but that was the point. I didn't want anyone coming near me, so the worse I looked, the better.

But one day, someone *did* recognize me.

"Hey, I know you!"

The voice belonged to a tall, gaunt man sitting by the side of the brook, naked from the waist up, washing out an old dress shirt. I didn't recognize him, but with my memory of everything before 1923 wiped, that wasn't surprising.

"No, you don't," I sneered, and tried to walk on, but he stood with surprising speed and caught hold of my arm.

I was all ready for him to spout off about how I'd given him a bad tip that had wiped him out. But he didn't say anything like that. Instead, he just looked me straight in the eye and said, "You killed her."

I gave him a menacing look, but I was intrigued. He seemed to know something about my past, and despite my better judgment, I wanted to know what it was. "I didn't kill anyone," I said, indignant. "If I had, I wouldn't be standing here right now…"

I made like I was trying to pull away, but it was a feeble attempt, and he held on like he was trying to arrest me.

"Just who do you think I killed, anyway?"

"Dot King," he snarled. "Don't act like you don't remember her."

"Doesn't ring a bell."

"I stuck around and saw you running out of her brownstone that day. I saw you get hit by that car. When they found her body, they wanted to pin it on my boss, but I knew he didn't do it. I knew it was you. The boss wanted me to put a tail on you, but I told him you were dead. I thought you were... but here you are."

"I didn't kill anyone. At least not that I can recall." I smirked at him and made it sound sarcastic, even though it was the stone-cold truth.

He grabbed me by the collar of my green-and-yellow plaid shirt. "My boss went through hell because of you," he growled, pulling my face up close to his so I could smell his reeking breath. He'd found some stash of spirits and was somewhere between tipsy and blotto. "He wasn't just my boss, he was my friend."

"So where's he at now?" I asked.

"He's 'doin' all right. Not that it's any of your business."

"He's 'doin' all right' and he leaves you down here to rot in this hellhole? What kind of friend is that?" I spat in his face, which flushed red. "I didn't do that," I whispered. "Your friend did. And I didn't kill anyone, either, but I might have to start with you."

He still had hold of my collar, and I tried to break free, but he held on tight, kicked his leg out behind my knee, and threw me to the ground. The guy was a lot tougher than he looked.

"Get up!" he taunted. "Get up and *try* to kill me!"

I was done with this. I got up on one knee, fully intending to turn around and walk away from this lunkhead, but before I could get up any further, I saw his booted foot headed straight for my head. I felt the impact, but that was the last thing I remembered before waking up after nightfall with the dirty water from Molly Ann Brook running by my ears and one hell of a nasty headache.

Dante

MR. FEATHERS

Anyone who tells you that the cure for a knock on the head is another knock on the head doesn't know what the hell they're talking about. If anything, the Thin Man's boot had scrambled everything up even more.

I had to admit I wasn't quite right in the head. I had flashes of thought that *seemed* like memories but couldn't have been. I sat through a showing of *The Girl of the Golden West* while I was camping out during a late-night showing at the Orpheum, and it felt like I was there... but different. Other faces, different from the ones in the movie, popped into my head, along with other names, like Tommy and, in particular, Jewel. Or was it Jule? Julia?

The memories that did come to me were mostly like that: faint echoes that were always triggered by something. I came across a copy of an old Mark Twain book, *A Connecticut Yankee in*

King Arthur's Court, without the cover and with a lot of the pages missing, just sitting there in the Hooverville. But the mirage that arose in my mind then was even more convoluted. One minute, I was standing in front of the king himself, shouting something at him I couldn't make out; the next, I was talking to Twain.

"You have forgotten yourself."

I was shaken from my reverie by the sound of a voice that wasn't quite human and wasn't even a sound. It was more of an impression in my brain. Another aspect of my delusion? Perhaps, but it seemed to be coming from a specific direction: up and to the left.

Despite myself, I shifted my gaze upward toward the bare branches of a dead hickory tree. There, in its branches, sat a peregrine falcon of impressive size. The very name of the bird seemed to trigger something, sending me back to King Arthur's court again.

The falcon's head swiveled this way and that, as though it were looking for prey. It seemed to be ignoring me, but the voice I had heard came from its perch. There was no one else there but the bird.

"Are you so far gone, then, that you would turn down an offer of some polite conversation?"

"Who's there?" I said in a whisper, looking around.

"You are looking straight at me." The voice was obviously coming from the falcon, but its beak didn't move. It just ruffled its feathers in avian indignation and continued looking around distractedly. Not only had that kick to the head failed to restore my memory, it had me hearing things as well.

"Do I know you?" I whispered.

"Speak up!" the voice said.

I'd been trying to keep my voice down so no one would

notice me talking to a bird. I repeated myself, a little louder, grateful that no one was around at that particular moment to hear me.

"Of *course* we know each other," the falcon replied. "We were allies of a sort—albeit with some reticence on your part—many lifetimes ago, and we share a bond that transcended that lifetime."

"What are you talking about? Stop speaking in riddles." I had a feeling I was actually talking to myself, struggling to sort things out in my own head and projecting it onto a bird. But if my mind was trying to use some creative strategy to get everything straight again, having a heart-to-heart with Mr. Feathers wasn't helping me make any better sense of the jumble.

"I told you plainly before that you would pass through many lives, and that you would need to be cautious lest the journey drive you mad."

That *did* sound vaguely familiar, but maybe I was just trying to figure out why my brain was on the fritz. But I already knew the answer to that question: My memories had been jarred loose by that car accident back in '23 and then that kick in the head.

"I am not referring to the crash or your more recent unfortunate encounter with Mr. Wilson. No, that's not his real name, but it isn't for me to undermine his anonymity if he wishes to maintain it."

"Then what *are* you referring to?" My impatience was getting the better of me, and I was talking a little louder now. A young mother passing by, carrying her baby around in a grocery basket lined with rags, turned her head and gave me an odd look, then quickened her pace and moved on.

"Women," I muttered. "They're the devil's spawn."

The falcon chuckled. Could a bird chuckle? I was definitely

losing it. "Oh, they *can* be a handful," he said. "I fell for a woman who swore I had reached my final incarnation—this was fifteen centuries ago—yet here I am, still flying about. I'm not sure whether she knew the truth and was lying to me or was simply not as informed as she let on. Either is possible, I suppose. But the devil's spawn? I think that's taking things a bit far."

"I don't," I spat. "At least when it comes to one woman."

"And who might that be?"

"I can't remember."

"Ah, yes, the amnesia. Maybe it's doing you a favor, if she was such bad influence on you. But I suggest you also consider the possibility that the fault lies not in her, but in yourself. Perhaps *your* many lives have driven you to the point of madness, or beyond."

"I'm not mad!" I nearly shouted, then looked around and lowered my voice again. "I just need to... be rid of her. I loved her once. Hell, I still do. But it's *her* that's driving me mad. And *you're* mad for suggesting that I lived other lives before this. I don't remember..."

"Because of those bumps on the head. Their effects won't last beyond this lifetime, and the problem may resolve itself before you breathe your last."

"Stop it! Just stop it! You're not real!" I grabbed my head on both sides and shut my eyes tight, but when I opened them again and looked up into the tree, the falcon was right where it had been before.

I shook my fist at the bird. "I have to..." I began, then lowered my voice to keep any meddling drunks or tramps from hearing me. "I have to *kill* her. I need to be rid of her."

The falcon cocked its head to one side. "You said you loved

her."

"I did... I do... And she loves me, but she won't admit it. She won't allow me to get closer to her, no matter how I try. I could be a gentleman or a soldier or a... I don't know, some guy in a laundromat."

"In many different lives."

My eyes bulged out. This bird was determined to make me feel like I was going crazy—not that I needed any help with that.

"Tell me," the falcon inquired, "if you do not even know who this woman is, how do you intend to kill her? How do you know, for that matter, that she isn't already dead?"

"I. Don't. KNOW!" I shouted as I picked up a rock and flung it toward the falcon's perch.

But the falcon had vanished. Had I scared it away, or had it ever been there in the first place? Not that it mattered. Whether I had encountered a real talking bird or it was a figment of my imagination, I was obviously having trouble dealing with reality. Maybe I *was* at the point of madness. If I was, this was all *her* fault. And if so, I *would* find her. Maybe then I could recover my memory and stop this insane pounding in my head. No matter what, I would find my dark paramour and make her pay for what she'd done to me.

With her life.

Sharon Marie and Stephen H. Provost

Dante

HEY THERE, GEORGIE GIRL

I'd worn out my welcome on the East Coast. Not long after my encounter with the falcon, some of the folks who were slumming it in Hooverville got wind that I was—or had been—Wall Street's notorious Bull Rider. And just as I'd feared, they were out for blood.

Without a car, I wasn't exactly in a position to drive off into the sunset. But on the bright side, I didn't have much to weigh me down, so I could make like a banana and split at a moment's notice. I could hop on a boxcar head west. Why west? Because you couldn't very well go farther east from the Atlantic Seaboard, and, more importantly, I knew *she* was there.

I didn't know her name.

I didn't even know what she looked like.

But I knew she was there, or would be there. All I had to do was bide my time and go looking. I would know her when I saw her.

It didn't turn out to be that easy, though. I made it out to L.A. and started checking out all the places I thought she might go. My amnesia was as bad as ever, and I was starting to think it was permanent, but if anyone could jog my memory, I knew she could. Lots of dames were headed out to California in those days, hoping to land a movie contract, so I figured that was as good a place as any to start. I got a job working on sets at Warner Bros., which put out a film with Errol Flynn and Humphrey Bogart in 1940 called *Virginia City*. They didn't actually film it there, but it was another one of those things that triggered a fragment of some weird memory. I realized I'd been to Virginia City, but I had no idea when or why. I only knew that the idea of it gave me a sick feeling in the pit of my stomach.

I quit the studio mid-production and caught on as a bouncer at Ciro's on Sunset. I was in pretty good shape from hauling all those set pieces around. I might have been a little long in the tooth compared to some of the other muscle, but I carried myself like I was pissed at the world. Which I was. But mostly, I was pissed at the gal I was certain would walk through that door on the arm of some producer or A-lister. Plenty of them came and went, and I saw plenty of starlets up on the screen, too, but none of them was *her*. Not Betty Grable. Not Lana Turner. Not Ava Gardner. None of 'em. The gal I was looking for was a nobody who wanted to be a somebody but would wind up as a never-was... because I would get to her first.

On my nights off, after the war started, I'd head down to the

Evermore

local USO and hang around outside, scoping out the women who came looking to land some soldier boy as a hubby. Then, Bette Davis and John Garfield opened the Hollywood Canteen at Sunset and Cahuenga. The idea was to provide meals for servicemen free of charge and give them a place to blow off steam on the dancefloor. That meant there would be women there, too. Maybe the one I was looking for.

Naturally, I started volunteering there. Ciro's hosted a fundraiser to get the place off the ground, and I was more than happy to help. I was one of the few non-celebrity servers, but between my time at Warner Bros. and Ciro's, most of the folks there knew me.

Then, one day in 1944, someone who didn't know me walked in. Her name was Georgette, and she was starting work at the Canteen as what was called a junior hostess: a young woman who volunteered to dance with the servicemen. She was from New York, like me, so it was natural that we would strike up a conversation. I might have been thirty years older than her, but she didn't find that creepy. In fact, just a few minutes after she got the scoop on what she'd be doing, she walked right up to me, bold as brass, and introduced herself.

"I'm Georgie," she said, sticking her hand out and standing straight up, her head thrown slightly back. "What's your name?"

"Dante," I stammered. She'd thrown me off my guard, which wasn't easy to do. For a moment, my anger melted away, and I just stood there, unsure of what else to say.

"How long've you been serving here?" she asked.

"Off and on since it opened."

"I don't recognize you."

I laughed. "How could you? You just started. But I'm not anybody, really. I'm surprised you wanted to talk to me with all these stars around."

"Oh, I already know everything about most of them from the gossip columns. You I don't know. But maybe I want to." She winked.

"Don't you think I'm a little old...?"

She put her hand to her mouth and giggled. "For what?"

"For... never mind." She still had me off balance, which made me uncomfortable. The best way I knew to rectify that was to be the one asking the questions. She was opening her mouth to say something else when I blurted out, "What made you want to come and work here?"

She closed her mouth, nodded approvingly as though she knew exactly what I was doing, then opened it again to answer: "A girl's gotta start somewhere, doesn't she? This isn't my main gig: I'm only here on Wednesday nights; the rest of the time, I work at the Women's Service Bureau over at the *Times*. But I want to be an actress, so I thought this would be a good place to make some contacts. If nothing else, maybe I'll land me a man. He's got to be a good dancer, though. Are you a good dancer?"

She'd turned it right back around to me again.

"I..."

She smiled broadly, her eyes fixated on mine. "Don't answer that. I want to find out for myself."

"Aren't you supposed to be dancing with the G.I.'s?"

She shrugged. "That's my job, but I get breaks. I don't have to spend them in the powder room. My first one's at 8. I'll come get you. You don't even need to sign my dance card!" She giggled again, then turned on her heel and walked away as quickly as she'd walked up to introduce herself.

That's the last I'll see of her, I chuckled to myself, but I had to admit the attention felt good. Could she be the one I was looking for? Anger flashed behind my eyes, and my head started pounding. Her magnetic pull to me. Her flirtations. I felt a twinge of something, but I couldn't be sure what it was. It was probably nothing, though. I'd get a better idea if she actually followed through on her promise—or threat—to dance with me on her break. If she did, I couldn't let myself be drawn into her web again.

I heard the falcon's voice, or my own voice, in my head. *That would mean she's from one of those past lives.*

I told myself again that I'd never had any past lives. That this Georgie girl was someone I'd known before the accident. Yet she *couldn't* be. She couldn't have been older than twenty, and the accident... had been twenty-one years ago. *But if she died twenty-one years ago, that would have been perfect timing for her to be reborn in a different body... a year later.* The falcon had been right. This *was* madness. My head was pounding again. I thought about excusing myself and heading home. This was a volunteer gig, after all; I didn't need to be here.

But something kept me from leaving. My feet wouldn't move, because part of me had to know whether Georgie was the one. There she was, out on the dancefloor, whirling effortlessly to "That Old Black Magic" and "Boogie Woogie Bugle Boy." From the look of her, she just might have what it took to be an actress: wavy brown hair that flowed down onto her shoulders, innocent eyes that made her look even younger than she was, and a winning smile.

Then it hit me why she'd come right up to me: She knew I wasn't a star, but she'd probably seen John Garfield slap me on the back and thank me for showing up and Jane Wyman give me a peck on the cheek. Both of them knew me from my time at Warner Bros., but she had no way of knowing that. Because I was older, she thought I was a producer, and had designs on winning me over with some flirty attention so I'd cast her in a bit part.

That's just the sort of thing *she* would do: use me to get what she wanted, then push me away. I didn't have any specific memories of it, but seeing her triggered that feeling. I balled one hand up into a fist. She was dancing now with a tall soldier boy —he might have been 6-foot-4—and didn't seem to be enjoying herself. He was trying to hold her a little too close and, at one point, tried to lean in and steal a kiss.

She pulled back.

Good girl.

It had to be *her*. Her attraction to me wouldn't allow her to get close to anyone else. But what would it matter if she just pushed me away once she'd lured me in. Push, pull. Push, pull. Like I was a doll to do with as she pleased.

My face felt flushed, and before I realized it, I was halfway out onto the dancefloor. Georgie saw me coming their way, and nodded her head once, frowning. That was all the confirmation I needed: I quickened my pace over the last few steps, thrust out my arm and insinuated myself between her and the soldier boy.

"Hey!"

"I'm cutting in," I said, scowling and pushing him back a step. At 6 feet even, I was tall myself compared to most guys, but I felt like a midget staring up at him. Not that I was intimidated. No one intimidated me.

"You're a damn civilian," he said, putting his hands on my chest to give me a shove. My arm shot up and brushed them away.

"Careful, buddy boy," he said. "If you weren't an old man with an ugly puss, I'd deck you here and now." His arms came up again to push me, but I grabbed one of his wrists and bent it back the way it wasn't supposed to go.

He screamed.

"Who you callin' old, punk?"

"Stop!"

I didn't let go. I kept pushing back on the wrist until I heard a loud snap, then finally released him. You learn a few tricks from being a bouncer.

The dancefloor had cleared out, and everyone was standing around in a circle, watching us. I was a little worried that the other G.I.s in the joint would back him up, but everyone seemed more interested in seeing how long an old man like me could last against this tall, strapping lad.

They should have been asking that question the other way around.

Mr. Hotshot took a wild swing at me, but I didn't have to duck far to avoid it, with him being so tall. That put him off balance, so I lowered my shoulder and plowed into him, knocking him to the floor. He put out his hand reflexively to break his fall, but it happened to be the one I'd just broken, and he screamed even louder when he hit the floor.

"All right! All right!" John Garfield came out and stood in front of me, staring down at Mr. Hotshot—who wasn't even trying to get up. He was just sitting there, cradling his hand like it was a ragdoll mommy had given him. "Get outta here," he said to the guy. "Stop givin' our boys a bad name. The point of this place is to boost morale, which means everyone's got to get along, understand?" That had been addressed to Mr. Hotshot, but he shot a warning glance at me, then said under his breath, "This isn't Ciro's."

I nodded.

Georgie, who had come up to stand behind me, apparently overheard and said, "It wasn't his fault, Mr. Garfield. Dante here was just looking out for me. This... person..." she glared at Mr. Hotshot, who had finally stood up and was trying to dust himself off "...was taking things too far."

"She wanted it!" Mr. Hotshot snarled; then, to Georgie: "You know you did."

"I told you to get outta here. And don't come back unless you get a Purple Heart. Come to think of it, maybe you deserve one for tangling with Dante." Everyone laughed, and the band struck up "Sing, Sing, Sing" as Mr. Hotshot crawled out the door like a pup who'd been caught pissing on the carpet.

"Thanks," Georgie said, planting a kiss on my cheek. "Maybe you should be fighting the Nazis." She giggled.

"I'd give 'em what for," I said, trying to play along, but I was still fuming. And not just at Mr. Hotshot. I was pissed at Georgie for dancing with him in the first place. It didn't matter that she couldn't have known he'd be such a jerk. That wasn't the point. The point was she should have been spending time with me. "But be careful who you dance with. Just because a guy's in uniform, that doesn't make him a hero."

"*You're* my hero," she cooed, running her fingers over the back of my hand. "Hey, I've got an idea. I don't want that guy or one of his friends following me home. Mind if I grab a ride with you?"

"Be happy to." That was more like it, but I still saw the ulterior motive. She just wanted me for protection, and she probably still thought I was some bigwig producer, especially after Garfield had blamed the other guy for our altercation—rightfully so, but still...

"Good. Meet me inside the front door at closing." She smiled and flitted away as another soldier beckoned her out onto the dancefloor. He was careful to act like a perfect gentleman, but that didn't mean I had to like it. I also noticed it was past 8 o'clock, the time Georgie had said she'd be taking her break. To spend with me.

I brushed it off. She'd just lost track of time with all the excitement, I told myself. Nothing to worry about. I'd see her at closing.

Except I didn't. She wasn't there waiting for me inside the door, like she'd said she would be. In fact, I didn't see her anywhere. I'd been busy serving up grub, so I hadn't been watching her every minute. *She must have slipped out when I wasn't looking. Trying to avoid me.*

I should have known.

Sharon Marie and Stephen H. Provost

Evermore

Georgette

LAST DANCE

I was beat by the time 9 o'clock rolled around, so I decided to knock off early from the Canteen (it was a volunteer gig, so what could they say?). I walked over to Junie and told her I was ready to go: "I've had enough excitement for one evening."

"Me too," she said. "Let's scat."

"Like a cat!"

We both laughed.

I lived 3 miles west of the Canteen, which was too far to walk, so I figured I'd drive there and back in my Olds or get a ride from Junie. She worked with me at the *Times* and had signed up to volunteer Wednesday nights at the Canteen like me. She'd offered to be my chauffer this time.

"What about that guy you said you were gonna meet after?" she said.

I frowned. "Drat. Well, he's a nice guy. He'll understand. He's a volunteer here too, like me. If he's interested, he'll be back around. I think I poured it on thick enough to whet his appetite."

"You're not thinking...?"

I laughed. "Of course not. He's ancient, and he told me he wasn't anybody special. But I think he's a producer or something. I saw some of the stars being all friendly with him, like they were cozying up. If it's good enough for them..." I winked.

Junie shook her head as we walked to her car. "Be careful you don't push it too far," she said. "He doesn't much look like a producer to me."

"And what's a producer supposed to look like?"

She shrugged. "Maybe wearing a goofy French hat and a scarf and carrying a megaphone?"

I nudged her playfully. "That's a director," I giggled. "Even I know *that* much. But if he was a director, that'd be almost as good. Besides, who takes a megaphone out for a night on the town?"

Junie laughed. "I don't know. But if he told you he wasn't anyone special..."

"I'm sure he didn't want to be bothered. He probably gets a lot of girls coming up to him and trying to make chit-chat."

She gave me a side-eye. "But you're different than those other girls," she said sarcastically.

"Darn tootin'!" I flashed my biggest come-hither smile and batted my eyes.

Junie smiled back. "Yeah, I guess you are."

When next Wednesday rolled around, Dante was there serving up beef stew and baked potatoes. I smiled at him, but he didn't smile back. Maybe I'd been wrong. Maybe he *was* still sore at me for standing him up. I started to walk over to him to make amends, but he turned away at just the moment I was about to open my mouth.

Well, that was fine with me. I could wait for later. If I gave him the cold shoulder, he'd probably forget about it and come chasing after me. Men liked to pursue a girl. The trick was to get them to think it was their idea, then turn it around and get what *you* wanted once you had them hooked.

A lot of gals wanted money. I didn't. I lived alone in a swanky Fountain Avenue apartment paid for by my Daddy, who'd earned a fortune as an oilman. He could afford to put me up in those snazzy digs at the El Palacio, as the building was called. And boy, did it live up to its name. Mahogany doors inside. Little balconies outside. There was even underground parking. What wasn't to love? My apartment was more like a home than a flat, spaced over two stories, with the living room, dining room, and kitchen on the first floor and a couple of bedrooms up top.

I was living the good life.

No, I didn't need a sugar daddy. I needed someone to notice me so I could be in pictures where I belonged. That's where Dante came in—or so I thought.

Then I found out the truth.

Junie took me aside after a couple of dances and pulled my ear close to her lips. "I've been asking around," she whispered. "That Dante guy you're sweet on...?"

"I'm not sweet on him."

"Well, whatever you are to him, he's not what you think. Those stars you saw talking to him? They know him from Ciro's. He's the bouncer there. And before that, he *was* in movies, but he was never a producer, a director, or anything like that. He helped build sets at Warner Bros."

I frowned. "Then I don't feel bad for standing him up," I said.

"I guess I'll have to start over."

"Guess so," Junie said. "It's too bad, though, because he really did seem to like you."

"If he liked me, he would have told me the truth about who he is."

"He did. You told me he said he was a nobody."

"Nobody in this town says that and means it. And if he *did* mean it, he's not worth it anyway."

A few weeks later, I came home exhausted. I hadn't made any real headway in my search for a studio connection, and I was starting to think about quitting the Canteen.

Daddy's secretary, Rose, had been there attending to some of his business earlier, and had remarked that I'd seemed out of sorts.

She was right.

Men kept hitting on me at the Canteen, but they were mostly drunken servicemen. Dante was still there volunteering, but he either didn't notice or didn't care. The one time I'd tried to approach him, he'd mouthed the word "whore" and turned away. He'd seemed like such a nice guy when we met, but he stopped hiding his true colors once he realized he couldn't get me in the sack. That's what it seemed like, anyway, and since most men behaved that way, it was as good an explanation as any.

The El Palacio was mostly dark when I drove home around midnight and parked my car. I'd asked Junie to sleep over when we met up for our shift, and it seemed like an even better idea to me after what happened at the club. One of the soldiers had insisted on cutting in and doing the jitterbug with me; he was too pushy, and I was too tired for his games. I preferred a nice, formal waltz, and I wanted a gentleman—which he definitely wasn't.

I shot a glance over at Dante, hoping against hope that he might intervene, but he just smiled and nodded as if to say, "You made your bed, now go lie in it."

Junie saw what was happening, but it was a busy night and she was in high demand among the G.I.s She was stuck on the dancefloor and couldn't break away. By the end of the night, she was as beat as I was and begged off sleeping over: "I think I need a good night's sleep in my own bed."

She'd said goodnight outside the club, and I'd gone home alone.

I changed into my pajamas, but I was too keyed up to go straight to bed, so I went back out to the kitchen, where I grabbed a cantaloupe and a can of string beans from the kitchen and put it on a tray for a midnight snack. I set them both on a silver tray and looked for something else, but nothing appealed to me. What I would've *really* liked was a hot fudge sundae, but I had to stay in acting shape for that "big break"—even if it was beginning to look like it might never come.

I turned around suddenly at a sound behind me. The apartment door was open; I'd forgotten to lock it! I dropped the tray and it crashed to the floor as I stood there, looking at a familiar figure staring back at me.

"Dante?"

"Sorry I spooked you," he said, an apologetic half-smile on his face. "I saw that guy bothering you at the Canteen, and I wanted to be sure you got home safe."

"You followed me?"

"After the way you stood me up the last time, I didn't want to intrude by offering to accompany you. I just wanted to be sure you got home safe."

He'd just said those words. Now he was repeating them. But

he didn't seem nervous; it was more like he wanted to be sure I heard him. It was important to him that I "got home safe," but why? He'd said two words to me since I stood him up. And one of those words... "Why did you call me a whore?"

He looked stunned. "I never said that! What do you mean?"

"That time I went up to you a couple of weeks ago. You mouthed the word 'whore' before I could reach you. You made it perfectly clear that..."

His face fell, then he lifted it slowly again to meet my gaze. Were his eyes wet? "I was telling you I *adore* you. I couldn't bring myself to say it out loud, because I knew you didn't feel the same, and what would everyone think if I said that to a woman half my age? No matter how beautiful she might be."

My eyes widened. "You mean...?"

"Yes, Georgie. I haven't been able to stop thinking about you. Not for a single moment since we first met." He reached back and closed the front door behind him, locking it. "There," he said, "all safe and sound. No one will get in now, and even if they do, I'll protect you."

"Protect me? You lied to me," I told him. My eyes went to the door he'd just secured, but he was standing between me and the exit. Even if he hadn't been, I knew I couldn't escape if he wanted to catch me. Part of me was scared. But I also felt something else from him—something like genuine remorse and affection.

"Can we talk?" he said, moving away from the door and walking over to the sofa, sitting down and patting a cushion. At least he wasn't trying to block my exit. That was a good sign. But I couldn't very well run out of my own apartment and leave him there.

I sat down beside him but left as much room as possible between us.

"What did I lie to you about?" he asked.

"About being some Hollywood big shot."

He shook his head. "I never said I was that."

"But the way you acted led me to *believe* you were. It's the same thing."

"The way I acted?"

"Palling around with those stars, acting like you belonged there at the Canteen. Most of the people serving food are stars, but you're not. I just assumed you had to be a producer or at least a director."

"That's not *my* fault." His tone was less remorseful now and more offended... irritated. "You have to learn to listen more carefully."

"You're right," I said. "I was stupid." My anxiety was rising again. I couldn't leave, but I didn't like to think about what might happen if I made him angry. Why hadn't I locked that stupid door behind me?

"Oh, but you thought you were smart, didn't you? You thought you'd use this big-time Hollywood producer to get your foot in the door. Admit it."

He shifted closer to me.

"No... no... I really did like you."

"If you liked me, you would have let me kiss you." He leaned in closer.

"I would have... You never asked."

"Well, I'm asking now. Just one kiss. That's all I need, and everything will be forgiven."

I nodded nervously. I didn't have much choice but to believe him.

He leaned in, and I felt the heat of his breath on me. I didn't trust him, so I tried to keep my eyes open, but his face became

275

blurry as he pulled in closer. I closed my eyes involuntarily. This wouldn't be so bad.

Just kiss him and get it over with. If he tries something...

I didn't have a way to end that sentence. I waited for his lips to meet mine, but the sensation never came. Instead, I felt something different... something pressing against my throat.

My eyes flashed open to see his eyes, filled with rage, boring into me, his teeth clenched as he held what felt like a piece of torn cloth to my throat. It was stretched taut, with either end held in a clenched fist. "You thought I was going to kiss you," he growled. "But I'm going to KILL you!"

I screamed as he pressed the cloth in hard, struggling against him, buffeting that face of his with my hands. He hadn't bothered to tie me up... thought I would just give in to him. But he had another thing coming. I brought my knee up into his groin, and he lost his grip on one end of the cloth. I was free!

...almost.

He tumbled backward, wincing in pain, but before I could scramble off the sofa, he lunged back at me, landing the full weight of his body on top of me.

"Whore!" he shouted. "You'll pay for that!"

I reached up and pulled hard at his hair, yanking a fistful out by the roots, then I reared up from beneath him and bit his shoulder as hard as I could. The feeling of my teeth sinking in to his skin made me want to vomit, but I didn't have time to think about it. I was fighting for my life.

He balled up his fist and hit me hard in the left eye. I tried to blink, but I couldn't stem the tide of liquid clouding my vision. It wasn't tears. It was red. I tried to wipe the blood away, but he was pinning my left arm to the floor. The cloth was in his left hand, so my own right hand was free. I swung it at him, palm open, but without any leverage, it did nothing to slow him down. He dropped the cloth and began pummeling me with both fists.

"Stop!" I shouted. "Stop! You're killing me!"

"That's the idea," he seethed.

He wasn't going to stop. I knew that. But if I couldn't fight him off, maybe someone had heard me shouting and trying to fight back.

But if they did, they didn't bother to check on me. It was past 2 in the morning now, and everyone would be asleep. I tried to kick him in the groin again, but his unrelenting assault had sapped most of my strength. He was sitting on me now, and I couldn't push him off. He got that cloth again and pressed it hard to my lips, but I bit down on it and yanked my head to one side, tearing it in two.

I held it there between my teeth like a trophy, mocking him. That's when he took both hands and put them to my neck, leaning in and squeezing. I sputtered, but I couldn't scream now. He was crushing my windpipe. I tried to focus on something, anything, to keep from passing out, but I was looking up at a ceiling that seemed to be fracturing like a looking glass into a kaleidoscope of darkness.

The last thing I heard was the sound of his voice in my ear. "You thought you could escape me. Don't you know you never will?"

Sharon Marie and Stephen H. Provost

Dante

FATAL DISTRACTIONS

"NOOOOOOOO!"

She was still there. I could still feel her out there somewhere, which meant I'd killed the wrong girl.

Not that Georgie hadn't deserved it. But I'd put in all that effort, and for what? I wouldn't have given Georgette the time of day if I hadn't thought she was *the one*. The one I'd been looking for. The one whose presence still tormented me, making my head pound.

My memories were as lost to me as ever, but I wouldn't stop—*couldn't* stop—until I'd ended this once and for all. But how would I find her?

Careful, I heard my inner voice tell me, masquerading as the falcon's. *Stay focused on what you want to achieve.*

Stay focused? I'd spent the last two decades trying to stay focused, and what had it gotten me?

Nothing!

But I had to clean up my mess before I could start looking again. I took Georgette's body and threw her face-down into the bathtub. That piece of cloth she'd torn from my fingers was still there, clamped firmly between her teeth. I pulled her pajama bottoms off and threw them into her bedroom to make it look like sexual assault, but I'd never raped a woman, and I had no interest in doing so now. I would not break the bond I had with *her* by having intercourse, forced or consensual, with another woman. And I would never force myself on her.

You won't rape her, but you're going to kill her? Do you think that makes you honorable?

"Shut up!" I shouted aloud at the inner voice, then clamped my hand over my mouth. I couldn't allow anyone to hear me.

I ran back to the front room and saw Georgette's purse on the kitchen sink, next to her keys. As an afterthought, I opened it and pulled out $100, then threw the bag on the floor to make it look like she'd been robbed. Then I picked up her keys and slipped them into my pocket. I'd seen the car she drove—a '36 Oldsmobile Coupe—so I ran downstairs, found it, and made my getaway.

I swerved to avoid another car as I ran a red light, denting the fender on a light pole. The engine wasn't damaged, so I threw her into reverse, then shifted to drive again and kept on going... until the gas ran out. I'd only made it ten miles from the scene, but the town was still asleep, I was guessing it would be far enough for me to slip away without being noticed.

No one was gonna find Georgette's killer.

I lay low for a while after that, but *her* presence still taunted me the way Rocky Graziano taunted the bums they threw into the ring with him. And the pounding in my head only got worse.

What if you never find her? the voice asked.

"Oh, I'll find her all right. And in the meantime, I'll show her what will happen to her when I finally do."

I meant it, too.

I killed another 21-year-old girl, strangling her with a silk stocking and dumping her body in the gutter outside L.A. City Hall. If she was watching, and she had to be, she'd know I was coming for her.

But she wasn't the one.

I walked up behind a 15-year-old girl and tried to put my hands around her neck to choke her, but she slipped out of my grasp, so I stabbed her in the heart with a stiletto.

But she wasn't the one, either.

Then, late in 1946, I found her at last.

Sharon Marie and Stephen H. Provost

Elizabeth

TROUBLE IN MIND

No one would have called me a good girl. Trouble seemed to follow me around, and when it didn't, I'd go chasing it.

My father took a flying leap off the Charleston Bridge in Boston after the Market crashed in '29. Before that, he'd built miniature golf courses for a living—talk about a weird gig—and everybody thought he'd killed himself. I was just 6 at the time, but I remember him cursing someone under his breath: a stockbroker named Dante who'd steered him wrong on his investments.

Everyone thought Daddy was dead, but he wasn't. He sent Mother a letter thirteen years later, with a brief apology for disappearing on her. I probably should have just left it alone, but he was my father, and I hadn't seen him since I was little. I wanted to get to know the guy, even if he'd been a jerk to Mama.

I'd dropped out of high school and had just turned 18 a few months earlier: I was old enough to be out on my own. So I left Miami, where I'd been living because of my bronchitis, and flew out to Vallejo.

Big mistake.

I lived with Daddy for about a month, but we were always at each other's throats, so I wound up moving out.

I got a job at Camp Cooke, an Army Air Force base down in Lompoc, and hooked up with a sergeant there. He let me stay with him, but then he started hitting me, so I moved on after a few months and headed farther south to Santa Barbara. I promptly got myself busted for underage drinking at a local bar, and they shipped me back to Massachusetts.

But I liked Florida better, so I tried my luck there again. Things were starting to look up when I met Mike, a hotshot pilot who was training there before shipping out to Southeast Asia. He was hurt in a crash there, and while he was recovering, he wrote me with a proposal of marriage.

I accepted.

Then he crashed again... and died. Just like my life always seemed to be crashing down around me.

I couldn't stay in Miami. There was nothing to keep me there, so I decided to head back to the West Coast, where one of my friends from Florida, an Air Force lieutenant named Joe, had relocated. Yeah, I had a thing for a man in uniform. I can't deny it. Maybe it was because they seemed so put together, all clean-cut and gussied up: everything I wasn't.

But I didn't hook up with Joe. I got a job as a waitress, and set my sights on an acting career. I stayed here and there, but never let on much about myself to the people who took me in. There was too much in my past I was ashamed of, and since bad luck seemed to follow me, I didn't want to let on about my plans... not that I had many. I beat the proverbial pavement in my off hours, but I didn't get any auditions or casting calls. Keeping my dreams to myself didn't seem to help, but at least I didn't have to admit my failure to anyone.

My boyfriend was a traveling salesman, so he wasn't around much, which was fine by me. I wasn't on the lookout for anyone else, but then *he* fell into my lap like kismet. Not my lap, exactly, but a table at the place I was waiting tables.

"What'll it be?" I asked without looking at him, but I felt his eyes on me, pulling mine to meet his gaze.

I looked up from my notepad.

I knew this man.

I'd never seen him before, but I *knew* him. It wasn't the grey on his temples or the complexion of his skin. It wasn't his eyes, either, but it was what lay behind them. Mysterious. Hidden. Captivating. Yes, he was more than twice my age, but that didn't make him any less handsome.

"Eggs," he said. "Over hard. I don't like them running on me. Give me a side of bacon and a cup of Joe."

I stood there staring at him for a minute, but then he started drumming his fingers on the table and I realized I hadn't written down his order. "Oh... right," I said, scribbling hurriedly on my pad. "Where have I seen you before? You're not a regular."

"Not here," he said, with what looked like a devious smirk, but he didn't elaborate. He played things just as close to the vest as I did. That made me want to know more about him, but it also scared me.

"No...," I stammered. "Not here."

"Right. Meet me tonight at my place." He pulled out a piece of paper and scribbled down an address. I didn't have anywhere to stay that night, so it was convenient.

"Okay," I said, "but no funny business."

He laughed. "You've made it abundantly clear you have no interest in me *that* way."

"Well, I didn't say that. We only started talking this minute. I just want to get to know a guy first."

"Oh, you know me," he said, winking. "But I get it. I'll be a perfect gentlemen. Separate beds. Separate sofas. Separate bowls of cereal. The whole shebang."

I laughed. "You've got a deal," I said. "I'm sorry, but I didn't get your name."

"Dante," he said, and I froze for a second. "Dante Martin at your service."

I wanted to ask him if he'd ever worked on Wall Street, but I wasn't sure I wanted to know. I was on the outs with Daddy, so what did it matter? Pops had never been there for me, and what were the chances this was the same Dante who'd made him go jump off that bridge? If he was, did it matter? That was my father's problem, and I wouldn't make it mine.

"Hey, Liz," the cook called from the kitchen. "Order's up."

I glanced at the scrap of paper he'd slipped me. The address was within walking distance of the place I was staying. "See you tonight," I said.

"Seven o'clock," he said. "Don't be late."

"I won't." I spun on my heels and headed toward the kitchen. He obviously wanted to get out of buying me dinner, but that was fine. I just needed a place to crash the swede, as Mike used to say.

Dante

LIFE IS SHORT

It was her. I knew it the moment I saw her. I'd spent the past few years driving a taxi, hoping she'd be one of my fares. But I always came up empty. Who'd have thought I'd finally find her waiting tables? She was certainly a looker, without being the cookie-cutter pinup type. Her wild dark hair made her look taller than she was, and those eyes! It was like she was looking right through you.

But I couldn't let myself fall into the trap of admiring her. I had to have her, but I *couldn't* have her. This was the fate she had consigned me to. I had accepted it, true enough, but I was also determined to punish her for it.

I couldn't delay any longer.

Once I had dispatched her, I was convinced, those memories from so long ago now would return. Then I could finally be at peace.

I'd told her to be there at 7 o'clock promptly, but I thought it would be fun to show up late myself. To make her wait. This would be the beginning of her torture. I knew she wouldn't give up on me arriving, not with our connection, but she wasn't there when I arrived at 7:45.

Thinking I'd miscalculated, I pulled out my keys, unlocked the door, and stepped inside... and there she was: half-sitting, half-reclining on the sofa, staring like a tiger at the door, ready to pounce.

"I know where you saw me, before today, I mean," she said coquettishly as I shut the door behind me.

"Oh? And where might that be?"

"MGM. I went there looking for a job. They threw me out on my ear," she laughed. "Said I needed an appointment. But I got a look around before I left. Saw this guy directing a movie. I don't remember the title, but I know it was you. I'm right, aren't I? I never forget a face."

I put both hands in front of my face, touching the tips of my thumbs together and pointing my index fingers up. "You oughta be in pictures, Liz," I said, trying to hide my anger. She was trying to use me, just like Georgie had. That's why she was here. Because she thought I was some Hollywood mucky-muck.

She frowned. "Are you making fun of me?"

"No," I said flatly. "But you're wrong. I used to work at Warner as a set designer, but I've been out of that business for a while now. Sorry to *disappoint* you."

She sat forward and shrugged. "Just more of the same for me. My whole life's been a disappointment."

"I know what you mean."

"I don't think you do, but it doesn't matter." Her voice was harsh, and it was rubbing me wrong.

You have no idea.

"Make yourself at home. It ain't much, you only make so much on tips when you're driving a cab."

I saw whatever enthusiasm she had left drain out of her face. *Did she just roll her eyes?* "Look, if you don't wanna be here, you know where the door is."

She nodded once firmly. "Right. I guess I'll be going then."

She stood up and brushed past me. Was she *really* going to leave? *Of course she is. That's what she always does.* I didn't know how I knew that, but I did. That was why I needed to kill her.

I caught her by the arm and turned her roughly around. "You're *not* leaving."

"Oh yes, I am!" She tried to wrench her arm free, and I slapped her hard across the face.

She slapped me back with her free hand even harder, raking her nails across my cheek. I released her arm from the shock of it, and she ran out the door. I shouted after her, "I'm gonna kill you!" I put my fingers to my cheek and brought them up in front of my face, watching as the blood dripped down them. I smiled. *Blood for blood.* I grabbed a large cleaver from my kitchen, which I'd kept razor-sharp for just this occasion.

I don't know whether she realized I was following her, biding my time until she stopped so I could confront her. She ran up to a cop on the sidewalk, and I saw her body convulsing in sobs as she no doubt told him about the man who'd hit and threatened her. She was hysterical. The cop must have thought she was drunk or crazy, because I saw him shake his head and heard him tell her to move along.

She stumbled on and turned into a field in an empty neighborhood that was waiting to be developed.

No one was around. Everything was dark, and nothing stirred. It was perfect. This was exactly where I'd planned to kill her, but she'd made it easier by arriving of her own accord. It was our connection that had brought her here. She knew instinctively where I wanted her, and she had no choice but to comply, even if it meant the end of her life. I'd thought about choking the life out of her the way I had with Georgie, but strangling was too good for her. I had to make her *hurt*.

I snuck up behind her, holding the cleaver behind my back, careful not to make a sound. I wanted to savor every moment of this. I had a vision in my mind of what I was going to do, but I was so fixated on it that I wasn't looking where I was going. I must have put my foot down next to a scorpion, which had started crawling up my leg. I felt the tickle of it just before it stung me.

"Argh!" I shouted in surprise and pain.

Liz spun around and those haunting eyes of hers, still wet from tears, widened when she saw me. "I'm sorry," she wailed. "I'm sorry... so sorry... I'm so sorry... I didn't realize who you were."

I stopped in my tracks. Was it possible? Did she really know me? Could she tell me who I was? All the things I had forgotten? Maybe I was making a mistake by killing her. Maybe there was just that little thread of hope for us after all.

"Who am I, then?" I asked.

Then the thread snapped.

She stared at me for a minute, then opened her mouth, running her tongue across her upper lip. "I'm not going to tell you," she said in a peculiar tone that danced on the borderline of pity and ridicule. Did she *really* know the answer and was just refusing to tell me, or was she playing with me like a cat with a mouse?

290

Evermore

She leaned forward. "I'll go to the grave with it," she hissed. "I *am* sorry: I'm sorry for *you*, you piece of shit!" She started laughing hysterically, and I realized that, even in this relatively isolated field, someone was bound to hear it if I didn't shut her up.

I lunged forward and grabbed her, cupping my hand over her mouth as she struggled and tried to bite me. I had no time for this. I pulled the cleaver out and thrust it deep into her stomach, dragging the blade from one side of her to the other. She passed out and crumpled to the ground. It was my job to ensure that she would never wake up again.

I dragged her into a nearby shed, where I had stored some cleanser, buckets of water, and some brushes earlier that day, leaving it unlocked.

Yes, I had planned it all in short order. I'd been waiting to find her for so long, I'd known just what I would do when I did. And I'd known just what she would do as well. I'd known she would run, and I'd known we would wind up here. This, was where it would all end.

Coming around to stand over her, I took the blade and finished what I'd started, slicing in a clean, straight line clear across her midsection, then hacking again and again to sever her spine. Bending over, I reached into her gut and yanked her intestines up and out of her, the blood spurting and cascading in every direction. I wanted to be sure she bled out. "The life is in the blood": Isn't that what the Bible said? I needed her completely dead. I needed there to be nothing left of her except the husk of a body she had formerly occupied. I ripped out her organs with my bare hands, leaving the best for last: her heart. That belonged to me. I wrapped it up in a newspaper I had stuffed into my pocket. Then I pulled both halves of her body out of the shed one at a time and left them in the middle of the field, looking like a severed mannequin.

I returned to the shed and used the cleanser I'd left there to remove every trace of blood, intestines, sinews... every trace of *her*. Then I washed down the shed with the water I'd left there and walked away, tossing the cleanser and brushes down into a ravine.

Something was still wrong, though.

My memory hadn't returned, and my head had started pounding again.

I hurried back to my place to take off my blood-drenched garments and wash them thoroughly by hand. I showered and put on a clean set of clothes. Then I cut up the old ones, went out again and buried them in a different corner of the neighborhood where I'd killed *her*.

I started back toward my place, but the pain in my head was excruciating. Was this my punishment for what I'd done? I was suddenly dizzy, and I had to narrow my eyes to focus. Even then, I wasn't sure where I was. Nothing seemed familiar. Had I taken a wrong turn? All the streets looked the same... what little I could make out. Everything was blurry, and the stars were spinning. I stumbled forward, crashing into a mailbox and falling to the ground. I felt like my head was going to explode, and I grabbed it with both hands, squeezing hard to make the pain go away. But that just made it worse. I closed my eyes, and then...

I heard voices, but I couldn't open my eyes. "He's been out for three days since we got him here."

"He's not going to make it..."

"Cerebral hemorrhage..."

"It was just a matter of time before..."

Evermore

"Brain damage..."

"...irreversible."

"Did you see the papers today...?"

"Werewolf killer..."

"Woman's body..."

"What kind of person...?"

They started fading into background noise. I strained to hear them, but I lost consciousness again.

When I awoke, I had my memory back. Finally! I was lying in a hospital, but I when I opened my mouth, nonsense came out. I looked down at myself. I was no longer Dante Martin. I was someone else.

I hadn't ended it after all. I would have to find her again.

Fresno, California, 1985

The Fiery One

Seraphina

Someone Wicked This Way Comes

I felt that eerie, skin-crawling feeling you get when you know you're being watched—that some unknown person's eyes are following your every more. Standing in the middle of Fashion Fair Mall, I was surrounded by people flitting left and right, busy with their shopping. Friends were chatting over lunch in the food court. Young couples walked arm-in-arm, with wistful smiles on their faces. Harried mothers and fathers tried to keep their hyper toddlers and wandering teens together for a "fun" family outing to buy school clothes. How would I ever pick out a pair of eyes fixated on me through this chaotic throng?

But then I saw them. Dark, penetrating eyes burned right through me, seeing every part of me like they had x-ray vision. The tall, dark-haired man, handsome and unnerving at the same time, flashed me a small, knowing smile. But *what* did he know? He certainly didn't know me. He raised his hand and gave a small wave, just before my eyes flashed down, unnerved by the intensity of his stare.

Even though people described me as beautiful and charismatic, I was not one to date often. I was a shy, quiet girl who preferred riding my horse, attending college classes, preparing for my MCATs to qualify for medical school, and spending time with a select group of friends I'd made in college. The few people I'd dated were boys I'd known through school or sons of my mother's friends. I'd always been uncomfortable receiving attention from strangers, especially strange men like the one standing across the plaza.

The frustrating part of this experience—how very uncomfortable I felt right now as he stared at me—yet I somehow felt strangely drawn to him. Every cell in my body screamed danger, but my heart... my emotions fought to draw me closer to him. My mind was a chaotic whirlwind of thoughts that I couldn't make sense of. The only solution I could draw for this enigmatic situation:

Run, bail, get out of Dodge.

I'd kept my eyes down ever since I first saw him, so I had no idea what he was doing now. I noticed a payphone next to me, so I picked up the receiver and pretended to make a call as I flicked my eyes up to find a way of escape.

"Hey, Brittan...," I stammered as my eyes met his, standing only two feet away from me.

I hung up the phone as my mouth hung open, desperately trying to find words to say.

"Hello, angel. Did I interrupt a call?"

"Umm... uh... no. It started to ring, but the line disconnected."

"I was wondering. I didn't see you deposit a dime."

"Do I know you? How did you know my nickname is Angel?"

"You don't know me yet, but you will. Just call it a lucky guess, but you glowed from across the room. There's a fire inside you that drew me to you."

"Umm... okay. Well, I really need to be going. My friend is expecting me." I looked down at the watch on my trembling wrist. "In fact, I'm already running late." I turned to leave but froze when I felt his hand grip my arm gently. He pulled out a small bit of paper and hastily scrawled his name and number on it, then passed it to me.

"Give me a call sometime. I just know we were meant to meet."

"Sure. Great. Nice to meet you... uh... Tristan."

I power-walked across the mall and out to my car. I wanted to put as much distance as possible between us as quickly as I could. I got in the car and locked the door. Leaning over the steering wheel with my head resting on my hands, I took several deep breaths to calm the swirling emotions inside. I slid the key into the ignition and was about to turn it when I saw him exit the mall, scanning the parking lot as he walked.

Is he looking for me? Chill out, Seraphina! He is probably looking for his car just like all the other people out here.

Just the same, I ducked down behind the steering wheel and waited for him to leave before starting the car and pulling out of the parking lot. I still felt uneasy, but I couldn't get him out of my mind. I spent the rest of the afternoon studying for my upcoming Organic Chemistry midterm. I'd arranged to meet my roommate, Brittany, for dinner at Me-n-Ed's Pizza before hitting The Wild Blue to celebrate our friend Anthony's 21st birthday with some friends.

I put on a yellow off-the-shoulder dress, embroidered with eyelet flowers, and slipped on my cowboy boots. I used the curling iron to make soft ringlet curls in the golden blond hair that framed my face. I applied shimmer lip gloss and grabbed my wristlet purse before heading out the door. I'd promised to pick Brittany up from the library, so I headed there first.

A car had been following me since I left my apartment. As I merged into the turn lane on Shaw to enter the campus on Barton Avenue, I noticed it was still there.

To my relief, the driver continued east on Shaw when I turned into the school parking lot. I parked near the door and saw Brittany come bouncing out when she saw me. She hurried to the car, ready to start our afternoon.

"Girl, are you ready to parrrrttttttyyy?" Brittany screeched as she yanked the door open.

"I'm ready to eat some yummy pizza and have a drink with Anthony while the rest of you party hearty."

"Don't be a party pooper, Angel. Just cuz that's your nickname doesn't mean you have to act like one."

"The O Chem exam is in two days. I need to be ready to study tomorrow. I've got to keep my grades up if I want to get into the right medical school. Maybe I will be 'wild and crazy' and have two drinks. Deal? Besides, I didn't say I wouldn't have fun... just not drink like a fish. And I agreed to be the designated driver anyhow. Remember?"

"True. I take it back. You're an angel here on Earth. God knows I don't intend to stay sober, and I sure as hell don't want to walk all the way home."

I giggled as I pulled into traffic and made the short drive to our favorite pizza place. We shared a large sausage and olive pizza with pesto sauce. Neither of us had eaten lunch, so we scarfed it all down, leaving not so much as a crumb or a dot of sauce on the pan. While we ate, I told Brittany about my experience at the mall. All she could do was roll her eyes. She couldn't understand why I felt so unnerved. Just before we left, Brittany called Anthony to let him know we were headed to the bar.

We left the pizza parlor and got on the freeway, heading down toward the Tower District, near downtown. Brittany had me laughing so hard I almost missed the highway exit. I quickly hit the turn signal and swerved over into the exit lane.

Then I noticed a black Volvo just two cars behind us make a similar move. A sickening feeling rose in my stomach as I realized it looked identical to the car that I thought had been following me earlier. But it couldn't be! That had been almost two hours ago.

"Brittany, I think someone is following me. And they were earlier, too."

"So, pull over, girl. Do you think it's that 'man' who was interested in you? Take advantage of it. You need to get some. It's a miracle you found someone who ignored that rampant 'leave me alone' vibe of yours."

"I'm not joking here, Brit. This is really freaking me out. I'm telling you that man earlier was weird. I don't know how to explain it. I have never met him in my life—never even seen him before—but I feel like I know him. He gives me the creeps, but at

301

the same time, he fills me with longing to know more about him. It's just too weird that, on the same day I find him staring at me, I suddenly seem to have someone tailing me."

"You're paranoid. You're just not used to someone hitting on you. Do you know how many black Volvos there are in this city? I'm sure that it's not the same one. Just relax and have some fun please."

"I..."

"Pleasssse."

"But..."

"Pleeeeeeasssssssssssse!"

"Fine! You're seriously relentless. I will."

"You will what?"

"I will relax."

"And?"

"I won't worry."

"Annnnnd?"

"I will have fun."

"Yes! That's my girl."

I made it a point not to look in the rearview mirror for the rest of the drive. Thankfully, it wasn't long before we reached the Tower District. We found a parking spot near the bar without too much trouble... surprising for a Saturday evening. When we went inside, though, we found it as crowded as ever. Anthony was already seated in the back, with three tables pulled together.

"I was beginning to wonder if you girls got lost." Anthony jumped up with a big smile and hugged us both.

"Oh, Seraphina was trying to hide from her stalker."

"Stop it, Brittany."

"Excuse me? I feel lost." Anthony's face was awash with curiosity.

Evermore

"I know. It's shocking to me too. A *real live man* wanted to date our little Angel here. It was a simply terrifying experience for her. He approached her in the mall and gave her... his phone number! Can you imagine? The horror! Then she thought somebody was following her car on our way here, and she was just sure it *had* to be him."

The two of them burst out laughing, along with three other friends sitting at the tables. I flopped into the chair nearest me, my face a bright red. It was useless trying to convince them. I knew I wasn't wrong. With any luck, I'd never see him again. I tried to calm down and focus on the music. I hadn't seen this band before, but they were pretty good, playing covers of current hits.

Our friend group grew over the course of the night, and the next few hours passed in a blur. I ended up having a few beers to relax, so when Brittany's and my roommate, Katrina, arrived, she offered to drive us home in my car. All thoughts of the midterm or the strange man vanished from my mind.

We were laughing at Ryan's impression of Professor Stewart when I suddenly felt nauseated. I looked at Melanie next to me. "I think I'm going to ralph." I started to stand up but collapsed back into my seat as a wave of dizziness hit me. I grabbed at my throat as I gasped for breath. Melanie thought I was choking and tried to pull me up out of my seat to give me the Heimlich.

"Can't... breathe."

Brittany grabbed my wristlet off the table and dug out my asthma spray. "She must be having an asthma attack."

I knew that wasn't the problem, but I didn't know what was wrong. As I looked around the room, fighting for air, I saw him.

Tristan!

He was standing at the bar only twenty feet away and

staring right at me. I couldn't explain it, but I knew he was the cause of my distress. I waved my hand toward the back door of the bar. "Air," I croaked. Brittany realized what I wanted and helped Melanie support me and lead me out into the cool evening air. With distance, the tightness in my throat eased, and I sucked in great lungfuls of air.

"Are you okay, girl?" Anthony asked as he rushed out the door.

"Yes. I'm better. Thanks."

"What happened?" Melanie asked.

"I'm not sure." I wanted to explain, but I knew no one would believe me. I wasn't sure I believed it myself, but I could feel it in my bones.

Anthony and Melanie returned to the party a short while later while Brittany sat outside with me for a few more minutes. I couldn't bring myself to look her in the eyes, but I had to say it.

"He's here."

"Who?"

"Him. Tristan... that man."

"Are you serious? Is that what's wrong? Did you seriously have a panic attack over a man?"

"Damn it, Brittany! No! It wasn't a panic attack."

"But you can't seriously be blaming him though, are you?"

"Yes... no... I don't know. That's not the point right now."

"What is then?"

"The fact that he's here. I told you someone was following us. I told you I was afraid it was him. Now he suddenly shows up. What are the chances?"

"Let's go back in. Show me this boogeyman. I'll send the boys over to talk to him if you want."

I followed her back inside, and he was still standing in the exact same spot. His eyes turned toward me the instant I returned to the table.

"See. There he is. Staring at me right now."

Brittany looked over and started giggling. "You can't be serious. Are you talking about that guy over there in the acid-wash jeans, white V-neck T-shirt, and white tennis shoes? He looks kinda like a tall version of Tom Cruise?"

"Well, now that you mention it, I guess he does."

"Well scoot over, babe, and send him my way. You kept saying 'man' in this ominous way. I was expecting some lecherous 40-year-old or some scary old man like from *Phantasm*. I'd hardly call him a man. He looks like he's our age."

"Yes, I suppose he does."

"So, are you truly surprised to find a guy our age out at the coolest club in town? Where else would he be on a Saturday night looking that hot?"

Brittany was making me feel like a fool. Yet I still couldn't get over the overwhelming feeling of unease washing over me. As I sat there, I realized I had my chin balanced on my hands, which were crisscrossed over my chest and covering my throat. I could still breathe, but I felt pressure at my neck.

I changed seats with Melanie so that I didn't have to see him standing at the bar. I could see that Katrina and Brittany were deep in conversation—about me, by the looks they kept throwing my way. I closed my eyes and tried to ground myself.

"Let me go get you another beer," Katrina said as she moved over beside me and saw my pale face.

"Thanks."

The band began to play another song, and I recognized the electronic beat and the desperate, haunting lyrics of "Obsession" by Animotion. Just as the chorus began, I felt a pair of hands rest on my shoulders near my neck. I turned and looked up as I said, "Thanks, Kat..." But I found myself looking into the eyes of... Tristan.

"Would you like to dance? I've always loved this song."

I began to tremble. My eyes grew wide. I couldn't find my voice. My breath came out in a rush.

"Are you okay?" he asked, looking concerned.

Katrina rushed to my side, sloshing the beer on me as she stopped abruptly. "What's your damage? Can't you see she's not feeling well? I don't think she's up for a dance. Buh-bye!" Katrina pushed in between us and sat back down. I was relieved to see him take the hint—not that Katrina was subtle—and walk away.

"Seraphina and I are going to bounce, Brittany. Do you want to come, or can you get another ride?"

"I'll take her!" Melanie piped up.

I waved goodbye and mouthed "sorry" to Anthony, who was so tanked he didn't even notice my departure.

"Thanks, Kat. You're a lifesaver." I walked alongside her down the block to her car. I felt weak.

"No problem. You've saved my ass more than once. I don't care what Brittany says. Gag me with a spoon. He's *not* hot, and I don't blame you for being creeped out. That was so bogus the way he put his hands on you like that."

"I know. And did you notice the song? That can't have been a coincidence."

"No, I didn't actually. What was it?"

"It was 'Obsession.' He touched me just as the singer came to the part about capturing you. Total creep factor. I was about to freak out again when you came up and saved me."

"What is he, mental? That is totally warped. Stay away from that guy."

Evermore

"Don't need to tell me twice. You know what Brit would say though, don't you?"

Katrina pinched her nose and held her head up a little, adopting a superior demeanor. "You know," she said, mimicking our friend, "'Obsession' is still one of the hottest songs out there. They play it on MTV all the time."

I started cackling. "You nailed that perfectly."

"I love that girl, but she can get on her high horse sometimes."

"I'm way too busy with school to deal with that shit. I just want to go to bed and forget this night ever happened."

"Oh, come on," Katrina said. "Can't you veg out with me for a bit... watch a movie? I just rented Purple Rain. Now if you want to talk about *actual* hot men, Prince fits the bill."

"Sold! I do love Prince. But then I really do have to get to bed so I feel up to studying tomorrow. I have to pass my midterms if I'm going to go to Santa Cruz on spring break."

"No way! You're going?!"

"Only if you are."

"That's totally bitchin'. Count me in!"

Tristan

My Angel

Her sudden appearance at the mall had taken me by surprise. I'd been looking around, trying to find the Wherehouse so I could pick up the new Tears for Fears album. Then I came around the corner, and my heart began to race. A surge of excitement washed over me as I saw her—my soulmate—followed by the dark thrill I felt whenever I watched the life drain from her eyes. I'd always been drawn to her, but our love was doomed. We were fated to perpetuate an endless cycle of disappointment, heartbreak, and death.

She'd once been the source of all my joy and hope for a future, but she dashed those hopes and ripped my heart out every time. Now my only enjoyment came from seeing her fear and pain. For us, love only hurt.

It had always been hard to tear my eyes away from her beauty. But at that moment, I'd gotten lost in thoughts of how to leave the same scars on her body that she had left on my heart. I wasn't surprised that she felt my stare—or that it alarmed her.

My smile only widened as I watched her fidget uncomfortably.

I had hoped for a small scream when she found me standing by her side, but instead she was dumbfounded. This time my love was meeker and milder than in the past... a timid little mouse. This was going to be fun.

She was so uncomfortable that she didn't even remember she was wearing a gold necklace with the word 'angel' in cursive. It was a safe bet that it was either her name or a nickname. When I used it to address her in such a familiar manner, she was down for the count.

I'm not sure it would have been possible for her to escape the mall any faster. I missed seeing her get in her car, but my patience paid off, and I caught her trail as she pulled out of the parking lot. She must have been lost in thoughts of me because she didn't notice me follow her to her apartment.

In fact, she didn't realize anyone was following her until she left home again and was just about to turn into Fresno State. I drove on and parked down the road, out of sight. I didn't want to freak her out too fast. Slow, mounting terror was the way to go with this shrinking violet.

She picked up a friend who kept her busy talking and laughing, so she failed to notice me tailing her again.

At first.

But she saw me again when I had to make the same hasty lane change she did for the highway exit. I took a chance and dropped back, taking a couple of detours before parking on Olive Avenue. I was betting that she was probably headed for The Wild Blue where all the co-eds hung out on Friday and Saturday nights.

Once again, my intuition was correct. I saw her and her friend on the street just about to enter the bar. I killed some time reading my psychology textbook in the car before heading in myself. It gave her some time to feel safe and comfortable amongst friends before I dropped the bomb.

The band went on a break just as I arrived. I walked over to say hi and found my biology lab partner was the leader of the band. He readily agreed to my song request. I headed over to the bar and looked over at the table where my angel was hanging out with her friends. They were the loudest group in the club, and I overheard one of her friends call her Seraphina. I filed away that tidbit of information for another time.

It wasn't long before she felt my presence—even across the crowded bar—and our eyes met. Her reaction far exceeded my wildest expectations. She started hyperventilating and went into a full-blown panic attack.

It was hard not to laugh, but I couldn't blow my cover just yet. I had to make allies of her friends and chip away, bit by bit, at her comfort zone.

I had to leave her alone, with nowhere to hide.

No one she could trust.

I was going to systematically deprive her of everything she held dear, including her dignity, until she begged me to take her life. And I would.

Slowly.

And painfully.

Step One was to make her friends question her mental health. That one was easy. She came back inside after her outburst, just moments before the band returned.

I knew my girl was intelligent, even if she wasn't brave. There's no way she'd fail to notice the significance of the song I'd requested. I made my way over and kindly asked her to dance just as the chorus began. This was the '80s—people were chill. How could anyone get so rattled by a simple touch on her shoulders? But she nearly had a complete emotional meltdown. And poor, innocent me just walked away rejected.

As if!

Step Two sent me back to the mall on a mission. I needed to get a gift made for a special occasion.

Seraphina

Spring Break

Midterms went even better than expected. I'd always been an excellent student, but I totally aced my exams without even breaking a sweat. By the time I finished on Thursday afternoon, I was ready to go celebrate—in more ways than one.

Five minutes after I got home, Brittany burst into my room.

"Are you done packing yet? Kat and Elijah are ready to hit the road. Santa Cruz, here we come!"

"I just got in. Give me ten minutes. Okay?"

"We have something special planned for your birthday Saturday. You're finally going to be 21. No more fake ID for you! I still can't believe we convinced our 'perfect little angel' Seraphina to get one in the first place. You're always such a goodie-goodie!"

"I know, I know. But I've been *such* a goodie-goodie, I knew I wouldn't blow it if I let myself have a little fun. So what are the plans?"

"I'm not going to ruin the surprise. You'll just have to wait

313

and see."

"Well get out of here and let me pack. I'll be out in a jiffy."

Five minutes later, I had packed my cosmetic bag and grabbed the last few items I needed. As I walked into the living room, bags in hand, I heard Katrina laying on the horn and bellowing, "Last call for alcohol!" I ran out to her Jeep, and we were off, the wind in our hair.

We were staying at Brittany's parents' beach house for the week. Twelve of us packed into three bedrooms. It would be cozy but fun.

We arrived in town about 6 p.m. and headed to the Boardwalk for fun and food. We went on most of the rides and played a few carnival games. I even won a goldfish that I gave to a little kid standing off to the side. Then we ate until we thought our stomachs were going to burst. Brittany and Katrina went down to the beach while I went on a few more rides. Elijah was going to go to the haunted house with me, but at the last minute he saw some of the other guys who had just arrived.

I never grew tired of the exhilaration I felt as The Giant Dipper slowly clack-clack-clacked up the steep hill before its thrilling high-speed descent. There was just something special about old wooden roller coasters. And while I might not have been the bravest person in the world, I did enjoy the adrenaline rush I felt when some cheesy monster jumped out at me in the haunted house.

I'd been coming to the Boardwalk since I was 5. I'd probably been through the haunted house two dozen times, and not much had changed. Even though I knew what was coming, I still jumped every time.

The first half of my trek was par for the course, but then all of a sudden, my fear spiked. I knew there were teenagers just ahead of me and a few behind me because I could hear them, but I could hear something else as well. Furtive footsteps trying to sneak up on me. Menacing whispers that I couldn't quite make out... at first. I'm sure I heard "pain"... "blood"... "love hurts." They felt like threats directed at me.

I was on pins and needles, waiting for the unexpected. Maybe one of the teenagers was trying to play a trick on me, waiting to jump out of the shadows. Teenage boys did things like that all the time, but this felt more serious... and frightening.

As I turned each corner, the feeling of being stalked increased. I kept turning around quickly, trying to catch sight of my pursuer each time, but there was never anyone there. I even ran back around a corner suddenly, but I still didn't see anyone.

As I turned into the funhouse mirror maze, I caught sight of him. Only for a second.

Tristan!

The look on his face terrified me. It was pure evil. He was enjoying this: getting off on scaring me. I knew the path like the back of my hand, so I began to run. I could hear his rapid footfalls behind me. I didn't know what he planned to do to me, but I wasn't going to stick around and find out. I ducked behind a horror tableau depicting a scene that looked straight out of *Texas Chainsaw Massacre*.

I sat on the floor with my knees tucked to my chest, hoping I wouldn't be seen. I felt my heart pounding and tried to quiet my ragged breathing. I closed my eyes as the tears squeezed out unbidden. I heard his steps slow as he came around the corner. He didn't see me and kept moving slowly past, but then I lost track of him. I knew the exit was just up around the next bend, so I was hoping he thought I'd left—and had done the same.

I lost track of time. I don't know how long I sat there. I was too afraid to come out. I heard other come people come and go, but I was still afraid he was out there waiting for me, whether he was up around the next bend or just outside the exit door. I didn't move until I heard Elijah and Katrina calling out for me as they walked through the haunted house. When I realized they were nearly to me, I burst out into Katrina's arms, bawling.

"He was here, Kat! Chasing me."

"Who was chasing you?"

"Tristan!"

"Did he try to hurt you? I swear I'll kill him."

"No. I hid from him. But he was trying to get me. He was following me through this place and trying to stay out of sight. When I ran, he started chasing me. I hid here, and I was too scared to come back out."

"Oh my god, Seraphina!" Elijah yelled in exasperation. "This is ridiculous! He's not fucking Jason chasing you with a machete."

Katrina whirled on him, fire in her eyes. "Leave her alone."

"No. This is so stupid. He's a cool guy."

Katrina's eyes narrowed. She surveyed him with suspicion, ready to lash out like a rattlesnake. "How would you know?"

"Last weekend after you guys left, Brittany told us about Seraphina's 'terrifying' encounter with him." He held his curled fingers in the air, like a creeper reaching to grab his unsuspecting victim. "A couple of us talked to him later that night and, like I said, he's a cool guy. He even came over to Brittany and apologized for upsetting you. He just wanted to ask you out on a date, and he's a bit awkward."

"Guys always think other guys are cool. I'll always trust another girl's impression. If she says he's a creep, he'd have to be a magician to convince me he's anything *but* a creep. Besides, I agree with her. He bugged me out too."

I smiled at Katrina, thankful for her support. I just didn't have the strength to defend myself right then. Katrina wrapped her arm around me and led me out of the haunted house. Brittany and the rest of our friends who had arrived recently were sitting on a bench nearby.

"What's wrong?" Brittany asked.

Kat gave her a look. "We'll talk about it later. Let's just go back to the beach house."

Elijah piped up, "Seraphina is losing it about Tristan. Poor guy can't catch a break."

If looks could kill, Elijah would have dropped right then. He shut up when he saw Kat's eyes on him.

Brittany didn't get the hint. "What about him? She hasn't seen him in a week."

I replied weakly, "He was chasing me in the haunted house. I'm sure of it."

"How? He isn't even here. He's back at school. He had to work tonight at the bookstore."

"How would you know his schedule, Brittany?"

"Umm. I just do."

"Spill it. Now!" Katrina demanded.

"I was just talking to him the other day. He happened to mention it. We were talking about spring break plans and all. I said we were leaving town on Thursday night. No biggie!"

"And?" Katrina prodded.

"There's more to it, Brit. I know you."

I started to feel nervous. I couldn't bear to utter the question that had come to my mind. Katrina must have read my mind when she saw the fear in my eyes.

"Oh shit, Brit! Tell me you didn't."

"Didn't what?" she asked innocently.

"Tell me that you didn't invite him down here to stay with all of us this week."

"Would I do that?"

"Yes!" Katrina and I yelled in unison.

"Of course not. But..."

"But what?!"

"I may have invited him down for the party on Saturday though."

"No! Not Seraphina's birthday party? How could you do that?"

"I didn't mean to do anything wrong. He's really a nice boy. All the guys can tell you." She looked around at our friends seated around her, and they all nodded in unison. "We all thought Seraphina needed to relax and have a little fun for once. We just thought if she met him again on neutral territory amongst the safety of friends, she'd see that he was okay. Maybe if she got some, she'd chill out a bit. You know?"

"Leave it to you to be a crass bitch, Brit. It's not your decision to make. It's *her* birthday party."

"At *my* house! Can't I invite who I want?" Brittany whined.

"Everything's always all about you, isn't it?" Katrina retorted.

"I'm not some pathetic virgin," I protested. "Just because I don't whore around like *some* people doesn't mean I'm a frigid bitch either. I have other priorities right now."

I couldn't ignore the feeling that he was watching this entire exchange, but I was too amped up to let it go. I was about to bail out of this whole week anyhow, so it didn't matter. As I turned to walk away, I asked Katrina to drop me off at a nearby motel.

"I'll take a bus home tomorrow," I told her.

"I'll take you back to Fresno if you want. Let little *Miss Busybody* find her own way home."

We'd gotten about 100 feet away when Brittany came running up to apologize. "I'm sorry, girls. I swear. I'm a bitch sometimes. We all know that. I'll make it up to you... both of you... I swear. When we get back to the beach house, I'll call him and leave a message uninviting him. Deal? Just please stay and enjoy spring break with the rest of us."

Katrina shrugged her shoulders and looked over at me, leaving the decision to me.

"Fine! But if Tristan shows up, I'll bounce."

Brittany must have succeeded in reaching Tristan because he didn't show his face at my party or the rest of the time we were there. I had a great time that week, and the time away at the beach was just the break I needed before finishing the semester.

The next few months would be some of the busiest and most important ones to my future success. It was nerve-wracking to consider that I still had an entire year of school left after this semester, but these next months would determine if I started med school next year in the fall.

I would be taking the MCAT in May. Then the application process would start a week later and finish up in June or July.

When we pulled up to our apartment, I stopped to check the mailbox. The landlord had left a note that there was package to be picked up in the office—a gift bag with a card attached. I told Brittany and Katrina I'd run down to get it, and they lugged in my bags for me. The landlord told me someone had dropped it off Saturday.

I walked back up to our apartment, excited to open the

present. My brother had been out of town and told me he would be dropping something off for me while I was gone.

I was still like a small child when it came to opening gifts—the present first and then the card. Inside the gift bag was a small jewelry box. I opened it to find a gold necklace. It was like one of my angel necklace, except it was a word, not a name.

"Evermore."

It seemed a little odd, but I thought maybe my brother had gotten it as a cute tongue-in-cheek gift to reflect my love of fairy tales with princesses, love, and the happily-ever-afters. When I opened the card, my heart stopped.

It was from Tristan!

The blood drained from my face. I began to shake, and the gift and card fell from my hands. Katrina was just entering the room, and she came to my side rapidly when she saw my reaction.

"What's wrong? Sit down before you pass out."

I pointed to the items on the floor.

She picked them up and looked back at me, shocked. "What the fuck? Is this the package you went to pick up?"

I nodded.

"How does he know where we live?" I asked.

"Two guesses, and the first one don't count." Kat got up and angrily called out Brittany's name.

Brittany arrived a moment later, looking perplexed at Kat's anger.

"Did you tell Tristan where Seraphina lives?"

"No, of course not. Give me some credit. I wouldn't go that far." She sounded offended, but then she gasped.

"What?"

"Umm... nothing."

"Tell me, Brit," I demanded.

Evermore

"Well... umm... he's in my psych class," Brittany said hesitantly.

"Yessss?" Katrina prodded.

"Well, he missed class on Tuesday. He needed the notes, and he asked if I would mind sharing mi... mine."

Katrina slammed her hand on the desk beside her. "Don't tell me. He came here to pick them up?"

Brit nodded sheepishly.

"Goddammit, Brit! Sometimes you don't use the brains your momma gave you. I really wonder just how you even got into college sometimes."

Brittany broke into tears and joined me on the couch, where I had slumped during their verbal altercation.

"I really don't think she has to worry. I told you he's a sweet guy."

Katrina held out the necklace to her. "Does this seem normal to you? This guy doesn't know her. He's never had a real conversation with her. Is this an appropriate gift in your world? Is any gift appropriate from one total stranger to another for an occasion that you were *uninvited* to attend?"

"Well, it is a bit much. But like we all said, he is a bit socially awkward."

I stood up, angry. I was *not* going to let him control my life with fear. This was going to end today... *now*, in fact. I snatched the items from Katrina's hand and shoved them in the bag.

"Since he's your new best friend, Brit, do you know if he's working today?" I asked, red-faced.

"I think so."

"I'll be back!" I slammed out the door and walked down to my car. I heard Katrina run up behind me.

"I'm going with you."

"Fine! You can stand back and watch, but I'm handling this alone."

"Got it." She looked down at her hands in her lap. "I just want to back you up. You know, just in case."

I softened my tone. "I know. I appreciate it. You're a good friend."

We pulled up on campus a few minutes later and walked over to the campus bookstore. There he was, sitting behind the desk at the front. I walked up to him. "Do you have a moment to talk?"

Tristan called back to a co-worker stocking a display with graduation caps and gowns in the back, who came up to relieve him. We walked out front to a bench and sat down. Katrina was sitting on a brick wall surrounding a garden nearby.

I handed him the gift bag.

"I just got home and opened your present. I really can't accept this. It's too much. We just met a few weeks ago."

He moved his hand toward mine to touch it, and I pulled it back involuntarily, sliding back on the bench. He stopped and held his hand in the air awkwardly. "No really. I want you to have it. It belongs to you."

"What does that even mean... Evermore?"

He looked me straight in the eye, the intention behind his eyes overtaking me. "My affection for you will grow evermore."

My own feelings for him were overwhelming me as well. My heart and soul... my very body... were being sucked inexorably into his void. But at the same time, I felt like I was being torn apart by equal parts revulsion, anger, and fear pulling me back from the edge. If I looked at him much longer, I felt like I would fall into his eyes, never to be seen again.

I tore my eyes away from him and looked down at the

ground. "But you don't even know me."

I heard him mumble, "I've always known you." I fought to ignore the creepiness and absolute absurdity of that statement.

"You talk about affection. Affection for what, exactly? My pretty face? Because that's as deep as our connection goes at this point. We've never had a real conversation. You know my nickname and now my real name because of my friend... not because I had the occasion to tell you. And to be honest, that's as deep as our connection *is going* to go. I'm not interested in a relationship with you."

Anger flashed across his face.

"Or anyone else," I hastily added. "I'm too busy with school and working toward a career. It's not you. I don't even know anything about you. I'm not trying to hurt your feelings here."

He picked up a rock from the gravel garden beside us and hurled it at the trash can, denting it. "Yet, here you are doing it again. Like you always do. Love hurts, right?"

He jumped up and stormed off, mumbling as he walked away. Katrina ran over to my side, blocking him from my view.

"Are you okay? That looked really tense."

"Yes. No, not really," I started sobbing. She sat down beside me and wrapped her arms around me. "Did you hear what he said as he walked away?"

"No. Why?"

"It might sound crazy, but I'm positive he said, 'I'm going to make you feel the pain you've caused me.'"

Sharon Marie and Stephen H. Provost

Seraphina

A Turn for the Worse

When I thought things couldn't worse, life proved me wrong. Most of my friends thought I was an asshole for the way I'd treated Tristan. Brittany said she understood and agreed with my decision to return the gift, but I still felt a rift in our previously "close as sisters" relationship.

My professors were piling on the homework and final projects as we neared the end of the semester. When I wasn't studying for my MCATs, I was preparing for finals. Then, if I found a free moment, I was running around to get letters of recommendation—all while writing and rewriting essays to go with my applications. To say I was stressed was an understatement.

I'd been through counseling, and had, over the years, learned to deal more effectively with my natural tendency toward anxiety. But those coping methods were starting to fail.

It had all started when I'd begun having night terrors as a small child, waking up screaming and desperately trying to pry invisible fingers from my throat.

My parents had taken me to a psychologist for an assessment, afraid that I was emotionally damaged. The therapist, who dismissed it, chalked it up to me seeing an inappropriate image from a horror movie.

I hadn't.

Those early traumatic nightmares had developed into paralyzing fears that controlled my life. Any foreign sensation near my throat made me feel that same paranoia about not being able to breathe. In my preteen years, it had spiraled to the point where I had to seek formal counseling after all.

I refused to wear turtlenecks, sweaters, scarfs, or necklaces—especially chokers. I was always careful to chew each bite of food 15 to 30 times so I wouldn't choke. A sore throat could send me spiraling down Alice's rabbit hole, wondering if I'd been strangled during the night. I began sleeping on my side with my arms pressed to my chest and my hands crisscrossed against my throat.

I developed agoraphobia, making me fearful of strange places where I might become trapped. That morphed into enochlophobia, a fear of crowds. I didn't know who I could trust. I feared there'd be a panic, and I'd get crushed and suffocated by the masses.

It had taken a lot of therapy until I was 15 to relieve me of my phobias and most of that anxiety. After all that, my parents had sheltered me from everything—until I was nearly 16 and finally demanded some freedom. Today, I still didn't like anything around my neck, but it didn't cause me the cascade of anxiety it once did. I'd never grown out of sleeping in that strange position. But at least I no longer found myself adopting that pose in other situations that caused me anxiety.

I hadn't had a strangulation nightmare for over five years, but they'd returned with a vengeance since the night of Anthony's party—at first just intermittently, but nightly since I'd returned the gift.

Since I began seeing Tristan everywhere every single day.

It seemed I couldn't avoid him, no matter how hard I tried.

Tristan began to frequent the school gym, even though he never had before. I paid to go to a private gym, and then he showed up there. He shopped at the same market I had used since moving into our apartment near campus. We began to run into him on our Friday pizza nights at Me-n-Ed's.

If I was alone, he would follow me. If I was with friends, he was careful to act as if he'd never even noticed me. At first, I tried to tell people, but they began to accuse *me* of stalking Tristan. They said how convenient it was that I always noticed Tristan and wanted to roust him when he was just minding his own business. Only Katrina believed me.

The semester was almost over—there were only two days left in final exam week, I'd taken my MCATs, and I felt confident in my performance overall. I just had to wait 30 to 35 days for the results to come in. The situation with my friends had been resolved when I shoved down my feelings and hid my fears.

I would be spending the first month of summer alone at my parents' house. They were going on a whirlwind tour of Europe—just like they had in college—only this time in five-star hotels with fine dining. I wasn't worried about being lonely because I'd be busy filling out and sending in medical school applications. In fact, I was looking forward to some alone time.

Katrina knew how hard the last few months had been for me. She kept offering to come stay with me, but I knew she had plans to travel with her boyfriend. I told her that I would keep in contact and let her know if I needed anything.

I could tell she was worried about my emotional health. I'd opened up to her about my struggles when I was younger. She knew how often I was having the nightmares because I'd woken her up screaming or gasping for breath more than once. She kept trying to convince me that I wasn't crazy, and there was more to my fears about Tristan and the corresponding return of my nightmares.

The conversation started up again Thursday, when neither one of us had a final.

"Seraphina, will you do me a favor?"

"Maybe. I'm not agreeing without knowing what."

"Please go see this psychic that my grandmother knows. See what she has to say. Then tell her about your fears and your experiences with Tristan. I really think she can help shed some light on this situation."

"I don't know, Katrina. I don't really believe in that kind of stuff."

"I know you don't. I'm not sure that I do either. But my great-grandmother is Romani. She came from the Old Country as a little girl, but she grew up believing in 'fortune telling.' It can't hurt, right? I'll even pay if you want. I just want to see if there is anything she might say that can help you. I'm worried."

"Are you going to drop all this if I do?"

"Fine. I'll do it."

"Great. We have an appointment in an hour and a half. Let's

go get lunch first."

"Sneaky girl! If I didn't trust you…"

"Then you'd have no one you did trust."

"True."

The shop wasn't as over-the-top ridiculous as I'd feared. There was no sign shaped like an open palm with an eye in the center. No table covered in a red tablecloth with a crystal ball in the center. It was just a plain building with modern décor and the word "Psychic" on the door.

The woman who greeted us was dressed in a chic pantsuit and led us to a small room that reminded me of an exam room, minus all the medical equipment. Two comfy armchairs awaited us, situated in front of a desk. The woman sat down in an office chair behind it.

"Hello. My name is Lydia. So which one of you is Seraphina?"

I held up in my hand, feeling awkward, like she was taking roll in a classroom.

"Nice to meet you, Seraphina. How can I help you today?"

Before I could speak, Katrina jumped in. "I'm her best friend. I set this up for her. She's been having some issues lately with being afraid. I was hoping you could help us… just give us your impression."

"I can do that. Are you comfortable with me touching your hand?"

It felt silly, but I agreed. I laid my arm out on the desk. She placed my hand in her open palm and placed her other hand on top, closing her eyes. Katrina and I both sat there silently, not sure what to expect.

After a moment, she began to speak. "As your friend said, I am sensing some very deep fear. Fear for your life."

Her eyes shot open and flew up to mine, fixing me with her gaze. "I feel surrounded... like I can't move... I can't even breathe. There is a great pressure on my chest as my lungs scream for air." Lydia's hand moved to her throat as she spoke. "Is that right?"

I nodded solemnly. I didn't know if I could speak. Her expression showed she knew exactly what I had been feeling.

"There is someone... a man in your life... he is the one making you afraid. I feel a strong bond to this man. Were you engaged to him before?"

"No. Never! We've never even dated."

"That's puzzling. I'm not sure why, but I definitely feel a connection between the two of you—and it is not one-sided. There is great love, but there is also immense anger. This man is a danger to you. You need to stay away from him."

I pulled my hand free and started to stand up. What she'd said rang true... reflecting the feelings I'd felt for him all along. I couldn't stand to hear any more. "Enough! That's more than enough to convince me. Thank you very much for your help."

Katrina grabbed my hand. "Wait."

Lydia's eyes pleaded with me. "I really think we should explore this more. There's more to this story. I just can't quite see it yet. There are other things I can try that might help me explain what is going on. Please sit down."

"No. I really must be going. You've been a lot of help."

"If it's a matter of money, I won't even charge you, Miss. This could be a matter of life and death."

"It is. It's time I go live my life and quit letting him control me. He's lived rent-free in my head long enough. I'll be fine. I'll be very careful." The need to flee was impossible to ignore. I felt like we were coming terrifyingly close to a revelation that might send me back down a rabbit hole from which I might never emerge.

Evermore

I ran out the front door and halfway down the block before I slowed down. I heard Kat yelling for me to stop, but I couldn't. I couldn't breathe, but I couldn't stop running from this real-life nightmare. I felt her grab my wrist and pull me to a stop. I turned around and fell into her arms, sobbing.

When we returned home, I went to bed early. Katrina begged me to eat, but I had no appetite. My sleep was plagued with the same nightmares, only it was Tristan's fingers wrapped around my neck, tighter and tighter, until I heard bones snap.

The next morning, I arose exhausted, with dark circles under my eyes. My last final exam was set for later in the day. I had felt prepared before, but my thoughts had become jumbled.

I walked into Human Anatomy II, running the names of all the bones in the body through my head. I felt as confident as one could, given the situation. The hour and a half passed quickly, but I finished the exam without any major hiccups.

I was lost in my thoughts as relief flooded through me. I was done. Everything was going to be okay. I would start packing tomorrow, and I'd be in the safety of my old bedroom by Saturday night, at the latest. Everyone else was headed toward the parking lot to go celebrate at The Wild Blue or the frat houses.

My head was down as I turned down the hallway headed toward the counselor's office. I wanted Miss Collins to take one more look at my essay before I started submitting it with my applications. I never even saw *him* standing in the shadows between the hedges.

One minute, my thoughts were on my essay, and the next my head was bouncing off the wall. He grabbed me by my shoulders, spinning me around and pinning me against it. His hands wrapped around my throat without applying any pressure—an unvoiced threat—as he brought his head down to my eye level.

He was nearly boiling over with rage. I could tell he wanted to do more than just threaten me. His fingers thrummed with the desire to throttle me. It was like I could read his thoughts: He wanted to be covered in my blood as he squeezed every last breath from my limp body.

Love should never be expressed with the venom behind the words he spat at me.

"You are mine... always have been... always shall be... evermore."

With that, he turned and walked away. I fell to the ground in a heap, sobbing soundlessly as I fought to breathe.

Seraphina

Love Hurts

The first week at my parents' house brought me the kind of peace I hadn't felt in months. No more hiding—hiding from Tristan, or hiding my real thoughts and fears from everyone who doubted me.

I could just be me. The fearful, nerdy girl who loved her independence and solitude. The one who could get lost in books for hours. The one who enjoyed the adrenaline rush of a good jump scare in a horror movie or a thrill ride, but in reality, just wanted a serene, quiet life.

I was an hour away from campus. No one knew where my family lived, not even my roommates. I felt truly safe because there was no way he could find me.

I was hoping an entire summer of not seeing me would kill this obsession he had developed. Everyone knew long-distance relationships didn't work, because absence did *not* make the heart grow fonder... at least I hoped it didn't. It certainly hadn't with my high school romance or for countless other people I had talked to at school.

The old Roxy Theatre in town was having a movie marathon of old black-and-white tearjerker movies... *Casablanca*, *It's a Wonderful Life*, and *Camille*. I called Katrina to check in and then headed out. To my relief, she reported that no one had seen Tristan hanging around lately, in town or on campus.

I loaded up on movie snacks and spent an enjoyable afternoon watching some classic romantic flicks. When I returned home, the house was dark and quiet. As I crossed the living room, I stubbed my toe hard on the end table. I turned the knob on the lamp, but it didn't come on.

Cursing my forgetfulness for not having left a light on, the way I usually did, I held my hands out in front of me as I took slow steps toward the kitchen. As I reached for the switch, I heard a soft noise behind me. I turned to peer into the dark, thinking I might have knocked something down.

I had come home blissfully happy and relaxed, but everything changed. As I turned around, the hairs on my arms stood at attention. I felt like I was no longer alone. I felt eyes on me, watching my every move.

They were just waiting for me.

My heart began to race as I pondered my next step.

I couldn't see a damn thing. Ominous shadows drifted around the room: the kind enhanced by fear. But they all seemed to be cast by items I knew belonged there. I heard no sound but my own ragged breathing.

What is wrong with you, Seraphina? No one's here. Tristan couldn't have found you.

I questioned why my paranoia had been so easily triggered. I wondered how I would ever get past this trauma and return to school in the fall. As I focused on breathing deeply, in through my nose and out my mouth, I suddenly heard the slow, steady beat of a bleak love song I knew so well, lightened only by the dulcet tones of the Everly Brothers' vocals: "Love Hurts."

NO! NO! FUCKING NO!

I whirled back toward the kitchen, diving for the light switch. As my hand flicked it up, I felt him tackle me from behind. I crashed to the floor on my stomach, the wind knocked out of me. The weight of his body was crushing me.

My mouth gaped open trying to convince my body to draw in a breath.

I felt dizzy.

My vision darkened...

I woke a short time later on my back. Tristan was straddling my waist and looking down at me, a wicked smile on his face.

"Hey there, dollface! You look surprised to see me."

I nodded.

"Cat got your tongue? I thought you were going to sleep the night away, but we have too much to do for that."

My mind spun, grasping for a way of escape. At the moment, he had the upper hand.

"I can see you thinking, my clever dear. I highly suggest you don't try anything. There's really no use because it ends the same way every time. And to be honest, I've grown quite tired of that. My feelings matter too. It's not going to be quite so easy for you this time. One thing I can guarantee—the more you struggle, the angrier you'll make me, the more I will hurt you."

As I listened to him and the music continued to play in the background, I knew he had chosen this song for a reason. His insane love for me hurt him, and he was going to scar, wound, and mark me. There was going to be pain in abundance.

"Get up!" Tristan grabbed both of my wrists in his large hands and pulled me up as he stood. Once I was standing, he pulled my arms behind my back and looped his arm through, pulling me tightly against him. He pulled a butterfly knife out of his pocket and flipped it open with practiced ease. The tip of the blade was pressed against my side as he led me through the house and up the stairs to my room.

He pushed me down onto the bed and began to rip off my clothes.

I found my voice again. I fought back tears as I begged him, "Please don't do this, Tristan. I'm sorry. I didn't mean to hurt you."

"Don't even start with me. I heard you talking to your friends. I know you're not some bastion of virtue. You've spread your legs for others. It's time I have what belongs to me."

My anger flared. "You were there! You made everyone think I was crazy. That I'd imagined you."

He laughed cruelly. "That I did. I was always there. Even when you didn't realize I was. Watching you sleep at night, having those awful nightmares."

"You're a monster!"

"Enough talking." He undressed quickly and climbed on top of me. As he thrust himself inside me, he wrapped his hands around my throat. He squeezed harder and harder with each rough thrust—grunting and moaning with pleasure at my pain. Tears streamed from eyes, and my lungs ached for air. Droplets of spit sprayed on my face as he laughed. My body was covered in his sweat.

After what felt like an eternity, my vision began to fade to black as I lost consciousness.

Some time later, I awoke again to find his mouth wrapped around mine, breathing air into my lungs. I coughed and tried to push him away.

"There you are! I brought you back again. Couldn't let you leave quite yet."

"Bastard!!"

"What? Would you rather I'd just left you dead?"

"No! Just leave! You got what you wanted."

"No, I haven't. Not by a long shot. You are mine for eternity. You always have been. If you'd just come to me, we could have been so happy. You made this choice."

"You're sick."

"I suppose you would see it that way. But I don't care what you think. You lost that right lifetimes ago."

This man was utterly insane. Or maybe we both were.

The way he kept referring to me "always being his" or "lifetimes ago" made no sense, yet it struck me as right. How could that be? But I had to put those thoughts out of my head. It was not the time to think of such things.

His hands were roaming around my body again—at one moment soft and tender, almost loving—only to become brutal as he used his fists to punch me all over. I could feel that he truly thought I was his to use as he saw fit. And that is just what he did.

I was left with only foggy memories of what happened next as he raped me and strangled me to death, only to resuscitate me, to begin the cycle again. How long before he wouldn't be able to bring me back again? How long before he crushed my windpipe?

My throat ached, and I could barely stand to swallow.

Breathing was getting more and more difficult as the delicate tissues began to swell. I ached everywhere and was so exhausted that I couldn't find the energy to fight him.

As dawn began to break, I noticed a change in his behavior. He seemed to be getting ready to leave. But I could sense that he didn't intend for me to do the same. At that moment, I remembered that I had one possible way to effect my escape.

Thank God for this one instance of paranoid planning!

He walked over to his pile of clothes and began to dig through it. While his back was turned, I leaned over and slid open the drawer on my bedside table. I pulled out the knife I'd stashed there the day I had arrived home. I tucked it under my pillow quickly because he was turning back, his own knife in hand.

He sat down on the bed beside me. He brushed the hair back on my forehead. "This could have been something special, Seraphina. My fiery little angel!"

I saw him bringing his other arm, holding the knife, from behind his back. It was now or never. I reached up and yanked the knife out from under the pillow. It got caught on the headboard for just a second—removing the element of surprise—giving him a moment to lunge forward and plunge his blade into my chest.

He pulled the knife out, just as I freed mine, and I sliced deeply into his arm. He cried out and lurched backward, giving me the opportunity to lean over and grab the lamp off my nightstand. I'd begun to have trouble breathing as my lung collapsed.

I swung the lamp with all the strength left in my body. This was my only chance at survival. He fell to the ground, dazed but not unconscious. My own fortitude and the adrenaline coursing through my body carried me out of the room and down the stairs. I threw open the front door and ran for my life down the center of the street, headed for my neighbor half a mile away.

My own heartbeat thundering in my ears kept me from hearing whether he was following me. I couldn't risk focusing on that and losing any ground I had gained. I just ran until I reached the Johnsons' door and began beating on it.

The last thing I saw was Mrs. Johnson's worried face in the crack; then I slumped against the door and lost consciousness.

I didn't reawaken until the next day at the hospital. The police had called my parents, and they were on the way home from their vacation.

I spent nearly a week in the hospital, recovering from my wounds. They'd nearly had to intubate me because of the extensive damage to my throat—including a crushed larynx.

The police assured me I had nothing to worry about. They said it'd only be a matter of time before they caught him. In the meantime, they felt sure he wouldn't dare come anywhere near me. But I didn't believe them. I knew I'd never be safe. One or the other of us would have to die before this would end. I knew that I needed more information to deal with this problem.

There was only one place I could go for that.

Katrina had arrived in town before my parents returned from Europe and started babysitting me like I was a small child. I hated losing my independence. Kat wouldn't let me out of her sight either. Luckily, she was the only one my parents trusted to watch over me—other than themselves. I knew they'd never understand what I needed to do.

A week after my release from the hospital, I had Kat

take me back to see Lydia, the psychic. Lydia's eyes widened when she saw me. There were still prominent bruises around my throat. I was weak and looked like I had been through a war.

I had.

Lydia grabbed my hand tenderly and led me back to the consultation room.

"Dear girl, I'm so glad to see you alive. I knew you were in terrible danger. I'm afraid the danger has not passed, but I think you already know that. Is that why you're here? Will you let me help you?"

I broke down into racking sobs. Katrina wrapped me in her arms and rubbed my back. "Please help me," I whispered hoarsely. "I'm sorry it's so hard to hear me."

Lydia's stoic face melted, and I saw her eyes well up for just a second. "Don't you apologize for anything. Of course I'll help you, dear. I will do whatever I can. Are you ready to start?"

"What do we need to do?" Katrina asked, a grave look on her face. "I'll pay whatever it takes."

"Nothing. As I said before, I just want to help. I think you should start by telling me how all this started. Spare no details, no matter how small, trivial, or silly. I assure you everything matters in cases like these."

I nodded.

She interjected again before I began: "I understand now why I felt such an oppressive sense of pressure, and I couldn't breathe." Her eyes flicked briefly toward the bruises on my neck.

A tear ran down my face. Lydia smiled and gave my hand a squeeze. I took a deep breath and began my story. It took nearly an hour to tell her everything that had happened over the past three months.

Had it only been three months? It'd felt like years... an

eternity.

I even told her how I'd always felt a connection to him. How that feeling grew stronger every time he mentioned me always belonging to him. How when he said those things was nearly the only time I felt he was telling me the truth.

She nodded and didn't seem surprised. I had been worried that she would laugh at me. Instead, she grabbed my hands in hers as she said, "That's just as I suspected, dear. Remember, I sensed it when you were here before. In fact, I think that's what made you run out of my office. You weren't ready to hear it."

I nodded again, too scared to look her in the eye.

"We need to investigate this connection more. We have a couple of ways of doing that. I have a theory about what's going on. I don't know if I can find a way to stop it, but I can give you the most important tool in your arsenal. Knowledge is power, Seraphina. If anyone can figure this out, it will be a fiery, intelligent girl like you."

I smiled for the first time in weeks. "What's first?"

"Let's go for knowledge first. Then we'll go to the hocus-pocus mumbo jumbo."

I tried not to laugh, but I couldn't hold it back.

"I know what people think about what I do. I could see your reluctance to come in here the first time. You may doubt the next part, but it could be important. Even I don't know yet what I'll see. Now, I need you to go lie on the couch over there and get comfortable. I'm going to hypnotize you and lead you back."

"Back to what? I don't want to relive the events of the past few months."

"I want to do what is called a past-life regression. You feel like an old soul to me, one that's been around before... repeatedly. If I'm right, it will explain a lot."

Lydia began to speak to me in a soothing voice, with the sound of a metronome ticking slowly in the background. She had me picture a time and place in my life where I felt the safest and happiest. She then asked me to picture an impenetrable dome surrounding that location so that no one could get in. After I was done, she told me to take a seat and turn on a television inside my safe place. The television would broadcast stories for me to see.

At that point, she reminded me that Tristan couldn't hurt me before asking me to picture him. She told me to follow my feelings of love and connection with him to see where they led.

I began to see Tristan and myself—I'm not sure how I knew it was us because we looked so different—living in a variety of times and places. Some were immediately recognizable, and others not so much. Each time we had this unbreakable bond... an immense love for each other... but circumstances always got in the way. Tristan became more broken and bitter each time. I could see the anger building up until he'd completely lost his mind, becoming consumed with the idea of causing me a painful death. It was terrifying and heartbreaking at the same time.

I could feel myself lying there, but it felt like I was watching it from a distance. I was crying because I felt so bad for him... and for myself. But the one thing I could feel above all else was the hopelessness of the situation. There was no fixing him. There was no making our love go right. It was too far past that point. I feared there was only one solution, but I couldn't go there... yet.

Lydia snapped her fingers, and I awoke with tears streaming down my face. I remembered every detail. I'd been Teagan, Dot, and a slew of other women, and all of us had died at his hands. Katrina came and sat beside me, holding me in a bear hug as I sat up.

"I don't want you to blame yourself, Seraphina. You need to

understand this. I'm sure you've heard that some people believe that with reincarnation, if you relive the same experience over and over, it's because you didn't learn a lesson you needed to before moving on. I think that's crap. In case you had any doubts, I don't subscribe to any one particular religion or accept any of their texts verbatim. I don't think it's that simple."

"Okay."

"I'm sure you've heard of soulmates. I do believe that sometimes certain people are born with a soulmate. You might have heard of them referred to as twin flames or intertwining souls... the proverbial other half. I think that one is the best description. Just like cells divide, I think sometimes souls can be cleaved—how, I don't know—so those two halves of the soul will follow each other throughout time... through all incarnations until one day they—or should I say it?—cease to be. Am I making any sense at all?"

It sounded crazy to me on the one hand, but on the other, it sounded exactly right. I nodded and waved for her to continue.

"Those two souls are not always lovers, but they will always be close. They could be mother and child, brother and sister— frequently identical twins, or even best friends, but most often they are lovers. I think most, if not all, the great romances you've heard about throughout history have been soulmates."

"Then why would it go so bad? Why would our connection be just as absolute, but so dark and horrifying?"

"That's not as clear, but once again, I think it comes down to simple biology. Do cells always divide or replicate perfectly? Of course not. Incompletely divided cells result in conjoined twins. Unchecked cell replication is cancer. Nature is not absolute or perfect. As your parents probably told you as a child, bad things happen. I think that's what happened here. There's a flaw. A deadly imperfection. Sometimes a woman's body can sense such a flaw during pregnancy, and her embryo is aborted. But this time, that system of checks and balances failed."

Katrina elbowed me playfully in the side, a little too hard. "Why didn't you think of that, Miss Pre-med?"

I winced.

"Sorry, Sera."

I chuckled softly, wincing again. "You've got a point, but I never knew any of this was possible."

"Don't feel bad. Most people don't believe in this stuff at all. I'm glad you have an open mind." Lydia patted my hand.

"Are you ready for the last part? I don't know if this will be helpful, but I need to look."

"I'm a little scared. What do you mean exactly?"

"I want to look at your lifeline. My granny, an old Romani woman, taught me to look at your dominant hand. Please give me your dominant hand, palm up."

I looked over at Kat and raised my eyebrows.

"Okay, you got me. Lydia is my aunt. I didn't want you to doubt what she said because we are related."

"I don't. I trust you," I turned my head to Lydia and met her eyes. "Both of you."

I laid my right hand in Lydia's outstretched hand. She frowned and stared long and hard at my hand. I began to worry. What did she see? Was I going to die?

"First, you need to know that your lifeline shows both your past and your future. Yours is very interesting. I've only seen this once before. Granny told me that it is extremely rare and special. I can't give you a good picture of the future. I don't want you to fret though. This is neither definitively good nor bad news, but it could be promising. It means your future is not determined at this point, which, most importantly, means you may be able to help determine where it goes."

"I don't understand."

"See this line here... that's your lifeline. Give me your hand, Katrina." Katrina laid her hand on top of mine. "See hers... see how it is long, curved and unbroken? You can clearly follow the path from beginning to end."

Katrina removed her hand.

"Now look at yours. It starts out and then stops after a short distance, and then picks up again, only to end once more. That repeats over and over. That shows exactly what you described. You have lived many lives... each time for only a short span of time... never reaching middle age."

"I see that. But how does that affect my future?"

"The exact length of your lifeline cannot be determined. Do you see how there is a blemish or scar on your hand? That patch of unnaturally smooth skin where your lifeline and skin ridges just seem to disappear from sight? That lifeline is in there somewhere, but its length and whether there are any interruptions can't be seen the way they can at the beginning. Your ultimate destiny is not determined yet. This knowledge can give you the power to help set its course, one way or the other."

I smiled. Hope was bubbling for the first time since Tristan attacked me.

I knew just what I had to do. I needed to go somewhere safe far away. Hopefully I would be able to hide from him for the rest of my life, and maybe that would break our vicious cycle. In the meantime, though, I would devise a Plan B. I hoped I could come up with some other way to stop him. I couldn't keep being viciously murdered, over and over again. It would drive me insane, just like him.

A month and a half later, just as I was getting settled into my new surroundings, I had an unexpected visitor. My period didn't come on time, but a positive pregnancy test did.

Aiden... 10 years later

Not Again

Life in a small highland village near Loch Ness, Scotland, was everything I knew it would be. I'd always dreamed of visiting one day, but I never imagined that I would come to live there.

But necessity is the proverbial mother of invention. I needed to find someplace to live that I'd never been associated with. Since my life hadn't gone the way I planned, I had to find happiness in whatever way I could.

There was one source of unending joy that I couldn't imagine living without, and that was my beautiful daughter, Bridget. She was my strength. I'd always wanted to be a mother. I'd never imagined that motherhood would come out of such adversity. I'd had so many other plans for my life at that time, but I wouldn't have changed a thing when it came to her.

After my visit with Lydia, I'd returned home and told

my parents that I had to leave. My issues as a child had turned them into overprotective helicopter parents. It hadn't been easy to assert my independence at 16, and I knew it would be even harder, now that I'd almost been killed. But I had to make them understand.

Tristan's vanishing act reassured them at first that all might be well. But with time, I convinced them that he was just lying in wait until the right moment—when I was vulnerable. In the end, my safety was all that mattered to them. I was fortunate that my family was well off, so they were able to fund my disappearance as I established a new life.

At first, I didn't know where to go to be safe. But then I eventually realized the location itself wasn't as important as anonymity. I would travel far away and, during that journey, I would erase every trace of Seraphina.

First, I flew to Madrid, Spain, where I stayed in a small hostel, registered under the name of Sally. Changing my name was just the first step toward giving up everything that made me *me*... my entire identity. I wanted to be completely unrecognizable.

I spent the next day changing my appearance. I dyed my hair cocoa brown and began to grow it out. No longer would I have the shoulder-length golden curls I'd so loved since I was a teenager.

I dressed in jeans and a plain-colored T-shirts, rather than the chic, sleeveless sheath dresses of the past. I had never been one to dress sexy, but I did like the way those dresses tastefully flattered my figure, allowing me to transition from a day at the medical office to a night on the town.

Evermore

Over the next several weeks, I traveled across Europe on the Eurail, exploring as I tried to recover both mentally and physically. I had to figure out a long-term plan for my life. I knew part of hiding meant I wouldn't be able to pursue the career that I'd wanted since I was 5 and playing doctor with a toy stethoscope. But what would I do instead?

Everything changed one day when I realized that I'd need to find a place to settle down as quickly as possible and decide what I would do there. I'd been vomiting for two weeks; it was difficult to eat in the morning, and some foods sent me running away. I felt tired all the time.

It was only when I looked at the calendar that I realized just how late my period was. My heart dropped. It wasn't possible.

Please tell me I'm not carrying that monster's child.

I stopped at a drugstore to grab a pregnancy test, and before long, my worst fears were confirmed. Over the next few days, I locked myself in my room, lost in a tumultuous sea of emotions. My first instinct was to end the pregnancy. I didn't know how I could ever love a child that had come from such a violent, hate-filled act.

But at the same time, I was torn. It was not the child's fault, and I'd always felt children were a blessing. I'd always intended to be a mother. Not this young and not alone, but I didn't know if I ever could or would trust a man after all that had happened.

This might be my only chance.

Then there was a memory... one from long ago... one that was not even truly *my* memory but belonged to Alba. She'd had a conversation with The Falcon about how he had been reincarnated many times, and he was cursed with remembering all of them. He'd told her that his son with Vivian bore the same "gift."

The Falcon had then told Alba—or I guess it was really me —that this son was Angus, or should I say Tristan. Did that mean my child would bear the same "gift" as his father? Would he or she have the same capacity for indifference to the suffering of others as The Falcon and Tristan did?

After days of soul searching, I knew what I had to do. I couldn't hold my child's father against him or her. I couldn't worry that my child would be evil. It was simply impossible. My child would grow up knowing only love and having compassion for all life, great or small.

Thus began the life I had lately come to know. I took a boat from the Continent to Scotland, where I fell in love with the countryside. I spent weeks traveling from one small village to the next, visiting all the old castles I'd dreamed about as a child.

When I came to the highlands around Loch Ness, I knew I was home. After some time, I found a small farm with a large barn and a tiny stone cottage that was up for sale.

That was the start of Seraphim Crofts.

With that, I became Aiden. I couldn't let go of every vestige of me... the fiery girl who had overcome so much. While Aiden was often considered a boy's name, it meant "fiery one." It seemed the perfect name for my rebirth.

I set about repairing the place as my pregnancy progressed, and it was ready in time for Bridget's birth. I started out with a small flock of sheep, whose wool I sold at the market.

Over the years, Bridget and I expanded the size of our flock significantly. We also built up a fold of about a dozen Highland cattle for our personal use, and then there were the horses I raised to ride our land and herd the livestock. With the increase in our animal population came another barn; a corral and a bullpen for training the horses; and outbuildings for our workers. We even started a garden to grow vegetables.

When Bridget was at school, I'd spend hours riding the highlands. When the wind blew through my hair, I remembered the freedom I'd once enjoyed—and now finally felt again.

I eventually began offering free riding lessons to the children in our village who didn't live on farms. I found a way to give back to this community that had welcomed us with such open arms. I'd found family and friendship in a way I never thought I'd have again.

I realized just how valuable those relationships were when Kellan, my neighbor down the road, came up to me as I returned from a ride.

"Hullo, Aiden. Everything awrite?" Kellan had a puzzled expression on his face.

"Yeah. Why do you ask, Kellan?"

"There was a tall lad looking 'round yer place this mornin'. I asked him what he be doing, and he said you's lookin' for a buyer... ya know, money troubles and all." Kellan looked down sheepishly.

I felt that familiar pang of anxiety grip my chest. I tried not to let it show, but I could hear the strain in my voice.

"What did he look like?"

"Tall fella, dark hair and eyes. He was a serious-lookin' lad, which is why I was concerned."

"Thanks for letting me know. There's nothing wrong here. I wouldn't sell this place for all the money in the world. I don't know who he was, but if you see him lurking around here again, please let me know."

"You can be sure of that, lassie. I'm glad to hear everything's fine. We'd miss you around here."

As soon as I was alone, I began spiraling downward into a dark and scary place. My breath caught in my chest. That same familiar feeling of being choked or suffocated.

It had to be him. Who else could it have been but Tristan? Kellan had described him to a T.

Over the years, I'd dreaded this moment and imagined what I'd do if he ever showed up again. How I'd stop this once and for all. I'd racked my brain, going over everything I knew from all my lifetimes. Finally, when Bridget had just turned 2, I'd figured it out. It might have been a longshot, but I knew I had to try. There was only one choice. If I died again, this hellish cycle would just keep repeating itself. And what would become of my precious Bridget?

Only death would stop this nightmare... his death.

Aiden

This Has to End

There was no way I was going to let Tristan win. I had too much to live for. I had to be there to raise *my* daughter—he had no place in her life. My plan was already in place. I just had to make a couple of quick arrangements to set it in motion.

I couldn't imagine how Tristan had found us, but part of me knew that, with the whole soulmate thing, it had been unavoidable. I hoped that he didn't know about Bridget, or at least not that she was *his* daughter. Either way, I had to get her out of here until this was over. I knew Tristan would come for me first either way, and I didn't think I had long to wait.

I mounted my swiftest horse, Starfire, and rode

through the fields until I reached Margaret's house on the other side of the village. I knew I could trust Maggie to care for Bridget. I'd never explained the whole story to her, but she knew I'd had a stalker—who was also Bridget's father. I told her I was pretty sure he'd found me and asked her to pick Bridget up at school and keep her for the night.

I told her that, if I didn't pick Bridget up by 9 the next morning, she should call the police.

After leaving Margaret's place, I stopped in the village to pick up a few supplies. I hadn't felt that sensation of being watched yet, so I knew he must be laying low somewhere, probably waiting for darkness to fall before attacking. I used a payphone to call Kellan and ask if he'd seen the man return.

He hadn't.

I rode back home, and when I got there, I had my farmworkers feed the livestock and secure them for the night so they could head home early. As the afternoon wore on, I began to sense his presence. I could tell he was nearby, keeping an eye on me.

After I bid goodbye to Lachlan, my livestock foreman, I entered my cottage, making sure to bolt the doors and windows and close the drapes. I only left the window in my bedroom open a crack. I'd developed a chill that I just couldn't shake, so I stoked the fire in my hearth.

I knew he would have the upper hand. He was stronger than I was and sustained by a rage that had burned for centuries. But he didn't realize he was coming up against a momma bear with an iron will to survive, born of pain and love.

Still, there was no room for error.

Evermore

As the sun began to set, I made sure that I had everything in place. I'd turned on the lights in the living room and dining area. I settled myself in the dark corner of the back bedroom just under the window. I felt confident that would be his point of entry.

Thankfully, he didn't disappoint me. It was about 11 p.m., and I had started to doze off when I heard the crunch of gravel under my window. I stood carefully and pressed myself into the dark corner, arm raised.

I held my breath as I saw him slip through the window and drop stealthily to the floor. He stopped and listened to the sounds of the house. I had left the television on, with the volume low, in the living room. When he felt confident of my location, he took a step forward.

At that moment, I pressed the play button on the stereo remote in my pocket, starting the CD player. The haunting tune to *our* song began to play. "Love hurts..." I saw his body tense in the millisecond before he realized, too late, that he had walked into a trap. At that moment, I lunged forward, bringing a large cast iron pan down on his head with all my strength.

He dropped to the ground in a heap.

I couldn't take a chance that I hadn't knocked him out, so I pulled the syringe from my pocket.

Years ago, when the local vet had come out to examine my sheep, I'd stolen one of his vials of ketamine. All this time, it had been locked in the metal lockbox mounted in my closet—where I also stored my gun—for just such an occasion.

I jammed the syringe into his neck and gave him a

walloping dose of ketamine. I couldn't have him waking up before I was ready for him. I had such surprises in store for him.

I dragged his body down the hall and out into my living room. I began by tying his hands together, then his feet. I'd learned a lot running a farm for ten years. Like how to tie knots that couldn't be loosened.

I'd also built up some muscles of my own, which I used to hoist his body onto one of the work tables I'd had Lachlan bring from the barn in before he left. I tied his body down to the table across his knees, waist, chest, and his throat—*just* tight enough to make breathing feel more difficult. I wrapped a bandana around his mouth and tied it tight, gagging him. I couldn't have him caterwauling too loud and drawing the neighbors' attention.

He still hadn't woken up, and it was time to get this party started. I walked over to the hearth and picked up a special gift... just for him.

It was red hot. "Wakey, wakey," I called out in a sing-song voice as I pressed my branding iron against the skin of his forearm. He woke up, his muffled scream of agony music to my ears. His skin sizzled and smoked as my personalized livestock brand burned into his skin. The blacksmith in town had created it just for me... a stylized "S" (for Seraphina) made to look like a lightning bolt.

When I pulled it away, his angry, red skin was blistered and raised. "Welcome to Seraphim Crofts, Tristan."

I couldn't understand his irate mumbling. I pulled down the gag. "What was that, dear?"

"You fucking bitch! I am going to make you pay. You

and that little bitch of yours. You're going to feel so much pain that you'll beg for me to kill you. You'll come find me next time just to make it end faster."

But I had the upper hand this time. He wasn't going to get away. Neither I nor Bridget would be dying tonight.

"You won't be setting one finger on our daughter."

The startled expression on his face brought me the satisfaction I had been looking for, but then it turned to horror."

"You have to let me kill her. I can't let her survive. She'll be just like me and the Falcon, cursed to live time after time, remembering every painful mistake. Desperate to make things different, but going mad when she realizes it never stops."

"She's nothing like you, and she never will be. She's been raised with love. She has the kind of compassion for others that you could never come close to fathoming. Even if she shares your curse, as you call it, she'll recognize it and see it as a gift.

"Those who don't learn from history are doomed to repeat the same mistakes. The way *you* have. But unlike you, she will use that knowledge wisely. Our daughter is remarkable, and very intelligent. She will learn from her own mistakes and those of others. She will make the world better."

He shook his head no, a mocking sneer on his face.

"By the way," I said, "I'm so glad that you mentioned the Falcon. You see, I remember him too. I remember all of it. Every time we have been together. I have your gift as well. And I'm going to use it to eradicate one evil from this Earth: *you!*"

He started laughing, shaking his head in disbelief.

"You see, my pal The Falcon... your dear old dad..."

"Stupid bitch! He wasn't my father."

"Oh, you didn't know that part, did you? It seems he told me a lot more than he told you. I know things that you don't know. Important things."

I couldn't help mocking him. I'd turned the song on repeat. It ended and began again as I continued speaking.

"The Falcon told me about the gift you share. He met the love of his life, Vivian, and he knew he couldn't live without her. She knew he was a seer and begged him to tell her about her future, but he refused. Then, one day, in anger, she told him that she had seen *his* future, and that the life he was leading would be his last."

"You're making this up."

"I am not. I thought you should know your future. Let me finish, and you will see."

He stopped talking and turned his head away, so I resumed.

"In anger, he looked into the future and saw that he and Vivian would not stay together in that life—or in any other. That was something he couldn't handle. He vowed that the life he was living then would be his last, only realizing afterward that his wishes matched the fate she had foretold."

He turned back to look at me, unable to hide the curiosity beneath his rage. "So! Let's say I believe you. What does any of that matter now? How does it apply to us?"

"Ding, ding, ding, we have a winner! I'm so glad you asked. As I said earlier, I am gifted as well. I can and will break this cycle here... tonight... by killing you. My determination to survive and end this cycle of violence you've perpetuated against me will change our fate. It all ends here. This is our last life. Yours ends now, and mine will end years from now—after a long, happy life."

"Fuck you! You can't do that. It's not your choice to make. I'll find you again and again. I'll make it hurt more each time."

I didn't care to hear his voice any longer. He had controlled my life long enough. It was my turn to be in charge. I pulled the gag down and applied a strip of duct tape across it for good measure. The song had restarted again.

"You hear our song? I played it just for you. I see now why you picked it. Your love does hurt. You made me tough enough to defeat you. But *you* aren't strong enough to handle the truth, and you certainly can't avoid your fate. I bet you wish you hadn't been such a good teacher when it comes to inflicting pain. Love..."

I dug my finger into his freshly burned skin. "Scars!"

He screamed again and tried to pull away, but his bonds were too tight. I walked into the kitchen, where I pulled the large, heavy metal meat mallet out of the drawer and a butcher knife from the block.

I returned to the living room and set the items down on the table beside him. His eyes grew large, but he didn't make a sound. I couldn't help but laugh at his fear.

I'd been through lifetimes of terror. The past-life regression had made me experience and retain vivid memories of each one of them. If I focused on them, I could hear the sound of the hyoid bone in my throat cracking; smell his sweat as his body was pressed to mine; and feel the pain he inflicted on my body.

"You look scared, Tristan. I still remember all the times I've been scared. I remember running for my life as Dot when you pursued me in a car. And feeling you thrust the blades into me when I was Elizabeth and Seraphina."

He looked at me with a question in his eyes.

"Yes, I said my own name as if it belonged to someone else. Because I *do* feel like an entirely different person now. I still remember the crushing betrayal Emma felt when you strangled her.

"I think you've blamed me from the beginning, even back when I was Alba. But how could that possibly have been my fault? I'd been taken prisoner and forced to marry my conqueror. After my affair with Angus... you... was discovered, I was sent to languish in a convent. My heart was broken. I thought I'd never see you again. I couldn't live without you, so I took my own life."

He mumbled, so I ripped off the tape—along with some of his skin—and pulled the gag down again.

"I didn't know that's how you felt. I felt abandoned."

I cut him off. I didn't want to hear his excuses.

"That's just it. You don't know what true love is. You're selfish. You only love yourself. Part of me does love you now and always has, and that's why this has to end for both our sakes."

"That's not true."

"Shut up!" I pulled the gag back up and continued.

"Other lifetimes brought other challenges, but we could have made it work. As someone once explained to me, soulmates don't have to be lovers. We could've been an important part of each other's lives, regardless of our connection."

I grabbed the knife and held it to his throat.

"I was your sister, and I was dying from tuberculosis. I asked for your mercy. For your help to end my suffering. But you killed me in anger. I could feel your rage toward me. That wasn't love! You're a sick, twisted bastard! Love? It hurts!"

With that last statement, I grabbed the meat mallet and began to beat his lower legs. I heard loud cracks as first the fibula, then the tibia broke. A few more swings, and the skin ripped open on his left leg from the blunt-force trauma. Blood oozed from the wounds, especially on the right where a compound fracture of the tibia had torn through his shin.

"Let's not forget that it wounds!"

Bones healed with time. I couldn't have him running after me again. He needed to be handicapped. I grabbed a log from the pile in the basket next to the hearth. I untied his bound ankles and placed the log between his legs at the level of the ankle bones. It only took a minute and a few hard swings to break his ankles and feet so devastatingly that he'd never walk again. Not that I would give him that chance.`

His screams were so loud that my ears rang. I began to fear that my neighbors would be roused from their slumber, but he passed out from the pain.

I grabbed a chair and pulled it over to the table. I'd have to wait for him to reawaken. I turned off the music while I waited. I couldn't bear to hear it one more time, or ever again for that matter. I wanted him to feel the same terror that I had over and over again. The best was yet to come.

I heard him moan as he began to stir. "Hi there, Tristan.

I was beginning to think maybe I'd lost you. Tonight's the night, darling. My eternal torture will be ending soon and so will yours. But... not... quite... yet."

I had the knife in my hand, its razor-sharp point on the table. With each pause in the sentence, I was rocking the blade and walking it forward toward his abdomen. I smiled down at him as I raised it. His eyes widened as he realized what I was going to do.

"Mmmpphhhh... no... noooo!"

"I can't understand you. Could you speak a little clearer?"

I cackled at the unintelligible sounds he made.

"Hmmm. Let me think. There was one more thing about love. It'll come to me. Just give me a minute here. Oh, yes! That's it. It marks!" I screamed as I plunged the knife into his abdomen just under his breast bone.

I began to use slow, sawing motions to cut through the tissue down to his groin. The blade was more than sharp enough to slice through his skin like butter, but that wouldn't hurt enough.

Blood was pouring from his body, so I had to hurry. I couldn't have him dying before I was finished. I was glad that I'd laid out tarps underneath the table. I couldn't have Bridget finding her beautiful home covered in blood. I wouldn't have much time to clean up before dawn.

I remembered who I was each time that I'd been murdered. I'd looked up the cases that had been covered by the newspapers. I knew that the last time I had been murdered, it had been called the Black Dahlia murder. I knew exactly what he had done to me.

It was time to gut him, just as he had done to me when

I was Elizabeth. I reached into the bloody chasm of his abdomen and pulled out his intestines. Feeding the long, slippery ropes of entrails through my hands and slopping them on his chest for him to see.

The last thing he saw was the wide grin on my face as I said, "Fuck you. Game over, motherfucker!"

I hastily dismembered Tristan's body and wrapped it in the tarps I'd laid out, along with some heavy rocks to weigh him down. I used the wheelbarrow to cart his remains to my truck and drove him down to the Loch. I rowed my little boat out as far as I dared on a nearly moonless night and pushed his remains over the side. They sank into the water never to be seen again... at least not in my time.

Nearly 46 years have passed since that night in my home. In that time, I've watched Bridget grow into a beautiful young woman who got married and had children of her own. She has traveled the world over with her husband, helping those in need, just as I knew she would. She became the doctor that I had always dreamt of being.

She's never asked about who her father was. She never even asked me why I had her go stay at Auntie Maggie's that night. I've seen no hints of any psychopathic or narcissistic behavior, just as I knew I wouldn't.

And even if she is reincarnated repeatedly, I have no doubt that she will only spread more joy and goodwill throughout the world just as I told Tristan that night.

I know that I broke the curse, for me at least.

I'm not sure whether I believe in the existence of a

heaven or hell. Before that day in Lydia's office, I didn't believe in reincarnation. I only hope that, if there is a hell, Tristan is burning there for evermore.

As my breathing slows and I inch ever closer to my own death, I just wish my eyes will be closing for the last time—that I'll never open them again.

And if I do, that I'll never see him again.

Norfolk, Virginia, 2060

LIFE GOES ON

Molly

HURRY HOME

"Are you sure you can't get out of it? Don't they understand that I'm due in two weeks?"

"I'm so sorry, sweetheart. I know this is the worst possible time. Trust me! I'm not any happier about it than you are, but frankly, we need the money. And if this don't clinch that promotion we've been hoping for, nothing will." Mark raised his eyebrows as he said that last part. He knew me too well—I had been worrying about finances.

"Well, I can't argue with you about the money part. The fertility treatments cost us so much, but it's all been worth it." I rubbed my big belly, smiling. "It's finally going to happen."

Mark walked around my back and wrapped his arms nearly all the way around me. "Yes, it is, Momma," he whispered in my ear. "I promise everything will be okay. Like you said, you're not due for two more weeks. I leave early tomorrow, and I'll only be gone three days. One day of travel each way, and one day to give the presentation. This partnership and expansion into the market with Tokyo is important."

"I know. I get it. I'm a worry wart."

"Yes, you are. That's why we're the perfect pair. You do the worrying, and I'm the voice of reason."

Mark had arrived in Tokyo without incident. He called me the next morning just before he walked into the meeting, so I could wish him luck. I'd just sat down for a late dinner. I'd been feeling antsy all day—arranging and rearranging items in the nursery a dozen times it'd felt like.

"How's the little momma doing?"

"I'm doing okay, Mark," I said with a sigh.

"What's wrong, babe?"

"Nothing really. Please don't worry."

"Then why the sigh, McFly?"

"You're such a dork, you know?"

"That's why you love me. I'm serious. I have a few minutes."

"I'm just tired, I guess. And missing you. I think I'm just getting excited. I'm... what do they call it? Hmmm. Nesting! I'm nesting. I rearranged the room like fourteen times. I just hope he will like it."

"He's a baby. He isn't going to like anything except us and milk for a long time to come. When he's old enough to care what his room looks like, we'll redecorate. Deal?"

I couldn't help but laugh. He was right. I was being ridiculous.

"My husband, the genius. You are right as usual. Now I should let you go. Call me when you get back to your hotel room."

"Babe, I probably won't get done until somewhere between 3 and 5, which will be the middle of the night for you."

"I don't care. I'm so fat and uncomfortable that I don't sleep good anymore anyhow."

"Your wish is my command, darling. Have a good evening. Give slugger a rub for me."

I hung up the phone and rubbed my belly. "Daddy says goodnight, baby boy."

I finished my bowl of macaroni and cheese and curled up on the couch to watch some television.

I woke up about three hours later to an intense cramp in my belly. I felt some anxiety, but I tried to convince myself it was just Braxton Hicks. An hour later, as the cramps intensified and grew closer together, I knew I couldn't wait any longer.

I called Mark's phone, but of course, he didn't answer. I left him a message letting him know that I was going to the hospital. Then I called my friend Lisa and asked her to drive me.

My phone finally rang just after 3 a.m.

"Babe, is everything okay?" I could hear the concern in Mark's voice, but he was trying to sound calm for my sake.

"I'm fine. We're fine. Apparently, your baby boy is an impatient man, just like his Daddy."

"What do you mean?"

"He's coming. It's time."

"Oh, God! Just wait for me. First babies always take forever, right? Twenty hours of labor and shit! I already booked a flight for two hours from now, but it'll be like 18 hours or so till I get there. Can you wait?"

I groaned and gripped the bed railing as another contraction hit. When I caught my breath, I began laughing.

"What's so funny, woman?"

"You, dumbass! This isn't a reservation for dinner. I can't just call the restaurant up and move it back. I said he was impatient, and I meant it. I'm already 8 centimeters dilated. It won't be long."

"Damn it! I'm so sorry, babe. I'm such as ass."

"Relax, honey! Just travel safe and get here as soon as you can. We'll be waiting. Lisa's here with me, and everything is going fine. Textbook birth, albeit a little faster than normal."

"Hey, Mark! She's a trooper," Lisa called out from the background.

"Tell her thanks, Molly. I'm on my way. Bye! ...Wait! We haven't even settled on a name yet. We thought we had time."

"Don't worry. Not all babies are born with a name ready. We'll find the right one for him when we see him."

I had to give Mark credit: When he made a promise, he always came through. Just over eighteen hours after we'd hung up the phone, he walked through the door and into my hospital room. The nurse's aide was just helping me back into bed after a trip to the restroom, and the lactation nurse was waiting impatiently to help me learn how to get the baby to latch.

The nurse's aide eyed him warily as he approached my bed and sat down next to me. She pulled my covers up quickly and dropped them. "I've got to go." She rushed out of the room and closed the door behind her. The lactation nurse shook her head and mumbled, "Young girls these days. It's so hard to find good help."

Mark removed his jacket, setting it behind him, and rolled up his sleeves.

"No worries." I smiled at her as she reached out to hand me the baby.

"Can you hand her to him?"

"Her?" Mark's eyes grew wide.

I giggled as the nurse harrumphed and came around the bed. "Apparently, ultrasounds are still not 100 percent accurate. She was the one in a rush to debut on the world's stage."

The nurse's expression grew serious as she looked at Mark's forearm. That's an interesting... um... mark there. Is that a scar or a..."

Mark chuffed. "You talking about my lightning bolt?"

The nurse nodded.

"In case you were wondering, I didn't have a run-in with Voldemort."

I snorted when I broke out laughing. "Owww! Does anyone even know who Harry Potter is anymore?"

The nurse apparently didn't think we were funny. She was just staring at him hard.

"It's just a birthmark. No interesting scar story here."

"I've got to get going."

"But I thought..." I started to ask as she neared the door.

She didn't even turn her head. She just waved her hand dismissively as she exited, calling out, "Just let another nurse know if you need my help later."

"Well, that was interesting. I'm so glad to see you, babe. Thanks for rushing home."

"What else would I do? I needed to be here for you and... her."

He looked down at her so strangely, still coming to terms with having a daughter rather than the son we had prepared for.

Just then, the doctor walked into the room. "I have good news for you. All the tests on your baby checked out. You have a perfectly healthy baby girl. How would you like to go home late tomorrow morning?"

"Great, doctor."

Mark

FATE OR FREE WILL

Another sleepless night. I got up and put on my bathrobe as I walked down the hall to turn off the monitor in the baby's room. The baby ran like clockwork. She'd wake up sometime soon, and there was no sense waking up Molly, since I was already up. The baby was frequently fussy, and Molly was exhausted. She needed to catch up on her sleep.

I'd found it increasingly difficult to sleep ever since that night. I'd walked into Molly's hospital room ready to meet my newborn baby, and there *she'd* been with my wife. Then there'd been the way that nurse had looked at me...

Life had been so perfect. Even though I remembered *her* and all our lifetimes together, I had somehow convinced myself that it was all over. I had put it all behind me.

Or at least I thought I had.

I'd been an angry teenage boy in trouble all the time. Outsiders blamed it on my difficult home life with an alcoholic father and an abusive mother. But they didn't know the truth. I remembered what had happened with that bitch Seraphina. All I could focus on was revenge. I was the injured party, after all. She was the one meant to suffer, not me.

Against all odds, I had made it into college, bent on escape rather than education. And that's when life changed for me in a way I hadn't expected. That first semester, I'd sought help at the tutoring center. I hadn't paid attention in high school as well as I should, so I was struggling in my trigonometry class.

That's where I met her. Molly was the math tutor available on that first day I walked in. She was a breath of fresh air. She was beautiful, sweet, and she seemed interested in me as well.

It wasn't long before we turned into best friends. We studied, ate pizza, and hung out in the rec room together whenever we weren't in class. Over time, almost without us realizing it, that friendship blossomed into love.

And the rest, as they say, was history.

Each moment that Molly and I spent together pushed Seraphina further and further back into my mind. She was there deep inside, but I never thought about her anymore. Rage and the desire for vengeance disappeared. I had everything I could want.

After we graduated, we followed the expected trajectory: marriage, career, and children. Except we weren't getting pregnant. Eventually, we went to the doctor and found out that we had fertility issues.

Tens of thousands of dollars and a lot of stress later, we finally got the news we'd been hoping for. Molly was pregnant. My life was perfect until that moment when I walked into that hospital room.

I looked at the letters on the door to the baby's room that I had nailed up earlier in the evening. We had finally come up with a name for her. Her glittering eyes led us to the only name that fit.

Lucy.

Her beautiful eyes made us think of "Lucy in the Sky with Diamonds."

That bitch Seraphina had been so sure that she could end this connection between us. And I'd been stupid enough to let myself believe it. Leave it to her to fuck everything up.

I picked up the pillow in the rocking chair in Lucy's room and sat down, waiting for her to awaken. I tried one last time to convince myself to forget about Seraphina. I had just the life I'd always wanted... a gorgeous wife and a bouncy baby girl. Why would I throw it all away just to get back at her?

As I walked toward the crib, pillow in hand, Lucy opened those sparkling eyes of hers and began to cry as they focused on me.

This is the last time, Alba. You're not going to control me anymore. I won't go through this cycle again. You wanted it to end last time, Seraphina, and I wasn't ready. But now I am. Our fates shall truly intersect with our wishes.

Tears streamed from my eyes as I pressed the pillow down on her tiny, angelic face, and a scream of anguish erupted from my throat as her struggles ceased.

Authors' Notes

Many historical details, and some figures from history, were used in compiling this book. If you recognized some of the characters, places, and cultural touchstones depicted here, that's no accident. Portions of this book are alternative history, and each section takes place against a specific historical backdrop.

Queen Charlotte's Ball was a high point of the social season in Regency-era England, a coming-out showcase for well-born debutantes, and the words in the funeral committal ceremony are quoted directly from a standard prayer of the day. The Wherehouse record store really did exist at Fresno's Fashion Fair Mall back in 1985, and the Wild Blue was a popular nightclub on Olive Avenue that featured an eclectic group of musicians and catered to customers ranging from hippies to coeds.

We've even included references to several song titles in our chapter titles to help tell our story: "The Maiden and the Knight" by Groundstar; "Nevermore" by Queen; "Gallows Pole" by Led Zeppelin; "Georgy Girl" by the Seekers; "Last Dance" by Donna Summer; "Trouble in Mind" by Dinah Washington; and of course, "Love Hurts" by the Everly Brothers.

The following is a list of some people and events from history we used to weave this story that spans the centuries.

Part I

The reader may recognize many of the characters in this section as historical figures—but under different names. The Bear is King Arthur, a semi-mythical figure who is said to have ruled shortly after the fall of Roman Britain from a capital called "Camelot."

Several locations have been proposed for Camelot, including Scotland and Cornwall on the southwestern coast of Great Britain. For the purposes of this story, we have set it in Camulodunum. The similarity of the two names is obvious, and London was shortened in similar fashion from the Roman name Londinium. Since Camulodunum was the provincial seat of power in Roman Britain, it stands to reason that it would have been the seat of power in the post-Roman period as well.

Arthur's name comes from the Welsh word "Arth," meaning "bear," with Arthur possibly meaning "bear-man." Pagan hunters were known to wear the skins of their prey, both in celebration of their conquest and in the belief that doing so would endow them with the attributes of the slain animal. A bear would have been particularly powerful, so it seems natural that a Pagan king of this era might well have worn a bearskin into battle.

Alba is, of course, Guinevere. Both names carry similar meanings: with Alba meaning "white" and the Welsh Guinevere meaning "white and smooth" or "white ghost." The ancient name of Britain, Albion, has a similar meaning: "white land." Nothing seemed more fitting than naming one of the country's most famous queens in honor of the land she ruled.

The Falcon is Merlin, who shares his name with a small falcon known as the pigeon hawk. Anguselaus, meanwhile, was a name associated with Lancelot in some old manuscripts.

Part II

The siblings Laurence and Teagan are fictional characters. But fears about vampirism—and the sort of "remedy" for it depicted in this section—were not uncommon in late 18th century New England. Similar fears and activities were also known in Europe during various periods and probably were imported from there to the New World.

Part IV

The murder of famed Virginia City prostitute Julia Bulette by Jean-Marie Villain (his actual name) was a real event in history. The manner in which Bulette was murdered is depicted here, as well as much of her personal history: She really was born in England, and she really did come to California to ply her trade at mining camps there before moving on to Virginia City. Villain really did serve in the Crimean War and lived in California both before and after that conflict. There is no record of him having encountered Bulette during his time there, but it was theoretically possible. This coincidence was used to set up the romance between the pair.

The manner of Bulette's death and the subsequent hanging of Villain depicted here are based on details from the real events. The fire at the St. Charles Hotel precipitated the destruction of Downieville, which led Abraham Curry to leave town for Genoa and eventually found Carson City.

Tom Peasley, the real-life fire chief in Virginia City, did take a shine to Julia and became her protector. He died in the manner described in this chapter, and Julia's visit to the opera house on the night of her death is also a part of history. Eilley Bowers and her husband, Sandy, struck it rich in Gold Hill, and she earned fame as a fortune-teller, using a peep stone. Mark Twain never interviewed Villain, but he was in Virginia City and witnessed the hanging, reporting on it for the *Chicago Republican*. The actual text of that article is included in the story.

Part V

The mysterious murder of one of the Roaring Twenties' "Broadway Butterflies" served as fodder for this section. It was billed in newspapers as a "locked-door puzzler" because neither the arrival nor the departure of the perpetrator could be explained.

Dot King's colorful life inspired Hollywood to make several movies dealing with this case. She had run-ins with a number of people in the days leading up to her death, but none of them were viable suspects. "Mr. Marshall" and "Mr. Wilson" were prominent people in her life and in society at large. Her boyfriend, Albert, was an abusive con man, as described.

The case will never be resolved because multiple mistakes were made and evidence was overlooked during the investigation.

Part VI

A string of unsolved murders in the Hollywood area during the 1940s serve as the basis for this section. The most famous of these was the "Black Dahlia murder" of Elizabeth Short, which was originally attributed to the "Werewolf Killer." In seeking to solve this gruesome homicide over the years, some investigators have suggested a link between Short's murder and the others—perhaps most prominently, the strangling death of Georgette Bauerdorf.

Many of the details of the Bauerdorf and Short murders are included here as part of this fictional account, in which our character, Dante, is revealed to be the murderer. Bauerdorf, for example, did indeed work at the Hollywood Canteen on Wednesday nights with her friend, June. Many of the details of her life were used in weaving this tale.

Similarly, many of the details of Short's real life are used in the section that introduces her, and the details known from the night of her murder (down to the can of string beans and cantaloupe), are included as well. The tray that crashed to the floor, the police officer who found her sobbing, and the place where her body was discovered—along with its condition—were all taken from newspaper and historical accounts.

Sharon Marie and Stephen H. Provost

About the Authors

Sharon Marie Provost specializes in horror, thrillers, and speculative fiction. Beginning her career in late 2023, she has published a novella, two short story collections, and two collaborative collections of short stories with her husband. Her first novel, *Dark Arts: Love Me Tinder*, was published in 2024. This is her second novel collaboration with Stephen H. Provost, following *Azrael's Assassin*. It has received acclaim for its detailed and chilling story of a serial killer who turns his victims into works of art. Sharon is the chief operating officer of Dragon Crown Books. She has lived in Carson City since 1987.

Stephen H. Provost is a former reporter and columnist with more than 30 years of experience at daily newspapers. Over the past 11 years, he has written more than 50 books. In addition to six novels and three novellas, he has produced an extensive collection of nonfiction works on topics ranging from

Sharon Marie and Stephen H. Provost

Nevada's pioneer days to the history of retail in the United States. He has written more than 20 books on U.S. history in the 20th century focusing on highways, towns, and culture. Stephen is the founder and publisher of Dragon Crown Books. He lives in Carson City.

Books by
Sharon Marie Provost

Dark Arts
Shadow's Gate
Shades of Love, Vol. 2
The Last Train to Clarksville
Azrael's Assassin (with Stephen H. Provost)
All Hallows' Nightmare's Eve (with Stephen H. Provost)
Christmas Nightmare's Eve (with Stephen H. Provost)
The ACES Anthology 2023 and 2024 (contributor)

Books by
Stephen H. Provost

Fiction

Azrael's Assassin (with Sharon Marie Provost)
The Memortality Saga
  Memortality
  Paralucidity
Meteor Ridge
Academy of the Lost Labyrinth
  The Talismans of Time
  Pathfinder of Destiny
The Only Dragon
Identity Break
Identity Forge

Sharon Marie and Stephen H. Provost

Crimson Scourge

Nightmare's Eve

Christmas Nightmare's Eve (with Sharon Marie Provost)

All Hallows' Nightmare's Eve
  (with Sharon Marie Provost)

Shades of Love, Vol. 1

Need

Death's Doorstep

Feathercap

Madeline the Redheaded Witch
  The Reluctant Little Witch
  Madeline's Dragon Quest

The Adventures of Mark Twain in Nevada

Waffles the Poodle Dragon

Nonfiction

Mark Twain's Nevada

The Comstock Chronicles

Virginia City Then & Now

The Legend of Molly Bolin

A Whole Different League

California's Historic Highways series
  Highway 99
  Highway 101

America's Historic Highways series
  America's First Highways
  Yesterday's Highways
  Highways of the South

Evermore

Highways of the West series
　　America's Loneliest Road
　　Victory Road
　　The Lincoln Highway in California
　　　　(with Gary Kinst)
　　Sierra Highway
　　Bonanza Highway
Roadside Illustrated series
　　Happy Motoring!
　　Signpost Up Ahead: The East
　　Signpost Up Ahead: The West
The Great American Shopping Experience
Fresno Growing Up, 2024
Martinsville Memories
The Century Cities series
　　Cambria Century, Carson City Century
　　Charleston Century, Danville Century
　　Fresno Century, Goldfield Century
　　Greensboro Century, Huntington Century
　　Roanoke Century, San Luis Obispo Century
The Phoenix Chronicles
　　The Osiris Testament
　　The Way of the Phoenix
　　The Gospel of the Phoenix
The Phoenix Principle
　　Forged in Ancient Fires
　　Messiah in the Making
Please Stop Saying That!
50 Undefeated

Praise for Other Works

"The writing was superb, the attention to detail shows she knows what she's doing when it comes to police procedure, and the kill scenes are very detailed and disturbing... For fans of serial killer stories with plenty of graphic imagery. Highly recommended."
— Justin Boote, author of *Soul Searchers*,
on Dark Arts by Sharon Marie Provost

"One of the best books I have EVER read! Messed-up, cringy, tense, sickening, thrilling, exciting, disturbing and complete!"
— Kim Sloan, author of the *Billy Bob Adventures* series,
on Dark Arts by Sharon Marie Provost

"Haunting and beautiful. This book is so good! All the stars!!!"
— Angel Van Atta, author of *In the Tall Trees*,
on Dark Arts by Sharon Marie Provost

"I read this book in one sitting, something I rarely do. The story is fast paced and crisply written, the description of the crimes, though tough to read, are expertly and vividly written. There are plenty of believable twists and turns. The ending is fabulous."
— Catherine Riddick, former *Fresno Bee* assistant managing editor,
on Dark Arts by Sharon Marie Provost

"Heartwarming, heart-wrenching. The romance broke my heart and then mended it."
— Carol Purroy, author of *Tiara*, on
The Last Train to Clarksville by Sharon Marie Provost

Evermore

"I loved the story and the twist at the end. It's my kind of book! I had no idea and I love to be tricked and intrigued by an ending! Highly recommend it if you are a fan of everlasting love!"

— Sue C. Dugan, author of *A Slow Climb Up the Mountain*, on **The Last Train to Clarksville by Sharon Marie Provost**

"The complex idea of mixing morality and mortality is a fresh twist on the human condition. ... **Memortality** is one of those books that will incite more questions than it answers. And for fandom, that's a good thing."

— Ricky L. Brown, Amazing Stories

"Punchy and fast paced, **Memortality** reads like a graphic novel. ... (Provost's) style makes the trippy landscapes and mind-bending plot points more believable and adds a thrilling edge to this vivid crossover fantasy."

— Foreword Reviews

"The story feels so close, so intimate, we as readers experience the emotions, the events, and the conflicts, in what feels like real time. Gut-wrenchingly so."

— Stephen Mark Rainey, author of *Blue Devil Island*, on **Death's Doorstep by Stephen H. Provost**

"The genres in this volume span horror, fantasy, and science-fiction, and each is handled deftly. ... **Nightmare's Eve** should be on your reading list. The stories are at the intersection of nightmare and lucid dreaming, up ahead a signpost ... next stop, your reading pile. Keep the nightlight on."

— R.B. Payne, Cemetery Dance

Sharon Marie and Stephen H. Provost

"**Memortality** by Stephen Provost is a highly original, thrilling novel unlike anything else out there."

— David McAfee, bestselling author of
33 A.D., 61 A.D., and *79 A.D.*

"Provost sticks mostly to the classics: vampires, ghosts, aliens, and even dragons. But trekking familiar terrain allows the author to subvert readers' expectations. ... Provost's poetry skillfully displays the same somber themes as the stories. ... Worthy tales that prove external forces are no more terrifying than what's inside people's heads."

— Kirkus Reviews on
Nightmare's Eve by Stephen H. Provost

Did you enjoy this book?

Recommend it to a friend. And please consider **rating it and/or leaving a brief review** at Amazon, Barnes & Noble, and Goodreads.